BEYOND the MUNDANE
FLIGHTS of MIND

AN ANTHOLOGY OF SCIENCE FICTION AND FANTASY

Beyond the Mundane Series:

Flights of Mind
An Anthology of Science Fiction and Fantasy

Unravelings
An Anthology of Mystery and Horror

BEYOND the MUNDANE

FLIGHTS of MIND

AN ANTHOLOGY OF SCIENCE FICTION AND FANTASY

Edited by DANIEL J. REITZ

Mundania Press

Cover Art © 2004 by Regina Brytowski
Titling and Layout © 2004 by Stacey L. King

A Mundania Press Production

Her was first published in Black Petals Magazine, Spring 2003.
December Morning was first published in Tomorrow SF, Issue 2.
Meeting Mr. Wright was first published in Strictly Romance, 1997 Summer Issue #4.
Just Don't was first published in L. Ron Hubbard Presents Writers of the Future, Vol V.
The Bonda Prophecy was first published in First Line magazine, Jan/Feb 2001.
Catch of the Season was first published in Twilight Times, Spring 2002.
Oracle of Cilens was first published in Pegasus Online, Fall 1999.
Survival Instinct was first published by Quantum Muse, May 2003.
The Old Green Door was first published in Stardates, 1998.
Drink My Soul...Please was first published by The Eternal Night, January 2002.
All other stories appearing in this anthology are original.

Trade Paperback ISBN: 1-59426-023-0
eBook Edition ISBN: 1-59426-024-9

Library of Congress Catalog Card Number 2004107184

Mundania Press LLC
6470A Glenway Avenue, #109
Cincinnati, Ohio 45211-5222

To order additional copies of this book, contact:
books@mundania.com
www.mundania.com

First Printing, May 2004
10 9 8 7 6 5 4 3 2 1

Printed in the United States of America

ACKNOWLEDGMENTS

Introduction © 2004 by Daniel J. Reitz
Her © 2004 by Nick Aires
December Morning © 2004 by Eolake Stobblehouse
The Carnival © 2004 by C. J. Winters
The Chosen © 2004 by Sandy Cummins
Devotion © 2004 by Loren W. Cooper
Learning Curve © 2004 by Jackie Kramer
The Storyteller's Thanksgiving © 2004 by Linda Bleser
Maybe Next Time © 2004 by J. Brian Jones
The Lightning Bug © 2004 by Frances Evlin
Hunters © 2004 by Loren W. Cooper
My Brother, My Brother © 2004 by Jane Toombs
Meeting Mr. Wright © 1997 by Chris Grover
The Gargoyle Who Loved Me © 2004 by Nora Santella
Transcendence © 2004 by Loren W. Cooper
Butterflies © 2004 by S. Joan Popek
The Plague Bearers © 2004 by Loren W. Cooper
The Bonda Prophecy © 2001 by Nick Aires
Catch of the Season © 2002 by Vicki M. Taylor
Thunderstruck © 2004 by C. J. Winters
Stones of Destiny © 2004 by Linda Bleser
Unmarked Planet © 2004 by Nick Aires
Oracle of Cilens © 1999 by Kathryn Sullivan
The Takers © 2004 by Loren W. Cooper
Survival Instinct © 2003 by Elaine Corvidae
Mr. Fate © 2004 by Kenneth E. Baker
The Old Green Door © 1998 by Julie D'Arcy
All The Fires Of Home © 2004 by Loren W. Cooper
Drink My Soul...Please © 2002 by Rie Sheridan
Just Don't © 2004 by Eolake Stobblehouse

CONTENTS

INTRODUCTION

by Daniel J. Reitz

While growing up we all dreamed of more exciting times. Somewhere, there was a knight slaying a dragon to rescue the damsel in distress. Somewhere, the engines roared to life as the rocketship blasted off into the blackness of outer space. Somewhere, the old wizard was losing his patience with his clumsy young apprentice. Somewhere, there must be these amazing adventures happening, and we longed to experience them all.

Fantasy and Science Fiction genres are more popular today than ever. Each year thousands of die-hard fans flock to hundreds of conventions to catch a glimpse of their favorite sci-fi star, purchase marvelous treasures from the hucksters, and dress up as their favorite fantasy characters. The imagination of fantasy gamers run wild with the excitement of hacking and slashing some vile creature and then dividing up all the gold pieces. Just a few more XPs to the next level!

Do you need a little escape from the daily grind of your busy world? Then come along with us on a fantastic journey to far away lands where strange and wondrous sights are beheld around every corner. We invite you to visit the wild and wonderful worlds created by 19 of today's most talented authors in fantasy and science fiction.

Contained here are 29 stories that are exciting, funny, thought-provoking, and entertaining enough to take you beyond the mundane.

So sit back, relax, and let your mind take flight...

HER

by Nick Aires

Nick Aires is a Writers of the Future finalist, and he has published dozens of stories in anthologies such as EN-CHANTED REALMS II, magazines such as Futures Mysterious Anthology, in ezines such as Antipodean SF, and on Story House coffee can labels. With James Richey, he is the coeditor of FANTASY READERS WANTED—APPLY WITHIN from Silver Lake Publishing.

Her smile. It seems like it's been so long since I've seen her smile. She's smiling now and her whole face is aglow. In all the time I've spent at this house, the "living room" has never been more alive; the twinkle in her eyes is like two bright suns radiating warmth and light.

Her beauty touches my heart and arouses my ardor. I cannot stop staring at her.

She turns off the television. Sadly, the show that made her smile is over, and the smile has gone with it. She gets up from the couch and heads towards the bedroom, glancing briefly in my direction. I smile at her, but she does not seem to notice. At times I feel that I am no more significant to her than a fly on the wall...but I shove that thought from my mind. This is not the time for self-belittlement, nor is it the time to wonder how I ever had the fortune to cross paths with this otherworldly enchantress. Now is simply the time for *her*.

In the bedroom, she undresses—slowly, erotically. Sweat rises unbidden to the surface of my callused skin. Although undoubtedly unintentional, her natural movements create a paradox of innocence and titillation that serves to make her even more desirable. All too quickly, the striptease is over, and she stands before me in all her naked glory. I am speechless—her beauty knows no bounds. I admire every inch of her as if for the first time. Never have I seen a body so smooth, so flawless.

She steps into the adjoining bathroom and bends over the tub to put in the plug. Seeing her in this position excites me at the basest of levels. I try to get closer to her, but only succeed in banging my head against the window.

The thud is loud in my ears, but she has started the bath water, which apparently masks my cranial collision, for she does not turn around. Nonetheless, I back away, not wanting to disturb her.

While waiting for the tub to fill, she attends to bodily functions. I look away from her private acts, and check the date. It is Friday. She showered this morning, as she does most days. Normally she takes a bath on Sunday nights, but her louse of a boyfriend stood her up again. I would never stand her up, would that I could.

The rumble of the water has ceased. I look back through the window. Perfect timing: she is stepping into the tub. Such grace of movement; she never fails to hold my rapt attention. As she settles in, the water laps gently against her bosom. I admire the buoyancy of her breasts as she picks up a soapy sponge and rubs it leisurely across her chest.

Too enraptured to be concerned with disturbing her, I glide in to get a closer look. The motion catches her attention. She finally looks right at me. Our eyes lock. My heart is so full of love at this moment that I fear it shall burst.

Without warning, my darling raises a hand to me! She swats at my starship, as if it were nothing more than an annoying insect.

Although physically I am able to avoid her attack, emotionally I am crushed. If she would only take the time to look closer, she would see that I am not so different from her. She would see all the similarities and compatibilities of our physical forms. It is such a pity that with all the technological marvels within my control there is nothing that can compensate for our insurmountable size difference.

The transceiver buzzes. It is time to file my mission report. I keep it brief.

After several cycles of observation, it is my firm resolution that this planet be slated for immediate terra forming, starting with the eradication of the present populace.

If I can't have her, nobody can.

DECEMBER MORNING

by Eolake Stobblehouse

Eolake Stobblehouse was born in 1963 in Denmark, and works with art, photography, and writing. He is writing for various international markets with science fiction, fantasy, and non-fiction writing. He currently lives in Lancashire, England, with his two Macs named Susse and Dariya.

It is a cold December morning. The old house is creaking quietly in the biting cold outside. Old willows are standing uncomplaining like islands in the snow. The sun is veiled by a thin layer of clouds. A black cat is walking through the garden.

The inside of the house is dark wood, and old things, things rare and worth much gold. A gray-haired man sits by a table. A young woman stands by a mirror. He is in a morning robe, she is wearing a bath towel, and combing her hair. The curtains are only drawn from one window, the largest one, facing the large snow-covered garden.

The man looks at his hands on the bare table top. He looks at a painting on the wall. He looks out the window, he looks at the floor. He looks at the woman. He puts his hands on his face. He rubs his face, rubs his eyes, rubs his head, he sits back in his chair. He sighs silently.

The woman finishes combing her hair, and puts down the comb. She turns from the mirror, and takes off the towel, hanging it over a chair. She turns back to the mirror and flexes her body, stretches her arms backwards. She makes a musical humming, then massages her breasts and her ribs. She stretches lazily, and then, still humming, goes to the window, leans on the window sill, and looks into the garden.

The man is silently watching her, unmoving.

The woman speaks: "Oh, I do so love Winter, I do. It is so cold, so white, so merciless, so virginal. Any old evil can hide in Winter, hiding in the open, in broad daylight, invisible due to the numbness and the blindness coming from the cold." She puts her hands further apart, leans forward, stands still.

Outside, it begins to snow. The man rises from the table, and walks to the window, slowly. He wraps his robe tighter. He stands still, close to the woman. He lifts his hand, puts it down again. He sits down on a nearby chair.

Not looking at the woman, he speaks to her. "You shouldn't stand naked by the window. It is cold."

She turns, smiling. She straddles his knees, facing him, puts her arms on his shoulders. She looks into his eyes, still smiling. "I think you know that doesn't hurt me," she answers. She plays with his hair. The man's face is turned away.

Outside, a black bird lands in the snow. The house creaks someplace.

With a sudden movement, she grabs his face with one hand and turns it towards her own. With a quiet, precise voice she says: "You haven't spoken to me in days. What is the problem?"

He looks into her face. She has dark blue eyes, long, arched eyebrows, a thin nose, pale skin. Her dark hair is falling in wet strands over her forehead and shoulders.

He says: "I love you, you know."

"Why, thank you. I appreciate that. What is new?"

"I am tired, Marlene. I am so tired." He sighs, puts his hand to his forehead.

"You have been tired for a long time, Michael."

"Exactly. It isn't changing, except for getting worse. I haven't done any work in months."

"You don't need to work, Michael. You are rich."

"Yes, I am rich, but I can't live my life doing nothing. I am not made that way. And I like what I work with."

The girl gets up. She walks around, waving her arms. "Michael, you are hopeless! You have everything a man can dream of! You have a beautiful home, important friends, ten cars, you have me. What do you want!?"

The man is watching her. He is leaning back in the chair, stroking his chin. "Marlene, what are you? I don't see you sleep. You can stand any temperature with or without clothes. You hardly eat anything. I saw you the first time fifteen years prior to marrying you, and you don't seem to be getting any older, though you are changing. What are you?"

Outside, the snow is coming down harder, and a wind is starting to blow. The woman sits down in front of her husband.

"Well, the legends don't quite fit," she says, "but you should be able to figure it out, Michael. You are nothing if not intelligent."

"No, the legends don't quite fit. That's what stopped me for a long time. But you must be what we call a vampire."

She looks, down, smiling. "Thank you, Michael. Yes, I am a vampire."

"But you can stand sunlight, and you make a reflection."

"We don't mind sunlight, but we don't tan, that's probably the cause of the misunderstanding. People that pale must be afraid of the Sun, people reason. Of course we make reflections. We hate all strong spices, including garlic. The crucifix means nothing to us, that is merely a desperate hope. And yes, we live from the blood and spirit of human beings."

The man looks at her. "But why me? And why us." He feels his throat.

She laughs. "Why don't you have teeth marks? You have felt my teeth often enough, when kissing. You know you should have punctures. It is simple, really, as a survival mechanism. We wish to keep victims ignorant as long as possible. We secrete something that heals the puncture marks almost instantly."

She looks down at her slender hands. "And why you? Well, I like you, Michael. You are a strong man, a good man. You taste good. You keep me strong. You are a good living. Delicious. Nutritious." She smiles at him. "Of course you! I love you!"

He looks at her with a still, neutral expression. "You love me like a snake loves a rabbit. Like I love roast beef. You love me like a hammer loves the nail. You love me like thunder loves the sky. You love me like a car loves the road. What do you know about love?"

The young woman gets up again. "What do I know about love? What don't I know about love? I love the night. I love the frost of winter. I love the wild life of the forests. I love hunting. I love exhaustion. I love fear. I love to kill. I love...I love the taste of your blood. I love the feeling of you growing smaller and weaker in my grasp. I love to have a life in my hands."

She has picked up a flower from a vase. She is sniffing its scent. She holds it delicately in both hands. Then she puts it back by its stem.

She stands in front of her husband. "You see?"

Her husband regards her pale, slender figure standing in front of him.

"Yes," he says. "I see." He continues: "Why don't you leave me be? I have done nothing bad to you. I have done nothing to deserve this." He looks into her face. "You are killing me. You are draining my life away. I am dying day by day at your hands. You can't do this to anoth.... You can't do this to a living, thinking human being. You can't do this."

The woman turns from him, and goes to a nearby closet, and takes out a dress. The dress is dark blue, of thin fabric. She pulls it over her head and straightens it down her slender body.

Taking the man's hand, she says, "Shall we have some breakfast? Here, go sit by the table, I'll make you some breakfast. But first, a question." She sits down opposite the man.

"Let me tell you something," she says. "I'll leave it up to you." She takes both his hands in hers. "What you say, goes. I will only stay if you want me to. I'll stay, and we will continue our life as before. Be assured, I will not kill you. I want you to live as long as you can. You may be able to do less and less, but you will be alive, and you will be with me. Then, on the other hand, if you so desire, I will leave right now, and never return. I will walk out your door, and you will never see me again. You will return to health, you will be able to start working again, you will be active. You can start living. You are still not an old man, you know. It just feels that way at the moment. You have potentially half your life left for you."

She lets go of his hands, and sits back. "I just need your word."

The man sits for a while, then puts his face in his hands. "Don't," he begins.

"*Don't* what?" says his wife. "I can't hear what you're saying."

"Don't leave," says the man.

She leans forward, holds his face, looks into it. She smiles, a broad, happy smile with her whole face. "Say 'please'. "

"Please," says the man.

"Good," she says. "Thank you." She pats his hand. "What do you want for breakfast, Darling?" She gets up.

THE CARNIVAL

by C. J. Winters

C. J. Winters was always more interested in Tomorrow than Yesterday. Then she discovered the American Past offers a wealth of backgrounds for some of her offbeat story ideas. Combined with her fascination for the extra-normal, she has ten books published or soon-to-be published in electronic formats and paperback. Paranormal romances include three time-travels: RIGHT MAN, WRONG TIME; SLEIGHRIDE; and MOON NIGHT...plus A STAR IN THE EARTH (sequel to MOON NIGHT), and the AUTUMN IN CRANKY OTTER series. Other works include a paranormal cozy mystery, SHOW-ME MURDER, and the non-paranormal, MAI'S TIES.

"...go with the flow...go with the flow..." Carla snapped off the radio in disgust, giving up finding a tune with more than a single catch phrase for lyrics.

*Go with the flow...sure...Friday night, let my hair down, let it all hang out. Had it with corporate structure? Have a drink with the girls after work...grab a pizza and a video on the way home...pour a glass of Chablis...*and fall asleep on the sofa before the flick is fifteen minutes old.

Carla Sommers, forty-nine, widow, mother of two, granny of one, and underwriter by occupation, hated living alone. However her apartment lease didn't allow dogs, cats ignored her, and fish hardly made for cozy palship.

So on impulse that late September evening she swerved off Highway 40 and into the parking lot of a forlorn shopping center where a weekend carnival had drawn in hundreds of visitors.

Nothing like cotton candy to brighten a sour mood!

She parked under a pole light between two sedans with child seats. Then, cell phone in one blazer pocket and Shock-jock defensive spray in the other, she eye-surveyed the area, stepped out and locked the Taurus.

Tinkling music from half a dozen rides plus the high, excited voices of children and loud calls of barkers and vendors combined in a cacophony of life and energy. Jostled by youngsters pulling their parents this way and that, her shoulder bag clutched tight under her arm, Carla permitted herself to be swept into the current.

Maybe I'll go really wild and ride the merry-go-round!

Instead, a fortune-teller's tent, its multi-color stripes sporting their faded patina with something like quaint dignity, caught her eye. Outside the flap opening a double-sided sign proclaimed *Madame Leticia's Crystal Ball Holds a Message for YOU! Readings, $10.* Business appeared anything but brisk; no line stretched from the entrance, and no money-taker waited to entice her inside.

What the hell. The last time she'd had her fortune told was thirty-five years ago, at the State Fair in Sedalia. *That* gypsy woman declared Carla could be the next Marilyn Monroe if she moved to Hollywood and bleached her hair. Carla and her friend, Monica, had giggled all the way home. She sighed, for a second regretting she'd never bleached her hair. *Time* was working on it now, threading silver strands through the blackness.

Hesitantly she lifted the flap and peered into the stale, incense-scented interior illuminated by a single lamp with a red shade. Seated at a small table and wearing a shiny turquoise caftan and pink turban, a heavy-set woman of possible middle-European descent looked up from a large crystal ball that glimmered eerily in the dusky light.

"Come in," said the woman with a languid wave of one large, bejeweled hand. "I have waited for you."

It was more of a command than an invitation, and Carla found herself obediently moving to a chair opposite the reader.

The woman's dark eyes measured her client as she extended her palm. "The reading fee, please."

Why not? It beats going home to the weekend.

The seer turned her gaze to the crystal ball and got right to work. "You seek your other," she said in a husky voice seasoned by tobacco. "The man to replace the one you lost."

Carla gulped, then nodded. Although Tom had been sixteen years older, they'd looked forward to an active retirement. Instead he'd left her one night in a heartbeat.

Her gaze fastened on her psychic tool, the seer droned, "*He* is here. Open your heart–" Then she halted and looked up. "Ah...so soon."

Carla swiveled on her chair and followed the seer's gaze to where a man stooped half in and half out of the tent, still holding the flap. "Sorry," he said, starting to back out. "I didn't know anyone–"

"*Come in!*" barked the reader. "Your place is *here.*"

The man straightened, and while his posture indicated he was accustomed to being in charge of his movements, like Carla, he obeyed.

The seer rose to her feet and said, "Now go outside. Enjoy the carnival and one another." She raised her hands in dismissal. "Life is short. *Go!*"

Well! Carla also rose, and with an ironic smile for the intruder, said, "Congratulations. You got your reading for free."

When they were outside the tent, he said, "What the hell went on in there?"

"Couldn't you tell? Madame Leticia is a matchmaker."

"But all I did was–"

"Give her an excuse to take a break. C'mon, don't tell me you think I buy this 'coincidence'? Take a hike, fella. I'm not in the market."

"In the market for WHAT?"

Behind silver wire-rim glasses sparks glinted in the man's grey eyes. Carla glanced around for help in case she needed it, and spotted a uniformed policeman. "You go your way, I go mine. No questions asked. 'Bye."

The man's eye-sparks darkened with temper. *"Oh, no you don't!* I stick my head into a tent and get told to buzz off by a fortune-teller *and* a woman who acts like I'm some kind of scam artist, I want to know *why!*"

The stronger light showed Carla that her adversary's pinstripe suit was too expensive for a carny-con. He was about her age and height, making their gazes level. She indicated the cop. "Don't make me call him."

Their gazes tangled.

Then he said, "I won't if you don't." And grinned.

Carla burst out laughing. "So why did *you* go in there? You don't look the type to want your fortune told."

"Neither do you."

"I'm not. It was a whim. I was really hunting cotton candy."

"I just passed the stand. I can show you."

She eyed him. The parking lot was brightly lighted and swarming with people. "Okay. Then you can sneak back to the tent."

"I don't have to sneak!"

Ah, a male raw spot. "Sorry. Show me the candy and I'll buy yours."

"No way. I spent the morning at the dentist. His name is Marcos, in case you need him after the candy." He took a business card from his inner coat pocket and handed it to her. "His office is across the hall from mine."

Carla read the card, *Pericles Jonathan, Account Executive, Marley Advertising,* and suppressed a smile. "I'll bet nobody forgets your name."

"Right. That's why I chose it. I was born 'William'."

"And they called you Billy Jon in grade school?"

His startled expression said she'd hit the nail on the head. "Why do *you* need a fortune-teller?"

Almost without her realizing it, he'd guided her to the cotton candy stand. She chose lavender from the clouds of rainbow pastels and paid for it before replying. "I think I may be having a midlife crisis. Along with a sudden yen for cotton candy, I was thinking about leaving my job and becoming a beachcomber. Or something equally lucrative."

"What are you doing now?"

"Insurance underwriting. It's become very old." She nibbled at the airy sugar. It was revolting, but having made such a production about it, she was going to finish it. "I think the worst part is the time on the freeway."

"Me too!" *Pericles– Perry?– no, Pericles suited him better,* pointed at the ferris wheel, its lights tiny earthbound stars against the dark heavens. "How about a ride? I love the view from the top. Haven't been on one since my kids were little."

Carla nodded. "I was going on the merry-go-round, but you're right, the view is better."

He insisted on buying their tickets. "*My* idea, *I* pay."

"Then if we don't get stuck up there, the ice cream's on me."

"You live dangerously. Marcos told me to cut out sweets or he'd own my house one day."

Is that my cue to ask about your wife, Pericles, so you can tell me you're widowed or divorced or about to be? If so, forget it.

She sat down on the right side of the ferris wheel seat in case she needed to use the repellent spray in her right-hand pocket. Or she could tip him overboard— except he looked as fit as she did, so it might be a tossup. She swallowed a chuckle. Fifteen minutes ago, she'd have said *Never!* to such a risk. At this rate, she'd be heading for the casinos next!

"You like casinos?" Without waiting for a reply, he said, "I used to. Then I found out my ex- and her boyfriend are going through her share of the divorce settlement at the faro table. I figure a carnival won't wipe out my 401k."

"It's hard to watch such things happen. I'd rather spend my play money on travel."

The ferris wheel operator loaded his last customers into their seat, pulled a lever, and the wheel backed into a slow upward journey into the night.

As the garish carnival scene receded, Carla said, "It *is* beautiful. Do you have children or grandchildren to take on the rides?"

"Not yet. You?"

"One, but she's only ten months old. Next year I'll take her on the merry-go-round."

"I've thought about carving a carousel horse," Pericles mused. "You like wood-carvings? I sell an occasional cigar store Indian."

"I'm impressed. I used to garden. I've thought about opening a nursery in a small town, someday."

"Some days get in the way, don't they? Of doing what we really want, I mean."

Carla caught her breath as they hovered on the brink of space and began the descent. "It sounds like we're both having a mid-life crisis."

Pericles turned to her, a sheepish, almost callow, expression on his unremarkable, yet attractively modeled features. "That's why I went to the fortune-teller. To see what she'd say when I told her I want to move to the mountains and carve wood for a living."

"Why ask? Why don't you just do it?"

Pericles' eyes probed hers. "Why don't *you* open a plant nursery? Your husband too hidebound to change?"

"He died two years ago."

"Oh. You still wear rings, so I figured– Sorry."

"A habit." She stared down at the rings, as familiar as her hand, thinking. Then she said, "I'm going to start changing my habits. I'll start small. Just do some things differently. And then maybe I *will* start that nursery!"

Once more moving backward toward the top of the wheel, they rocked and swung in comfortable silence.

Nearing the top Pericles said, "What's your favorite thing in the world? Not counting people."

"A kaleidoscope."

"Because...?"

"It always creates beauty, even though the pieces are broken."

He nodded appreciatively. "That gives me an idea for a carving."

"A cigar store Indian in rose-colored glasses?"

Laughing as they once more swung out into space, she said, "I haven't had this much fun in ages. Thank you, Pericles."

"Let's do more." His grey eyes brimmed with mischief. "Let's go back and wring our fortunes out of the teller."

"Done!"

The wheel jerked to a halt and the operator hustled them from their seat.

"Come on," Pericles said. "There's the cotton candy, so the tent is to the right."

Behind the Toss-n-Win, however, they stared at the Shoot-a-Duck-Win-a-Teddy booth.

Carla said, "Maybe we should've gone left."

Pericles' scowl of frustration reminded her of Tom's whenever they became lost on a trip. "I'll ask," she said, and before he could refuse, marched over to the officer she'd seen earlier.

Still scowling, Pericles followed.

"A fortune-teller?" The cop shook his head. "There isn't one, ma'am. There's a city ordinance against fortune-telling."

"No," put in Pericles, "it was a striped tent, right over there." He pointed at the Shoot-a-Duck. "There was a woman in it, with a crystal ball..."

His voice trailed off at the young cop's expression, a blend of skepticism and sympathy.

Carla nudged Pericles' arm. "Come on. I owe you an ice cream."

"He thinks we're senile!" stormed Pericles as she pushed him around the corner.

"I *know!*" Hearing the tinge of hysteria in her voice, Carla took a deep breath and expelled it slowly. "But if the tent isn't here, *it isn't here.*"

"Then where the hell is it?"

Another time she might've smiled, his reaction was so like Tom's when he hadn't grasped something. "I don't know, but...I think...I understand."

"Understand *what?*"

She smiled into the bewildered grey eyes of Pericles Jonathan...and Destiny.

"My name is Carla Sommers. And I believe."

For a long moment he stared at her, uncomprehending. Then his grey eyes widened. "So do I," he said, and smiling, drew her into his arms. "What say we go buy some start-your-own-business magazines?"

THE CHOSEN

by Sandy Cummins

Sandy Cummins is an Australian writer with many non-fiction articles to her credit. Her writing has ranged from Christian Parenting Columns, home-schooling advice columns to fantasy short stories. Sandy spends most of her time as a publisher rather than writing, and is the owner of Writers Exchange E-Publishing.

The woman lashed out with her feet, a grunt from an Acolyte the only acknowledgment of her accuracy.

"Feisty; Kamar will appreciate that."

The woman continued to struggle, her eyes darting wildly. Ropes bit painfully into her swollen belly as they lashed her to the altar. Smoke from the myriad of candles wafted over her. The pungent scent of incense drugged her senses.

"Divine Kamar, behold your sacrifice!" shouted the priest as he plunged the ceremonial dagger between her breasts.

Her dying scream echoed around the chamber, bringing dread to unbelievers and exultation to the faithful.

≫≪

The Gods called; no-one answered.

Spurning the Gods of their ancestors, the villagers had turned to a new God, an evil God, a God of their own creation.

A girl child was born, torn from her mother's cooling flesh.

The Gods chose; they chose her.

≫≪

Caitlyn strode down the village street towards the home of Akbah, the High Priest of the "Ancient Gods".

The Ancient Gods, whose names have been lost to human recollection, never enter the world they toiled so hard to create. Instead, a believer worthy to lead their church is chosen as High Priest. The High Priest and a few select priests can draw the Gods' powers into their bodies to augment their own magical powers. Only the most talented and disciplined priests survive this ritual, and their power is phenomenal.

This system had worked well for generations, the people faithfully worshipping their creators until the renegade god Kamar appeared. Kamar demanded human sacrifice from his worshippers. It was this foul practice that had cost Caitlyn's mother her life.

Akbah had taken Caitlyn in after the midwife had delivered her from her mother's corpse. He had generously assigned his priests to raise and train her.

She turned to an old warehouse that backed onto a dark alley. She knocked on the stout oak door. The peephole opened and an eye raked suspiciously over her. The guard was unable to identify her in her cowled robe.

"Who is it?"

"Caitlyn, Akbah sent for me."

Recognising her voice, the doorkeeper gave a satisfied grunt and slid back several bolts.

Since the King's conversion to Kamar worship, the worship of the ancient gods had been outlawed. It was no longer safe to live in the temples and the High Priest now lived in hidden apartments at the back of this warehouse.

Placing two fingers in a concealed knothole she flicked a switch; the wall parted.

Two bodyguards roughly searched her for hidden weapons.

She glared at the hulk on her left. The manhandling had been less than professional. "If you want a female, try a brothel." She tugged her robe back into place.

He grinned.

She didn't.

His eyes glazed, his large body crumpled to the floor.

"Don't even think about it—" emerald eyes blazed at the remaining guard— "you're not paid to protect him."

"My priests have taught you well," rasped a voice like sandpaper.

Caitlyn turned her back on the bodyguard. Barely discernible in the dimness at the back of the room sat a figure. Eerily young eyes stared out from an ancient visage. Eyes that demanded attention and obedience.

Caitlyn felt like a moth with its wings pinned helplessly against a board. Struggling against the power of his gaze, she dragged her eyes from his. Resolutely she straightened her spine and approached the Master.

Caitlyn lowered her cowl and bowed her head respectfully, her auburn hair obscured her face as she knelt at his feet. "You summoned me."

"Yes my child." A bony hand grasped her chin, raising her face to his inspection. The Master studied her pretty face, the creamy complexion and long coppery hair, which reminded him so painfully of her mother. The jade green eyes sparkled with intelligence and glowed faintly from the powers stored within. "It is time."

"What do you wish of me?" she asked humbly. Her instructors would have been proud. Their wilful student setting aside her pride as she faced the man to whom she owed everything.

≈≈

The road extended flat and dusty to the horizon. Straggly bushes stretched withered branches into the parched desert air. Travelers rarely ventured far these days, but Caitlyn knew of no danger for one of her training. The Master had commanded and she had gone; she didn't like it, but she didn't have to. She had a job to do and she would succeed or she would die. Caitlyn had no intention of dying.

The cutthroats who attacked her camp that night obviously didn't share her intention of a long life.

Only a fool would attack someone wearing the Temple's famous black robes. A journeyman's saffron robes, maybe; a novice's white robes, certainly; a master mage's black robes, never.

The outlaws must have felt that their numbers would make a difference. Caitlyn shrugged, their evil intent suppressed her usual compassion. Turning to the men before her, she stretched out a small slim hand.

A hand of beauty.

A hand of death.

Caitlyn called her Gods; their power augmented her own, shining as a beacon from her glowing emerald eyes. Her long hair crackled with the energies converging on her small body.

As the power receded, she sank to the ground staring sorrowfully at the charred craters surrounding her, all that remained of the men who had so foolishly wasted their lives. She said the words of passing and cried for their families.

≈≈

Two weeks of cross-country traveling had shortened Caitlyn's temper. Navigating the scrambling throng jostling to enter Pyron's Main Gate further added to her annoyance.

"What I wouldn't give for a bath," Caitlyn muttered, adjusting her backpack and wiping ineffectually at the road dust which stuck thickly to her. Her travel-stained robes clung damply to her tired body as she maneuvered her way through the current to the first Inn's welcome doors.

Once inside she waited a moment for her eyes to adjust to the dimness. Quickly she scanned the room, and seated herself at an empty table which afforded her a clear view of all three entrances. One doorway lead to the upstairs rooms, one to the kitchen and the last was the entrance from the street.

She had scarcely settled herself on the rough wooden bench before a waitress approached.

"What ya havin', luv?"

"Mutton stew, beer and a room."

"Sure thing, just get comfy and we'll see about feeding you up. Look like ya haven't eaten in days. Never mind, my Bert's stew'll put some meat on ya bones. What ya doin' here by yourself anyway? You're too young to be in a place like this, you'd best be in bed before the drinkers come in. Not that we have a rowdy pub, but the guys aren't used to pretty young girls at the tables..."

"Miriam, leave the kid alone will ya? You've nearly put her to sleep with your yabbering."

Indeed Caitlyn did feel somewhat bemused by Miriam's motherly fussing. But she enjoyed the novelty, people rarely talked to black robes, let alone mother them!

"Sorry about that, child," Bert continued, pushing his wife in the direction of the kitchen. Then recognizing her robes under their disguising film of grit he started, only the most powerful priestess would wear the robes of office in public.

"Sorry ma'am, please excuse my wife, she didn't mean any harm."

Caitlyn sighed, "It's all right. Tell your wife I appreciated her concern for my welfare."

"I will ma'am, and she'll be back with your stew any moment."

Leaning back, Caitlyn closed her eyes wearily. Outwardly relaxed she sent her mind searching through the pub. Five rooms upstairs, only two were occupied. Both occupants appeared to be harmless merchants with naught on their minds but profits. Bert and Miriam were the only others in the establishment and they were busy in the kitchen.

Sensing no immediate danger, she allowed herself to relax and rest her tired muscles.

Miriam reentered the common room with Caitlyn's supper. Thrusting the plate of steaming stew and the cold beer onto the table, she backed away apologizing for the delay.

Caitlyn felt the weight of the temple reputation settling on her like a cloud. *Most sixteen year olds are considered children yet I'm feared by everyone, even battle-hardened warriors.*

Wishing for acceptance was new to Caitlyn, but so too was being out of temple grounds away from the strict supervision of her trainers.

Caitlyn finished the stew quickly, famished from her trek and mentally congratulated Bert on his culinary skills.

Retiring to her chambers, she luxuriated in a warm bath. Soaping her hair she was dismayed by the grey suds that ran back into the tub. She must have looked a fright, she grinned, she'd be lucky if Bert and Miriam recognized her when she returned to the common room.

⚘

A few hours later, refreshed from a nap, she entered the large room clad in a clean set of priest's robes. From the doorway she observed the drinkers, still unaware of her presence.

Three burly men sat at the bar jesting with Bert. Their brown beefy arms and callused hands proclaiming them farmers or labourers.

Sitting at one of the tables, a group of respectably dressed young nobles were drinking and gambling.

Noting her arrival, Bert broke off his friendly chatting and cautiously approached her.

"Anything I can get for you, ma'am?"

"Dinner and another pint would be nice," Caitlyn said, heading for the table she had occupied earlier.

Seating herself, she watched the patrons return to their pursuits, somewhat less boisterously than before.

As the evening progressed and Caitlyn sat savouring her rabbit pie, ignoring the activity around her, the atmosphere relaxed.

The card game was progressing well, at least for one nobleman. As the pile of coins in his stack grew, his florid face beamed exuberantly. His rich satin shirt shone from the reflected light of the coins. His long fair hair was swept back from his face by a sapphire-encrusted band. In keeping with latest fashion, his sword and scabbard were also festooned with precious gems.

Satisfied at his suitability, Caitlyn placed a light compulsion upon him.

Laying down his cards, the noble swaggered over and without invitation, sat at her table.

"So Priestess, wanna join us for a hand, or aren't your kind allowed to gamble?"

Noting his glazed eyes and slurred speech, Caitlyn smiled to herself. "We are, and yes, I will join your game."

"I'm Count Nelson." He thrust his hand out at her.

"Caitlyn," she said, placing her delicate hand in his, wincing at the strength of his grip.

Count Nelson fell back into his chair and pointed to the other two cardplayers, "Geoffrey and Ronald Haversham."

With practiced skill, Nelson deftly dealt a new hand.

"Your wager?"

After a quick glance at her cards, Caitlyn removed a solid gold coin from a concealed pouch. She laid it on the table in front of her, "One Samaris."

Breath whistled sharply from between the Count's teeth. "Big wager for a first hand." Pushing a large quantity of smaller coins from his hoard, he saw her bet.

Geoffrey hesitated before grudgingly folding. "I'm out."

"Me too," agreed Ronald, avidly watching the tableau before him.

Count Nelson turned to Caitlyn, eyes suspiciously clear for one so drunk.

She placed her cards on the table.

Nelson groaned, "You win."

Caitlyn continued to win and soon whittled away his stash.

Geoffrey and Ronald were pleased to see Nelson getting a taste of his own medicine and cheered her on.

"I fold, I daren't ask Dad for another loan."

"I haven't enjoyed myself so much in ages," Caitlyn gushed, "You can borrow some off me if you'd like, I can certainly afford it at present."

Eyeing the coins that used to be his, Nelson agreed.

Caitlyn was hard pressed to conceal her triumph, the bait had been swallowed, Nelson didn't know it yet, but he was hers.

The game continued, the horrified Havershams keeping tally of their friend's increasing debt. They urged Nelson to stop, but all gamblers know their luck will change, if only they persevere. And persevere he did, until he owed Caitlyn more than he could ever possibly repay.

Suddenly realization dawned, "You did this deliberately," he whispered. "What do you really want from me?"

"A loyal ally," Caitlyn reassured him, "friends can come in handy on occasion."

"I'm sure they can," Nelson agreed weakly.

"I'm fortunate to have made your acquaintance this night. The Priests of the Ancient Gods are usually fortunate." Caitlyn smiled.

"I'm sure they are." He grimaced, hearing a lock snap into place, *What have I gotten myself into now?* he wondered.

Hearing his thoughts, Caitlyn felt a tinge of pity, which she ignored.

სᲠᲔ

The palace dominated the city. Black marble towers pointed into the cloudless sky. The flower gardens spread like a colourful carpet from the main gate to the pink-veined marble portico.

The beauty of this extravagant structure contrasted dramatically with Kamar's temple which blighted the northeast corner of the grounds.

Caitlyn looked upon her destination and shuddered, the obscenities practiced by the cult were anathema to her and her Gods.

I see it Master, it will be destroyed. This I vow.

Within this gilded cage the heart of the King rotted. He must die. But was there a suitable successor? The Priests of Kamar had corrupted the Princes since birth. They were at least as depraved as their father.

"Nelson, does the King have any bastards?"

"His Grace's only publicly acknowledged illegitimate son lives in a coastal village. Far enough away not to cause trouble to his rightful heirs."

"Who raised him?"

"His mother, I suppose."

"Then we must go to this village."

⚜

The village of Seahaven clustered in a tight knot around the pier, docked with many small wooden fishing vessels. The pervasive salty tang of sea and fish was strange to the desert-raised Priestess.

She stopped a brawny youth and inquired after the King's ex-mistress Bella.

Following his directions, Caitlyn and Count Nelson headed for a small cottage near the centre of the village.

Caitlyn knocked politely on the thick front door. While waiting patiently for a response, she looked at the wooden structure curiously.

It was well-made and strong, shielding the occupants from the cold ocean breezes. *A small house for an ex-mistress to the King.*

"Yes?" A small thin face peered through a crack in the door.

"Are you Mistress Bella?"

The woman looked startled. "I was."

"Please may I come in and talk to you?"

The woman hesitated. "Why would a Priestess wish to see me?"

"Please let us in and I'll explain."

Bella opened the door. At her gesture, they seated themselves at a rough-hewn table in the kitchen.

Caitlyn scrutinized her critically. Her fine-boned face dominated by large stormy grey eyes bore remnants of beauty faded by twenty years of poverty. Her raven tresses were traced with silver but were still thick and lustrous, though pulled back severely. Bella's work-hardened hands bore no resemblance to the silky smooth hands of a pampered socialite.

"Why were you looking for Mistress Bella? I haven't gone by that name in many years."

"We needed to locate you and your son."

"What do you want with Simon?"

"The church needs his help."

"For what?"

"Before I answer that, may I ask you one question? Do you hold the King in high regard?"

Her face twisted bitterly. "No."

Caitlyn looked uncomfortably at Bella. "Normally I wouldn't pry but this is important. As his mistress, surely you cared for him?"

"The King has absolute power over his subjects, it was against my will that I went to live at the palace."

"I see... would you like to revenge yourself against the king?"

"Possibly," Bella replied noncommitally.

"I have been sent by The High Priest on a holy quest. If you and your son help me to succeed, 'Kamar' and his worshippers will be banished, their blasphemous temples destroyed, and worship of the ancient Gods restored."

"Why should we help?"

"Revenge and wealth. We need to remove the King from power and replace him with someone who will help restore the true religion, someone the populace will accept. As a direct descendent they might accept Simon."

"I'll have to consider your proposal," Bella said escorting them to the door.

Outside, Caitlyn and Nelson exchanged a disappointed glance, Bella didn't seem very enthusiastic.

And so the quest faltered.

⁊ ⁊

They returned to Pyron discreetly that night.

Count Nelson had borrowed a townhouse from a relative for them to use. Situated on Pyron's outskirts, the rambling complex was enclosed by a nine foot brick fence. The nearest neighbour was off traveling with the absentee owner.

Caitlyn bestowed a rare smile on Nelson and said, "This place is perfect, very secluded, well done."

"What's next?" Count Nelson was starting to enjoy himself.

"We need to find a way to convince Bella to help us. A job I'm sure I can leave in your capable hands."

Count Nelson preened.

Nelson waited a few days to give Bella and Simon a chance to discuss their proposition. Returning to Seahaven, he found the cottage deserted.

Had Bella and Simon informed the King of their plan? With no way to know, they had no time to waste, the King's removal must be accomplished at once!

⁊ ⁊

After Nelson returned from Seahaven with the bad news, Caitlyn started her preparations for assassination in earnest.

Bribing a servant of the King was not too difficult. The debauched monarch inspired loyalty through fear, but a Priestess wearing the master mage robes inspired more.

As the sun set, Caitlyn entered the palace through the side door. Guided by an anonymous servitor, she was lead to an empty room across from the King's suite. She had been informed that after dinner the King usually attended the temple and returned late in the evening rather the worse for wine.

Sitting quietly, she slowed her breathing and communed with her Gods. Around midnight her meditation was disturbed by the King's arrival.

Caitlyn focused her will on the guards standing at attention outside the King's door. They never noticed the ten minutes missing from their lives. As their eyes glazed over, Caitlyn pulled her robe closely around her and followed the King quietly into his chamber.

The room was richly adorned with colourful tapestries depicting ancient wars and ornate carvings of wild beasts. In the centre of the room was a large canopied bed upon which the drunken monarch had passed out. Caitlyn concentrated her mind and reached out to the sleeping figure. Without disturbing his slumber, she stopped his heart and stilled his breathing.

Although granting the inhumane king a peaceful death went against her instincts, she decided it was better than risking discovery.

Feeling saddened by the task that lay ahead, Caitlyn left the royal chamber and proceeded to the suite of the two princes.

≈ ≈

With the legitimate heirs removed, Caitlyn proceeded to her final task, the destruction of the temple and the "God" Kamar.

Knowing the strength of the God depended on the belief of his disciples, Caitlyn chose to destroy the main temple in a showy fashion. Killing the priesthood and the faith of the surviving believers all at one time.

≈ ≈

The bells of the temple called the faithful to morning worship. As the last peal echoed around the palace grounds, Caitlyn joined with her gods and drew some of their power.

Appearing outside the temple, she announced in a voice supernaturally amplified for the entire city to hear, "See the judgement of the Ancient Gods. Kamar and his false prophets have been condemned for their blasphemy."

She turned to the large marble temple blighting the city. She raised her hands and a bright light streamed from her fingertips and engulfed the structure. Screams sounded from within as a golden nimbus shimmered around the temple.

The gathering crowd watched in horrified fascination as Caitlyn waved a negligent hand and the temple crumbled as the golden cage contracted, crushing the priests and devout within.

Turning to Count Nelson, Caitlyn said for all to hear, "As none of the Royal line are left, you must govern the city. Good luck and remember the Ancient Gods." Without a backward glance, she turned and headed for the city gates.

As her figure faded from view, Bella stepped forward from the crowd. "This traitor helped kill our rightful King, imprison him!"

Some of the older people, recognizing her, supported Bella's charge. As the guards closed in around him, she said quietly, for his ears alone, "You and the priestess dealt with the King, now I only need to avenge myself against the Ancient Gods. They should never have abandoned us to a Kamar-worshipping King, calling us apostate for his depravity. Now Simon will see that their worship remains outlawed. Her quest has failed."

DEVOTION

by Loren W. Cooper

Loren W. Cooper has published numerous short stories in the last few years. His recent collection THE LIVES OF GHOSTS AND OTHER SHADES OF MEMORY won the 2001 Eppie award. His favorite authors range from Aquinas to Zelazny.

Once there lived an upright man. At his right hand stood a painfully bright figure, containing all vastness, and at his left hand stood a figure of incomparable darkness, in which peace and violence marked the borders of infinity. He walked between the two, giving his heart to the one and his devotion to the other.

As he rose from the depths of night, blind need filled the man. He could only sense dimly the purpose behind the need, and that purpose brought him pain, so he shied away from it and rose into the awareness of gray light. He moved carefully, his body clean and well-rested but his mind pulsing with obscuring filth. He reached...and identity failed him, knowledge failed him—only need remained without clear purpose.

He lay still, examining his surroundings. Gentle warmth, an absence of movement in the air, and an absolutely neutral environment combined into a somehow familiar strangeness. He lay on his back in a confined area only slightly larger than his body. A soft gray glow enveloped him, reducing vision to comfortable blindness when he opened his eyes. The pleasant durability of cloth stretched firmly around his limbs. He almost relaxed into the comfort, but need prodded insistently. He reached upwards with one hand, felt the keys beneath the gray gloaming, and depressed them rapidly, without conscious volition.

A harsh glare hit him and an opening flowered into existence above his head. He wormed out of his metal and plastic cocoon into a world of movement and sound and light, which did not, on some level, surprise him. Around him men and women, dressed in many fashions but the most common of these being a utilitarian bodysuit like the one he himself wore, milled through the curving corridor. Sleeping cap-

sules identical to that from which he had just crawled lined one wall
of the corridor, stacked like the compartments of an enormous hon-
eycomb. His vision doubled, blurred, then cleared. He blinked slowly,
but showed no other outward sign of discomfort. He did this instinctively. He allowed himself bemusement as his body sealed the sleeping cubicle without any real direction.

The gravity felt strange, yet comfortable, a thing he had felt often
before. His very bones seemed to fibrillate, dancing to the subatomic
waltz of an induced gravity well. He knew this and did not question
the source of his knowledge. Need prodded again and cold spread
through him. He moved, merging with the walkers around him
smoothly. As he looked up the curve of the long corridor, an echo
moved once again within his vision, then faded. He maintained his
pace, showing no trace of the shadows within.

Not a tall man, he walked with easy grace, slipping through and
into the crowded passageway as if he had lived in that place for years.
As he moved, his blood warmed and his mind turned inward, wondering, fighting inner obscurity, trying to feel something other than the
pressure of the need. A name? He could find none. A place? Nothing.
Only pressure with shadows before and behind.

Around him, he could see numbers over passages that led out,
away from the inside curve of the corridor, into and from which people
flowed. As he walked, he surreptitiously ran his hands over the
jumpsuit he wore, felt the hard flat presence of something in an inner
pocket. He stepped into an alcove on the inner curve of the corridor
and took it out carefully, every movement made with a flow of familiar
certainty that would give any casual observer the impression that this
man stood where he belonged. He had been alone and needed to be
inconspicuous often before this. He made note of that fact and bent
his gaze to the object he had retrieved from his pocket.

The white card fit neatly into the palm of his hand, nearly as
small as the tag attached to it by a loop melding smoothly with the
substance of the card itself. On the card he read a name, Memnosyne,
which meant nothing to him, and a number, 1120A, which also meant
nothing to him. A slight ache accompanied by a shadow passed across
his vision as he glanced back up at the numbers atop the corridor
across from him, and he smiled as he read 900-950. Now he had
something.

He followed the corridor until he came to 1100-1150, and hoped
that the letter would become clear. The corridor he followed orga-
nized itself in blocks numbered consecutively, each block having heavy
doors with card slot and keypad facing each other across the hall. He
showed none of the satisfaction he felt as he saw that each door number trailed an A or B.

Need burned him then, and he increased his pace, noting that he
walked alone but for a few others as he passed into the side hall. One

man paced him as he increased speed. Intrigued, as much by his own casual noting of the man as by the presence of such a one, he slowed slightly, watched the other adjust his pace, maintaining the distance between them. Some instinct confirmed what he knew should be paranoia, and his mental picture of the man had such clarity that it surprised him. The other bulked relatively large, perhaps an inch over average height, his stride powerful, his body taut as a bowstring.

He resisted an urge to *tsk* disapprovingly as he considered his shadow. Without consciously considering the source of his criticisms, he decided that the other displayed too much tension and should not have allowed himself to be detected so easily. His shadow began closing the distance as he approached 1120, so that they stepped into block 1120 almost together. He turned at the door, and saw his pursuer stop.

The larger man kept his hands well away from his body, a fleeting smile crossing features tight as a drumhead. "Aristodemus. Why are you here?"

He tensed, tasting the name as the other rushed on, through his confusion. "You came alone, but you came here. You're with them, aren't you? You wouldn't have come this close to her unless you were with them."

He flushed, felt the halflight press back as the name settled into place. That felt right, that he had been Aristodemus. In him, he saw a face suspended against the velvet night, light against the darkness, smiling. Something moved gently within his own darkness, when he saw that face, then stilled. Need attached itself to that face, the "her." He hedged. "I'm alone. I'm not with anyone."

The other's eyes narrowed. "Don't be a fool, Aristodemus. Just coming here was a declaration of intent."

He, who accepted himself as Aristodemus, for lack of anything better, chose his words carefully. "I'm alone. I'm acting on my own, because I don't know enough."

"You don't..." The other man stepped back, pity in his eyes driven out by fear. "They've taken the choice from you."

The man who had known him once tensed, then his hand dipped inward, a quick, sure movement that should have caught Aristodemus off guard. As the other man began the movement, Aristodemus reacted on a level below conscious thought, a level clean of the muddying of enveloping shadow. Aristodemus stepped beside him, slipped an arm companionably around his neck, and then torqued the larger man viciously backwards, down against the corner of the alcove. The molded metal of the wall crushed the back of the larger man's skull with a small sound, a sound broken only by the clatter of the weapon as it hit the floor.

Aristodemus quickly shifted to the doorway, carded the door, and stuffed the body through the opened hatch. Scooping up the pistol, he glanced around, noticed no one, and entered, closing the door behind him. Only after he had closed the door did he wonder at his reaction, the spreading cold fire, the clean pleasure below the obscuring darkness in his mind, the ease with which he had reacted, and the almost instinctual act of concealing the kill. The roll of sensations felt familiar to him. He had killed and felt the reactions many times before. All of that was a part of him, along with the natural camouflage of survival.

He nodded to himself, shelving that as another piece of the puzzle, something to push back the shadows a bit further, and obeyed the need pressing him. Aristodemus located a closet, secured the body there, and briefly allowed himself remorse that the other man had forced the confrontation. He had given Aristodemus his name.

Aristodemus turned away and walked through the compartments, satisfied when he reached the forward deck and found a chair and console. Slipping into the chair, he closed his eyes. Need replaced pleasure, so he let the need drive him, filled himself with need, closed his eyes against a momentary swelling pain, and found his fingers scrawling hastily across the keyboard. Finished, he leaned back and touched the final entries on the projection, exiting.

He did not recognize the coordinates he had entered, and he did not waste any time thinking about their source. He waited for the formal query from the routing station, giving the necessary verification. Once routed, the computer did the rest of the work. He leaned back, the need satiated for now, but still present, waiting, a prod that had been removed after he had dredged up the necessary information.

He paused on that, the need as a prod. Eyes narrowing, he shook himself out of the stupor that had begun to fall upon him and pulled the information back up. Matching with the model provided by the computer that was the actual pilot of the craft, he placed the coordinates—outside of the normal path, a vector thrust applied to distort the quasimatter holding the passage together and throw the ship out of the passage early. Could he be followed? Unlikely, he decided, and he smiled.

The longest part of the trip was not the time taken to cover the greatest amount of distance. Once the data feed had been given to Transit Control, position confirmed, the contact made, and the assent given, forty-five percent of transit time had been accomplished. Over fifty-four percent disappeared into normal transit, pushing the ship out to the appropriate coordinates at the end of a fusion trail. The jump itself took less than one percent of total transit time, no time at all to the senses. That hole in the perception of his world disturbed Aristodemus in a familiar way.

The driving need became one with the throbbing in his temples, pushing him to his destination. But strangely intense pleasure mixed with anticipation distanced the pain as he made his approach to the world that loomed above him as he exited the corridor. He recognized the place, knew its fickle temperament intimately, but shadows moved between him and the rest of it, cloaking even the name. Need burned him as he moved in, fire streaking the sky to announce his presence. The coordinates led him to a familiar set of buildings, huddled against the savage landscape. He recognized the place, and knew it for an abandoned research station. Though the need throbbed and pulsed, insistent, demanding, he dressed carefully and, once outside, savored the bite of a clean wind, blowing cold and fierce.

She was waiting for him, pale hair gleaming in the light of an alien sun, her body still and straight despite the lash of the wind. She did not move, nor did she speak as he approached, but in her hooded gaze he saw something small, something still, a thing he knew well of old. His vision blurred lightly, and her upright form doubled and swayed in a field of light. Purpose moved within him, demanding that he take her, as cleanly and efficiently as he had taken the man on the station. Some tiny thing, something central and almost lost to him, refused to move, denied the need quietly, and the purpose shattered into glittering fragments of time, shards of spent possibility.

He watched her standing there, bright angel, White Lady, and unbidden tears washed his vision clean. Cold awareness burned in him then, as he reached deep, grasped the sheeting light of old memory blocks, and dropped them against the alien purpose in his mind. He opened his eyes and sighed, relaxing. She watched him closely, nodded once and turned back to the warmth of her refuge.

As Aristodemus fell in behind her quietly, memories glittered against the shadows. He clenched his teeth as he felt tenuous fingers of thought flutter gently against his ragged blocks. They would not have thought him capable of such control, and yet, and yet...they knew him better than anyone. Why the charade?

He bowed his head as the great doors fell into place behind them. Neither of them said a word as she showed him to their place, the roof and walls a clear dome that let the occupants feel exposed to the bite of this ungentle nature, and let the violence and motion of the wind and the earth and the snow surround the room. He knew it well, this place that was a part of both of them, and knew no more. Still the shadows, though pierced by light, wrapped him in tattered fragments.

She seated herself quietly across from him, moving slowly and deliberately, demonstrating a quiet certainty in her movements quite separate from fear. "I did not expect to see you here."

She smiled slightly, but he did not return her smile. "Death walks in my shadow. Your death."

She leaned further back into her seat, and her smile faded like a dying ember losing its glow. "Yet I live."

Aristodemus wanted to sag, but he did not allow it, fearing to show weakness as the memories started to flow, as he began to catch an inkling of the depth of her need. "What have you done?"

His voice softened more than he had desired, and she caught it, leaned forward, and stared sharply at him. "Bringing the policies of the elite before the judgment of the masses is unpardonable sin. Why did you come here?"

He bowed his head, broken memories flooding past the barriers of his artificial desire, the manmade shadows fading as bright, fragmented images spilled into him. He saw the same face, young, laughing and conspiratorial as she led him from the boredom of formality into new worlds of experience. He walked in darkness then as she introduced him to the pull of life and love under the pall of violent death.

He smiled in spite of himself as he felt again the warmth and brightness she stirred within him. She had been born of the elite, a child of bright stars. Reared walking in the light, she should never have chanced upon one of the chained wolves of the elite, a dark servant of the rulers of the bright gardens of the Concilium.

Aristodemus nodded, clutching at his fragments and assembling the puzzle. She had fought them, as she would have when they eventually came to disagreement. Fleeing, she would have come to their refuge, this old research station, and they, unable to find her, would have turned to the key, her old lover. Unreliable, perhaps, but breakable if unbending, and expendable as wolves must be, even those turned to the hunt.

The shadows still danced in the corners of his mind, but he knew that they could trace him, and he could feel how another's mind had been on his all through the station, in the ship, on the fields, until old training had reasserted itself and he had forced the bastard out. Aristodemus could still feel the ghostly pressure and knew that the telepath, probably the same one that had taken him apart, would break through eventually, and would at least be able to follow them. They would know the coordinates. That nameless other had seen the flight corridor as he had keyed it in, and they would be following.

He turned back, his face deliberately hard again. "Can you run?"

She flinched from the harshness in his voice. "I have a ship, and the unit here can establish a rider link to the transit Tunnel. Remember? We chose it deliberately so that if we had to run, there would be enough quasimatter only for one Tunnel. Any pursuer would be trapped. Except them. It was their station, and they would have their own resources." She paused. "Come with me. Even though we are no longer what we once were."

Aristodemus steeled himself, made his face harsh. "We were young then, and foolish."

She shook her head slowly. "You were never young."

He laughed mirthlessly. "I was young before I met you. Or at least innocent. Life was simpler then. So was death."

She smiled slightly. "You once told me I was life to you."

Aristodemus lied as he did most things, flawlessly, feeling fingers probing gently against the walls of his mind. "Life is pain, however sweet. You showed me that."

She took a step back, pain in her eyes. When he saw her about to speak, he deliberately turned away from her. "Angel, you fool, don't you know that if I'm with you, I'll be the death of you?"

He sighed and sank into the comfort of the chair, and stayed there until after he had felt the rumble of her departure, and seen the streak of her passage defile the purity of a savage sky. Pain burned beneath growing acceptance as the fact of her absence came home to him. And with the pain another presence grew. He snarled softly, stood, and stepped over to the console.

Using the memories he had as a guide, he put up every defense the station had, defenses that would fog even their sensors. All but the one he could feel even now digging through old and crumbled blocks.

The telepath had to be deceived. Aristodemus settled deeper into the chair and began his last deception. Sorting through the mosaic of his past, he picked out pieces of memory from times they had spent together. Her laugh, clean and gentle in the shadows. The sense of duty she carried like a badge of honor. The sense of justice that had turned her against her own kind. He closed his eyes and felt again the soft touch of her hand on his arm. He smiled as she leaned against him, the sweet, clean scent of her hair rising through her warmth as her head lay against his shoulder.

Each newfound memory brought new delight, and he lived again all those things in her he had loved once, and in the process he found that he loved them still. As he lost himself in the memory of her, he felt his inner vision blur, and then the alien presence dropped away from his mind. He opened his eyes to the heart of the storm and waited quietly as the shadows lengthened and the storm spoke softly to him in words of thunder.

They came in swiftly, his first knowledge the glimpse of the sleek dark shape flowing around the mountain as dusk drew gentle folds around him. Hugging the ground, moving at subsonic velocities, the warhead gave him a balcony view of the most graceful of dances. And, as he watched Death dipping sweetly down through the gathering darkness, he raised a lover's arms in greeting.

The light rose above the sound and the fury while below, in that place, the darkness swept in to cover what had once been its own.

LEARNING CURVE

by Jackie Kramer

Jackie Kramer started her writing career penning Star Trek short stories for fanzines. While working as a pediatric nurse and raising two sons, she decided to "go legit" and switched to professional writing in romance. When her first book, BABY BONUS, with Silhouette Desire hit the USA Today Bestseller list, she went on to publish several more contemporary romance novels and a paranormal romance. With LEARNING CURVE, she returns to her first love, science fiction.

Jaycee Bradley, third watch communications officer of the *Solar Rose*, pushed aside the branch, wincing as a six-inch spike gouged her cheek. The fading shouts from behind convinced her to ignore the stinging injury and keep running. Fire burned along her side and in her labored breathing. Her legs hurt, her chest hurt, in fact, her entire body hurt, but Jaycee knew if she stopped, the aliens chasing her would kill her as quickly as they had her fellow crewmate. Of the five-member survey team, only she and Dan Markeet, second officer on the *Rose*, still lived. Jaycee gritted her teeth against her exhaustion, and forced her body to keep moving. She didn't intend to end her brief spacer's career on this slime ball planet on the Rim.

Ahead of her, she could see Markeet as he splashed through a shallow, meandering creek. Clutched in his left hand was the large metallic artifact they had found in the ancient D'kilz ruins. He ran with ease, seemingly oblivious to the heat and humidity and entangling vines in his path.

No doubt he'll have something to say to me about being out of shape, she thought sourly. Markeet had seemed to delight in ragging on her ever since she signed on to the *Rose*.

He dashed through a clearing in the jungle growth, then halted on the opposite side, his chest barely heaving as he scanned behind them. Jaycee sank to one knee, drawing in huge gulps of the fetid air. God, she hated hot, humid worlds.

"I think we lost the bastards," Markeet said as he scanned their back trail. "But we'd better put some more space between them and us." He glanced at her, his expression disdainful. "Can't you get through to the ship yet?"

She ignored his derisive tone, and shook her head. "No, sir. There is some kind of interference in the atmosphere, something the sensors didn't scan."

He shook his head. "You'd think a communications officer could do better."

Jaycee bit her tongue against a heated reply. Markeet was still her superior officer.

"Let's go," he continued. "The ship's bound to send down a shuttle when we miss the deadline. All we have to do is stay free...and alive until then."

He started walking, and Jaycee forced herself to her feet, biting back a groan as sharp pain darted down both of her calves. "Yes, sir." She took a couple of deep breaths. "Though when I signed aboard the *Rose*, I didn't figure I needed to be a long distance runner," she groused.

Markeet smiled coldly at her over his shoulder, his teeth making a shark's grin against skin burned black by the suns of a thousand worlds. "Didn't you read the fine print in your contract, kid? 'Sign on with the Survey Corps and see the Universe. Bring your own running shoes.'" He examined the device in his hand briefly before tucking it into his backpack. "C'mon, let's get going."

"And don't call me 'kid'," she muttered under her breath as she followed him through the thick brush. Around them, unseen animals rustled in the shadows, and she felt eyes watching. Grotesque insects swarmed them in a cloud, and Jaycee wrinkled her nose at the faint scent of rotted plant-life. This was only her seventh planetfall, but she'd already learned that each world had its own smell, its own character.

From orbit, Epsilon 149 appeared like any other class M planet. Mean temperature 42 Celsius, nitrogen-oxygen atmosphere, and more water than most planets. What the sensors hadn't shown was the D'kilz ruins and a surface laden with natural booby-traps that had already killed three of the *Rose* crew. They also hadn't revealed that Epsilon 149 had a sentient race.

When the team first found the device Markeet carried, the certain knowledge of vast wealth had sent excitement through the entire team. After all, D'kilz technology was centuries beyond Earth's, and the Companies would pay top credits for even the simplest relic. But then everything went wrong. The natives had shown up. Twelve feet tall, reptilian, armed with only primitive spears, they had silently appeared among the stones of the age-old ruins.

Markeet had gone through the usual first contact, attempted to set up a trade for the device, but her translator hadn't been able to crack the alien language. Almost before she knew it, tempers had flared.

Sam Reever must have thought the group was in danger because he suddenly drew his blaster. And in a blink of an eye, the big, bluff security man lay on the jungle floor, cut down by a streak of silent lightning that flashed from one of the spears. The rest of the humans had managed to blast their way clear, but the aborigines had proven persistent.

Jaycee slogged behind Markeet, determined not to be the one to ask for help. All her life she'd wanted to be in the Survey Corps, exploring new worlds, discovering new resources. So here she was, trudging through primeval slime, being chased by hostile aliens, all for the sake of a hunk of machinery no one probably knew how to operate. She quirked the corner of her mouth in derision. She must be out of her mind. Right now, she could be safely on Earth, sitting at Murphy's Bar with—She walked slam-bam into Markeet who had halted without her awareness.

He gripped her arms. "Steady, kid. It doesn't pay to daydream when you're planetside, especially on a rock this adverse. Remember Wiley?"

Memories of Rod Wiley, the botanist, filled her mind. He had become excited about a plant he'd spotted and unwisely started studying it without checking for surrounding danger. The hidden reptile's bite had him yellow-faced and dead on the ground before any of the team could reach him. And when the natives had first attacked them, Sanders had blindly stumbled into a patch of poisonous barbs during his panicked escape from the aliens. His body had swelled, his features distorted, as they hid from the aliens. At last he had slowly strangled to death despite every drug in the medkit.

"We'll take a break here."

Markeet's words broke through her stupor, and Jaycee gratefully dropped to the ground. She took a drink from her canteen, mindful of the need to ration her water, then pulled her communicator from her utility belt. Twilight was stealing across the jungle. She wouldn't have much time to get it working. But all she got from it was a few flickering lights and a pitiful whine. Useless, she decided. Maybe the translator had been able to crack the natives' language. It had had enough time to work on the problem.

"Still can't get it to work, communications officer?"

Jaycee kept her gaze on her work, refusing to respond to his baiting tone.

He snickered. "Then maybe you'd better sleep the first watch." Markeet eyed her, the corner of his mouth lifted in mockery. "You can manage that, can't you?"

"Yes, sir," she responded stonily as she glared at him. She set the translator beside her and curled up where she sat. She watched Markeet settle beneath another giant fern, his blaster across his lap. Her last thought as she drifted into a restless sleep was that if Fate was kind, when she awoke, this planet...and Markeet would be gone.

⊱⊰

A soft chittering sound penetrated Jaycee's exhaustion and she slowly awakened. A thin fog glittered in the rising sun. Jaycee rubbed her dry, gritty eyes, then cautiously sat up, every muscle in her body stiff and sore. she saw a small bird-like creature on a nearby branch, watching her. A pale, blue fuzz covered the tiny avian and, it stared at Jaycee with large, multi-faceted golden eyes.

"At last," she murmured. "One animal on this god-forsaken mudball that is cute and furry." She extended a forefinger to stroke its soft coat, but the winged beast pounced on a lizard scampering through the thick growth and savagely demolished it with a mouthful of razor-sharp teeth. Jaycee shuddered as she snatched back her hand. "Yuck!"

She looked around, wondering if Markeet had seen her careless action. Ten feet away, she spotted him, still sitting under the giant fern, his head bent and his eyes closed. Jaycee grinned. She couldn't believe it. The mighty Dan Markeet had fallen asleep while on guard duty. She cautiously rose and slipped closer. She couldn't wait to see his face when she awoke him with a shout.

As she approached, a sliver of dread cascaded down her spine. He was too silent, too unmoving. She reached his side, then noticed a trickle of dark liquid seeping from his left ear. A hard fist seemed to form inside her chest.

"Markeet?" Her voice came out in a thin whisper. She swallowed the hard lump in her throat, kneeled, and tried again. "Mr. Markeet. Wake up, sir."

She touched his shoulder as she spoke and he toppled to his side. She squealed, then terror surged through her. The back of his head writhed as if alive. An eight-inch gray slug crawled out Markeet's ear, trailing blood and gray matter.

Jaycee jerked away from the sight and landed on her butt. "Ohgod, ohgod," she sobbed as she pushed with her feet, scooting backwards on her rear.

The slug undulated down Markeet's cheek, plopped into the grass, and disappeared, leaving the dead officer with his skull flattened. Jaycee's stomach heaved and she rolled, just in time to expel her stomach contents into nearby bushes.

Numbly, Jaycee lay with her cheek on the damp ground. She was alone, lost on a deadly planet. Her translator lay a few feet away, humming gently, a tiny green light flashing. Vaguely, Jaycee realized the machine had finished its job, but she didn't care. All she wanted was off this hellhole. And if she was going to achieve that, she had to get moving.

Pushing away all her fear, all her weariness, she gritted her teeth and rose. She grabbed her translator and headed for the jungle. A metallic flash caught her eye, and she hesitated. She spied the D'kilz artifact, laying innocently beside Markeet's body. Revulsion swept over her. Because of that damned thing, all her crewmates were dead. For a moment, She considered leaving it behind. No, her team wasn't going to die in vain. She scooped up the relic and plunged in the rainforest.

She glided from tree to tree, watchful for danger. When she suddenly rounded a bush and almost ran into a native, she instinctively whirled and ran. The sound of her pounding feet matched the throb of her heart. All of a sudden, the ground beneath her gave way and she screamed as she fell. The D'kilz mechanism whined as it flew from her hand, and she felt a momentary pain slice through her. She landed hard and realized she was laying at the bottom of some sort of sinkhole. She saw her translator, wedged in a tangle of roots poking out from the wall.

She couldn't feel her feet. She couldn't even hear herself breathing. Glancing down at her body, she saw a gaping wound across her chest. There wasn't any bleeding from the neatly sealed edges, but she could see her severed lungs. Tears pricked her eyes. She didn't want to die...here...all alone.

Movement caught her attention, and she looked up. Two natives stood at the lip of the hole, staring down at her.

"I wish we could save it."

Jaycee heard the voice, but as if in a dream. At last, the translator had figured out the alien language. She could understand them. She tried to talk to them, ask them for help, but couldn't. Darkness crept closer, and as her spirit released life, she saw the other alien shrug.

"It's too bad the creature will die. But, she did run with scissors."

THE STORYTELLER'S THANKSGIVING

by Linda Bleser

Linda Bleser began her writing career publishing short fiction for women's magazines. Since then, she's completed several award-winning novels in a variety of genres, from rib-tickling comedy to bone-chilling suspense. Reviewers have hailed her work as unique, original, and impossible to put down.

The storyteller's wife chopped vegetables while her sister rolled out pastry crust.

"Doesn't he ever come down?"

Her knife missed the onion and came down with a fierce smack on the cutting board. No, he hardly ever came down anymore, but she wasn't about to give her sister the satisfaction of knowing how it gnawed at her, bringing new worry lines to an already wrinkled brow. There were enough rumors whispered about her husband and his dangerous hobby.

Her glance shot upward, as if she could see him hunched over the keyboard, sending useless messages that could one day destroy them all.

 ❧ ❧

Upstairs, the old man wiped his brow and reached deep into his memories. For a moment he almost forgot that the words were only dark symbols on a cold screen. His arthritic fingers tapped slowly on the keyboard, but in his mind he spun tales around a blazing campfire.

"...and when the farmer noticed that the destructive birds and animals came back when he left, he built a human form of straw and old clothes to stand guard in his absence. This came to be called a 'scarecrow.' The scarecrows stood in the fields, animated by the breeze and given substance by the human scent that lingered in worn threads.

The scarecrow kept watch over the field, fooling the predators and protecting the harvest."

The storyteller sat back and rubbed his throbbing knuckles. Immediately a response came back on the screen. "Are there scarecrows still?"

The old man felt the sadness churning inside him. So few fields left, so little need for scarecrows except as a symbol of what used to be—before *they* came and took his land and his people—his very language—away.

"Some," he answered. "On isolated reservations where our people still keep the old ways."

"Tell me more, grandfather."

The old man wanted to reach out with a reassuring touch, but he knew it would be a useless gesture, soothing only to himself. He could give them words and nothing more.

"There were ceremonies," he continued. "Ceremonies of birth and death and rites of passage. All the people would gather and celebrate with song and food."

"Tell me about songanfood."

He sighed. Sometimes they asked the impossible. How to explain song to a race that had no concept of music? What was food to a body that needed no sustenance? Still he tried.

"Songs are stories put to music, a way of communicating feelings. Voices lifted to the sky, capturing dreams in bubbles of sound."

No, not enough. The old man felt impotent. If only he could let the child hear a song, smell bread baking, feel the soft grass bend beneath his feet. Perhaps then he could truly communicate what this world had once been like.

But he had to be content that at least he could pass down some of their heritage in words, as ineffective as that sometimes might be, and somehow that knowledge would be kept alive.

Soon their time was over. The old man knew it wasn't in the nature of the young to be idle for long in useless chatter, and it was dangerous for him to stay online. His messages could be traced, putting their village in danger.

But this one would be back, as his hunger to know made him once more call for the memories the old man shared. As a parting gift, the old man gave him a name to use the next time he called—*Hummingbird*.

As for the old man's name, only those in his tribe spoke it. The questions that came on the screen were simply addressed to "grandfather," a term of respect he answered to with pride.

When he looked up, his wife stood in the doorway, wiping her hands on a dishtowel. "Why don't you come away from there for a while?"

"Not yet. Just a few more."

She sighed. "Couldn't you let someone else answer their questions?"

"Someone else," he murmured with a shake of his head. "Who? So many of our people are gone, their memories dust."

She came to him, warm comforting hands on his leathery brow. "Maybe the time for remembering is past."

"Not while I still breathe." He straightened and turned back to the screen where more requests had stacked up.

"Tell me a story, grandfather—Darting Minnow."

"Grandfather, tell me a story—Wild Rabbit."

"Tell me...tell me."

"Look." The old man gestured to the screen. "So many questions. I can't simply turn them away."

She bit her lip. "I was wondering. What if it's a trick?"

He shook his head, seeing the worry on her face and knowing who had put it there. "You mean your sister has been wondering."

She lowered her eyes. "What if she's right?"

"Why should she start now?" he muttered. As soon as the words slipped out of his mouth he was ashamed and wished he could take them back.

"I'm sorry," he said. "Maybe she's right. Maybe they're *all* right and I'm just a foolish old man."

Her hand rested on his shoulder. They had never let cross words come between them before.

"Old men, old memories," he muttered. "What are they good for?"

She shook her head and left the room.

The old man refilled his coffee cup and lit a cigarette, listening to the soft, tired footfalls of his wife's retreat. He turned back to the screen, but his heart was no longer in it. The questions were too many, the answers too few.

How could he even begin to explain the pleasures of eating, drinking, even smoking—all things that were now illegal. These were pleasures only the old ones could still enjoy here where they were allowed to retain the traditions of their former society on small, isolated pieces of land.

But for how long? Soon even this would be lost as the elders died out, taking their memories with them. It was said that when a man died, a thousand stories died with him. Soon they would all be gone, all the elders and all their stories.

The old man's only pleasure now was passing down the ways of his people, as more and more the young ones came with longing questions. The requests had become more frequent lately, as if what was once human in them could no longer resist searching for their roots.

He rubbed his aching shoulders where old age had settled in the joints and once again, as he did more and more often these days, appreciated the appeal of an indestructible body.

In his youth, with strength and vitality surging through his bones, it was easy to despise those who chose to replace their natural bodies with metal parts. He'd felt it was a sin against humanity. But now, as his body failed him, he could appreciate the allure of a body immune to disease, decay or death. Like the ones who reached out to him through this terminal.

Cyborgs they were, but *Boors* his people called them, spitting the name with disdain. The word itself felt evil on the tongue, a curdled, rancid curse against nature.

They'd begun as a transplant here, a patch there. Soon all that was left was a brain, a small piece of meat, acting as the central processing unit to a mechanical body. It worked so well that people became impatient. Why wait for the body to fail? Why not begin all life encased in virtually indestructible metal?

Before long, entire generations matured never knowing a hug, a touch, human warmth or song. Knowledge was hardwired directly to the brain and no other sustenance was needed.

Until now.

Lately more and more requests came across his computer screen, young Boors curious about the ways of their ancestors who lived in soft fragile skins; wanting to experience human conditions they had no use for.

Why this sudden surge of interest in the old ways?

Perhaps in remaking themselves the Boors now realized that they had lost a vital human link—their heritage, their culture, their very history.

Another message came on the screen. The old man smiled. It was Blustering Wind, an insolent youth who enjoyed baiting him. The storyteller tolerated Blustering Wind with amusement.

"Grandfather, what good is it to suffer in soft skin that bleeds?"

The old man placed his hands on the keyboard, prepared to quench a thirst that had no name. "How can you improve if you don't suffer? What is there to rise above?" he answered. But he knew Blustering Wind could neither fathom the answer nor the question. Sure enough, he disappeared, only to be replaced by another with equally challenging questions.

Today Blustering Wind hadn't irked him, but sometimes the questions he raised made the old man wonder whether he had made the right choice. He was the last of his family to adhere to the old ways. Even his own kin had left him behind as easily as a snake sheds its skin.

≈ ≈

Downstairs his wife shook her head sadly. Her husband's hobby might be the death of them. He didn't hear what the rest of the village whispered behind his back. Many in the tribe wondered if he was losing his mind, taking chances by talking to the Boors. They worried that his stories were flags leading the Boors to their door to destroy them once and for all.

Even if she had been able to coax her husband away from the screen, she knew his thoughts would have remained with the faceless Boors on the other end. She couldn't compete with these strangers who stole so much of his time. She was too old and tired to try.

She pushed her thoughts aside. There was too much to do to worry about an old man's foolishness. Tomorrow was a celebration of thanks and she, being the eldest female in the village, would oversee the cooking, making sure the feast conformed to the traditional table, and recreating recipes she had learned at her mother's knee.

"Haven't you started the pudding yet?" She snapped at her sister, who raised her hands as if to say, *Don't take it out on me*. But the look in her eyes was smug.

≈≈

The storyteller squashed out his cigarette and drained the last of his cold coffee. He turned to the computer terminal where a growing list of messages waited. Lately the requests were unending, but something inside him couldn't let a question go unanswered.

Despite the reassurances he gave his wife, the old man worried as well, for each message could be a threat in disguise. He smelled onions simmering in the kitchen, and wondered again if he was putting his wife and neighbors in danger by answering these requests.

In the last few years distrust had developed among some militant Boors who declared the few remaining elders to be dangerous, spreading unrest with their stories of a world whose time had come and gone.

At first these few remaining villages were ignored, with the arrogance of science that they would succumb or become extinct. Now, though, the Boors looked on them as a threat, a dangerous provocation of unrest. For this reason he kept his replies short, to avoid being traced and accused.

The Boors had set out to destroy the few pockets of resistance, his pod village among them, where vestiges of the old society remained and generations died and were born and stories continued to be passed down from father to son—stories that told of the old ways, traditions and religions.

He turned back to the screen and reached into his mind to retrieve a story, saddened by how many he had already forgotten. He realized that even the memories he'd retained seemed meaningless now—the Taj Majal, fireworks, parades, the Statue of Liberty, and even the ugly blanket his wife's mother had woven. Each held a story and there were so many stories to tell.

Some stories were not even his own; only wisps of memories given him as a child, borrowed from someone else's vision. He worried that he wasn't being true to their meaning and wondered how many of the shared memories which had deep significance for him would be twisted in the retelling years from now? It all seemed so hopeless.

≈≈

The storyteller's wife was elbow deep in corn stuffing when the knock came.

"Just a second," she called, wiping stuffing from her hands and then rinsing at the sink. It was probably one of the neighbors with a last minute emergency—*I need more sugar*, or *How long should I soak the leeks?*

Drying her hands on her apron, she shuffled to the door, opened it, then let out a quick gasp of surprise.

A Boor stood at the threshold, blocking out the sunlight.

She took a step back. Then another. What was he doing here? Had her husband finally led the enemy to their door? At the stove, her sister turned, spied the Boor and screamed.

But the storyteller's wife simply stood, staring in wonder at this strange marriage of man and machine. She'd expected that when this day finally came she'd be terrified. Instead she felt a strange sense of relief. Now she could stop expecting the worst.

The Boor tilted his head/screen at her. She knew that this gesture enabled him to receive data from his input sensors, but the gesture looked so human that it momentarily disarmed her.

She slowly scrutinized the Boor. She hadn't seen one in over fifteen years and they had changed quite a bit since then. Evolving, as all things do. In the beginning they had retained a human look, but it appeared they had given up form for function now that their dealings with non-Boors were kept to a minimum.

The data screen, no longer perched precariously on the torso like a human head, was now suspended within the metal life-support pack. Arms that swiveled 360 degrees at four joints were covered with sensory pods, reminding her of suckers on the tentacles of an octopus. Instead of legs, the Boor moved on fat, treaded wheels that functioned independently. Its case was the same gun metal blue of her father's antique shotgun. She couldn't help shivering in the Boor's shadow.

"What do you want?" she asked, ignoring her sister's open-mouthed look of horror. Perhaps he was just lost. She tried not to glance at the curious metal appendages that served the same purpose as her two sturdy arms.

"I have come to see the grandfather," he said, in that strange mechanical monotone that left no room for emotion. She knew the Boors were capable of speech, although they never used it among themselves. They spoke to each other in binary transmissions, but the speech ability was a throwback to the old days when humans outnumbered

Boors and communication was a necessity. Now communication between man and Boor was rare.

It was not in her nature to turn someone away from her door.
Even a Boor. She considered herself much less naive than her husband, however, and kept her response deliberately circumspect.

"I'm sorry. You must have the wrong pod. We have no children
and therefore can be no one's grandparents. Perhaps I could direct
you further if I knew who you were seeking?" She could hear the un-
truth beneath her stiff words, and hoped the machine, being unfamiliar with human inflection, wouldn't detect a lie.

The Boor entered the room without waiting for an invitation. His
wheels sent sinister whispers across the floor. He seemed even bigger
and more threatening inside the small room, and his approach was
more than her sister could take. She ran screaming out the back door,
the hem of her dress pulled immodestly above her knees. It wouldn't
be long before the whole community knew the enemy was among them.

"I seek the storyteller," the Boor said. "I believe I have come to the
right place."

The storyteller's wife turned away, unable to lie and unsure how
to misdirect. But the Boor persisted in that strangely over-precise way
that made him sound like an educated foreigner.

"He calls me 'Morning Star.' If you would tell him that I am here,
I am sure he would see me."

She straightened, unconsciously mimicking his stilted speech. "I
will tell my husband of this. Perhaps he will know how to help you."

Somewhere deep in her heart she'd always known this day would
come. Whatever happened now was out of her control. She hurried
upstairs, her heart fluttering like a trapped dove beneath her chest.

The sight of her husband sending electronic signals that made
them all sitting targets unleashed a surge of anger. She charged across
the room and screamed into his astonished face. "They're here. Are
you happy now?" She swept the keyboard off the desk, sending it clattering to the floor. "You and your stupid stories have led the enemy
straight to our door."

"A Boor? Here?"

She put her hand to her mouth, afraid to say more. She nodded
and glanced toward the doorway, sure that the Boor had overheard
her outburst and was now looming behind her, all threatening metal
that could crush her dead in an instant.

But the doorway was empty and soon her husband's arms were
around her, soothing, comforting. His assurances were useless, however. She knew that things would never be the same. From this day
forward, her once safe kitchen would always carry the stain of Boor.

❧❧

The storyteller welcomed Morning Star, as his wife knew he would.

The Boor bowed his head/screen in what seemed a genuine sign of respect. "Grandfather," he said, "I've come for a story."

The storyteller studied him thoughtfully. Finally he came to a decision, nodded, and gestured to the Boor. "Let's talk."

The storyteller's wife lowered her eyes. She knew her husband too well to hope he'd turn this stranger away, but a secret part of her wished he had stood firm and thrown the Boor out of their house.

She made busy motions in the kitchen, but listened as her husband told the Boor of the ceremony they were about to celebrate. He spoke of the first Thanksgiving and how the Indians shared their harvest with the settlers who would eventually take everything they had.

No longer limited by the words on the screen or the need to finish quickly, he seemed to come alive in the telling, recreating different aspects of the story with gestures like an actor on stage. Even his wife, who had heard this story told many times around the table, felt as if she were hearing it for the first time.

The Boor listened quietly, without interrupting. She watched him carefully, though, filled with mistrust. She had often thought herself a good judge of character, but how do you read a screen and polished metal? No human heart beat within the life support pack, and Boors could neither cry nor bleed.

He could be exactly what he professed to be—a student in search of his teacher. Or he could be a scout for the enemy. How easy it would be to steal their memories and then report them to the government. They would be wrenched from their village and imprisoned.

Or worse.

She decided right then not to be as trusting as her foolish husband. She shifted her attention back to the gentle cadence of his voice and realized that his story had changed.

Her husband was now telling the Boor about the most hated man in history...*Benedict Arnold?* She listened closely, for this was a story she could not remember hearing before, and wondered whether her husband might be making it up.

Perhaps he was not as naive as she suspected, for this story told of a man who betrayed his own people; a man whose very name became synonymous with the word traitor.

Would the Boor understand the implications?

Her wonder quickly turned to amazement as she heard her husband offer the Boor lodging for the night and a place at the ceremonial table tomorrow.

This was unheard of!

She tried to signal her discomfort with her eyes, but then stopped herself. Her husband looked so happy, like a father teaching one of his own sons. Perhaps that was why it meant so much to him when the voices called through the void for his memories. They filled an emptiness he never spoke of to her. Perhaps this was his way of ensuring that a part of himself somehow lived on—if not through a son of his own, then at least through this strange hybrid creature.

But to welcome a Boor to the ceremonial table?

This would be the final straw. She felt a rush of embarrassed panic at what would be whispered about her husband's state of mind among the others of the village.

~ ~

She didn't have to wait long. Word spread quickly through the small community that they were harboring a Boor. Despite her own fears, she found herself forcefully defending her husband's choice when the elders came to question his decision. Her own sister was the loudest among them.

"How can you let him into your house?"

"He's already here. What should I do, throw him out?"

"But a Boor!"

"He's here to learn..."

"Learn? He's here to destroy us. I knew your husband would set them on our trail. You should have put your foot down long ago."

"Like you put your foot down with *your* husband?" That finally shut her sister up.

While arguments flew around the room, the Boor sat quietly, watching. No one asked his motives or directed questions his way. He sat, seen but not heard.

And no one seemed to notice when he wheeled quietly away.

"How can you trust him?" someone asked from the back of the room.

She heard her husband's voice, soft and gentle, but filled with authority. "Trust," he said, "is a choice that reveals more about the man who makes it. What else could we do?"

"Leave," one of the elders spoke up.

"Like we have in the past? How long can we keep running? What if we're wrong and they *are* seeking us out with a genuine desire to understand and accept the old ways. Should we let this opportunity slip by us? Should we ignore the chance to heal the rift and truly let our legacy live on?"

She heard a soft chittering coming from the other room. The Boor was transmitting. Who was he sending information to? She suspected he was a scout, mimicking innocence before leading an army of Boors their way.

~ ~

That night, alone in their room, she questioned her husband.

"How can you take him into our home so readily? Didn't you listen to the story your lips told of how the Indians welcomed and fed the enemy, only to lose everything they had?"

"I know the story," he stated calmly. "But what other choice do I have? If I assume, without proof, that the Boor has come to gather information against us, than I am less human than the Boors themselves."

"But..."

"However, I choose to trust," he continued, holding up a hand to stop her arguments. "And hope. Hope that maybe one day after we're gone our heritage will live on. Maybe there will be other Boors to spread the word and keep the traditions alive long after we're dead. It's a risk I choose to take." But his shoulders slumped, betraying his bravado.

"No," she said firmly. "I don't understand and I don't agree."

He looked at her, surprise evident on his face. They'd never disagreed so strongly about anything before.

"I'm afraid," she said with quiet conviction.

"Don't be."

"I can't trust as easily as you." She had already made up her mind. "I won't spend a night under the same roof as the enemy. I don't have the same faith that you do."

"What will be, will be." The storyteller muttered the words to the old folk song.

"I'm sorry," the old woman said and turned away. "I'll be at my sister's house tonight."

When she left, she passed the window where the Boor would be spending the night. She spied guiltily into her own home. He was transmitting again, the soft chittering sound blended with that of the crickets and peepers outside. Who would have expected the end of the world to sound so peaceful?

She hated leaving her husband alone, but it was his choice, not hers, and she could only save face among the village wives by leaving. But she knew she had a much harder decision ahead of her. Along with many others who would have to decide whether to stay or go.

⁀≈

The next day the storyteller led the Boor to the communal hall, afraid that when he opened the door it would be to an empty room. He took a deep breath and listened, surprised to hear sounds coming from inside.

When he opened the door, all conversation stopped. Heads turned in his direction. Ignoring the openly hostile expressions, the storyteller took a seat. He glanced around the ceremonial table. There were nearly half as many people as should have been there. So, some had chosen to leave. Very well, it was their choice. Each of the celebrants glared at the Boor as it wheeled up to the table beside the storyteller, but no one stopped him.

The old man looked each of them in the eye, daring them to question his right to bring a guest to the ceremonial table. This, of all days, was the day to welcome strangers. Even a Boor.

His heart sank when he saw his wife's empty place, but he stood, with steel resolve and addressed the group. "This Boor is named Morning Star," he told them. "He is here to learn about our ways and to share our culture. He is my guest, so please make him welcome."

He looked around the table. Heads leaned together whispering, staring. The air was filled with mistrust, and the smell of fear competed with the aromas of the ceremonial table. Someone stood and the old man worried that both he and the Boor would be sent away after all.

Suddenly his wife came to the table and put a restraining hand on the shoulder of the man who was about to speak. She turned to the Boor. "You are welcome at our table, Morning Star." Then she nodded to her husband and sat at his side.

The storyteller gave his wife a grateful smile.

As they joined hands around the table, the ceremony began. The storyteller spoke the words that had been handed down from his father's father. Around him other voices joined in, stronger, as they gave thanks and celebrated their brotherhood.

He stood, looking years younger than he had before. His voice was strong and firm. "I have wondered why more and more the Boors have come seeking stories about the old ways. I think I now understand.

"It seems," he said, addressing his friends around the table, "that this is the way it has always been. Progress is not a straight thread from yesterday to tomorrow. It twists and curls, circling back to touch the past, then stretching forward once again.

"One generation produces another that marches off into the future, never looking backward at its primitive roots. Their children return, however, embracing the rich culture their parents shunned. And so in this way we are assured continuity, a twisted cord of old and new which strengthens rather than weakens with time. That's why," he explained, "I accept him so readily. This new generation of Boors has come back to reclaim their heritage. It is the way of the world."

"What will be, will be," his wife murmured. She nodded in agreement, then closed her hand around his.

He smiled back, remembering the old folk song. Their eyes spoke silently, the way only two people who have been married most of their lives can communicate.

He reached over and stroked her hair. "Would you sing the ancient folk song for us?" he asked. Her family had always kept the sacred music alive and her voice rose sweetly in answer.

"Kay-seera, sera. Whatever will be, will be. The future's not ours to see. Kay-seera, sera."

When the song ended, one by one they raised their heads in shocked silence, stunned to see that they were circled by Boors.

An army of Boors.

So this was the end. The storyteller's wife took no pride in having been right.

Dozens of Boors circled the table, their bodies casting sharp shadows over the bare floor. A quick chittering began, led by Morning Star, then taken up by the group around them, until the soft noise was almost deafening. They circled the table, leaving no room for escape.

"What will be, will be," the storyteller's wife murmured quietly, resigned.

Under the table her sister kicked her viciously. "I told you."

"Shush." She turned from her sister and embraced her husband. At least if the end came they would die together. And they would not die empty of humanity, a fragile shell unable to give the gift of trust.

Slowly one Boor broke away from the circle, wheeled up to the table and faced the storyteller. "Grandfather," he said, "I offer corn for your feast. I am Lone Fox."

Another. "My name is Hummingbird, Grandfather. I bring you straw for your scarecrows."

"Darting Minnow...

"Rogue Wolf...

"Turtle's Back...

Each gift echoed something from the story the old man had told the Boor yesterday. So, Morning Star *had* transmitted their location. But he had passed on the story to his friends, not so they could attack, but so that they could be part of the ceremony. A gesture of trust in return from the Boors.

One by one they came, sunlight twinkling off their screens as they offered their gifts to the storyteller. Then, quietly they sat at his feet.

The storyteller stood, tears misting the corners of his eyes. He opened his arms, welcoming them, and in a voice crackling with emotion, gave them what they'd come searching for.

"Once upon a time..."

MAYBE NEXT TIME

by J. Brian Jones

Born and raised in southwestern Pennsylvania, J. Brian Jones can often be found playing hockey, watching hockey, or thinking about hockey. When not focused on that particular obsession, he immerses himself in online RPGs and other various interests. During the few spare moments that remain, he sits under a bridge and writes while listening to his collection of Alice Cooper CDs.

Two powerful wings were folded comfortably against its sides, while all four of the gigantic beast's legs were tucked beneath its lizard-like torso. A row of pointed tines ran down the center of its back, all the way to the end of a lengthy tail that was curled against one wall. Coins from long forgotten kingdoms covered the floor in heaps around and underneath the slumbering dragon, forming a makeshift bed. Gems of all sizes and colors peeked out here and there, making their presence known. A faint glow emanated from the weapons and armor of various cultures and races and eras that dotted the miniature landscape of coin-mountains. A plethora of wands, liquid-filled bottles, jewelry, chests, and various other "treasures" were also scattered throughout the enormous oblong cavern.

Arzechytium slowly raised a scaled eyelid until it was barely a quarter of the way open. A piercing yellow eye stared casually at one smallish entrance to the domelike chamber that housed him during his peaceful rest.

"How long had it been? A few days? Weeks? Months, perhaps?" he thought indifferently.

It was always difficult to tell how long he had been sleeping. After all, one as wise and regal as Arzechytium rarely ventured forth into the world. And time didn't really matter to him any more. He was content to remain here in his home, enjoying his well-deserved peace, rest, solitude, and treasure.

"Let the young ones worry about the outside world and all of its goings on! And good luck to them! Especially if they plan on aligning themselves with pathetic humans! Or trolls or giants or any of those

other lesser creatures, for that matter!" the dragon mused.

All Arzechytium needed now was peace and quiet. Yet something had awakened him. A vague noise in the distance that came from the tiny opening on the far end of his sleeping chamber. It didn't sound like the shifting rocks and rumblings of the mountain with which he had become so familiar over the years.

"Years? Decades? Surely I haven't been here for more than a century," Arzechytium pondered.

Another strange sound echoed from the narrow corridor, interrupting his internal debate. The ancient wyrm knew that it wasn't caused by something natural such as a cave-in, small earthquake, volcanic activity, or the like. There were no vibrations of the floor, ceiling, or walls to indicate anything of the sort. And the sound didn't come from the stone itself, but through the small opening across the way.

"What, then, might it be?" the dragon contemplated curiously.

Surely it wasn't another band of those ignorant goblins, wanting to expand their complex of tunnels again. It was bad enough they moved into the natural caves and passages far above his resting place. But at least they served as somewhat of a deterrent to anyone or anything else that might venture into his home. And it was only a minor inconvenience when the stupid creatures occasionally sent small parties to explore the deepest recesses of the mountain. Of course, none of them ever returned to their comrades or homes or families or whatever it was that the smelly little things had up there. Come to think of it, Arzechytium realized that he hadn't had a snack in a long time.

"Maybe they finally ran out of brave volunteers," he reasoned, chuckling to himself.

Brave! The old dragon might have laughed to himself at that notion on a different day. The goblins that actually did make it to his chamber were hardly brave. Most of them panicked and froze with fear the instant they caught a glimpse of his magnificent form. He would usually eat one or two of the creatures, even though they didn't particularly taste very good. Of course a few would turn and flee, not that it really mattered. As soon as he raised his serpentine neck and bellowed forth a stream of fire, those paralyzed by his splendor were immediately turned to ashes and blown away. The ones who retreated back into the corridor had likely suffered worse than the goblins that stayed to admire him. After all, they probably writhed in agony as their flesh and bones burned away at a much slower rate, since they weren't directly in the path of the raging inferno.

"Cowards always get what they deserve in the end," Arzechytium smiled.

The ancient wyrm allowed his yellow eye to scan the cavern again. It settled on another wide crack in the towering gray walls. Misshapen mounds of gold, silver, gemstones, and other precious metals were fused together, resembling rolling dunes of sand or waves on the sea. The stone surrounding the opening was blackened, as well. Small splotches of various colors speckled the walls in the area, a result of the sudden melting and splashing of assorted coins, items, and other prized possessions that he had liquefied with his fiery breath. Arzechytium stared angrily at the twisted heaps for a long moment.

"The goblin raiders came through that hole," he reminded himself.

The great red dragon returned his unconcerned gaze to the opening from which he had heard the noises that had roused him. A faint repetitive pitter-patter wafted through the crevice.

"Footsteps... And it smells like one of those perpetually singing, pointy-eared, woodland creatures," Arzechytium noted derisively.

The wyrm heard one distinct set of footfalls coming from far down the corridor. He knew better than to think that someone dared venture this deep into the underworld all alone. More would be following this advanced scout, but only after he deemed the passage was safe. The pitter-patter stopped for several seconds then receded, growing softer and softer. Getting farther and farther away.

"Going back for his companions since the way is 'safe'," the dragon smirked.

Sure enough, a faint whisper drifted out of the opening.

"All clear," the melodic voice beckoned quietly, speaking in the unrefined common tongue.

"Poor elf has to lower himself to that level just to make acquaintances," Arzechytium concluded sarcastically.

A murmur of three—no, four—other voices answered in less than subdued tones. Two were obviously male and likely human. The third was high pitched, but not sonorous enough to be elven. A human female, the ancient wyrm guessed. The fourth voice was deep-pitched and gruff. Couldn't be a dwarf. They don't get along well with the elves. At least they didn't the last time Arzechytium had been in contact with the outside world. And that had been... He didn't want to rehash that debate again. Instead, he listened for more clues about the individual with the rough voice.

"Let's go," one of the human males directed. "Don't want to keep Aylwin waiting."

"I don't like the idea o' him bein' up there by hisself anyway," the gruff-voiced man grumbled.

"Rudiger, we all know that you'd rather be near the front since the goblins killed your brother," the woman remarked. She sounded rather sympathetic. "But you would need a torch and Aylwin does not," she explained.

"Yeah, 'n don't worry, you'll get your chance at revenge," the second man agreed. "We know they hafta be down 'ere somewhere. 'Sides, Aylwin promised he'd come n' get ya 'fore fightin' any of 'em," he added.

It also sounded like he slapped the disgruntled man heartily on the back.

The deep-voiced man muttered something unintelligible in response.

"A human from the savage lands. It has to be," the dragon decided firmly.

The scuffle of many feet reverberated off the walls, making Arzechytium wonder how any of these pathetic humanoids had survived so long. They certainly weren't going to sneak up on anyone or anything with tactics like this. Eventually, the corridor became silent again. The whole filthy bunch must have finally met up. The wyrm assumed that they were coordinating their next move through hand signals or something of the sort, since he didn't even hear the telltale sign of someone scratching a drawing on the floor. After the brief pause, the solitary shuffle of the light-footed elf began anew. Louder and louder. Closer and closer. In fact, Arzechytium figured that the elf was not much farther up the corridor now.

"Would he keep advancing if he knew that I was only a few hundred feet away?" he pondered insidiously.

The dragon heard the footfalls come to an abrupt halt. A gasp followed almost immediately. He knew that the elf had gotten his first glimpse of the treasure from somewhere down the passage. The unmistakable sound of a deliberate gulp occurred moments later. Then the expected footsteps again, though now they were much more tentative.

Arzechytium gradually closed his eyelid. He left a sliver of space open so that he could watch, although to anyone else it would appear that his eye was completely shut.

"Surely the elf doesn't think all of this is unguarded," he reasoned, opening his other eye—the one that the approaching invader wouldn't be able to see from the hole.

Nervous, almost labored breaths preceded the elf long before he ever neared the end of the tunnel. Soon enough, though, the dragon saw the shape of his expected visitor turn the final bend in the passage. The elf stopped suddenly.

"His first look at true majesty," Arzechytium suspected.

Of course the intruder could see him, even though the cavern and passages were pitch black. The elf's infravision, although much more limited than that of the great wyrm, would enable him to see as if the place were bathed in the noontime sun. After several seconds, the figure in the corridor deliberately backed away. The shuffle of hurried footsteps followed moments later, well after the elf had disappeared around the bend.

"What'd ya find?" one of the men whispered.

"D... d... dr... dragon..." Aylwin stuttered shakily.

"Not very eloquent for an elf," the red wyrm noted snidely.

The elf's words were met with a cacophony of hushed murmurs. One voice finally talked over the others, earning the full attention of the speaker's companions.

"Did it see you?" one of the men asked.

"I... I don't think so," the elf replied. "It appeared to be sleeping."

"Then let's get it 'fore it knows what hit it!" the barbarian growled, his heavy steps echoing through the passage.

"No! Rudiger!" the woman squeaked.

"Yeah, wait 'til Aylwin catches 'is breath at least," the other man suggested. The footsteps halted.

"We can not just march right in there, anyway," Aylwin panted.

"Why?" the barbarian grunted.

"He'd hear us first," the elf stated matter-of-factly.

"I have already heard you," Arzechytium mused, almost humorously.

"We can sneak up on 'im!" Rudiger argued.

"The entire floor of the chamber is littered with coins, weapons, and many other things that would surely rattle," the elf explained.

"Hey, how 'bout another idea?" one of the men proposed. No one answered, so he continued. "Why don't we jus' creep up t' the edge 'n pick a few o' the loose coins 'n what-not off the top? Then we jus' slip away wit' the loot. We're safe 'n sound, while the sleepin' dragon's none the wiser."

"We shall see who is lacking wisdom, foolish human," the ancient wyrm thought contemptuously.

The man's idea was greeted with enthusiasm from everyone, even the battle-hungry barbarian. They spent the next several minutes working out the details for their grand scheme.

Arzechytium listened for a few moments, but soon became disinterested. This ragtag group of visitors may be even less intelligent than the dimwitted goblins that lived in his mountain. This band of thieving intruders didn't deserve one copper of his magnificent treasure. He should simply incinerate them as soon as they neared the edge of his sleeping chamber.

"Or maybe..." the dragon pondered. *"Maybe I should let them think their plan is working... Lure them in by pretending to sleep right through their pilfering... Even let them pick up a few precious treasures to give them a false sense of security. Yes, then I shall 'wake up' and act lethargic, as if I can barely move after sleeping for so long. I'll feign surprise and allow them to attack first. I'll pretend that I am wounded, hurt, and unable to fight back... Hobble around the cavern for a bit to stretch my legs... all the while inducing my new playthings into a game of cat and mouse as if they are the aggressors and I am the helpless victim. I should fight back a little, though certainly not with all of my might. Too quick. Too easy. Yes, I'll injure a couple of them first, still letting them think that they*

have a fighting chance. Only then will I reveal my full power and majesty! I shall rise up and..."

A hint of movement attracted his attention and interrupted his contemplation. The band of adventurers had arrived at the opening. The one in front bent down and carefully reached for a gold coin.

Arzechytium snapped open his eyelid and glared at the thieves. All in one motion he turned his head, opened his mouth, and exhaled at the invaders. A stream of searing fire billowed from his throat. It danced across the treasure-strewn floor, brightly illuminating the entire cavern for a few rare moments. Coins, weapons, and other items in the path of the blaze immediately turned into a pool of seething molten fluid. The stone walls on the receiving end of the blast turned black, forever charred by the violent heat. And the intruders were nowhere to be seen, though some of their ashes still floated gently down into the boiling pond of liquid metal.

"*Maybe next time,*" the ancient red dragon sighed, laying his head down and returning to his slumber.

THE LIGHTNING BUG

by Frances Evlin

Frances Evlin is a Pacific Northwest native whose love for creative writing predates her years as wife, mother and office employee. In fact, her preoccupation with creativity dates to a first grade story about a square fish. She appreciates the power of language and enjoys working with words. This, along with her other interests—reading, traveling and photography—motivates her to glean story material wherever she goes, from whatever she sees. Alas, so far, no square fish. Two of her favorite storytellers are Rod Serling and Alfred Hitchcock, and you may see their influence in her work in this volume.

A thunderstorm was putting on a light show over the hills across the valley, and Tucker and me were sitting on the steps watching. On the porch behind us, Grammy sat in her big, oak rocking chair, the only piece of furniture she'd brought with her when she came to live with us.

She was rocking really slow, almost stopping between forth and back. Her eyes were half shut, and she acted as if she was listening close for something.

All of a sudden she stopped, and her hands gripped tight onto the arms of her chair. "Lightnin' Bug's gonna get someone soon. Mebbe tonight," she said. "I kin feel it." Then she relaxed and started rocking again.

Tucker gave me a funny look. I felt like, me being the oldest and all—I'm ten and he's only seven—I should set things straight. "Never heard of a lightning bug hurting anybody," I said.

Grammy speared me with one of her hard looks. "I'm not talkin' about a *firefly*, Joshua. I'm talkin' 'bout The Lightnin' Bug."

"The Lightning Bug?" Tucker asked.

Grammy bobbed her head up and down. "Ther's them as say ther ain't no sich thing, and ther's them as knows ther is. I know ther is."

"Tell us about The Lightning Bug," Tucker said, and when she lolled her head back on her chair and didn't pay him no mind, he started begging. "Please, Grammy, please."

Finally she leaned forward in her chair, flung a quick glance over her shoulder toward the kitchen where Mama was fixing supper and started talking softly.

"Ol' Lightnin' Bug don't come ever time it storms. No, siree. Only comes when someone done somethin' he shouldn't oughta done. Then the Lightnin' Bug seeks him out and *smack!*"—she slapped one hand hard on the arm of the rocker, making Tucker and me jump—"he's a goner."

"Golly!" Tucker's eyes were big and round, like they get when he's really caught up in something. "Who's the Lightning Bug coming after?"

Grammy pressed her lips together and squinted her eyes, like she was thinking. "Don't rightly know. Could be anyone done somethin' he knowed was wrong." She opened her eyes and looked straight at me. I couldn't stand looking back at her, for fear she would read what had just come into my head.

I was glad Mama called us to supper right then. Her and Papa were already washed up and at the table. After a little bit, Mama must have noticed that Tucker was quieter than usual, because she asked him what was wrong. He told her what Grammy had said about The Lightning Bug.

Mama shook her head and frowned at Grammy. "I wish you wouldn't tell the boys stories like that."

"Weren't no story," Grammy said. She didn't look up. She was busy eating mashed potatoes and gravy—that's her favorite. "Lightnin' Bug got Henry Osburne 'cause—"

"Hank Osburne got hit by lightning," Papa interrupted, "because he was dumb enough to stay out on his tractor during an electrical storm." He was using his stern voice on her.

Grammy stopped eating for a minute and looked him in the eye. "Anybody see the actual strike?"

"No." Papa had to admit. "But he was found beside his tractor, and he had died from electrical shock."

Grammy went back to eating her mashed potatoes and gravy, but after a little bit, she said, "Beat on his wife, that's why The Lightnin' Bug got him."

Papa shook his head. Mama gave Tucker and me a look that meant we'd better not say anything more, so we didn't.

After we ate and cleared the table, Grammy went back out onto the front porch and Mama and Papa sat down for another cup of coffee. Tucker wanted me to play catch with him, so I went upstairs to fetch my ball and mitt.

Just as I started back down, I caught the tail end of what Mama was saying. "...couldn't spend all that money around here without raising suspicion." I stopped dead in my tracks. They couldn't know about the purse! I got the gollywobbles and plunked right down on the steps.

"That's one reason why the sheriff thinks it was an out-of-towner," Papa said.

I took a deep breath. It wasn't me they were discussing. It had to be they were talking about the man who'd robbed the branch bank at Willow Creek and then shot the manager dead.

"But nobody got a good look at him," Mama was saying as I hurried past on my way out, "and Willow Creek is too close..."

During the following days, the coin purse was a constant worry on my mind. Especially when Tucker kept bringing up the Lightning Bug story. We couldn't decide who was right about that. Mama and Papa thought they were, but Grammy was really old. Maybe she knew things they didn't.

Hank Osburne did get hit by lightning, all right. And there had been some talk about how bad he treated his wife, but nobody knew anything for sure. Except, maybe, The Lightning Bug.

I couldn't help wondering, how bad did you need to be for The Lightning Bug to strike you dead? Did keeping something that didn't belong to you rank as high as beating up your wife? I waited for the chance to get Grammy alone so I could ask her.

One day Tucker was off somewhere with Papa, Mama was working in the house, and Grammy and me were sitting on the front porch, shelling peas. It seemed like a good time to ask, so I said, "Grammy, remember about The Lightning Bug?"

She gave a big sigh. "Your Mama said I wa'nt to talk about it no more."

"I won't tell her," I promised.

She kept shelling peas into the pan on her lap and ignored me. I needed to get her stirred up. "How big is it, Grammy? Big as this pea?" I held up an oversized one.

"Oh, Lordy sakes. A hunnert times bigger," she said, then looked around quick at the front door, like she was afraid Mama was standing there, listening. She wasn't.

"Oh," I said. "Well, I guess if it's that big, it must fly like a bird."

She waved one hand in the air, sending some peas rolling into the corner of the porch. "No. No. Don't fly like a bird at all." She eyed the peas on the floor, then went back to shelling into the pan. "Just kinda floats along," she muttered, "like a lady beetle, with its wings half open."

"But how does it kill the bad guys?"

Her voice got even softer. "Goes right for the chest, or sometimes the head. Sticks right on."

"You mean, like a tick?"

"Don't bite, no. Jist sticks ther'. Sucks the life juices right out, like a sponge sucks up water."

My throat suddenly felt dry. I wanted to go get a drink, but still needed to ask how bad you had to be for the Lightning Bug to come after you. Then the front door opened, and Mama came out onto the porch. Grammy pressed her lips tight together and gave me a warning look.

I didn't think Mama had noticed, but I guess she did, because that night she came into my room and asked me if Grammy had been telling stories again. I told her "No", because it hadn't really been a story.

"Well, I hope not," she said. "Because Grammy loves to pretend. Remember, she's very old. She's my grammy and your great-grammy. She still remembers old myths and legends she heard long, long ago. She likes to tell them, because when people listen, that makes her feel important."

She started toward the door and then turned back. "I don't know where she picked up this thing about The Lightning Bug, but remember, it's just a story. I'm counting on you to make Tucker understand that. Okay?"

"Okay," I said. As soon as she left, I closed the door behind her, went over to my dresser and pulled out the bottom drawer as far as it would go. I reached in behind it and took out the brocade coin purse hidden there. For a little while, I sat there on the floor, holding the purse, remembering how I'd found it in the planter box outside Benson's Hardware.

I snapped the purse open. It had a few coins in it and one bill, which I carefully unfolded. It was fresh and crispy and so clean that all the little letters and numbers showed up sharp and clear. A hundred-dollar bill! The first one I'd ever seen. I didn't want to give it up.

Trouble was, I knew who it rightfully belonged to. Even without any identification cards in it, I knew the purse was old Mrs. Bailey's. She lives the next farm over. Tucker and me used to shortcut through her apple orchard on the way to school. Most days, we'd carry her morning paper from the main road delivery box down the lane to her side porch. Once in a while, she'd give us a nickel from that brocade purse. One day, she got it into her head we were stealing apples, and wouldn't let us cut through any more.

Mrs. Bailey was pretty stingy with her money. Why she had stuck a hundred-dollar bill in that purse, I didn't know and didn't care. But it was wrong to keep it. Besides, what good was it? I couldn't buy anything with it because everyone would want to know where the money came from.

That made me think about the bank robber. Did he sit and look at his stolen money and wonder if it was safe to spend? I bet not. He probably never even heard about The Lightning Bug, much less was afraid of it coming after him.

I put the purse away and got into bed. I'd hardly got to sleep when a big ugly firefly started banging away at my window screen. Pretty soon he had made holes in it big enough to stick his legs through. I tried to get up to slam the window shut, but couldn't move. Then he poked his head in, and all the while, his tail light kept flashing on and off, on and off. Bzzzt! Bzzzt! Bzzzt! Just when he was wiggling in through the biggest hole, looking straight at me with his fearsome red eyes, I woke up. My heart was rat-a-tatting like a woodpecker drilling on a cottonwood tree.

It was likely a full minute before I figured out the flashes were lightning far off, and the banging and buzzing was a striped, old June bug smacking up against the screen. Or had it really been The Lightning Bug, and now he had followed the storm away? I thought about getting up to check for holes in the screen but decided that could wait till daylight. One thing for sure, that purse had to go back to Mrs. Bailey.

The next morning, it turned out the storm had caused our phone to go dead. Mama asked me to ride my bike over to Mrs. Bailey's and call in for repair service. I told her okay and went straight up to my room, got out the purse and stuck it way down in my pants pocket.

Tucker was waiting for me in the front yard. I started across the porch and all of a sudden, Grammy reached out and grabbed my arm. Her eyes were scrinched up and she whispered, "Be kerful. Lightnin' storm's comin'." She let go of me and I went down the steps and got on my bike.

I looked around at the sky. It was a nice day—just a few clouds way off west. Grammy must be wrong this time; still a creepy feeling crawled across the back of my neck.

Tucker rode ahead of me. We went down the Old Highway and turned right onto Culpepper Road. Mrs. Bailey's place was a little ways from the corner. It was a big old two-story house, plunk in the middle of a grove of oak trees.

When we got to where her lane meets the county road, we could see the garage door was open and her car was gone.

"She ain't home," Tucker said.

"Might be her car's around back," I told him. "I'll go check." A driveway went past her garage and on to the outbuildings behind the house.

Tucker went with me as far as the garage, then stopped and stood astraddle his bike. "I ain't going no farther."

The reason was the kids at school had scared him with talk about how Mrs. Bailey's hired man had threatened them with a shotgun. Personally, I was a whole lot more worried about the way the wind was picking up, pushing in a bank of black clouds.

Leaving my bike, I ran down the path between the garage and the screened porch. Everything was quiet except when the breeze tinkered with the wind chimes hanging from the eaves. It sure enough looked like she wasn't home, and that was so much the better for me.

I ran up the steps, opened the porch door and was going to toss the coin purse up against the kitchen door. It was open a little bit and another thought came to me. Maybe I could throw the purse under the kitchen table or somewhere like that, so when she found it, she'd think it'd been there all the time.

Another gust of wind hit and rattled the tree branches against the house. I sneaked across the porch, opened the kitchen door some more and peeked inside. The space between the refrigerator and the cabinets looked to be the best place to throw the purse. I took my time and tossed it easy, underhand. It landed on the counter and slid along, but it didn't go over the edge. It was like almost getting the ring over the prize at the Fair.

That made me feel as if I had to do it, so I ran over and pushed the purse down into the crack. Boy, was it good to get rid of it! The kitchen was getting darker by the minute. The storm clouds were coming over. Well, let them. I didn't have anything to be afraid of, anymore.

Just as I got to the screen porch door, I heard Tucker half-yelling and half-crying. Old Mrs. Bailey must have come back and grabbed him. But it was her hired man, Dallas, who had hold of Tucker's left arm, hauling him up the steps. Dallas pushed open the screen door and caught me with his other hand.

"Mrs. Bailey's not to home. What're you doin' here?" His voice was growly.

It was easy to see why the kids at school made up stories about him. If Mrs. Bailey wanted someone to scare people away from her property, he could likely do it. But he was just doing his job, and I had to show Tucker there was nothing to be afraid of, so I spoke right up. "Our phone's out. We came to call for repair service."

He acted as if he didn't believe me. "Sure you ain't just been snoopin' around?"

"No", I said. But I had gone in without Mrs. Bailey inviting me. Didn't that classify as snooping?

Dallas stopped at the kitchen door, frowning, like he was trying to think what Mrs. Bailey would want him to do. His grip was so tight around my right arm that my fingers were going to sleep. He was one of those big guys who didn't know his own strength.

The wind was blowing pretty good by this time. Thunder rumbled, and it didn't sound very far away. I wished Tucker and me were sitting on the front porch with Grammy, watching the lightning.

Tucker's face was white, and he looked as if he was about to throw up. The stories had scared him good. Another big crack of thunder came, real close this time, and that seemed to shake Dallas out of his puzzlement. He let go of us.

"Well, okay," he said, in a more gentle voice. "You kids hightail it outta here." He looked at me. "And I won't tell the old lady I caught you inside her house."

My right arm was stinging like a thousand needles were poking in. Tucker's must have felt the same. He was rubbing his left arm with his other hand.

We started toward the porch door, Dallas walking a couple steps behind us. "Tell your Ma to come over to call the phone company in an hour or so."

For the first time, I noticed a shotgun leaning in the porch corner and hoped Tucker wouldn't see it. I opened the screen door and put myself between him and the shotgun.

As he stumbled down the steps, all rubber-legged, another lightning flash came and a big crack of thunder right with it. It was so close I caught a whiff of the burned-dust smell and felt the little eddies of wind.

Tucker headed down the path toward the garage, with me close on his heels. Then came a tremendous bright flash, and Tucker dove face down into the dirt, his arms over his head.

A fireball was coming toward us down the lane, fifteen or twenty feet away and about five feet off the ground. It was big as a dinner plate, flat on the bottom, round on top, and glowing white hot. It sailed along, not real fast, but I knew there was no stopping it.

The Lightning Bug!

As it got closer, I saw its eyes. They were violet-blue, and they had a sad look in them. The kind the veterinary doctor gets when he has to put down a sick cow.

My legs gave out and I went down on my knees in the path. The strength was being sucked out of me and The Lightning Bug wasn't even clinging on yet! I waved my arms and yelled, "No, no, no! I put it back!" But The Lightning Bug kept coming.

Maybe it hadn't heard me. Or maybe it was mad because I'd sneaked into Mrs. Bailey's house. Or because I hadn't faced up and apologized for keeping her purse so long. Froze in place, I waited for The Lightning Bug to hit.

But it passed on over me. On its underside, it had suction rings, like you see on an octopus arm. But they were in a circle, six of them and a bigger one in the middle.

I couldn't take my eyes off it and swiveled around to watch where it went. Dallas had the shotgun up to his shoulder, pointed right at me. My heart about gave out. I flopped flat on the ground.

Then he must have seen The Lightning Bug. He got wild-eyed, jerked the gun up and fired smack into the fireball. The pellets melted right into it. Before he could shoot again, it slammed into his chest and stuck there, glowing red, then orange, then blue-white.

Screaming, Dallas tore at The Lightning Bug. Pieces broke off and he threw them away, but they went right back and fastened on again. It kept swelling up bigger and bigger, like a balloon being pumped full of air.

Dallas dropped to his knees. He leaned back and raised his arms toward the sky. His mouth was open, but he didn't scream anymore. He just kinda gurgled. The smell of his skin burning was awful, worse than when Mama singes a stewing hen. Finally, he toppled over, arms and legs atwitching.

I heard a soft sucking sound—like when a cow pulls one of its feet out of the mud—and then Dallas stopped moving. The fireball exploded and little bits of lightning went shooting every which way, like a thousand little rockets.

I got Tucker onto his feet, and we ran.

≈ ≈

Well, it turned out that Dallas was the one who had robbed the bank and killed the manager. On the radio news interview, the sheriff said that Dallas had hidden the bank money in Mrs. Bailey's garage. She had found it and was going to turn him in. He had her tied and gagged and was rigging up an "accident" when Tucker and me came along. He likely thought we'd found her, and that's why he wanted to get rid of us, too.

At the end of the interview, the sheriff said that Dallas died when lightning struck the shotgun he was holding. I looked at Grammy. She smiled and winked at me.

Grammy and me, we knew.

HUNTERS

by Loren W. Cooper

The body had not yet cooled when the priest and his boy found it. Blood darkened the earth, black stains pooling around the head and shoulders in a mocking halo. The man's throat gaped wide, torn open by something with fangs. Flies had not yet risen into the early morning light, but the hot copper scent of blood filled the air to the exclusion of all else, despite the warmth of late summer and the proximity of the fens.

The priest sent his boy running to the workers on the edge of the swamp to tell the foreman, who in turn sent a runner of his own to tell the Comte that his personal assistant had died an unclean death. The worst of it, the priest later said grimly, was the smile on the corpse's face.

They interred the corpse swiftly, at the Comte's command, despite whispered rumors among the workers and a general uneasiness in everyone from the farmers around Foregate to the servants in the old stone keep. Something wasn't right, or so the rumors said—and so everyone seemed to feel. The midsummer air was heavy with more than the rich smell of decay rising from the fens.

The hunter arrived two days later.

He rode a big bay up the wide stone road that had outlasted its builders by centuries, his mount's shod hooves loud against the ancient stonework. A glaive rested across his knees, the four-foot haft and three-foot blade all covered in symbols of power. A heavy coat of scale mail (every small metal plate meticulously inscribed with a rune) complete with helmet, scale coif, breastplate, greaves, and vambraces (all etched with runes) covered him even in the heat of the day. The token guard that the Comte kept stationed at the road gate sent a messenger as soon as he saw the newcomer, even before the traveler caught his eye and rode up to his station.

The rider swung down from the saddle, bent his head, and drew off both helm and coif in a smooth, well-practiced motion. Dismounted, he stood no taller than the guard, who was himself perhaps slightly above average height. "Oslo Jaeger, Viscount and Emissary for Dux Frederick. Send word to your master."

The guard rolled his eyes, wishing he had another runner handy.

"May I ask your purpose here, Lord?"

Oslo raised one dark eyebrow. "I am a hunter. Where are your stables?"

The guard pointed mutely down the main street of Foregate to the keep rising above town and fen.

"Of course." The hunter led his horse through the gate, then paused and turned back. "One last thing. Any strange deaths lately?"

At the guard's expression, Oslo's face hardened. "Tell me where to find any witnesses."

⁂

The priest had taken quarters just outside the old church grounds, and had acquired some local labor to help him renovate the sagging structure. "An accomplishment in itself," he told Oslo.

Oslo nodded. "I had heard that Comte Sigurd had an obsession with the relics of the Empire. Jodan artifacts can be quite valuable. I take it that he is miserly with his labor?"

The priest grinned wryly. "You could say that." He stuck out a calloused hand. "Father Joseph, Society of Light. Here to keep an eye out for the souls of the people."

Oslo took his hand, and looked up at the taller man out of dark, narrowed eyes. "And you discovered the body."

Father Joseph's gaze clouded. "My boy and I did."

"You were married before the new vows."

Father Joseph smiled. "My wife died bearing him. Taking the vow of celibacy was easy for me, though I still wonder if it was the right decision. Dangerous to separate the life of the shepherd too much from that of the flock."

"Dangerous for a priest to have too many worldly interests, as well. Or so says the Primate."

"He speaks from bitter experience," Father Joseph agreed. "Both sides have merit to their argument. We'll see how it works out."

"About the body, Father," Oslo prompted gently.

The priest closed his eyes. "It was early morning, two days ago. We went walking, down by the edge of the fens. I've been here a while, long enough to know where the safe edge is, but I'm no local. I know better than to enter the fen itself. Between peat bogs, sunken tar pits with a scum of water over them, and discounting the snakes and 'gators, a man who doesn't know what to look for in the fen can find death all too quickly."

Father Joseph opened his eyes to look up at the church, where two men, already shirtless in the morning heat, were nailing down a new layer of shingles, tarring each section as they went, dusky skin shining with sweat. "He lay at the edge of the fen proper. His throat had been torn out, but I found no signs of a struggle. He was smiling. It was Randolf, the Comte's personal assistant, the old man's right

hand, really, now that his health is fading and he can't be out oversee-
ing the drainage of the fens and the recovery of the Jodan dwellings
personally. Unlike myself, Randolf knew the fens intimately. Possibly
better than anyone else, save perhaps a few fishermen or peat cutters.
It's unlikely that he would have died due to any natural causes in the
fens."

"So it didn't look as if he had fallen victim to a 'gator or a snake,
and the body hadn't been mangled by scavengers?"

Father Joseph shook his head and brushed a pale, unruly lock of
hair out of his eyes. "He was untouched by scavengers. He had only
the one wound at his throat. No snake did that. As for a 'gator, the
animal would have taken him into the water. We would have found
nothing. And no 'gator ripped out his throat like that." He held two
arched fingers to the side of his neck. "Fangs. Two fangs. They entered
at the side, and then tore across the windpipe and jugular like knives.
The blood had sprayed all across the ground, but only in one direction. As far as I can tell, he simply lay there, smiling, as he bled to
death."

Oslo absently rubbed one gauntleted hand across his clean-shaven
face. "What do you suspect, Father?"

"I looked for tracks," the priest said obliquely. "Other than his
own, I found traces and prints of another pair of shod feet. Something
was out there with him that night. Something that walked like a man.
Given the circumstances of the killing, it seems obvious to suspect
one of the Children of the Night."

Oslo smiled slightly. "If you're right in most of the particulars,
Father, then you're wrong in one."

Father Joseph raised an eyebrow. "And what would that be?"

"There were at least two of the Children of the Night involved."

"Oh?" The good father almost kept the polite disbelief out of his
voice. "What makes you say that?"

The set of the hunter's smile had taken on a decidedly grim cast.
"Because I followed them here."

The hunter watched the priest's eyes widen. "I need to talk to the
Comte, and then I need to see the body. I need you there. And if it's
what I believe, I'll need a fire."

As the priest nodded, the hunter turned his eyes to the keep on
the hill.

≈≈

Comte Sigurd's white brows bristled as he rose with difficulty
from a leather chair worn comfortable and stalked closer to the fire
he had commanded built in the great hall. "Ridiculous! This talk of
the Children of the Night is nothing more than village rumor-monger-
ing. Randolf was a fine man, a great help to me in the trials of my age."

The Comte cast a venomous glance at his son and ran one liver-spotted hand over the skull of some long-dead predator, mounted on a heavy wood base over the fireplace so that the great saber-teeth would extend below and along the curve of the dark oak mantle. "The only honor I could give him after his death was a place in the crypts, and I will not have his body outraged!"

Oslo steepled his fingers, casually rested his elbows on the heavy table, and listened as Richard, the Comte's son, continued the argument. "Father, please. You know as well as I that the townsfolk are buzzing like hornets over these rumors of the Children of the Night. The Viscount would lay these rumors to rest with a simple, public examination of the body."

"I will not have it," the old man said quietly, iron in his voice.

Richard shook his head, throwing Oslo an exasperated glance. "And what of the work in the fens, Father? The recovery of the land for farming, and the recovery of the Jodan relics?"

"Well, what of it?" the old man blustered, but uncertainty had crept in to his voice, and his son capitalized on it.

"Your workers are bound to the land no longer. The old rules don't hold. Allow them enough resentment, and they will slip away. The work has already slowed. Men are afraid of the swamps, particularly in darkness. They leave early and arrive late, to make sure that the sun is well in the sky while they are outside locked doors."

Oslo decided that Richard had cultivated considerable skill at carefully playing on the old man's fears. He would have to tell his lord, the young Dux. Comte Sigurd at least had a certain predictability, but his son appeared to have an aptitude for games of manipulation.

The Comte turned on the last man in the room. "Is that true, Johann? Have the crews been abandoning their duty?" He interrupted the thickly built foreman before the man could more than begin to stammer a response. "Damn and blast the filthy lot of you!" The Comte's string of curses became even more inventive, and Oslo watched clinically, wondering idly how much longer the Comte could go before the inevitable stroke. Out of the corner of his eye, the hunter saw a similar speculative look on Richard's face. The foreman wore the tired, hunched expression of a man weathering a familiar and unpleasant storm.

Oslo leaned back and looked around as the Comte showed no signs of immediately slowing or repeating himself. The great hall, like most of the keep that he had seen, showed many signs of the Comte's obsession: in most of the other rooms it was pottery—vases and plates of startling color and beauty, all in a condition that would have fetched a small fortune from any collector. Throughout the parts of the keep he had seen, Oslo had spotted Jodan sigil tiles as well, marked with active High Script, and wondered if the Comte knew the power still held in that ancient calligraphy. Dominating the walls of the great hall were the remnants of fantastic beasts from the age of the Empire. The trophies seemed to be mostly skulls, ranging from herbivores bearing one to five or more short, long, straight and twisted horns, to obvious carnivores, in sizes from approximately that of a domestic cat to a monster skull that must have weighed several hundred pounds, many sporting fantastically enlarged canines.

Richard caught Oslo's gaze as the Comte wound down. "The bones from the fens usually still have the hide attached. Tanned, almost. But for the ones that can't be salvaged for mounting, the skulls make the best trophies."

Oslo watched the Comte lean against the stonework of the fireplace, and decided that the old man was gathering steam to continue the tirade. The hunter's words were clipped, measured, and calculated for effect. "You must realize that I don't need your permission."

The Comte's eyes narrowed, but he said nothing.

"If this man was killed by the Children of the Night, it wasn't a feeding," Oslo said bluntly. "He'll be...gestating down in your crypts. By law far older than the Dux Frederick, preventing the spread of the Children of the Night is the highest and deepest concern of every resident of the human realms. They are the most virulent of plagues. If you do not allow me to examine this man's body, you are declaring war on the human race itself. Are you willing to do that?"

Oslo saw calculation behind the rage, and decided that the Comte played some subtle game of his own. Perhaps against his son. The Comte threw up his hands. "Very well, then. I hardly need Frederick's ready armies to roll through my lands as he has through so many of my neighbors' demesnes. I will not stand in your way." He cast another sidelong glance at his son. "But if you have reason to burn him, Viscount, I want his ashes returned to the crypts. You understand?"

Oslo inclined his head.

Sigurd snorted. "I leave you gentlemen to your dinner. I've lost my appetite. Or perhaps my desire for company."

They all rose as the old man made slow and painful progress, though not without dignity, to the door at the far end of the hall. Once through, his voice came floating back as he verbally flayed some luckless servant caught in his path.

Johann, the foreman, bowed politely out of the room. "I have work in the morning," he said, only traces of polite regret in his voice. Oslo didn't blame him. He had already figured that the Comte must pay the man well, if he tolerated the verbal abuse that appeared to be the Comte's idea of constructive criticism on a regular basis. He also wondered if Randolf had been the Comte's only real companion, or merely a device to torment his son.

"I must apologize for my father." Richard gave Oslo a regretful smile. "He doesn't wear his age well. It chafes him, that his infirmities deny him proximity to his passion."

The door at the far end of the hall opened, and three servants came through, bearing trays with various dishes. The youngest, a pretty flaxen-haired girl, had the flushed face and red eyes of someone about to cry. Richard waited until the dishes were set out before them, then caught her arm. "Mary. Let me take Father's wine up to him, tonight. We need to talk, anyway."

She nodded gratefully, if a trifle jerkily, and fled. Richard set in on the food before him, and Oslo, still hungry from the road, followed suit, deciding quickly that the Comte, whatever his other shortcomings, had at least managed to retain a decent cook.

Leaning back from the ruins of his meal, Richard swept a hand around the room. "I've always wondered about the fangs."

Oslo raised a polite eyebrow.

Richard shrugged. "You hear stories about the Children of the Night. About the fangs that they develop after the change. Could these animals have had such a plague among them?"

"Possible," Oslo conceded. "Though I doubt it. First, the fangs on these predators are far more enlarged than a Child's. Second, the size of the fangs of a normal predator would be sufficient to a Child's needs, though the function is different. Third, we've never known of another species haunted by the same plague. And last, none of them have the eyes."

"Eyes?"

"Children are nocturnal. Two obvious physical changes occur. The eyes enlarge, change in structure, become more suited to the nocturnal hunt. Less obvious changes happen. Children of the Night are generally faster and stronger than they were before the Change, they age much more slowly, and their minds change as well. They develop...talents...that aid them in the hunt. And then the teeth, of course."

Richard nodded. "For killing. And feeding."

Oslo shook his head. "No. Children don't need to feed physically, at least as far as I can tell. Some may drink blood, in a kind of orgiastic frenzy, but most of that comes from the way the fangs are used. They're reproductive organs."

Richard flinched. "What?"

"Haven't you ever wondered why Children aren't more numerous?" Oslo asked. "Two very good reasons: the Change is a voluntary choice on the part of the victim, and the Children must deliberately choose to reproduce. I'm afraid that's what happened with Randolf. I've known Children to survive for decades in the midst of a town, never killing, feeding on the hopes and dreams of the town's inhabitants, feeding on their vitality, feeding on their souls, perhaps. When they kill by bleeding their victim out, they are preparing him for the Change. The throats of the victim are always torn out, perhaps signs of the frenzy I mentioned earlier. Three nights later, the 'victim' rises as a fledgling Child. Perhaps the person never really dies, or perhaps the person dies, and their body is taken by some sort of damned spiritual parasite. I don't know—no one does but one of the Children themselves." He stared moodily into the dying fire. "They become phantoms of themselves. Echoes of the past personality remain, but they are not the same, Richard. They are evil."

Richard apparently didn't know what to say to that, so he nodded, and punched up the fire. "I'll have one of the servants show you the guest room," he said after a moment.

"I believe that I'll take advantage of a short rest, but no more. Tonight would be the third night since the killing, so I'll check on Randolf tonight. He'll be showing the signs, perhaps even be ready to wake. All of that depends on when the Change began, and I can't afford to miss his Awakening, if he is Changing."

"And if he is Changing?" Richard asked.

Oslo drained the dregs of his wine. "Then I burn him. And begin the hunt for the Lair."

❧❧

Father Joseph met Oslo at the stables. "I feel underdressed."

Oslo grinned, slapping his armored breastplate with a scale gauntlet and raising the glaive in his left hand. "I like to be prepared."

"By the way," the priest said casually, "I couldn't help but notice the runes. They look much like Jodan High Script."

Oslo nodded.

"Relics," the priest suggested hopefully.

"Sorry father. My work. With the Church's permission, of course."

"Of course," Father Joseph said dryly. "Doesn't it seem strange to use those tools in your profession? The dangers of Jodan power..."

Oslo smiled crookedly. "It's one of the reasons that I'm still practicing my profession, Father. I'll take every advantage I can get."

"A dangerous statement. Be careful that you do not become what you hunt."

"It's a hazardous profession, with many dangers. The physical not greatest among them."

The priest nodded sharply. "As long as you recognize that, you might keep your soul intact."

"The continued health of body and soul, Father, is my goal every day. Show me the crypts."

Father Joseph led Oslo through the maze of courtyards that enfolded the old keep, stopping at last in a long colonnade, which ended in a black iron door. The walls of inner buildings rose above them, built, as was all of the oldest portion of the keep, from dark basalt blocks hauled from some distant quarry by Jodan slaves in the distant past. Four men holding torches stood around a pile of wood eight feet in length and three feet high that reeked of oil.

Father Joseph saw Oslo scanning the few blank windows overlooking the colonnade. "You won't wake any of them with the fire," he told the hunter. "The Comte sleeps on the first floor of the main keep, in the heart of his collection. The Comte's son has claimed the northern watchtower as his place, and the few servants that remain overnight stay close to the Comte."

Oslo's gaze swept across the men with torches. "And them?"

"Townsmen."

The men bowed slightly to Oslo.

"They prepared for a burning, at my request," said Father Joseph. "They're here to help. And as witnesses."

"Let's hope they don't see more than they bargained for," Oslo said grimly.

He crossed the length of the colonnade with quick, even strides, pulled open the door, and peered into the darkness. Two of the men with torches followed Father Joseph as he fell in behind the hunter, the three of them flinching when Oslo murmured a phrase and light burst from the runes that covered the blade of his extended glaive. Without looking back to see if the others were following, the hunter descended into the catacombs.

The marble stair led down into darkness, dropping for more than one hundred steps before ending in a large chamber. Oslo looked at the green hue of the bronze plaques set over the niches, inscribed with flowing Jodan Low Script, before pausing to study the three archways leading from the room. He turned to Father Joseph. "Which way?"

The priest nodded at an archway. "The more recent dead are further back." He took the lead, Oslo immediately behind, the blade of his glaive providing considerable light for the two of them, the townsmen taking up the rear with their torches.

The air felt chill in comparison to the heat above, and the place had a smell like autumn winds and dry leaves. The priest led them through six more large chambers, each stacked high with their burden of the ancient dead, more chambers visible through the archways opening on each side of each successive room. In each chamber, the plaques became successively a little less green.

Father Joseph stopped in the seventh room, pausing by a niche still draped in fresh white silk. "This is Randolf's crypt. The Comte laid his man close to his own future resting place."

Oslo pulled the draperies aside gently, the two men with torches maintaining a quiet distance, Father Joseph at his side. A sharp intake of breath hissed through the hunter's teeth as he drew the last layer of silk away from the body. "As I feared."

He glanced at the priest's white face. "Has he healed?" He brought the glowing blade down to the scarred but whole neck, pink with new skin.

Father Joseph nodded sharply. "His hair is longer, too. And his face has changed."

"The eyes are undoubtedly larger, more deeply set into the skull," Oslo noted clinically. "If you examined him closely, you would probably find that his nails have grown, as well as his teeth. The Change does that, probably as the metabolism increases to allow regeneration of the wound. They don't really die, you know. The body doesn't decay. Rigor never sets in."

The townsmen muttered to themselves and backed a step. "Burn 'im?" the larger of the two asked nervously.

"Immediately..." Oslo's voice trailed off as he saw the chest rise and fall deeply, the head turn, and the eyes twitch open.

"But why?" The musical voice caught them, and everyone hesitated but the hunter, who plunged the blade of his glaive into the chest of the fledgling Child of the Night, even as the lustrous eyes sought his own.

The larger townsman dropped his torch and ran as the Child began screaming and fighting his way up the blade. Father Joseph noted incongruously that the glaive had a short crosspiece below the blade like a boar spear for just this eventuality. The smaller townsman stood his ground, watching as the hunter slid back on the marble, spreading his feet to maintain his balance against the force of the fledgling's rush. Oslo spoke a single word, his face grim.

White flame curled out of the fledgling's mouth with the next scream, and the blade of the glaive could be seen through his skin, like the flame of a candle seen through wax paper. As Randolf convulsed, Oslo grunted and lifted the fledgling's feet from the floor. Father Joseph and the last torch man hurriedly cleared the way, then followed cautiously after the hunter, who moved in a series of quick rushes, slamming the Child of the Night against the opposite wall of each successive chamber to keep the struggling figure pinned on the blade.

The fire of the blade burned within and without, the graveclothes exploding into flame as the hunter reached the base of the stairs. Oslo took the stairs in a sprint, bursting into the empty courtyard. The smallest of the townsmen followed the hunter out of the crypts, and threw his torch into the wood at the same time that the hunter thrust the blade of the glaive with its fiery burden into the heart of the pyre.

Flames bloomed out of the oil-soaked wood, curling around the haft of the glaive and the armored and gauntleted hands of the hunter, who held firm as the struggles of the Comte's erstwhile assistant weakened. At last the hunter stepped back, pulling his glaive out of the body with a sharp, smooth motion. Flames from the pyre licked twelve feet into the air, almost obscuring the figure that struggled feebly in their heart for entirely too long for the comfort of the priest or the townsmen. Oslo watched dispassionately, firelight filling his eyes with shadows.

When the fire had died, and only embers remained, Oslo accompanied the priest and the small torch man to the gates of the keep, where a crowd had gathered, the townsmen who had broken and fled standing at its head. When the hunter stepped through the gates, soot still heavy on his armor, a collective sigh went through the crowd. Oslo, his eyes ever searching, caught the merest glimpse of a flicker of movement at the edge of the torchlight, movement that could not be resolved separately from the shadows cast by the torchlight. The hunter nodded inwardly, sparing only slight attention for the priest as he told the people of what he had seen.

While the priest spoke, Oslo turned to the small townsman, who had not panicked even in the depths of the crypts. "Do you know the fens?"

He nodded.

"Would you be willing to guide me? Tonight?"

The townsman's face set itself in grim lines. "My name is Carlo, Lord. I have two children. One almost ready to marry. And I knew Randolf. He was not a bad man. I will guide you."

When the priest finished, the people huddled together, muttering and refusing to meet one another's eyes. Oslo followed Carlo through the crowd, and down to the fens, to the boat that Carlo kept moored in the common little bay used by those who did not themselves live on the edge of the fens, but who did go there in the course of their daily business or pleasure.

In the light of the hunter's burning glaive, Carlo introduced Oslo to the fens. Oslo did not tell Carlo that they were little more than bait for the Children of the Night, lit as they were by the glaive's blade, and Carlo did not ask, though the hunter did notice that his guide had brought several flasks of oil, and kept a torch burning in a sconce at the rear of the boat in addition to his lantern. Though they hunted the fens through the night and into the morning, Oslo did not again catch any glimpse of the hidden movement he had come to expect. When daylight had again retaken the swamps from the hand of night, they returned to Foregate, walking with the heavy tread of men who had seen the night through hunting dangerous game. Carlo's wife met them at the gate, her eyes red with worry, her children at her side.

From her Oslo learned that the Comte had fallen to the Children as he hunted the fens.

≈≈

Oslo met Richard, now Comte Richard, descending the stairs of his watchtower. Richard covered a look of surprise. "I had expected you later. Any luck?"

Together they went down toward the courtyard of the crypts, where the townsfolk had laid the wood for the old Comte's fire on the ashes of his companion.

"No. How did it happen?" Oslo asked bluntly.

Richard's eyes were dry, but his face twisted as he shrugged. "I don't know. They must have come for him in the night, arriving and departing without alerting anyone. Father slept in the center of his collection, surrounded by servants, deep in the heart of the keep. I checked on him after I brought him his customary spiced wine. He was deeply asleep, but alive. This morning, one of the servants saw blood pooling under the door, and ran for me. Blood was everywhere, drenching his linens, spraying the room. I had the linens burned. After hearing about your discovery last night, I thought it best to do the same with my father."

Oslo nodded as he saw two of the servants appear, carrying a litter bearing a long bundle wrapped in white silk. As the townsmen averted their eyes, the bearers carefully laid the stretcher onto the prepared pyre. Oslo stepped forward, before the torches could be thrust into the wood, and drew the silk back. The wound ran jaggedly across Sigurd's neck, a great flap of flesh torn back from a gash made by two long fangs. The flesh of the corpse's face hung loose, the man's age weighing most heavily on him in death. He looked smaller than he had in life, and pitiful as he had not been while living.

Oslo's eyes narrowed, and he lifted the body slightly, noting the rigidity of the limbs and that signs of darkening in the flesh of the lower part of the body had appeared—a sign of the blood settling after it ceases to flow. He sniffed, and in the summer heat he caught the slightest hint of the gathering fetid sweetness of decay.

The hunter drew back from the body slowly, watching as the townsmen set the pyre alight. Flames burst around the corpse, glinting from the hilts and pommels of the weapons that the townsmen suddenly all seemed to be carrying.

"Would you like to see the room?" the new Comte asked solicitously.

Oslo nodded. "Though I doubt the killer left any trace."

Richard gave the hunter a sidelong glance. "I thought that you told the priest that there were more than two."

"Or killers," Oslo amended gracefully.

"Would it have been possible for more than one of the Children to enter and leave unobserved?"

"It would have been easy for them," Oslo responded as they crossed through the dining hall where they had eaten the night before. His eyes flicked across the skulls of the animals of a bygone age, wondering how much the old Comte had known, expected, and planned for.

When they reached Sigurd's bedchamber, Oslo saw that it had been stripped and scrubbed. Even the walls were clean, the unbroken inlay of Jodan sigil tiles free of any trace of blood.

Oslo blinked in disbelief at the tiles, every one of them active, the largest collection he had yet seen. "I had thought to try my hand at a scrying," he said casually to Richard.

Richard smiled. "Scrying would have done you little good here. Many of these tiles were for privacy and protection, or so my father told me. If even half were still active..."

"The Jodan crafted well. So what will you do, now that your father is dead?"

"Clear the area of this pestilence," the new Comte said firmly. "With your help, of course. The townsfolk are more than ready. And after that?" His eyes gleamed. "Strengthen our ties to the court of the Dux. My father was too much an isolationist—too much consumed by his passion."

Oslo's eyes narrowed, and then his face relaxed. He turned away.

"What will you do now, hunter?" the Comte asked.

Oslo wondered idly if he should tell the young Comte that his father did not fall to the Children of the Night. But then, he undoubtedly knew that.

"I need to go and prepare," Oslo told him thoughtfully, "for the next hunt."

⁊⁊

Oslo knew more hunting strategies than simple pursuit.

For his call, the hunter chose the square, crenellated roof of a squat watch tower still uneasily held by the slipping grasp of the fens. Exposed by the ongoing drainage efforts, half-submerged in brackish water, the tower stood far enough into the fen that the townsmen would not immediately distract him, yet not so far in as to have been chosen by the Children of the Night as a lair. He checked for occupancy anyway, rowing out in a flat-bottomed boat to ease gently into slimy stone passages, the blade of his glaive burning like a captive piece of the sun. He found nothing but solid stone, the wet scent of decay, and a few broken relics from a time and people long since departed.

Satisfied, he began his preparations as the sun waxed in strength. He drew the tip of the glaive's blade along the stonework, faint traces trailing the path of the blade and fading to the edges of perception. He worked swiftly but methodically, completing all but the last stroke of the pattern by mid day.

Then he waited.

The sun had gone to ground and the stars filled the sky with distant light when he spotted his approaching visitor. The motion was slow and deliberate, not unlike the lazy movement of the palm fronds in the breeze, or the 'gators in the water. An observer without Oslo's defenses and experience would have seen little or nothing, and even the hunter would lose visual contact with his visitor in the moments between movements. But when the other flashed into view, gliding across the water and flowing up the side of the tower to stand at the edge of the crenellation, Oslo nodded a greeting, leaning casually on his glaive, the tip of the blade resting at the last unfinished stroke of the pattern.

The long face of the Child of Night was lean, ascetic, and expressionless. "Oslo."

"Cyril," Oslo responded gravely.

Cyril studied the pattern covering the roof of the tower. "This isn't your usual method."

Oslo smiled slightly. "I'm versatile."

"I'll remember that." The huge eyes, most obvious sign of the Change, rose to meet Oslo's gaze, and he felt a feather-light contact at the outer wards of his mind. "So you haven't decided to join us and tonight you abandon the hunt. Unless I step into the pattern you can do nothing to harm me. So why are you here?"

"For this. To talk."

Oslo flinched at the laughter, like and unlike the laughter of the man he had known, the man Cyril had been. "You're getting soft, hunter. Talking is the first step. Soon you'll be seeing us as something other than monsters."

"Soon you'll be joining us." The new voice was soft, warm, and directly behind him.

The iris of Oslo's eyes expanded when he heard that voice, pain touching his features lightly. "Rhea. Not soon, I think."

Cyril stalked gracefully to Oslo's left, never leaving the crenellation. Rhea's voice moved as she spoke, mirroring Cyril's progress. "Oslo. You are wasted, serving this boy. Growing older with each passing day. Your reflexes slowing. Your eyes dimming. Your muscles weakening. We could show you the way. We could bring you the Change, and give you strength and speed and youth such as you have never known. We could remake you."

Oslo studied her, her skin so pale and her eyes so black. "And in the remaking I would be lost, as you have been."

She stopped, and regarded him gravely. "Is that what you believe? That none of me remains? That I am nothing but a vessel for an inhuman hunger? Hearing me, is that what you believe?"

Oslo shook his head. "How much of you is Rhea, and how much hunger? Do you even know yourself? Listen to you, both of you. Whatever you are, you are not what you were."

"No." Cyril continued around to stand at Rhea's side. "We are not. We are more than we were."

"And less." The Hunter's voice held not the slightest trace of uncertainty.

Cyril rocked forward on the balls of his feet, his face relaxing into speculation. "We could take you. You would weaken, given time. You would come to see."

Oslo cocked his head. "Could you take me? Do you believe that you could take me before I completed the pattern and took us all to hell?"

Rhea laid one hand comfortingly on Cyril's shoulder as he flinched. "You will come to see, my love. One night, you will come to me willingly."

"Not tonight."

She smiled fully, long teeth gleaming in the moonlight. "Perhaps not. If you did not come here to kill, and you did not come here to die or be born again, then why are you here? You were never one to dwell on old memories."

"Why are you here? That's the question I've come to ask. You knew I was following. And you stopped here, close to Church centers and garrisons—all the resources that could be used to hunt you down."

The edge of Cyril's mouth quirked. "You forget the fens."

"I forget nothing," Oslo snapped. "You never knew the fens, and a misstep there could be as dangerous to one of your kind as to a man or woman. What was Randolf to you?"

Rhea's eyes narrowed. "He would have been my child, had you not slain him in the time of his Change."

"You killed him."

Cyril reared back, his mouth twisting into a snarl. "She rewarded him. You killed him."

"She rewarded him for guiding the two of you."

They were quiet.

Oslo continued relentlessly. "He was the old Comte's right hand, or so I am told. Surely he would have done little without the Comte's knowledge. Did you kill the Comte as well?"

Rhea smiled suddenly. "You know better."

Oslo sighed. "I know that you did not Turn him. And I doubt that you would have made such a clumsy attempt at making him look like the victim of an aborted Turning. And I know that you, in the full knowledge that I was hunting this area, never would have left the Comte's body behind for me to find and burn. Was he a candidate?"

Cyril nodded. "He desired it. He was no fool. And we would have given him his desire eventually. He earned it. And he was not so dangerous as his son."

Oslo's breath hissed between his teeth. "Richard sought you out."

Rhea spoke slowly. "He lusted after it, as he lusted after his father's land and position. But we are careful who we Turn. Such a one could be dangerous to the Clan."

"He was that."

Rhea studied Oslo in a moment of silence. "He killed his own father."

"He took advantage of your presence," Oslo said evenly. "Drugged the old man first, I suspect, and tore open his throat with one of those fanged skulls to cast suspicion on the Children of the Night. Not a bad plan, really. Roused the countryside against you in revenge for denying him, and gained his inheritance in the same stroke. If the action weren't so contemptible, the execution would be admirable."

Cyril stroked his long chin with one thin hand. "So you'll hale him back to the young Dux."

"On speculation?" Oslo shook his head. "Sigurd slept in a room sealed with Jodan warding tiles. No traces to be found there. And no physical evidence remains since they burned the body. Richard was clever in his deception. He executed his patricide perfectly, under the eye of the young Dux's own Hunter. As he grows into his power, he will become ever more dangerous."

"Perhaps even to Frederick," Rhea said softly.

"Perhaps. He has ambition enough."

Cyril sank into a crouch, and wrapped his arms around his knees. "You won't find anything here, you know. The Clan started moving from the fens the moment you arrived."

"I'll make sure of that on my own, of course," Oslo said. "Though my progress has been slower than I would have wished, what with investigating deaths and attending funerals. Deaths in high places and the associated funerals do interfere with my other duties."

A silent moment passed while the three of them considered that. Then Cyril stood abruptly. "You grow ever more ruthless, my friend. My enemy. Ever more dangerous. Ever more like us. You too are more than you were, and less."

He turned and flowed down the wall and out across the water.

Rhea smiled sadly at Oslo. "Be careful that in your service to Frederick, you do not lose yourself."

Oslo watched as she, too, flowed into the shadows. He waited there, in the darkness, thinking about the past and about bargains made and kept. What price would he pay one day for the bargain he had just made? How many souls would be sacrificed to protect the interests of the Young Dux? And how much damage would a man as ruthless and self-interested as Richard have been capable of, moving in the highest circles?

Oslo had a good idea of how it would happen. He had been familiar with the Children's work for years; he had burned out more than one Clan in days past. The Children would move past the unprepared guards unseen, unfelt save perhaps for shivers running along spines held erect and at attention. Richard, with his fondness for high places, would be considering his plans for the future, perhaps savoring a cup of mulled wine before bed. He would hear the slightest sound, and turn, to see huge eyes filled with black purpose. The fledgling had been Rhea's. She would want Richard to see death come for him. Then the soundless rush, and the long fall. Perhaps in that last instant, Richard would guess who had sent them. Perhaps, as he was hurled from the tower, his last breath would be spent cursing Oslo's name.

Oslo listened to the whispering wind competing with the calls of the night birds and the rippling, wet sounds of the snakes and the 'gators until the rising sun smashed the darkness to pieces of early morning shadow. Then and only then did he break the pattern and loose the power he had bound in lines of flowing script. He made his way back out of the fen with methodical care. He heard the raised voices of guards and excited villagers well before arriving in Foregate proper.

The priest and his boy met him at the gate. The boy's face was flushed with excitement and speculation. "Lord Hunter, Lord Hunter! The Comte is dead!"

Oslo nodded, his eyes old and tired in the merciless light of the morning sun. "I know."

The boy shook his head. "No! I mean the young Comte. Comte Richard has fallen from the height of his tower!"

Oslo nodded again, his eyes dark and his expression unchanging. "Ah."

The boy looked up at the Hunter anxiously. "Do you think it was the monsters, Lord?"

Oslo let one hand settle on the boy's shoulder, turning him toward Father Joseph. "Go to your father, boy." The priest's face looked pale and expressionless in the torchlight, but he bent down, handed his son a copper coin, and nodded off toward the inn. "Ask Marla to give you some mulled wine, and get you to bed. We have a busy day tomorrow."

The boy disappeared into the crowd, and Father Joseph turned to face Oslo. "Anything to confess?"

"Not for a long time, now."

"Care to change that?"

Oslo paused, and met the priest's eyes. "Father, we are all of us monsters, or could be." The priest said nothing as the hunter walked past him, keeping to the places between the light and the darkness.

MY BROTHER, MY BROTHER

by Jane Toombs

Jane Toombs, author of 70 plus published books, enjoys reading and writing—especially paranormal fantasy. In the winter she admires the beautiful swans on mid-Florida lakes. In the summer, she lives where she grew up, in Michigan's Upper Peninsula wilderness where the wolves prowl. Wolves have always fascinated Jane and the occasional sight of one crossing the road near her house thrills her.

Hunter came to partial awareness when he felt himself lifted. Danger! He fought to will himself awake. Failed. Slid back into nothing until he began hearing voices over the throbbing rhythm of a motor. The words didn't make sense. "Far enough. Dump him."

"Mumble, mumble....tracks?"

"Blizzard on the way."

"Mumble, mumble, piss on his grave."

In a barely functioning corner of his mind he recognized the voices. *Yonke, the loud one. Nevins, the mumbler. Partners. Friends?*

Felt himself lifted again and tossed onto a surface that yielded some, but not enough. Breath knocked from him. Struggling to draw in air, he heard the whine of the motor growing fainter, leaving. Snowcat?

Lying on cold. Snow. Wind rising, could hear it in the pines. Pines? Where?

Got to wake up. Get up...

His eyes finally opened. Lying on his back, he blinked at gray sky, snow sky, framed by pine branches. Snow on the way, he could smell it. Someone had said blizzard. Yonke. On the snowcat? Mind like mush. Hard to think straight. Hunter tried to raise his head and everything blurred.

Dizzy. Sick.

With tremendous effort, he turned over onto his stomach and finally was able to shove up onto his hands and knees. He began to retch, vomiting brown gunk on the snow beside a stain of yellow. He crawled backwards, away from it. Reached a tree trunk and, using it as a prop, struggled to his feet.

He closed his eyes against the world whirling around him, leaning against the pine for support. His mind began to function, telling him this growth of pines must be thick, the trees old, because all the branches were overhead. Virgin timber?

Where? He risked squinting through half-open eyes. Vertigo less. But all he could see were trees and snow. He thought the ground sloped down away from him but couldn't be sure.

From overhead came a bird call, chick-a-dee-dee-dee. Words popped unbidden into his mind. *Little sister*. Strange. Hadn't thought about such things since he was a kid. Wasn't going to help any that he had. Got to remember what happened. Where the hell was he?

Yonke. Nevins. Yes. Flew with them from New York to Michigan's Upper Peninsula. Home. No, not any more. Not for years. Yonke said possible uranium site, all hush, hush. January, cold, but need to check it out before another investment company beat them to it. Everyone knew the stuff was up here—somewhere. He'd believed his partner, his friend.

Drove rented 4X4 to a lodge named Con-de-Con, after a supposed Indian chief. Hunter's lip curled. Bad phonics. Anishinabe words didn't fit English, didn't translate well. He'd translated better than the words.

Cut that off. How the hell was he to find his way out of wherever he was before the blizzard hit? Better get moving. He staggered away from the tree and wound up clutching at another to stay on his feet. Why was he so sick? The wind moaned a warning in the branches.

Drugged. That blasted too-sweet coffee. Those slimy bastards dumped something in it. His partners. Lured him into the north woods to get rid of Hunter, the man who owned half the business one of the conglomerates now wanted to buy. With no Hunter, they'd split everything instead of just sharing the other half. Greedy snakes.

Fury arrowed through him as he recalled them tossing him off the snowcat to die—poor Hunter, caught in the blizzard. The hell he'd die! He'd survive. Kill the bastards.

Anger cleared his mind. This was his home territory as a kid, should be able to figure a way out. Isolated country, the U.P. Still wilderness. They wouldn't have gone too far from the lodge, had to get themselves and the snowcat back before the blizzard white-out.

Left tracks. He'd follow them.

Couldn't stay upright—too dizzy. Crawl, then. On hands and knees, gritting his teeth against waves of nausea, he started off, hardly aware when snow began to fall until the wind began blowing it into his face, blinding him, obliterating the snowcat tracks.

Hunter stopped. No man who wanted to live stayed outside in a blizzard. He judged he was nowhere near the lodge yet. In the storm, impossible to find.

He needed shelter. No knife, nothing to cut brush. Dig, make a snow cave, no other choice. His hands, covered with gloves instead of thick mitts, were already so cold they were numb. Feet, too—he wasn't wearing winter woods boots. And the wind—old hawk from the north—sliced through his city jacket, leaving him shivering. Hypothermia a real danger. *Dig*.

Huddled in the shallow snow cave, all he could manage, he knew it wasn't deep enough, but he'd used up what energy he had. Living soft too long. Plus the drug. He felt his mind begin to drift and tried to control his thoughts.

Brown puke on the snow. Yellow stain. Had those scumbags pissed on his grave, after all? He'd stopped shivering. Bad sign. He knew he was close to dying.

"Help me," he whispered, unsure who he was addressing. From somewhere out of the past, words came to him. *My brother, my brother,* he cried inwardly, *remember Sheema*! Flickering images brightened and faded in his mind: He was a boy again, on the reservation, a boy called Sheema by his older sisters. It meant Little Brother. Sheema was still his name when he grew old enough to be sent into the woods without food or water on his vision quest.

Sheema chose a sturdy crotch in an old maple, hidden among the colorful oranges and yellows of The Moon Of Turning Leaves. Here he was safe from foraging bears, stuffing themselves for the long winter sleep. He hoped he'd be favored and his quest made short—hadn't old White Owl told his sisters he might be chosen at the next Mide ceremony if his vision proved a true one?

To be a Mide meant being looked up to. That's what he wanted above all—to be somebody. His seventh grade teacher in town had told him to take college courses once he got to high school and try for a scholarship, saying, "Don't waste your smarts."

Maybe he'd do that, though he knew in his heart he'd never be a Mide if he went off to college.

Sheema shook his head and concentrated on why he was in the tree. Soon night would cover him and he must try to stay awake as long as possible. Vision dreams didn't come to those who slept too soon.

By the third night he was hungry and thirsty and cramped, but he persisted, hard though it was to keep his mind off food and drink. He heard the hunting call of kookoohuhu, the owl, and the soft rustle of waushkashe, the deer, picking his way through the brush. The last sound he remembered was the death cry of waboos, the rabbit, as one of the night hunters caught him.

He was asleep and yet not asleep when a luminous shape drifted down from the sky, leaving a trail of faint light behind it. Sheema held his breath as the shape hovered close, gradually shifting until an immense gray wolf floated in the air before his eyes.

Who am I? the spirit wolf asked without speaking.

At first the awed Sheema couldn't find words, but at last the right ones came to him. "Nessia," he whispered. "My brother."

Brothers in the hunt. The spirit wolf said *Do not forget...* He vanished before Sheema could answer.

In the morning, when he told his vision to White Owl, the Mide who interpreted vision dreams, the old man gave him the new name of Hunter and cautioned him to always honor his very powerful spirit brother.

Hunter had set that aside as he'd put everything Anishinabe away when he graduated from college and was recruited by a New York brokerage firm. He'd done so well, he'd left and formed his own wildly successful Gray Wolf group. Which eventually had led him back here to his homeland. And death.

No!

My brother, he mouthed silently, his breath failing, *in my way I tried to honor you. Will you take me on the hunt with you?*

Hunter's world exploded.

～～

The gray wolf's lip curled as he sniffed at what lay on the snow, aware they were the clothes Hunter the man had worn, aware he was now Hunter. As a wolf, he mistrusted the stink of man permeating the clothes, but he knew he had to take care of them. He dug a hole in the snow and buried the garments, telling himself he'd come back after the storm and find them to wear when it was safe to be a man again. Meanwhile, even a wolf couldn't survive in this blizzard without shelter.

He loped into the cover of the big trees, finding by scent an abandoned weasel den among the roots of one, and dug his way deeper inside, out of the snow and wind. By the time the storm ended, Hunter was hungry. Every instinct focused on finding food, he left behind the hidden clothes to hunt for meat.

Catching the rabbit he stalked proved to be the most exciting experience of his life, the tang of fresh blood on his tongue the sweetest. As he crunched the bones, wolf scent flung his head up. Spotting two smaller, younger males peering cautiously from cover, he snarled, warning them off. But, when they trailed him even after he finished the rabbit, the part of his brain that remembered human matters reminded him wolves had filtered into the U.P. several years ago from Wisconsin, wolves that had been originally reintroduced into Minnesota. And wolves hunted best in packs.

Since he was both bigger and stronger than either of the other two, with snarls and snaps he assumed the alpha role and then they traveled together, with him as leader.

He soon found himself reveling in his freedom as a wolf. How clear and sharp the scents, how thrilling the chase, how satisfying to devour the prey they ran down and killed. His human self faded.

When the softer breezes of the Moon of Breaking Ice started to melt the snow, he began to recall he was not all wolf. Feeling his man part had unfinished business, he left his two bachelor comrades and returned to where the clothes were buried, pawed them free of the snow, sniffed at them with distaste and reburied them in the dirt. He wasn't ready.

Unsure what to do next, he lifted his muzzle and howled. From nearby came an answer, along with a whiff of female scent that drove everything else from his mind, shutting down the human corner. This is what he needed.

In his wolf eyes she was beautiful and infinitely desirable. After she decided to accept him, their mating brought a piercing pleasure unlike anything he'd ever experienced. Hunter knew as well as the she-wolf did they were now attached for life.

As a pair, they attracted the two young males, forming a pack of four, which he, as the alpha male, led. His female soon went off by herself to den. She bore three cubs, one male, two female, and he brought fresh kills to leave near the den for them all. By the Moon of Falling Leaves, the cubs were old enough to join the pack.

Soon after that the two men with guns came. The part of Hunter that remained human came alert when he recognized their smell. He reasoned that they might be posing as deer hunters, but what they'd come back for was to find the body of the man he'd been so they could prove his death. His hackles rose and he growled.

The pack watched him, ready to follow his lead. The human part of him assessed the rifles Yonke and Nevins carried and weighed the risk. Revenge—and the risk—was his and his alone. Hunter led his pack deep into the woods, to the almost inaccessible ravine where his female had raised their cubs. He returned without them to stalk the men. Formidable though he knew he was, he understood he couldn't kill both at once. The problem was, while he savaged one, the other could shoot him. He figured he was no more invulnerable as a wolf than he'd been as a man—yet he'd never be able to rest until both were dead. He trailed them, keeping out of sight.

Waushkashe come. Be ready. At the same time the words of his spirit brother flared across his mind, he caught the deer scent and poised himself. Moments later a buck burst from the pines and fled across the path of the two men. They raised their rifles, aiming.

Hunter leaped from cover and sprang at Yonke, the larger of the two. As he brought him down, he heard a rifle crack. From the corner of his eye he saw the buck falter, saw Nevins turn toward him and aim the rifle. The blood lust gripping him proved greater than his fear of dying. He tore out Yonke's throat, then, with a snarl, faced the other man. Nevins lay sprawled on the ground, the dying buck on top of him, his rifle out of reach. One of the deer's sharp hooves had torn a hole in the man's chest and his blood mingled with the animal's. Hunter trotted up to him, growling, seeing terror replace the pain in Nevins's eyes. "Gray Wolf," he mumbled.

Hunter's frustration at having no way to reveal his true identity faded when he heard the words. It was enough Nevins made a connection between the company he'd tried to steal and the wolf that stood over him, watching him die. His revenge was complete.

Catching wolf scent, he whirled and saw his female peering cautiously from cover. She and the rest of his disobedient pack had trailed him. Just as well. The danger was over and they could feast on venison.

When, bellies full, they retreated, Hunter remained. Nevins had died during the feasting, no doubt certain he, too, would be eaten. Hunter curled his lip in disgust. Loping to where he'd buried his human clothes, he dug them up again and sat staring at them.

He had no doubt Spirit Wolf could change him back to a man. He could resume his old life, in no danger of being blamed for the unfortunate deaths of his two partners. But he didn't intend to take that route. Once he was a man again, it wasn't too late to go home, to learn the Mide way, to truly honor his spirit brother.

He formed man words in his mind *My brother, I wait...*

The answer came as silently as his asking. *Too late for honor, brother. We will always hunt together.*

For a second or two he didn't understand. Then grief and anger stabbed at him, sharp as snake fangs. He would never be a man again; his plea to his spirit brother had bought him a one-way trip.

He howled in anguished betrayal.

Whose was the first betrayal? The words slashed knife-sharp across his mind.

As he recognized this was the price he'd paid for his rejection of what he was, his anger dissipated. After a time, he sensed his female's presence and, with her scent in his nostrils, the grief vanished.

He pawed at the discarded human clothes, then grabbed the jacket and the pants in his jaws. Trailed by the she-wolf, he dragged them with him as he trotted back to the dead men.

Hunter dropped the jacket over Yonke's face and the pants over Nevins's. Before leaving the world of men behind forever, he marked each garment with wolf piss.

MEETING MR. WRIGHT

by Chris Grover

Chris Grover writes what she most enjoys reading: stories with a paranormal twist, and mystery stories with a European background and a police officer as a major character. Recent published works include WHERE'S MICHELLE—where a nine-year old girl is kidnapped while on vacation in England; and WITHOUT A CLUE, which is set in Paris, France and concerns the disappearance of an antiquarian diary. Chris is currently working on a mystery series with a woman from Las Vegas and a British CID officer as the major characters.

The fallen leaves lay thick on the ground and Vicki's running feet sent them flying in all directions as she jogged through Gage Park. A pale early morning sun filtered through the bare branches of the trees, lighting up the rich carpet of reds, golds and browns and making it glow like the jewels in a pirate's treasure.

Fall. Vicki's favorite season. In another few weeks, cold winds would blow in from the North, turning Lake Ontario into a sheet of ice and frosting Hamilton like a giant birthday cake.

The scent of wood smoke from one of the houses bordering the park hung in the air and Vicki stopped to rest for a moment. With her back against the trunk of an old chestnut tree, she did a few stretches and looked idly around. At seven in the morning, with the kids getting ready for school and the senior citizens still in bed, the park was a haven for joggers. A group of guys she recognized from the health club had overtaken her as she came in, and a few moments ago she'd passed another woman and a couple of older men jogging in the opposite direction. But the only person in view now was a man sitting on one of the benches a few yards away with his back toward her.

Dark-haired and dressed in sweats similar to those Vicki wore herself, he looked ordinary enough. Like most of the other mid-thirties males she encountered on her morning runs.

Except there was something about this man that seemed vaguely familiar. The set of his shoulders? The way he sat with his head tilted a fraction to one side? Maybe, if she could see his face...

Just then the man turned and smiled at her. "I've been waiting ages for you."

"You have?" Vicki halted, mesmerized by the flash of strong white teeth against a deeply tanned face and the compelling gaze of dark honey-gold eyes. "But...but—" She snapped her mouth shut and pulled herself together. There was nothing threatening about the man's demeanor, in fact she felt perfectly safe. On the other hand, she knew from experience that first impressions could be very misleading.

"Nice try," she said, softening her words with a smile. "But if we'd met before, I'd remember."

"You're right. We've never actually met before now." The man's smile widened as he stood up and took a step toward her. "But we're all waiting for someone. And I've been waiting for you."

Vicki's nerves tensed. He was handsome, sexy and undoubtedly deranged. And so was she if she thought he was simply making cute conversation. Like her mom used to say, if a con man looked like a con man no one would ever get conned. "If you want money, you're out of luck. All I have is a bus ticket."

"Money?" His dark brows drew together in a perplexed frown. A moment later the frown was replaced with an amused grin. "You think I'm a mugger?"

"I'm not sure what I think." She glanced quickly to the left, then the right. But instead of the steady flow of runners she usually saw in the park at this hour, the paths were strangely deserted. She took a small step backward. He followed. "I've been coming here same time every morning for months, but I don't recall ever seeing you."

"Corporate transfer. I arrived in Hamilton a few days ago."

"I see." Actually Vicki didn't see anything at all except the advisability of making a hasty departure while she still had the chance. "Nice to meet you, Mr.—"

"Wright. Don to my friends. And you?"

"Vicki Anderson." His smile deepened and Vicki noticed a tiny dimple near his mouth. Nevertheless she started to edge away. "I have to go now."

"No!" Don bounded forward and grabbed her arm. "Please, Vicki. Don't go. Not yet."

Vicki's mouth felt dry as cotton and her heart hammered against her ribs as he held her gaze. Don was tall, with broad shoulders and the body of a well-conditioned athlete. If he did intend to harm her, she was powerless to stop him. The only thing she could do was scream and hope someone heard her. She opened her mouth, but to her horror nothing happened.

Don released her arm and stepped back, then held his hands up, palms out. "Hey. It's okay. I'm not going to hurt you."

Vicki held her breath and concentrated on the tiny specks of glittering gold in the dark honey of his eyes. As the seconds passed her fears gradually subsided, then disappeared as she became increasingly aware of the intoxicating masculine fragrance of his body and the handsome face only inches from her own. He had the kind of wide sensual mouth that was made for laughter and lips that made her fantasize about long slow kisses.

Her nerves tingled with excitement. Despite the early morning chill, she was on fire. She'd even forgotten to breathe and now her lungs were bursting for air.

Don dropped his hands and took another step back. "I'm sorry. I've frightened you."

Vicki ran a hand over her short auburn curls and did her desperate best to get her emotions under control. "I guess you did. At first, anyway."

The sun had disappeared, and she felt a couple of raindrops hit her face. She looked up at the dark sky. "I guess the forecaster was right when he said we could expect a wet day." As she spoke, the rain began in earnest, slashing through the leafless branches above their heads.

"Come on. We'll make a run for it." Don grabbed her hand, but when Vicki didn't immediately move he gave it a tug. "Let's go or we'll be soaked."

Holding tightly to Don's hand, Vicki ran, but she had difficulty keeping up with his longer stride. Gasping for air, she tried to slow the pace, but he urged her on and the next thing she knew they were back at the park entrance.

As they turned out of the gate onto the sidewalk, Vicki was dismayed to see her bus had left the stop and was almost to the end of the next block. "Damn!" she wailed. "Now I'm really going to get soaked. There won't be another bus for ages."

"You live far from here?"

"Not really." She shrugged and pushed a strand of wet hair behind her ear. "But in this weather it might as well be the South Pole."

"There's a coffee shop next to the bus stop. If we get a table in the window, we'll be able to see the bus when it comes."

But when they reached it the coffee shop was in darkness. A neatly lettered note taped inside the door read 'Closed Indefinitely'.

"I live there." Don pointed across the street to a house with blue and white siding. "You're welcome to dry off and warm up while you wait for the next bus."

Vicki didn't even hesitate. She was soaked, she was freezing cold, and she would probably wind up with pneumonia. But attractive as Don was, she wasn't stupid and she didn't take foolish chances. "Thanks all the same, but I'd prefer to wait there." She indicated an apartment building further down the block that had a canopied entrance. "There'll be another bus along shortly."

Don's face reddened. "Sorry, I wasn't thinking. But how about the porch? I could make coffee and bring it out to you."

Vicki looked over at Don's house and the open porch that stretched across the entire front. The porch was in full view of the street—nothing to prevent her from leaving if she changed her mind. And there was a glider exactly like the one her grandma used to have on her porch—white with deep blue cushions. She wrapped her arms tightly around her body to stop herself from shivering. She'd always loved gliders. And right now she would give a month's pay for a cup of hot coffee. "I don't want to put you to any trouble."

"No trouble." Slipping a protective arm around her waist, he hurried Vicki across the street. "Have you had breakfast?"

"I'll have it when I get home."

After Don went inside to make the promised coffee, Vicki glanced cautiously through the open front door delighted to discover the hallway and stairs were carpeted in her favorite shade of deep midnight blue.

Moving away from the door, she peeked into the wide front window. But with no lights on and the overcast sky, it was impossible to see anything beyond a desk standing immediately in front of the window.

Vicki sat down on the glider and closed her eyes. The house was about fifty years old. The kind of house she hoped to buy herself one day. The most important room in her house would be the den. She loved to read so there would be two walls with floor to ceiling bookshelves. It would take at least that much space to accommodate all the books she owned. Of course, the den would be carpeted in midnight blue and matching blue velvet drapes would frame the window. She'd put her grandfather's antique walnut desk in front of the window. A house this old was bound to have a fireplace, so her two easy chairs could go there, one on either side. The remaining space could be filled with a couple of small tables and her stereo unit.

The furniture in her den would have no particular style and be neither very old nor very new. Just a mishmash of the various pieces she already had that blended together and made a house feel like a home.

"Hope you're hungry."

Vicki opened her eyes as Don put a covered tray down on the wicker coffee table in front of the glider. He removed the cloth with a flourish to reveal two mugs of coffee plus a dish of scrambled eggs and buttered toast. Also on the tray was a miniature dark red rose in a tiny crystal vase.

The food smelled wonderful and Vicki leaned forward to look at the tray. "You have been busy," she observed with a smile as she stroked a fingertip over the velvety petals of the rose. She picked up one of the mugs and took a sip of the dark fragrant brew. "How did you know I was hungry?"

"I guessed." Don returned her smile as he sat down beside her on the glider and reached for the other mug. "Cold rainy mornings always make me hungry."

When she'd finished eating, Vicki piled the empty dishes back on the tray with a small sigh of contentment. Leaning back in her seat, she regarded him through half-closed eyes. "You're one terrific cook."

Don shook his head. "Not really. Just showing off for my lady."

His lady? Vicki felt a rush of adrenaline. A hundred boisterous butterflies began performing acrobatics in her stomach and she swallowed hard.

He touched her hand lightly. "I'm really sorry about scaring you back there in the park. Can you forgive me?"

"Maybe."

"Only maybe?" Don gave a soft groan of disappointment and Vicki looked up. But instead of disappointment, laughter sparkled in his dark honey eyes while amusement tugged at the corners of his mouth. There was also something else in his eyes, but before Vicki could decide what it was he ran a finger down her nose. "You have freckles."

Vicki shrugged and began rearranging the dishes on the tray. "That's what happens when a person with red hair tries to get a tan."

"Are they just on your face?"

"No. I have them all—" Although it was cold on the open porch, the intimate turn in the conversation sent Vicki's temperature soaring. With her pale coloring her embarrassment was impossible to hide, so she kept her attention fixed on the tray. "Do you like to lie in the sun?"

"With you I would."

Vicki lifted her gaze. His half-closed eyes looked dark and dreamy and she felt her body go limp.

"I can see us now," he murmured, "stretched out beside cool blue water, basking in the warmth of the sun, our skin slick with oil and perspiration. But every once in a while, a breeze comes to soothe and calm our overheated bodies." He gave a small sigh. "Can you picture us like that?"

Vicki's mind had pictured the scene all too easily. She ran her tongue over her lips unable to stop the tiny tremor of excitement that skipped over the surface of her skin. "Sorry. I don't have that kind of wild imagination." She quickly clasped her hands together before they could betray her. "I must have been on a coffee break when they handed it out."

"Liar." Don whispered as he gently grasped her shoulders and drew her close. "I saw it in your beautiful green eyes."

A lock of dark hair slipped forward to lay on his forehead. She wanted to reach up and smooth it back, but somehow she managed to resist the urge and keep her hands firmly clasped together.

As Don's arms tightened around her body, she made a token struggle to escape the embrace, but her heart wasn't in it. His hard body felt warm, secure, and she laid her face against his chest. "What exactly did you see in my eyes?"

"Your dreams," he whispered against her hair. "Your dreams of our future together."

Vicki pushed his arms away and moved a few inches along the glider. "You're crazy."

He reached out and trailed a finger down her cheek. "I am about you."

Vicki stared at him for a moment, then she closed her eyes tightly. She'd finally flipped out. She'd imagined everything from the moment she'd noticed a man sitting on that bench right up until now. When she opened her eyes she would be back in the park and there would be nothing but an empty bench and dead leaves on the ground. Right?

She opened her eyes.

Wrong!

Don was still there. He was sitting less than a foot away with his arms folded while he watched her watching him.

"When we met this morning, you said you'd been waiting for me. You were just joking around. Right?" Afraid of Don's answer but knowing she needed to hear it, she began fiddling with a tassel on one of the glider's cushions. "Guys always use lines like that to pick up women."

Don smiled, his dark honey eyes liquid and warm with desire as he reached for her hand. "It wasn't a line, Vicki. I've been waiting for you for a long time, and I knew that one day I would find you." He reached for her and Vicki moved back into his arms, nestling her head against his chest. "In our dreams, I believe we've been waiting for each other for most of our lives."

"We have?" The blood sped through Vicki's veins at supersonic speed. She felt dizzy, disoriented. And her heart was pounding eight to the bar because she knew what Don said was absolutely true. He was her dream lover in the flesh. The shadow that had filled her dreams for so long had finally taken on form and substance. She snuggled closer, her hands reaching up to caress his face as his fingers threaded through her hair and he skimmed her mouth with a tender but fleeting kiss that brought her emotions to fever pitch and promised bliss.

As she continued to look at him, his dark head descended, blotting out the light. His lips touched her forehead, then brushed gently against her lashes like a short-sighted butterfly before moving down her face to hover over her mouth. She gave a soft little sigh. Her body ached for his touch, ached for him to deepen the kiss. She hadn't realized it until now, but she'd been waiting for him, too. She wanted a man to hold her and never let her go. She wanted a kiss that would last forever.

Don's kiss was all she'd ever hoped for and more. A kiss made in heaven. A kiss that sent her flying to the moon securely clasped in her lover's arms.

Just then she heard a loud ringing. Not the telephone or the door-bell. An ambulance? The fire engine? She struggled to sit up. Rubbing her eyes, she looked quickly around. Nothing!

She snuggled back down and closed her eyes. The only sounds came from outside. The angry scream of gale force winds and heavy rain slashing against her bedroom window.

Her bedroom?

Vicki sat up quickly as the raucous ringing started again. The noise came from the old-fashioned alarm clock sitting on her bedside table—right next to the book she'd been reading before she fell asleep last night.

Reality had returned. Time for her to get up and go to work. She turned off the clock, then groaned as she noticed 'MEETING MR. RIGHT' scrawled in fancy silver script across the book's midnight blue cover.

Unsure whether to laugh or cry, Vicki made her way to the kitchen and plugged in the coffee pot. Don's face was still clearly visible in her mind's eye and while she waited for the coffee to brew she sat down at the kitchen table and rested her chin on her hands. Okay so it had just been a dream. But what a marvelous dream! A thousand times better than all the others because this time she'd actually seen his face and talked to him.

But still only a dream, she reminded herself firmly. Exciting and lifelike certainly, but a dream nonetheless.

A deep and unexpected feeling of disappointment settled over her like a black cloud. She tried to laugh it off, but the laughter wouldn't come. Instead, a fat tear slid down her cheek. Her dream lover was perfect—truly the man of her dreams, and she wanted him back. But that was the problem. He only existed in her dreams—not in reality.

"Grow up," Vicki admonished herself sternly as she left the table to pour herself a cup of coffee. "And stop reading mushy stories before you go to sleep. Dark-haired hunks with honey-gold eyes only exist in the pages of romance books." And in your imagination, she reminded herself silently.

It was still raining when Vicki got to the bus stop, but with her mind busy replaying the dream, she barely noticed. For some reason, unlike her other dreams, this one showed no sign of fading. She could recall every detail as clearly as if it had actually happened.

"Hey, Miss! You want this bus?"

To Vicki's surprise, the bus was waiting with the door wide open and the driver's grin stretched from ear to ear.

"Got to watch that daydreaming," the driver joked as she dropped her ticket into the box.

Vicki pushed her way into the crowded interior. With every seat taken, she grabbed a handrail and hung on tightly as the bus started to move. As they lumbered along, Vicki's eyes slid shut and she returned to her dream.

But suddenly the driver slammed on his brakes and she lost both her grip on the rail and her balance. As she was thrown forward, strong arms reached out to steady and then enfold her and the next thing Vicki knew she was being firmly held against a hard masculine chest.

As she tried to free herself, a familiar fragrance filled her nostrils. She couldn't quite remember where or when she'd smelled it before, but—

"Are you okay?"

"I'm fine." Vicki lifted her head to look at the man who held her, then she froze as she encountered a pair of dark honey-gold eyes. A lock of dark hair had fallen down over the man's forehead and a smile tugged at the corners of his wide mouth.

Was she dreaming again or what?

She squeezed her eyes shut. When she reopened them the man was looking at her with a puzzled frown.

"Something wrong?" she asked.

"I'm not sure." He gave an embarrassed chuckle. "This is going to sound really ridiculous, and I know you won't believe me, but last night I had the strangest dream..."

THE GARGOYLE WHO LOVED ME

by Nora Santella

Nora Santella, a Jersey girl who currently resides in America's Heartland, earned a Bachelor of Journalism degree from the University of Missouri and has worked as a newspaper reporter, photographer, freelance editor and corporate business communicator. She wrote THE GAR-GOYLE WHO LOVED ME as an affectionate tribute to para-normal romance stories and horror flicks, especially those populated by vampires, shapeshifters and bad boys. Her first published book, GUESS AGAIN, is a 2004 EPPIE final-ist in romantic suspense and a CAPA (Cupid and Psyche Awards) nominee.

"You'd tell me if I was dead. Right?"

Beryl Magia clutched the shot of tequila in her trembling hand and wondered if she dare toss it down her throat. She never drank, but the damnable present seemed like a good time to start. Besides, if the alcohol didn't kill her strange metabolism, it most certainly would scramble her yin with her yang. Given her iffy circumstances, she craved the oblivion tequila could offer.

"Wrong," the bartender snarled. "We don't serve *Milk of Human Kindness* here."

Beryl eyed the nasty spikes on his leather collar before noticing his pawlike hands as he drew beer from the tap into a mug to serve a nearby customer. On second thought, the guy looked a tad hairy, just like her situation. Guardedly, she turned to survey the torch-illumi-nated, subterranean lounge. The castle-dungeon décor of her deten-tion area made an "abandon hope" statement with as much subtlety as an emetic.

"Where exactly is *here*?" she mumbled. "Hell?"

"No. Prairie Village."

Such good ears you have. So, she hadn't left the Kansas City metro area, thank the goddess for small favors, although how the Peculiar faeries had dispatched her across the Missouri state line into Kansas quicker than she could shriek "help" remained murky.

"Lucifer's joint is down the road," the Gother-than-thou bartender added, a bit too helpfully, giving her the impression that he'd answered the question more than once and knew the drill. "As dens of iniquity go, we're still in our infancy, striving for five-flame status. Maybe if a few more lookers like yourself stop by here, though, our 'stock' will improve."

He chuckled to himself, obviously enjoying the "insider" joke. His guffaw sounded more like a growl and stoked Beryl's escalating sense of danger. With a quick flick of his massive wrist, he tossed a matchbook onto the scarred mahogany counter. If the ambiance of her surroundings didn't urge a woman in jeopardy to giggle hysterically, the glossy-white-covered matchbook heralding the club's name, *Night Breed*, in blood-red script, provided the pregnant pause.

"Surely Hell wouldn't scare you, Sugarplum, after what you've witnessed. You ranted something about shapeshifting gargoyles when you materialized a short time ago and quit screaming."

"Materialized?" She noted that her "dragon lady" sheath of crimson-and-gold, bias-cut satin remained intact, but she'd lost her strappy red shoes with the sassy high heels. "Drat! My purse is gone, too, along with my cell phone and money." Despite her wooziness, she felt the faint stir of her Talent as she glanced back at the bartender. "You're not surprised."

* Be careful, Beryl. *

Spectral fingers caressed her exposed shoulder and made her heart flutter. The invisible guardian, whose male voice only she could hear, had added a teasing, seductive touch to his counsel the past few weeks. If she didn't know better, she'd almost believe he'd grown possessive since the relationship with her would-be boyfriend had heated up.

"What do you bet the same fey creatures who knocked me senseless sent me to *Night Breed*?" As the last four words left her mouth, she winced. *Was the owner suggesting a pastime or classifying a species? Bet he's devious.*

The bartender shrugged his shoulders. His indifference rippled in waves along with the ruffles on his maroon poet's shirt.

"I'm not here by choice. Aren't you the least bit concerned that I've been zapped and transported to your, uh, establishment by an illegal act of magick?"

"No." He studied her like a dinner menu. "Wizardry happens."

There was no humor or softness in his sharply angled face, only a brooding melancholy to match the truculence of his not quite Homo sapient eyes. Predator eyes.

Wolf-man.

The instinctive perception of his lycanthropy hit her like a blow. She tried to slide off the bar stool, but her body wouldn't budge. Magick bound her to the seat. She could feel it slithering around her now that she'd reclaimed enough of her wits to open her Talent and probe.

"You're stuck here until The Master sets you free."

"Is this so-called Master anyone I should know and avoid?"

You're caught in a web.

The familiar scent of sandalwood caused Beryl to shiver with awareness. She didn't know why she connected so intimately to her phantom guardian, except for her erotic dreams of late. When the warrior summoned her to his shadowy realm, his molten gaze, hot hands and clever tongue tormented her body and set her ablaze, inciting a wanton need that felt almost unbearable.

"You'll find out," the bartender said. "Don't run off."

"Yeah, right." *Where's the Mage Corps when a girl needs them?* "Like I'm the first innocent victim to drop into this club."

"Innocent?" His scornful laugh prickled the back of her neck. "The fey must've thought otherwise. Did they catch you in the act of being naughty at their preserve?"

"For your information, Woofy, I'm not that kind of girl."

Hold your tongue, Beryl.

"But I do blame myself for what happened to my friend tonight," she continued, ignoring better judgment and her guardian, although sometimes the two intermingled. "No mortal man deserves to be turned into a gargoyle."

"Ouch. Sounds painful." The werewolf loped off to answer the bogeyman's hail at the far end of the bar. When he returned to Beryl, he leaned with deliberate menace over the bar, crossing deep into her comfort zone. "You're very savvy for a mundane. How did you sense that I'm not wholly human when you're not '*were*' yourself?"

"It's a Talent of mine."

Fear flared in his eyes for an instant before he pulled back. "The faeries hate to be hassled by...Are you a witch?" He emphasized *witch* like an expletive.

"No! Absolutely not."

The vehemence in her denial made Woofy scowl and retreat. *Good.* She could have told him about her wicked-witch mother, Maleva, the high priestess of a coven best left unnamed. Given her current run of good fortune, though, Mommy dearest might be scrying in the midnight hour and hear her estranged daughter's declaration. There was power in names. Beryl refused to give her own away.

Out of habit, she searched the shadows and wondered which one might be her guardian. None of the pallid-faced patrons in the tomblike chamber could horrify Beryl more than witnessing a faerie curse transform her once hunky, would-be boyfriend into a stone-cold gargoyle. It broke her heart to think of his demise.

Gone in the flash of a thunderbolt was the flesh-and-blood man to whom she'd surrendered her virginity. As if his grotesque form wasn't payback enough for mashing the faeries' sacred toadstool beneath his knees in a moment of passionate trajectory, the wee magicians opted to unfurl his monolith wings in perpetuity when he tried to flee from the scene of his crime.

"Damned faeries!" She studied her tequila with morbid fascination. "The little perverts have an odious sense of justice. They didn't even give Rockley a fighting chance."

* They could've shapeshifted your lover's manhood at a critical moment. Wouldn't that have cast anatomical hardness in a new light? *

"Oh, shut up. I don't want to hear it." The last thing Beryl needed was a lecture by that irritating, know-it-all voice inside her head.

Woofy looked askance at her. She didn't care. If she survived the night, she didn't plan to complain about the service or the one-gram-of-fat pretzels. Still, it seemed proper to wallow in grief before she met The Master.

* It's not as if your life was defined by that single moment in time, unlike mine. *

"Your life? Puh-leeze. You don't have a life outside mine."

* You'd be surprised. *

She stared suspiciously at the tequila while she clenched her open-fingered, ruby-mesh-gloved hand around the shot glass. Perhaps she'd already chugged the first drink and this was a refill. Her short-term memory still seemed a tad foggy.

* Look at me, Beryl. I'm standing at the end of the bar. *

"But that's impossible..."

Sneaking a peek, she did a double take. The bad boy biker gazing wickedly back could be the mace-and-chain poster model. In her secret fantasies, she'd often pictured such a man with that glorious mane of ink-black hair. The sight of this guy's awesome pecs and sculpted abdomen made her tingle. The barbed-wire tattoo circling his left biceps intrigued her, too.

"Fricky figment." She sighed, long and hard. Maybe he was a hallucination born of stress or one her evil mother had conjured up.

* Don't deceive yourself, truthsayer. Trust your senses. *

Shouldn't she be blind to his muscular physique? Wasn't she supposed to be in mourning? Rockley Marston was dead–no, not exactly dead, just "stoned" indefinitely in Peculiar, Mo., until she figured out how to reverse the spell.

"This conversation can't be real. You're imaginary."

* No, I'm quite solid for the moment, thanks to faerie magick. But the spell might not last long. *

The hint of a time limit snagged her attention. "I thought imaginary friends were indestructible. How did the faeries bespell you?"

* I protected you from their gargoyle blast. *

Beryl sucked in her breath. "Thank you, but you can't, no you can't be...my guardian."

* Maybe if you ask me nicely. *

"Who are you?"

* Belek. Know my name, woman. Belek. *

He radiated a magnetism that drew her, body and soul. Although unprepared to deal with a psychic warrior in her weakened condition, Talent surged through Beryl when she scanned everyone along the bar, feeling the veracity behind his or her facade, much like a human lie detector. But she failed to get a reading for Belek, except for his macho fashion sense. He definitely provided inspiration for a passel of sighs in his black leather vest and pants.

Oh, yeah. While she could picture herself climbing aboard his "hog" and riding off with Mr. Sun Tan Perfect into the sunset, Belek's smoldering presence disturbed her as much as their tenuous link. Strange, too, was how she couldn't psyche out his energy pattern like all the others from this distance. His crooked grin, however, confirmed that he knew her well enough to recognize her secret weakness for waist-long hair in a prospective mate.

Odd how the word "mate" resonated in her mind as she gazed at Belek. She'd always envied people who identified life partners with some mystical sense. Her dating frenzy of late, even her deflowering, seemed like such a waste of time while Belek stared back, willing her to get up close and personal. Could something other than hormones have prompted her sex drive? Surely not fate...

Stubbornly, she resisted the temptation to follow her heart, turning from Belek to watch the glut of wannabe vampires trolling for victims, one fire-challenged wizard who'd set his drink aflame, a trio of gremlins swinging from the rafters, and the token troll with a requisite snarl. The naked lepidopterist sporting butterfly wings, though a sight to behold, was either another faerie victim or a cruel joke of Mother Nature. And, oh boy, the Big Bad Wolf bartender acted ready to pounce.

If only she'd listened to the Gypsy, she could've avoided this penance. One minute she'd been cavorting close to the edge of the waterfall at the Saints Preserve Us botanical gardens with Rock and then, a heartbeat later, he'd brought new meaning to his nickname.

The carnival fortune-teller had warned them not to skinny-dip in the garden's magical water or they'd suffer grim consequences. "A rogue band of faeries makes their home in gourds there," the Gypsy said. "They're a horny bunch, fearsomely jealous of human affection, and impotent besides. You, child, being mageborn, and your boyfriend, gorgeous specimen that he is..." She'd paused and peered googy-eyed once again at the X-rated image inside her crystal ball. "Being that your boyfriend is, uh, handsomely endowed, well, you're both bound to attract attention. So, I suggest you think thrice before driving the wee ones berserk with even a kiss. Don't tempt fate."

No joke. Penis envy from the peanut gallery had robbed Beryl of a lover in his prime, not to mention her first orgasm. Then an unearthly compulsion forced her to run hard and fast out of harm's way until she'd arrived at Club Bizarro.

Faerie dust. Your steps were directed here by faerie dust, but I cannot fathom why. I almost lost you, Beryl Magia.

"I know how close I came to a fate worse than death," she said with a delicate shudder and leaned back to acknowledge Belek.

Beryl's shoulder bumped into the hard wall of a chest. She smiled, pleased that Belek had come to her rather than vice versa. A quick flare of unfamiliar Talent squashed that notion. So did the chill that raced up her spine when the stranger whispered his apology.

Uh oh.

Slowly she turned to face a heartstopper in a tux. Way 007. He flashed an irresistible grin as she gaped at his male perfection and golden-brown hair. One problem, though. No pulse. He was vampire to his libido-melting core.

You're so veined, girl.

"When facing death, I recommend champagne over tequila." The vampire spoke with a sexy Irish lilt as he lifted the shot glass out of her numb grasp to set it down. "Mind if I join you for a drink?"

"Suit yourself."

"Open a bottle of Dom Pérignon for us, Orton," he instructed Woofy who'd snapped to attention as Mr. Hidden Fangs sat down.

"Yes, Master."

Master as in *The* Master? "I just want to get drunk, not enthralled."

There was amusement as well as hunger in his gaze as it swept over her. "Appreciating a good wine is complex–not unlike you, sweet angel of sadness."

"I'm neither sweet nor angelic, I assure you."

"Tart works well for me, too. My taste in women isn't carved in stone."

Stone. Why did he have to remind her? Even though the bloom in Mr. Plasma Lover's ivory cheeks suggested he'd recently fed, she squirmed on the stool. Her pulse skittered when he captured her wrist between his cool, marble-smooth fingers. Turning her hand over, he pressed a kiss in the palm that sent currents of desire through her.

You must call me or I cannot save you.

As the words screamed inside her head, she yanked her hand back and glanced down the bar in search of Belek, but he'd disappeared. The hitch in her breath she attributed to the loss of her biker rather than the voltage in the vampire's kiss.

One of the larger shadows on the wall shifted from the rest and undulated between the worlds of reality and illusion. *Belek?* Did she imagine the pair of perturbed eyes that seemed to flicker in and out of existence as she glanced away or the sudden whiff of woodsy aroma?

"I don't believe we've met," she said while Woofy served two flutes of premium bubbly, "but I know what you are."

He stilled for an instant, as if listening to her thoughts to evaluate their validity. "I'll try not to flash my incisors unduly."

His eyes glistened in the candlelight like dreaming pools of midnight blue. Powerless to resist him, she clicked her glass against the one he'd raised in silent toast.

"I am Trevor of the Clan Beltane. You are...no, don't say your name...Beryl, the Greek word for seagreen jewel. It matches the color of your eyes."

"You can read minds?" She parked her drink after one dangerous sip.

"Sometimes. I was clairvoyant in life and vampirism revved up the volume." He shrugged. "I'm much better at seeing auras. I've been watching yours since you entered my club. It sparks with your anguish." He paused, cocking his head. "You're not straight human."

"I'm the get of an unknown demon."

* Not true. I can tell you the truth about your father now if you'll say my name and lose the Prince of Darkness. *

"And the daughter of a sorceress." Trevor pursed his picture-perfect lips.

"A source of contention. Let's not go there."

"I can feel you scrambling to edit your thoughts." He chuckled while he eavesdropped. "Did she really try to sacrifice you to the Elements?"

"Yes, but I got lucky. Only one deigned to answer her entreaty."

Torn from its hiding place, the buried memory made Beryl swallow hard. Nearly losing her life on her fifteenth birthday at the behest of an unfit mother had provided clear proof that her guardian existed and could obliterate any threat when he transformed from elusive shadow into solid terminator.

Trevor's intense Talent pierced her to the marrow. "FrisPyr? The minor fire deity?"

She could see the eerie flames reflected in his eyes as he turned his vision inward. "Yes." Fleetingly, she worried over the scope of his mind control, afraid that she might reveal her other secrets without so much as a whimper.

* Fight his compulsion, Beryl. He'll suck you dry. *

"I'm impressed. You're resisting me admirably well. I don't want to hurt you, Beryl. But you'll feel much better if you tell me about FrisPyr."

"Sinners in Hell want ice water, too." She blinked and severed their psychic connection. "Stay out of my head."

* Good girl. *

"And if I don't?"

"I'm not without protection." She murmured an incantation. Soon a dainty flame danced across the palm of her outstretched hand. At that same instant, she felt the magick wards around her dissipate as if one arcane act on the premises cancelled out the other. She was now free to escape and fervently hoped the vampire failed to notice.

"A gift from you-know-who," she added, withholding the fact that she'd begged her shadow warrior to spare FrisPyr's life when it'd sputtered into an ember.

Trevor's eyes widened. "You must've inherited your mother's knack for The Craft." He looked frightfully pensive as she blew out the fire. "Orton won't appreciate that. He doesn't like witches. His *condition* is hereditary, brought upon his family by a scorned witch's curse."

"We all have our cross to bear, Master Trevor. Just keep your psychic Talent to yourself and I might cooperate. I'd hate for you or your club to go up in smoke."

He glowered, exposing his fangs for an instant, but she heard resignation in his voice when he said, "I sense something fey about you, besides the faerie dust twinkling on your skin."

"I'm a truthsayer."

He quickly doused the amazement that flared in his eyes. "That makes you almost as rare as unicorn horns in this part of the inhabited world. So, your Talent brings the truth to light."

She wondered how long it would take her to escape through the milling crowd, but nixed the idea. She couldn't recall seeing an entrance door and she doubted that any *Night Breed*er would help her pull off a Disappearing Lady act.

"Are you a Druid?" she asked, hoping to distract him from her thoughts.

"No, I'm Kelt. The family motto is 'enlightenment through ecstasy.' Care to test it with me?"

Only a fool could misread the cat-and-mouse game in progress. "Thanks, but, no thanks. I'm commitment-shy and you strike me as a long-term-relationship type of guy."

He nodded. "A good thrall is hard to find."

Needing no further update on the vampire's plans for her, she shot up from her seat. Trevor caught her by the arm as she bolted past him and spun her round like a rag doll. His preternatural speed and strength stunned her.

"Stay with me, truthsayer." He loosened his grip. "Unlike your first human lover, I can offer an eternity of delight."

"My first...but...how did you know?"

His tongue moistened his lower lip. "I can smell the virgin blood on your thighs and it's arousing."

* He's in league with the faeries. *

Out of the corner of her eye, she glimpsed a shadow fighting to materialize as Trevor held her immobile. The air around them shimmered. Beryl felt herself tumbling inward without a foothold while a strange force clouded her mind. Someone close by her screamed with feral intensity as the fighting broke out. She felt herself torn asunder and convulsed in dread.

Beryl! Beryl!

She didn't remember blacking out or how she'd got chained with her back against the stone wall of a cushy prison cell, but she knew she was in deep doo-doo. Straining against the manacles, she took deep breaths until she felt strong enough to raise her head.

Oh, praise the Maker. You survived ta'harta. The Lord of Shadows shall be pleased.

Trevor flowed into view, still looking devilishly handsome, despite his change from formalwear into jeans. Under different circumstances, she might've chuckled at the Stonehenge photo screen-printed on his black T-shirt with "rocks" as its label.

"Are you all right?" he asked.

She glared at him. "Why have you chained me?"

His gaze raked over her. "You're not what you seem, and far more than I'd suspected. The faeries dropped you on my doorstep, marked for the ultimate punishment, but the little fools failed to consider how you'd charm me."

"And they say chivalry is dead," she said as Trevor pressed his lips against her hair. "Are you in cahoots with the faeries?"

"The Sidhe are my countrymen, not my colleagues. They have their uses, though."

She didn't need Talent to detect his evasion of the truth. Her scathing retort fizzled when he gently cupped and fondled her breast through the satin dress and then slid his hand across her ribs and down her abdomen. He touched her with surprising restraint.

"I've not seen your kind before, Beryl." He pressed her against the wall so she could feel the evidence of his arousal. "And, though I know it's foolhardy, I'm attracted to you."

"Let me go."

"I can't. Hear me out." He stepped back. "I don't think your ability to fade into shadow has anything to do with being a truthsayer. Initially, I thought it was another faerie trick, so I held onto you as you blurred. But you fought me, tooth and nail–or, rather, an otherworldly version of yourself did. I won this round, but I don't want to meet her again."

She laughed nervously. "My evil twin scared you? That's rich. I didn't know I had one." She couldn't tear her gaze away from his frightful beauty. "W-W-What do you plan to do with me?"

His tight expression grew suggestive. "First, I intend to lick you." He dropped to his knees and, lifting the hem of her skirt, tasted the skin between her thighs with tantalizing flicks of his rough tongue until she moaned softly.

* Are you wishing it were me? I know what you crave. *

The potent combination of external and internal seduction made Beryl struggle to catch her breath.

"You excite me, shadowshifter. If I were supernatural enough to hold you in bondage..."

Trevor sighed, rose fluidly and retracted his fangs. Beryl shuddered. If what he'd said about her shadow proved true, she was hardly more human than the vampire.

"But I fear my competition will intrude before I could sneak a sample love bite." He smiled sadly, staring at her neck.

"Competition?" Instantly, she emerged from her daze. "You saw him? He's real?"

"As real as the faerie wings splattered on his leather clothes when he staggered into the club shortly after you."

Before she'd even realized he'd moved, Trevor maneuvered closer, looking hellbent for a kiss. She stiffened as his face lowered and his breath teased her lips.

* I'd like to whomp a certain master vampire's ass, too. *

"Belek!"

Belek might've been all in her head before the faerie zap, but she needed him to be tangible now.

"Don't shapeshift on me again." Trevor hastily distanced himself. "You've got that look in your eyes." He snatched hold of a first-aid kit on the table by the curtained bed. "Maybe when you're feeling more human, we could..."

"Belek! I need you."

* In more ways than one. *

"I'm, uh, glad we met, Beryl, but not enough to lose my head over you." Inching towards the door, Trevor added, "Forgive me for leaving so abruptly, but I rather face a horde of pissed-off Sidhe than meet your shadow guardian and her sidekick again. Besides, someone needs to patch up the faeries. I've been told that your sidekick almost beat them to pulp when he showed up, out of the blue."

"Yes, run along," she said with a sneer. "Be sure to tell your countrymen to reverse their spell of enchantment on my lover or Berry the Maleficent will come back to finish the job her sidekick started. And Berry takes no prisoners."

Belek materialized and groused, "Sidekick?"

"Rockley doesn't deserve to be a gargoyle. Damn those faeries."

Trevor hastily retreated.

Beryl tugged at her restraints when Belek advanced her way. "Well, well, well. I'd say the faeries aren't the only ones with the ability to shapeshift you from shadow into a man. I believe you've finally mastered that trick on your own."

"True, but I'd never before been pulled from my reality into your universe as anything but a shadow. While I appeared 'solid' earlier, I was powerless except for our shared telepathic connection." He stopped within arm's length of her, giving her time to wrestle with her ambivalence towards him. "I'm glad the vampire trussed you up. This holds...possibilities."

His fingertip skimmed across her bare shoulder and she quivered. The thought of surrendering in passion to Belek made the memory of the gargoyle who'd loved her fade into nothingness. She felt a twinge of conscience at her fickleness, but she'd be a poor truthsayer indeed if she didn't recognize the truth when it stirred her libido with a very mortal touch.

Hating to be at anyone's mercy, however tender, she wished with all her might that she could slip out of her manacles. She managed to do so, slick as a pro. Rubbing her chafed wrists, she gazed up into Belek's steel-gray eyes.

"I suppose you know how I did that."

"Magick." A dimple curved in his cheek as he smiled.

She could only stare, spellbound, as he drew her into his arms. His mouth joined hers in a soulful, devouring kiss. Not one suitor to date had ever kissed her with such heartfelt need or made her feel so cherished and irresistible as a woman.

"Oh, yes." Her sigh sung of contentment and wonder.

"I've hungered to touch you like this outside the dream world," he said, nuzzling her neck, nibbling at her earlobe.

"You've had ample opportunity, especially tonight. Why didn't you?"

His hands explored her back in arousing increments. "I wanted us to meet in the flesh as equals, Beryl Magia. You were unaware of your true heritage. The Lord of Shadows, your father, bound me to serve as your guardian in this dimension and forbade me to shapeshift unless you were in mortal danger."

Her body hummed with wanting as his tongue teased the edge of her low décolletage. "W-W-Why?" she managed to croak.

"You are so precious and dear to..." His head snapped up. "...to my Lord." It took a minute for Belek to orient himself and that pleased Beryl as she emerged from the very same haze. "Lord Dharuk didn't trust your mother or her perverted use of power. He feared she might taint you. And he felt morally obligated, as your sire, to protect you from harm until you mastered The Changing and could cross over to his world."

She shifted her position in his grasp. "Is my father...? Is he, uh, a demon?"

"No. Dharuk is quite human enough to suit you."

She tried to read him with Talent, but it didn't work. As if he'd sensed her attempt to probe, he *tsk*ed good-naturedly.

"If I've never lied to you in the past, truthsayer, why would I start now?"

"I can't peer into you, Belek." The fact that his face brightened at the admission made her nervous, but she didn't fail to notice how quickly he changed the subject.

"Your father is blessed with Talent, too. He's what the Medieval Ones on your Earth termed 'an adept.' Because his skill level is so extraordinary throughout our realm, he commands our Serene Ruler's protectors–a league of shadow warriors."

Beryl focused on only one word. "Are we talking 'adept' as in sorcery? You know I have magick issues."

"And with good reason." Belek tilted his head to the side and sighed as she pulled free to stalk a circle around him. "Maleva brought Dharuk onto your plane of existence when she tried to summon the element of air and aroused his curiosity."

Beryl stopped in her tracks to face him. "She aroused more than his curiosity. I'm living proof."

"But your mother failed to bind the Lord of Shadows to her side here in this reality, try as she might. He is powerful, Beryl Magia, and no match for an earthbound witch." A fierce pride glimmered behind his eyes. "It is an honor for me to be his title-designate."

So, not only was Belek handpicked by daddy for her, but he possessed a destiny beyond her keeping. The idea troubled Beryl almost as much as another did. "But is Dharuk in league with the Devil?"

"No, woman. Perish the thought." He crossed his arms over his chest. "Dwell on this instead. Your father wants to meet you. The decision, however, is yours."

Briefly, she considered the invitation, still very much aware of Belek's dangerous masculinity, but wondered more about what The Changing meant in the grand scheme of her life. "Things changed for you and me when I took a lover."

He nodded. "Still shrewd as ever, I'm glad to see. You severed my bondage the moment that you lost your hymen. But, more importantly, the rending activated your true shadow anima. We call the ability to transform from one shape into another–*ta'harta* or The Changing. *She* is your birthright and will guard you from this day forward."

"She's a part of me...like my soul?"

"Yes. You summoned your shadow anima in fear this time, but you must learn to glory in her. That will take patience and training. Newborns can be savage. It's no surprise that your vampire was spooked by your shadow's eager intensity to flex some muscle."

Shapeshifter, not wholly human. She drew back, daunted by how his revelation altered her world. Would Belek leave her now that he was no longer pledged to serve and protect? "But what about us?"

He captured her firmly by the upper arms and reeled her closer. "We share a unique vibration, thank the spectrum. That will always exist between us, no matter whether you choose to stay here or explore alternate realities with me. But, it's only fair that I warn you. I'd like you by my side."

She smiled and dragged her fingernail down the center of his magnificent chest. "Just tell me you're 'solid' where it counts."

"Definitely." His gaze heated to a feverish pitch. "There is much for you to learn, woman."

"Will you teach me?"

The truth glowed in his eyes before he kissed her. "Try to stop me."

"Hey! Whose fantasy is this?"

TRANSCENDENCE

by Loren W. Cooper

The beginning of the end, as I remember, lay back in the stirrings of winter. I know that's right, because in my memory I can still feel the chill reaching ahead of that first big storm, the icy touch of the air promising the deeper cold that followed on the heels of the north wind.

I had come to see Crispin, because I knew that if I did not shake him out of his hole, he'd let the night slip by before remembering our agreement. Crispin threw himself into his passions like a man possessed, and when possessed by his passions, all the voices of the exterior world were like the ringing of distant bells.

You see, Crispin built worlds.

His place took up a tiny corner in the top floor of an old building in that part of town that had last seen heavy traffic in the years just following the Civil War. His building stood in the midst of a place where old businesses went to die, and new ones passed away stillborn. They had character, those old brownstones, and not much else, but rent was cheap, so Crispin settled there as he settled into everything, drifting through life following a sedimentary path of least resistance.

I said Crispin built worlds. By that I mean he was a prime example of that particular subtype of gamer whose personal thrill lies in breathing life into an alternate universe. Weaving threads of vitality into a tapestry of place and character until the world begins to beat and pulse in the maker's mind is the meat and drink of a world builder.

Now understand, by gamer I mean a role-player, someone who assumes an alternate identity in a game where rules serve only to define the interaction of the imagination of the participants. Cards and board games don't count. Role-players might also play the occasional card game, but for them role-playing is the passion: role-playing is *gaming.*

Crispin had worlds, whole universes constructed with such intricacy that you could walk down any street in any of his cities and Crispin could give you the personal details of every residential address, down to character references on the family pets. Moreover, he could tell you when in the timeline of that world the house had been built, who built it, and whether or not anything significant had ever happened there. Crispin also understood the natural laws that governed each world, if they differed from ours, as fundamentally as any physicist understands

the laws of thermodynamics, and could describe how those laws in-
fluenced the building of that particular house.

Grappling with those laws drove Crispin ever deeper into his passion.

The draft worked its way up my trouser legs and probed the seams
of my coat for weaknesses as I climbed the narrow stairway that led
up to Crispin's apartment. I could hear the voices from one landing
down, so in the pale light trickling through the heavy clouds beyond
the small dusty panes of the window, I shifted into stealth mode and
eased my way up to the head of the stairs, stepping as close to the wall
as possible to keep the creaking of the steps to a minimum. One voice
had that particular timbre best described as harsh and piercing.
Crispin's occasional feeble responses came as a low, nearly inaudible
rumble. From the sounds of it, his landlady was giving him hell again.

She wound up with a sharp sniff, closed the door with a crack of
abused wood, and stalked down the hallway toward me. She spared
me one disapproving glance before descending the stairway with quick
sharp steps. Her long bony frame, nervous energy, and unlovely personality had always made me wonder if her closest relations weren't
mustelid.

I tipped my hat to her back and wandered down toward Crispin's
door. I rapped sharply, then pushed the door open. Crispin being
Crispin, sometimes he'd hear a knock, sometimes he wouldn't. He
looked up as I came in and nodded to me absently. He reminded me of
a Dionysus sunk deep in his cups, presiding morosely over the after-
math of a party thrown by bibliophile maenads.

"Thomas," Crispin said, his face a grim study of lines and shadows. "Have a seat."

I stepped carefully between precarious mesas of books and papers, and gingerly transferred a short stack to a nearby pile. The resulting tower teetered on the edge of disaster before stabilizing reluc-
tantly. "Bad day?"

He turned to face me, his eyes feverish in his thin, pale face. "Bad,
but not without promise."

I chuckled. "I'd be down too, after a visit from Mother Stoat."

"That woman," he said with a grin. Then his face fell and he waved
a hand dismissively. "Not her. Her tune never changes. I'll make the
rent. She knows it, and I know it. She just doesn't like to miss an
opportunity to savage me a little."

"What then?"

He lifted a bundle of loose pages, some torn raggedly from dis-
parate notebooks, some old printed sheets covered on the back side
by his ragged scrawl. "All that time, wasted."

"The magic system?"

He threw the mass into the center of the room, where it exploded
into the broad white leaves of dead trees. "A waste. I've been on the

wrong trail for the past ten years."

I nodded sagely. "Couldn't resolve the differences, eh? I thought quarks and Zen were going to do the trick."

He gave me his best aloof. "Jeer if you must. Gloat while you can."

"I told you a fully consistent magic system was impossible," I said. "Someone had to contradict someone else. Thales and Aquinas make uneasy bedfellows, without throwing in the Sufis and Boole. If nothing else, Godel should have told you that. Besides, maybe now you'll actually put it together for play. What good is a system no one uses?"

He shook his head sadly. "Philistine. It wouldn't be right to use if it weren't perfect. Besides, Godel was the key."

I settled back and regarded him skeptically. "You're onto something else."

His eyes sparkled. "Godel says that no axiomatic system can be complete. Systematic reasoning can't describe everything in the system. You have to go outside."

"I told you that, remember?"

"But you never went anywhere with it," he snorted. "Tell me, what's common to all magic that's been practiced across the world?"

I raised my hands, palm up.

He shook his head disapprovingly. "Tsk. Read the Kabbalah. Read Mircea Eliade. Read Frazier. Read the Bible, you heathen. All magic is worked from the outside. True magic is calling and controlling Powers from beyond, usually but not always spirits. Remember Prospero, in *The Tempest*? Ariel did all the work."

"Interesting. Should be easy to translate into nearly any system. All you have to do is figure something for a will contest between the summoner and the summoned, and decide what the particular capabilities of any class of Powers might be. Are you ready for tonight?"

"Bah." He rose, grabbed his coat. "I'm not close to a system, yet. I haven't even figured out how a sorcerer would do his summoning. In the Hermetic tradition, in the Kabbalah, even in most every shamanic tradition, the first summoning takes long rituals or great trials."

"So. What do you think that means?"

He snickered and turned off the lights with the care of a man who stretches every dollar until it snaps. "I think it means they were no closer than I am to understanding the actual Mystery. Really, the true magic lies in transcending everything we know. Like Kant said, transcendent experience is reaching something ordinarily untouchable by hands of mortal clay. That's magic."

I followed him out and watched him lock his door. A needless precaution, since he had little enough of value for even the most resourceful of thieves.

"How's work?"

He led the way down the stairs. "About the same. Less than usual. Slow for tutoring. What about you?"

My lip curled reflexively. "The day never changes with the company. But I've taken the next step. I've come far enough that I tendered my notice. The freelance business will support me until the game is done."

He shook his head. "I respect your drive. Too much connection with Mammon, though. I couldn't handle it."

I laughed. "Trust me, I hate the rat race at least as much as you. I refuse to sublimate my personality to the hive. But that drive is my ticket out. Make enough to support my needs, and I bow to no man. That's the way the world works."

"Ah." He tried for interest in the regular debate and failed. "Everyone coming tonight?"

"Last I knew."

We cleared the doors and the driving wind swept into our faces. Shoulders hunched, our thoughts trapped in the cages we built for ourselves out of old dreams and discarded hope, we walked without speaking to the warmth and shelter of my place. I put on some music (Celtic, to fit the mood) and the others came trickling in out of the wind's frustrated grasp.

We had a good game that night. Crispin's breakthrough fed the fires of his creation, until the transformation became complete. I left this gray place and traded it for brighter colors. Instead of my usual calculated plots to gain financial independence, my head filled with the charming fancies of a ne'erdowell rogue and gentleman trickster, Abercrombie by name, one of my favorite characters. When I looked over at Joan, I did not see the face of a pre-law student with fragile eyes, but rather an outcast and a rebel, bound only by the chains of her pride to an ivory blade that thirsted for blood. Jerome's face aged, and grew wise, and he became a man who could command the elements, and drive the storms to fury with the keen lash of his will. And Crispin became the world, and everything else in it, and we gamed until late in the night, finding solace from the things we had made of ourselves.

As they filed out, I shook Jerome's hand, and bid him a good night, and he smiled just to smile. "Good game."

"Crispin outdid himself."

"He did that, but we were all a part of it. It couldn't have happened without us."

I closed the door behind him and went to bed, dreaming in vivid color.

The holidays came, and gaming slid into its seasonal hiatus as the group split apart to resume contact with the families. After the new year, I stopped in at the local used bookstore and saw Jerome behind the counter.

"How's the project coming?" he asked.

I shrugged. "Not so good. Lots of ideas, can't pin down a theme.

Good to see you working, by the way."

"It's not much, but it's better than nothing." He looked around. "At least I'm comfortable here."

Jerome could recite entire passages out of Plutarch's lives, knew Tacitus by heart and Pliny (the Younger) on a first name basis. He had some Greek, and a little Latin he'd picked up along the way, and a better feel for the ancient world than anyone I knew. He didn't have a degree, and his skills and native intelligence meant nothing in the marketplace. I'd always harbored the suspicion that the modern world confused him. He would have been happy as a clam in the Library of Alexandria before Caesar arrived.

His voice caught me as I turned toward the door. "Have you seen Crispin, lately?"

I shook my head.

"Me neither. He's been out of circulation for at least a month now. You probably haven't noticed, as wrapped up in your project as you've been, but we have."

I thought about magic systems. "Maybe I'll stop by. See what he's doing."

He nodded. "Do that. Let me know what you find out. Maybe we can get the game going again."

Jerome looking wistfully after me, I left that place with Crispin on my mind. His building looked the same as always, and the light under the door told me that he was home. I knocked, and no one answered. That didn't surprise me. When I tried the door and found it locked, that did surprise me.

As I stood there, thinking about it, wondering if Crispin had actually forgotten to turn off the lights, I heard faint, distant music drifting through the door. That did it. I banged, I hollered, I made myself obnoxious. No response.

Irritated, I started back down the stairs. I heard a soft sound and glanced back, to see if Crispin had actually wakened from whatever stupor possessed him. I saw the face of a girl peering around the corner of the corridor, her face elfin, her eyes luminous.

I stopped, and she vanished. I pounded back up the stairs and rounded the corner, but I saw nothing. I hadn't even heard the door close, but Crispin's place was the only available bolthole. I beat on the door some more, the old wood suffering visibly under my vigorous buffeting, but I heard no response other than that same faint music, playing no tune I could recognize but teasing me with a phantom familiarity.

"Fine." It came out as a snarl. "Stay holed up in there, Crispin. But she looks a bit young for you."

I stomped down the stairs, closed myself up in the house for a week, and tried to work on my project. I've written programs since the foolish days of my misspent youth, and I'd always regretted selling my soul to a corporation. I'd had this idea for a killer video game, working out most of the kinks in my head while doing my time.

But proprietary laws and contracts being what they are, I had to quit to work on the game, so I'd be able to own my brainchild. High detail, high graphics, a few mind games worked into an intricate plot, with hard and easy paths to everything. The hard paths took thought, the easy paths took considerable manual dexterity. But my theme fell through, and until I solidified a decent theme, I couldn't do any serious work on the rest of it.

A week of that found me back at Crispin's door. Again with the music, though this time the light rippled like a live thing under the door, and I wondered if Crispin had lost it completely and hung a disco globe from his ceiling. No answer, of course, and my discontent had reached epic proportions by the time I turned back and started down the stairs.

I met Mother Stoat marching her way up, and I noted the yellow slip of paper in her hand. I stopped her on the stairs. "For Crispin?"

She nodded sharply. "I've given him every chance. He's over two months behind now. Thirty days, and the law takes over."

She brushed past me, five foot four of whiplash mean, and I let her go. I was worried, of a sudden, rather than irritated.

I called Joan and Jerome, but Jerome had met with the same lack of response that had greeted me, and Joan was busy with classes. I moped around, thinking, until I couldn't stand it any more and headed back determined to break the damned door down, if necessary.

The door opened on the third knock, and I just stood there with my mouth hanging open.

Crispin's face glowed with health, and his eyes glittered like black diamonds. He stood in the doorway without displaying any intention of inviting me inside. "What do you want, Thomas? I'm busy."

I looked past him into the usual disarray, but over in one corner I caught a glimpse of a rippling fabric of light, shot through with fragments of ghostly images. It could have been sunlight splashing off the glass and my imagination, but in my memory I paint again an open sky broken only by joyous faces glowing with the ethereal light of another world.

Crispin stepped back, narrowing the door and blocking my view. I shook my head, regained my focus, and glared into his eyes. "I wanted to see if you were alive and well, Crispin. I'm at least happy to see that rumors of your death were premature."

"Now you know."

He started to close the door. I shoved my foot into the gap. "Not so fast. Are you just writing us off? If it's the girl, hell, bring her to the next session. We'd love to meet her. We don't even have to game."

He looked at me with cool hostility. "I don't know what you're talking about."

I shook my head. "Dammit, Crispin! What's the matter with you. You cut us off, and the land lady's about to throw you in jail. What's the deal?"

He tried to force my foot out of the doorway. "Leave me alone. Let me be."

I leaned forward and asked him, "How's the magic coming?"

He straightened and his eyes softened. "Thomas." His head bowed. "You're too far away. You're holding on to too much that isn't really important. You stink with it." He sighed. "But I'm close, Thomas. I can feel it. Nothing on paper yet."

I rocked back at the intensity that lit in his eyes, and with sudden force he kicked my foot out of the way and slammed the door. I heard the bolt slide home, and I turned away. He'd lost it. I didn't even know him any more.

I thought about what I might have seen past Crispin for those fleeting fragments of an instant, and put conjecture away with a snarl. He thought to infect me with his madness, but I would permit no weakness.

I wandered back to my home and started cobbling blocks of scenes together, hoping that something would happen. Every now and then, I'd look at the dismal state of my financial resources, and I'd calculate how many days remained until I'd be forced to don the corporate yoke again.

Turning around these thoughts in an ever-tightening gyre, I came at last to where I had begun, and found myself climbing the stairs back to Crispin's place. In the middle of that climb, looking up into the distance I had yet to go, I stopped and stared out the window at the endless horizon, under an unusually clear night sky stitched full of stars. My eyes sought that place where parallel lines meet, and I wondered what I was doing, and why I was doing it.

Gentle movement at my side drew my gaze back from converging infinity, and I looked down into large eyes, gray like the sea.

She smiled up at me, and I tried to place her age. Sixteen? Twenty-six? "Thomas."

I grinned. "What a coincidence. We share the same name."

She chuckled. "Crispin told me about you."

"Nothing but lies, I assure you."

She laughed like music. "Ah, Thomas, it's a shame we hadn't met earlier. He's not there, you know."

"He's gone, then. I was afraid of that. I waited too long."

She raised a hand and touched me lightly on the cheek, tracing the line of my mouth. "Don't be afraid for him, Thomas. He's happier now."

I said nothing.

She shifted restlessly. "I must go to join him. Come visit us sometime. You're already halfway there. The rest is easy."

She descended the stairs, and I called down after her. "You never told me your name."

She looked back up at me, her expression impish. "Call me Ariel."

She disappeared out into the starlight. I didn't try to follow. Instead, I made my way up slowly to Thomas' open door and his empty room. I paced around the narrow space, listening to the fading echoes of a haunting music that sounded like distant horns calling, and so I was still there when Mother Stoat arrived.

I paid Crispin's back rent, catching the calculation in Mother Stoat's eye and stopping that train of thought with a single sharp glance. I brought his books and papers back to my place, to keep for him should he ever want them. He had little else of value.

Crispin apparently left behind all of his worldly possessions, though I didn't find the radio, or CD player, or whatever he played that haunting music on. I still hear it, now and then. That music in my ears, the problems with my theme fell away, and I completed the game in the midst of a storm of inspiration.

In the game, the player rises up through progressively less gritty levels, until at last the player breaks through into a place of pure dancing light. I called it "Transcendence," and you've probably played it. Copies still sell, and I seem to be rolling in cash.

I'm not any happier, for all that.

I don't play roles much any more, and sometimes I think about Crispin, probably growing fat somewhere in quiet pleasure with his beautiful wife. And as his children grow, and his wife's beauty fades, Crispin will never notice the passage of time until Death himself taps him impatiently on the shoulder.

Other times, I think about the light in Crispin's place, and the images I caught in the corner of my eye for a shattering instant. And on clear, starry nights, when I raise my eyes to the horizon, I wonder if he might not be out beyond the place where parallel lines meet, guided through the company of luminous spirits by a ghost with eyes gray like the sea, Ariel by name.

But the world doesn't work that way, does it?

Now and again, I hear music in the wind, and I wonder.

BUTTERFLIES

by S. Joan Popek

S. Joan Popek is an award winning author who managed to chase an elusive Associates of Arts degree for five years until it finally gave up and let her catch it at ENMU-R. She is a graduate of Writer's Digest Short Story and Novel School. Her work experience includes a fun filled stint as a bartender. She has also been a counselor in Adult Basic Education, a small business owner, publisher, author, editor, public speaker and other vocations not nearly as impressive. She lives and works in New Mexico with her husband and a dog named Nubbins.

In a small corner of Paradise, violins strained to reach the ultimate melody. Exquisite tones fluttered like leaves in a spring breeze. Laughing party guests swayed and pranced around the elegant ballroom.

A cool breeze beckoned Jolene out onto the dark veranda. The waiting night tugged at her. She strolled through the open doors to stand on the threshold of time.

The city lights blazed below, dancing across the rolling hills as if they too heard the music. In the darkness beyond, the distant thunder of drums throbbed like blood pounding through the open channels of a beating heart. The graceful music inside competed with the savage primitiveness of the drums. Together, they celebrated the night.

The drumbeats pulled her to them. Her heart pounded in unison to the sensual, primal rhythm. Her feet inched toward the railing—toward the drums—toward the eternal night.

"Hey! Be careful there, lady. You're thirteen stories up!"

Jolene's hands clutched the cool railing, her knees turned to jelly, and she felt herself falling.

"Whoa there, lady—I got'cha—you okay?" Strong arms wrapped around her waist.

"Let go of me!"

"Yes Ma'am!" He raised his hands to hold them palms up. "I was only trying to help."

"I'm sorry," she mumbled. "You just surprised me, that's all."

"Well I didn't mean to scare you, Ma'am, but it's a long way to the bottom, and you were getting awfully close to the railing."

Jolene glanced over the edge, and something cold slithered across her shoulders. She shivered and twisted back to face this stranger. "What the hell are you doing out here? I came out here to get away from people. Who are you? What do you want?"

"Well excuse me for breathing your air. By the way, did you know that your eyes flare like fireballs when you're angry?" He grinned, and one stray lock of thick, dark hair tumbled over his forehead threatening to engulf one of his stone-gray eyes.

She fought an overwhelming urge to brush the lock of hair away from his eye. "You're a spacer aren't you?" She demanded.

"Why? Do I look like a spacer?"

"The way you talk. You sound like one."

"Oh really." He shrugged. "So, how come you're so angry? Paradise is the perfect vacation spot of the universe. A utopia. Nobody should be upset in Paradise."

Shivering, she wrapped her arms around herself. A flash of memory reminded her of Bill and the reason she came here—the reason she was angry at the world. "None of your business."

"Ouch!" he said with another grin. "Didn't mean to hit a sore spot. Just making conversation. Here, take my jacket. You're shaking like a bad gyroscope."

Glancing up at his space-tanned face, Jolene took the jacket and wrapped it around her shoulders. "You *are* a spacer, aren't you?"

"Yeah—well—I used to be. Been here on Paradise for two years now. Retired. Name's Corbin. Mark Corbin."

"Jolene Baldwin. Nice to meet you, Mr. Corbin."

His rough hand gripped hers with surprising gentleness. His eyes seemed to pull her into them...sensing...probing.

She pulled her hand quickly from his.

"I have to go."

"May I see you back to your hotel?"

"No. I can make it myself. I came here alone. I can leave alone."

"Well, at least let me walk you down and get you an air car."

She wanted to say no, but he seemed so sincere, she nodded.

His hand was warm fleece on her elbow as he steered her toward the door. Neither said a word in the lift on the way to the lobby. Her knees tried to buckle again as the lift halted abruptly.

"Whoa, steady there—almost lost you again. You just don't have your Paradise legs yet. Takes a while to get used to the higher gravity."

"I did just fine on the ship coming over."

He steered her through the ornate, gold trimmed front entrance and out onto the sidewalk. "Yeah. They keep the gravity at near earth pull on the pleasure ships. Wouldn't do to have the passengers getting space sick, now would it? Not with what they charge."

"That's a fact." She smiled. His easy going manner seemed to be softening the angry, hurt feelings inside her as they spoke. That made her uneasy, that a stranger could do that, but she couldn't help asking. "By the way, who was playing the drums? I thought there were no natives on Paradise."

His eyes strayed to the sky and a guarded look took the place of the glint that had been there a second ago. "The Butterflies."

"Butterflies? How do they beat drums with no hands?"

"Not drums. Wings. They were feeding."

"Feeding? All at the same time?"

"Yeah—always simultaneously." The sparkle came back into his eyes. "Since I retired, I've been living here and studying the Paradieseian Butterflies. I'm an anthropologist, and they are a fascinating species."

"Well, they do make haunting music, and it sure sounded like drums."

"Yeah. They do, and it does. Well, here we are. Stay here. I'll flag an air car down."

She watched him wave at a cabby and speak softly to him, then he turned and gestured for her to come over. When she was seated in the car, she turned to thank him, but he slid in next to her.

"I'm going that way anyway. Might as well save an air car." He smiled, and the car took off.

As the taxi lifted, the vertigo she had felt on the terrace returned. She rubbed her temple.

"May I?" He gestured toward her head with his hand.

Before she could answer, his hand had pulled hers down to rest in one of his while he caressed her forehead with the finger tips of the other. She relaxed onto the soft cushion of the air car. Visions of cool, green waterfalls and deep orange sunsets cascaded over her.

"We're here." His soft voice pulled her gently from her trance-like state.

"So soon?" she whispered. As full awareness returned, she stiffened, and her cheeks reddened. "I must have fallen asleep." She looked into his eyes and for a flashing instant, saw the sunset again. "How did you do that?"

"Do what?"

"You know—the-the—"

"You mean the waterfalls and the sunset?" He grinned again. "Just a little something the natives of Solaria Four taught me. I spent two years with them. Native doesn't mean primitive, you know." He held out his hand and chuckled. "May I see you to your room?"

"No." This haunting stranger frightened her and intrigued her at the same time.

"Okay. Sleep well, Jolene." He held the air car door for her, waited for her to reach the steps of the hotel, turned and said something to the cabby, then waved to her as the silver streak lifted him into the twinkling, night sky.

As she entered the plush hotel lobby, she felt numb. The events of the last two weeks seemed hazy—almost unimportant. She tried to remember why she had been so upset earlier. When she thought about her faithless fiancé and her rush to Paradise to forget, she felt only sadness.

Strangely, the sadness was for him, not for herself. All of her previous anger seemed to be gone. *Maybe the vacation is working. Or maybe Mark...no that isn't possible...is it?* She dismissed her thoughts as exhaustion and entered the elevator.

In her room, she collapsed on the bed still fully clothed. She awoke the next day feeling calm and rested. She remembered dreaming of a waterfall and orange sunsets. There had been something else too—hovering at the edge of her consciousness—unattainable— and this one was not pleasant. She rarely remembered her dreams, and she *never* consciously tried to recall one, yet...

The chime of the image-phone interrupted her reveries. She answered it blind—no image—she didn't want to see anyone right now. She was afraid the calm she felt would dissipate with the realities of life. It was Mark.

"Thought you might have breakfast with me." His voice resonated with energy.

"I just woke up." She tried to ignore the flutter in her stomach his voice stirred.

"I'll wait for you on the *Isle of Orchids* patio."

"But, I—"

"Hurry, or all the good tables will be taken." He hung up before she could answer.

Fifteen minutes later, feeling a bit embarrassed at her haste, she was sitting at a table with him watching the most extraordinary sight she had ever experienced. A field of almost transparent orchids, of every imaginable color and shade, lay in a vast panorama of beauty as far as she could see. Narrow, winding paths laced through the garden like honeycombs and were dotted with laughing people dancing among the blossoms. Above them, gossamer butterflies with wing spans of at least ten feet fluttered gracefully. Sunlight sent shafts of golden light glancing off their magnificent wings to shower onto the flowers and people below as if it were raining gold.

Jolene gasped when she first glanced through the window, then fell into awed silence as she watched the fantasy scene before her.

"Catches your breath, doesn't it? I'll never forget the first time I saw it," Mark said. "Would you like to see the butterflies up close?"

Something nibbled at the edge of her mind, something from last night's dream, then it disappeared. "Could we?" she asked. She was surprised that part of her almost hoped it wasn't possible.

"Sure. How about this evening? About seven?"

"Yeah. Fine. Why not?"

"Great! I'll go make the arrangements." He flashed her a smile and left quickly as if he was afraid she might change her mind.

Jolene watched him leave. She couldn't help noticing the assured, almost arrogant way he carried himself. She liked self confidence in a man. She smiled and mentally chastised herself for where her thoughts were leading. Sipping sweet, Voracian chocolate, she gazed at the beatific scene out the window. The translucent winged creatures above seemed to oscillate into and out of solid form as if they were holograms, but she knew they were real.

Interrupting the peacefulness, she felt a sudden chill of apprehension. She was suddenly cold, even in warmth of the scene.

⁂

He called for her at exactly seven o'clock and escorted her to a waiting air car. There was no driver this time.

Mark piloted the car with practiced ease. "See that emerald patch down there?"

Jolene looked out at a pink landscape of rolling hills. In the center sprawled a circular patch of what looked like grass from her lofty vantage point. "Yes. What is it?"

"Forest. That's where we're going."

The air car swooped into a lazy, gliding circle and descended slowly. As she watched, the green patch became a mass of tangled trees and vines. The plants entwined like lovers, forming a barricade that was impossible to see through or around.

"How are you going to land this thing in that twisted mess?" She felt dizzy when she looked down, as if she was looking into the center of a giant kaleidoscope. She tried to focus on the distant horizon, but the foliage beneath her pulled at her like a magnet.

"I'm not landing in it. We'll put down at its edge." Mark deftly brought the skimmer to the ground, and the engines whistled to a halt.

The sudden silence was overwhelming. Even the air was still, without a hint of a breeze.

Mark helped her from the air car. "Stay close to me. It's easy to get lost in there." He nodded toward the trees, then headed for them at a steady pace.

Hesitantly, she followed.

On the ground, the vines didn't make the impenetrable wall it had seemed from the air. A narrow path led into what looked like the center of the small forest. Once inside, the cool, musty air reminded her of a cave she once explored when she was in college. "That wasn't much fun either," she mumbled.

"Shh. They'll be coming back soon." Mark whispered.

"Why are you whispering?"

"Habit." He chuckled softly. "They're coming to feed."

"Feed on what?"

"Watch." He pointed toward the edge of the forest.

Her gaze followed his pointing finger. She gasped, "They're beautiful!" At the same time, she realized that she had been hearing the drum beat at the back of her senses since they entered the forest. Now the beat was getting louder, almost frenzied.

Hundreds of glimmering butterfly creatures swarmed in ever narrowing circles, spiraling into dive bomb rushes to the ground, then at the last minute, pulling iridescent wings up and soaring into the sky again. "What are they doing?"

"Feeding."

"On what?" She saw nothing moving on the ground that might be a target for a hungry, giant butterfly.

"I don't know. That's why I brought you here."

"What? But, I thought—"

"Yeah, I know. You thought I was just bringing you for the show. I have a confession to make." He raised his head and looked straight into her eyes. "We didn't meet by accident. I followed you onto that balcony on purpose. I knew who you were from the beginning."

"What? Why?"

"The drum sound of their wings, it pulled you the same way it pulls me. It doesn't affect everyone that way. You feel it now, don't you?"

Jolene stared at his serious face. She realized that her heart had begun to beat faster, picking up the beat of the wings of the creatures now circling directly above them. She looked up and gasped, "Oh!"

"Don't worry. They won't hurt us. Actually, I don't think they even see us. I don't think they are even aware of our existence."

"What do you mean?"

"I don't think they are really in the same dimensional space we are. That's why I brought you here. I was hoping you could help me figure it out."

"Why me?"

"Because your field is microbiology. I've followed your career for a while now...ever since I noticed some things about Paradise that just aren't quite right. I checked the incoming guest list, and when I found your name on it, I started making plans to meet you. And the fact that their wing-beats have the same effect on you as on me is a bonus. It means you'll understand what I'm about to tell you."

Jolene stared at him. "What do you mean, 'not quite right?' And understand what?"

"I think that we are as unnoticeable to them as an ant would be to us."

"That's ridiculous. They are huge all right, but not that much bigger than we are. Not like we would be to an ant."

"I know. That's where my dimension theory comes in. I believe that they are not really here—that we see them like we see a reflection in a mirror."

"But, that's impossible. Sure, they are almost transparent, but I bet I could touch them if I wanted to."

"Could you? You'd be the first. No one else has ever been able to, and believe me, I've tried."

One of the creatures fluttered onto a clump of greenery just a few feet away from her.

"Go ahead. Try," he urged.

Jolene glanced at him and began to inch slowly towards the towering, shimmering being before her. It sat, looking straight at her with unblinking, black bead eyes, lazily waving gossamer wings just inches from her finger tips. She reached. Nothing happened. No barrier stopped her hand, yet it did not pass through the resplendent wing either. It was as though she was waving in the air.

"See?"

She turned to face Mark. "I just misjudged the distance that's all. I just need to get a little closer." She moved forward, reached again. Nothing. She looked at the creature's black eyes, and withdrew her hand quickly. The creature was not looking *at* her as she had thought, but *through* her.

"There's something else," he said softly.

"Something else?"

"Look around you. Any direction. What do you see?"

"Trees, bushes, clouds, sky and butterflies I can't touch. What do you mean?" Her confusion was becoming anger. She always got mad when she didn't understand something.

"Do you see any animals? Insects? Birds? Any moving thing except the butterflies?"

She turned around slowly taking in the majestic, panoramic view, then staring at the soil beneath her feet for a long while watching for any kind of movement. She looked back up at him and frowned.

"No."

"That's why I needed you. I'll stake my life that you won't find any microscopic life either, not even bacteria."

"That's impossible."

"I know, but it's true. Follow me. I have something else to show you." He turned and started walking toward the thickest part of the forest.

Jolene followed silently. The sound of rustling leaves blended with the beat of wings.

"There. Through those trees. Do you see it?"

Jolene had to squint to see into the shadows. "Just a bunch of trees and shadows. It's awfully dark in there."

"Come closer. Look over there at the darkest shadow."

"It's just—just—oh, it's not a shadow—it looks. . .solid."

"Come on," Mark said as he took her hand. He led her to a giant, black disk-shaped object in the center of the forest. It slanted at a forty-five degree angle, one rounded edge almost touching the ground at one point with the angle rising slowly until the disk seemed to be suspended in mid air as it towered above them.

"Wow! It must be twenty feet across," she whispered.

"Twenty one and a half," he said quietly. "I measured it."

She reached to touch it and jerked her hand back quickly. "It's cold. Like ice."

"Yes, and solid, not like the butterflies."

"What is it?"

"I'm not sure. That's why I brought you here."

Something moved at the bottom of the disk. Jolene screamed as a shadowy, rope-like object slithered out of sight behind it. "What was that? I thought you said there was no other life here."

"There wasn't. Until yesterday. These snake things just appeared from nowhere. It's almost as if they were put here on purpose."

She peered around the disk. Nothing but trees and bushes behind it or around it. "It looks like a giant disk of black glass."

"Yeah, but it's impenetrable. I've tried everything. Stones, knives, even laser guns won't hurt it. Nothing even scratches it."

She stared at the disk. "Okay. You have my attention, but I need some equipment. I packed a few things just out of habit. I'll take some soil samples to examine the microorganisms at my hotel, then we can bring the other stuff I need out here to test the disk. Who else knows about this?"

"No one that I know of. Large parts of this planet are still unexplored. Amalgamated Travel didn't take the time to check everything out. They were too anxious to add another vacation planet to the list. The lack of harmful life was seen as a blessing. Nothing to clear out first. I doubt that they even noticed the absence of bacteria. If they did, they probably counted that as a plus for their development. I tried to speak to the Director of Travel Affairs at the consulate, but he just said to count my blessings and enjoy the planet. He's refused to see me since then."

"Have you talked to anyone in the Planet Security Commission?"

"Yeah. They think I'm crazy." He shook his head and ran his hand through his hair. "Hell, maybe I am."

"Maybe," Jolene said as she watched his troubled face. "Maybe not. I don't know why I'm doing this, but let's get a couple of samples and go back to the hotel. Lucky for us, I brought some of my equipment. I just tossed it in a suitcase at the last minute. I certainly didn't intend to work. Anyway, I'm glad I brought it. I'll set up a makeshift lab in my room. It would be great if we could get one of those snake things. Are they as insubstantial as the butterflies?"

"No, they're solid. I have a dead one at home."

"Dead?"

"Yeah. Yesterday, when they first appeared, some of them died for no apparent reason. I put one in a sample bag, but when I went to get more, they had disappeared."

"All of them?"

"Yes, the live ones and the dead ones."

"Maybe something ate them?"

"What something? There are no animals, or even insects, here, and I know the butterflies didn't. They were gone by then. Come on, let's go. We'll stop by my place and pick up the snake specimen."

Five hours later, Jolene called him. "Mark, you have to take me back to the disk. I think I know what it is, but I pray that I'm wrong."

"What is it?" he whispered into the visaphone.

"Just pick me up in fifteen minutes. I'll be on the landing deck with some equipment." She broke the connection and started to pack what she needed.

In the air car on the way to the forest, they were both silent until Mark asked, "What have you found?"

Jolene looked at him. She felt queasy, almost sick at her stomach. "Mark, you were right. There is no trace of any life in the soil—not even microscopic. Same is true for the foliage I tested. And the water samples. Only the water piped to the cities has microorganisms and those have Earth type DNA, so they must be added at the pumping stations. Mark, this entire planet is *sterile*."

"Sterile?"

"Yeah. I know it's impossible according the laws of science, but it's a fact. I won't know more until I test the disk."

"What about the snake thing."

Jolene was silent for a long time, then said in almost a whisper, "The snake things are bacteria."

"Bacteria? Like a germ?"

"Yes."

"So Paradise does have bacteria?"

"No. They don't belong on this planet. The DNA pattern is all wrong."

He whistled softly, "But, a germ three feet long? Where did they come from? How big would the being be that could harbor a germ that large?"

"Big, Mark, really big. I can only guess where they're from, and I hope I'm wrong."

Both sat in silence for the rest of the flight, and neither spoke as they lugged her equipment to the disk.

Jolene's face was set in grim concentration as she set up the equipment. Mark watched her intently as she measured, adjusted settings and tested the black disk.

Finally, she pulled the laser x-ray off of her forehead and let it swing limply from her hand at her side. She stood and stared at the disk for a long time, sighed and turned to look at Mark's questioning eyes. "Have you ever seen an ant farm?"

"An ant farm? You mean those glass things in science kits for kids?"

"Yes."

"Sure, but what does that—?"

"Say you want to perform an experiment. Introduce a new type of food, or disease, or something like that to see what will happen, but your ants die. What's the best way to get more ants into the farm?"

"I don't know. Lure them, I guess. A trail of honey or something."

"What if they weren't interested in food?"

"I'd find something they wanted and use that."

"Like something they found pleasurable? Beautiful? Exotic?"

"Yeah, whatever worked."

"Right. Then what?"

"Well, I'd perform the experiment differently, under more controlled conditions. I'd watch them closely, introduce the variables one at a time, measure the effects, and see if I could figure out what killed my first ones. What does this have to do with—?"

"The snakes are bacteria, Mark." She frowned and repeated, "Bacteria."

The realization hit like a thunder bolt. "Oh God!"

"God? Yes, Mark, perhaps it is."

She succumbed to the urge she had when they first met and gently brushed an errant lock of hair away from his shocked eyes.

"And the disk is a—a—"

Her throat was dry, and she thought of that disturbing dream she couldn't quite remember—the uneasy feeling it left. Her stomach churned as she listened to the beat of a thousand butterfly wings. It was feeding time again, and soon the barrier would be lifted to complete the experiment.

"Yes, Mark, the disk is the business end of a *microscope!*"

THE PLAGUE BEARERS

by Loren W. Cooper

"That's not a pretty sight." A brightly colored kerchief covered Cyril's mouth and nose. Silvered runes caught the sunlight as the cloth stirred with his breath.

Oslo gave Cyril a caustic glance as he dismounted. "Death is never a matter of aesthetics." He too wore a rune-covered piece of cloth over his mouth and nose.

"I don't know," Cyril retorted. "I could think of a few deaths that would be positively beautiful, given the right person." His eyes lifted to the winding hills that marked the border territory between the Young Dux Frederick's land and that of the Grand Comte Vehelian. "Vehelian springs to mind."

Rhea looked down at the two of them, making no move to dismount from her horse. A rune-inscribed kerchief masked everything below her eyes, but her eyes were expressively distasteful. "I wouldn't wish a plague death on anyone. Do we really need a closer look? We've all seen too much death, these last few days."

Oslo looked down at the body sprawled in the dust of the road. It had once been a man. It wore the coarse tunic and heavy trousers of a working freeman. A sweet, fetid odor rose from the corpse. Its splayed limbs thrust out awkwardly, as if expressing futile resistance to death.

Not even the slightest breeze stirred the late summer air, and the dust the horses had stirred from the road hung in the heat like a rotting silk curtain. A shabby hut and two ramshackle outbuildings stood less than one hundred paces down the road.

Oslo glanced up and caught Rhea's gaze. "Given the choice, I'd rather examine a body in the open than in the hot darkness of a shack that might hold the remains of a family." He stepped close to the body and knelt, studying the mottled flesh, swollen with the signs of bloating. "Lesions, this time. Buboes as well. Evidence of extensive bleeding around the eyes, ears, mouth and nose." His voice remained clinical as he heard the sound of Cyril retching behind him. "No scavengers have touched the body. Even the animals are keeping their distance."

Cyril coughed. "Which means what?"

"We're getting closer," Oslo said quietly.

He remounted in silence, and the trio kicked their horses into motion. The sun beat down like a hammer as they drew abreast of the shacks. More runes could be seen on them as they moved, sparkling chains of power that wound over and through the clothes they wore down to the gloves that held the reins of the horses. Delicate silver traceries of runic chains mottled even the hides of their mounts. Cyril and Rhea both wore swords and long daggers. Twin narrow sheaths crossed at the small of Oslo's back.

Rhea mused aloud. "No animals. Symptoms are worse here than elsewhere. Everyone and everything that didn't die fled from this part of the countryside, carrying the plague with them."

Cyril pointed at a spot in the shadows of the shack. "There!"

Oslo and Rhea both examined the spot. Nothing moved. "What?" Oslo asked mildly.

Cyril stood in the stirrups, his eyes searching the shadows. "Movement. I couldn't tell for sure, but it looked about the size of a cat."

Oslo's gaze sharpened. "A cat?" He reined up, walked the horse over to the spot Cyril had pointed out, and examined the sandy soil. "No tracks." His flat tone betrayed no sign of emotion.

Cyril rolled his shoulders uncomfortably. "What can I say? I saw a flash of movement, then it was gone."

Oslo and Rhea exchanged glances. "Keep looking," Rhea said firmly. "If we do find anything dwelling in this area, it might be resistant to the plague. If it is resistant, we could learn something useful from its blood."

"If we're lucky," Oslo said softly.

"If we're lucky," Rhea amended gracefully.

Oslo lifted himself back into the saddle of the big roan. Rhea and Cyril flanked him on their twin sorrels as he led them on down the road.

"It's stronger here, isn't it?" Rhea asked.

Oslo nodded without speaking.

Cyril studied them both. "Then if your theory is correct, we should be approaching the source of the plague. Will your runes hold?"

"They should," Oslo said. "It depends on how strong the source of the plague is. I hope they hold."

Cyril ground his teeth audibly.

Rhea laughed at him. "Why ask questions you don't want answered?"

Cyril tossed his head. "He could have lied to me. I wouldn't have believed it, but I might have appreciated it."

Even Oslo chuckled.

They rode deeper into the silence. Every so often they would stop, and Oslo would dismount and study a corpse, or pause to consider the age of crops late for harvest, and then they would take this turning, or that, or continue on, always winding deeper into the hills that bordered the Young Dux Frederick's lands. The hills rose to mountains, and the roads ran through lush valleys heavy with the silence of death.

They continued even after the sun set. They had an unspoken agreement that none of them wished to test the strength of the runes sufficiently to take the time to sleep in that place. The warm summer night lay heavy on the land, and as the silver moon rose over the shaggy hills, Oslo turned and led Rhea and Cyril off on a small track that wound back toward a sheer rocky wall.

Rhea pulled her horse to a stop. "Oslo!" she hissed. "Look!"

Oslo's eyes followed her pointing finger into the top of a nearby pine. "What did you see?"

Rhea shook her head. "It was too dark. Something small and quick. A squirrel, maybe. A cat, perhaps."

Oslo nodded, saying nothing.

Cyril regarded him curiously. "Where are you leading us, Oslo? I can understand using the bodies as indicators, but this little path to nowhere..."

"Was once a Jodan road," Oslo interrupted. He pointed down at the dull gray stone just visible where the horses' shod hooves had cut through layers of humus.

Rhea shot him a sharp glance. "A curse, you think? Roused deliberately, or accidentally?"

"This plague ravages Frederick's lands this soon after his father's death? So soon after the coronation? And flies like an arrow toward the heart of Frederick's lands? I have no doubt that some hand set this plague in motion. At first I thought it might have been tied to a coronation gift. Vehelian, Corosin, Otho...any number of neighboring lords would benefit from weakness in Frederick's lands, and an end to the line of the Old Dux. But I examined every gift, and I did not find a single trace of malevolent power in any of them."

"I know," Rhea said quietly. "And I agree with your reasoning, but several of those gifts were of old Jodan make, filled with traces of ancient power. How do you know you didn't miss something?"

"I don't." Even through the mask, Oslo's frustration was evident. "But I was wasting my time there, and tracking the plague back to its roots seemed to offer the best alternative."

Rhea and Cyril both studied him coolly, but it was Cyril who spoke. "You're a traveling mercenary, Oslo. You've been loyal to Frederick this last year in his service, and you've risen high in that time because of the rarity of your skills and experience. But we were born into service with our liege. He's family, and closer. So you'll forgive us the doubts we've had. Rumors in the court..."

Oslo held up one gloved hand. "I know. I heard the same things. Do you believe them, or not?"

He looked from one to the other. Their eyes were cold. He had not seen this side of them before. Of a sudden he understood the trust the Old Dux had placed in the twins.

"I believe evidence, not rumor," Rhea said firmly. "And we haven't seen sufficient evidence for any judgment yet. But either you're very good at what you do, hunter, or you know far more than you ought. Time will tell."

Oslo nodded, his eyes flat and expressionless, and kicked his horse forward. Cyril and Rhea followed, as silent as the land around them.

The track snaked back between the trees, and up to a sheer rock face. A narrow defile opened in the heart of the basalt. Oslo considered the defile for a moment, then dismounted and began hobbling his horse. Cyril and Rhea followed suit. They watched as Oslo walked the ground in front of the defile, his eyes studying the stone and clumps of vegetation. He stopped abruptly, and the others stepped closer to follow the sweep of his hand. "You can see where the soil has been cut by shod hooves, and the grass has been cropped." He turned over a brown dropping with the toe of one boot. "Someone was here with horses."

Cyril nodded. "And farmers don't shoe their horses." One hand came to rest on the hilt of his long knife.

Oslo turned and led them to the defile. Moonlight filtered in weakly from above, casting the gorge into darkness. A man could stand in the mouth of the opening and touch stone on each side with his extended hands. Oslo paused, looking into darkness, then drew a blade with his left hand. Cyril and Rhea paused, watching as he brought the blade to his lips and whispered in a tongue centuries dead. White light flared from the foot-and-a-half long blade, casting knife-edged shadows across the rocky ground.

No one spoke a word as the three of them entered the stone throat. Oslo led the way, Rhea followed at his back, and Cyril took up the rear. After thirty paces, the walls began to curve gently away from the path. Before thirty more paces had passed underfoot, the walls had receded until the three of them could walk comfortably abreast. A hundred and fifty paces later, the walls had drawn into the distance so far that they faded into the shadows.

At that point, the little party came to stand before an arch.

The arch appeared to be carved from a single stone, and reared fifteen feet into the shadows. Twisting runes danced along its curving length, to the point where it plunged into the rock floor of the gorge. Round, about three feet thick, it stood over the path like an errant loop of some giant's stone rope.

Cyril studied the darkness uneasily while Oslo and Rhea examined the surface of the arch carefully, Oslo standing on tiptoe and stretching his light source as far as possible to examine the center of the arch as closely as he was able. "Old Jodan High Script. There's still plenty of power in these runes. This is a marker and a gateway, to the Valley of the Masters."

Cyril frowned. "Masters of what?"

Rhea shook her head. "There's only one set of Jodan Masters that needs no further remark. This is a Runelord burial ground. And this arch will announce our presence to whatever guardian remains."

"Go around it, then," Cyril responded without hesitation.

Oslo raised an eyebrow. "The arch opens a pathway, of sorts. It's...more controlled. Going around would not be wise."

"What now, then?"

Rhea shrugged. "We came this far. We go through. Find out what lies on the other side."

Oslo's mouth crooked into a smile. He sheathed his blade, and studied the arch. As the darkness closed around them, the arch itself began to give off a soft white glow. Oslo stepped smoothly under the arch, and faded like smoke.

Cyril swore in frustration. "He hasn't left us much choice." He looked anxiously at Rhea. "He didn't do anything to the arch, did he?"

Rhea frowned. "Not so far as I could tell." Her eyes met Cyril's, and she winked, and stepped through the arch. Her body, too, ghosted away into transparency.

Cyril spat in disgust, took two quick steps, and hurled himself through the arch. When he faded from view, nothing remained in the rift but cold, silent stone.

On the other side of the arch, Cyril collided with Rhea, knocking her off balance. They stumbled together for a moment, before Rhea regained her balance and steadied Cyril. He looked up and out into a boundless plain.

White stone stretched around them, broken only by the angular lines of two score or more black pillars and the arch behind them. Dark clouds hung at the edge of each pillar, save one. Flickering movement danced in the heart of each cloud, the source of the movement never quite plainly visible. Familiar feline shapes prowled around the three of them, slit eyes glittering with alien awareness. An upright form walked toward them from the single pillar unbounded by darkness.

"Cats?" Cyril asked, his voice thick with disbelief.

"Not quite," Rhea corrected him absently. "Halfcats."

Oslo looked over his shoulder. "Jodan guardians of the dead. Dangerous. Very dangerous. But not as dangerous as the Shaped One."

Cyril looked more closely at the tall figure approaching them, and swallowed. Sparkling flows of light crossed branching veins of darkness in complex geometric interplays over the surface of a man-like form. As the Shaped One approached, Cyril thought at first that its flesh had been covered by a tattoo of runes, and then as he saw light wink through its shape as it moved, he realized that the runes alone composed its substance, and a chill swept over his body. The silhouette of the Shaped One had been cut in the pattern of a man, but the fabric of its making had been something quite different from flesh.

The Shaped One spoke as it walked toward them, its voice the dry rasp of sandpaper on rusty iron. "Thieves more clumsy than the last."

Oslo shook his head firmly. "We are no thieves."

The eyeless gaze came to rest on Oslo. Three quick strides, and it towered over him, its head bent down and twisting from side to side as it regarded him. "No thieves? Liars and thieves, then. What else would bring you to this place?"

"Plague."

The Shaped One rocked back at the single word, giving vent to a hissing laugh. "My servants bear my message well. Return what has been stolen from the Masters, and the sickness will end."

"What has been stolen?" Cyril admired Oslo's composure. He felt certain he couldn't have maintained a steady conversation with such a thing.

"Don't you know, thief? My servants hound the thing to earth. They will find it, and when they do, the sickness you have seen will be as nothing."

Oslo leaned forward. "Now you're bluffing. Your range is limited. The sickness loses power with every mile away from the rift, even with the halfcats pushing the boundary further every day. And I have told you once, now I tell you again, I am no thief. I will set this thing to right, one way or the other. I will return to you what has been stolen, or I will seal this gate, and the source of the sickness with it."

The Shaped One seemed to smile. "You are strong, little Maker, but you overestimate your own strength. Would you set yourself against the Making of the Old Masters? No one hand wrought me; no one Master raised this place and set its wards. Even if you did succeed, in your arrogance, more wait behind me to enforce the will of the Masters." Its hands swept wide, indicating the pillars and the bound darkness waiting behind each one.

"How can I prove my good faith to you?" Oslo asked.

The Shaped One paused for a moment before replying. "Take off the mask that binds your breath."

Oslo hesitated, then reached toward the rune covered cloth. Rhea caught his arm. "The plague!"

He nodded, shook off her grasp, and unwound the cloth that covered his lower face. "And now?"

The Shaped One stooped over Oslo, catching his jaw in one great hand and turning his face up toward its own. It lowered its head until it almost touched Oslo's mouth. "Tell me now, little Maker, that you are no thief, while I taste your breath for lies."

Oslo spoke slowly. "For the third and last time, I am no thief. I seek only an end to this plague."

The Shaped One paused, and straightened. "Not quite true." Cyril and Rhea stiffened. "You seek an end to this plague, and revenge on the thief who brought it. Not an unworthy goal."

Cyril and Rhea relaxed, slightly.

"You interest me, Maker. My plague bearers, my little pets, follow the stolen crown. Return that crown to me, and they will trouble you no more."

Oslo's eyes narrowed as he wound his mask back in place. He heard Rhea draw a sharp breath behind him. "How will I know this crown?"

The Shaped One held out his hands, and white light filled them, dripping down between his fingers. His fingers danced, dipping into the light, and wove a sparkling pattern in the air. The pattern traced out the shape of an ornate crown, crested with seven twisting spires. "It has this shape."

Oslo nodded sharply. "I will find it." He turned his back on the Shaped One. Cyril and Rhea backed through the arch ahead of him, never turning away from the Shaped One who stood unmoving in the midst of its feline company.

Oslo stepped out into the soft darkness, rejoining his two companions. Again he drew a long knife with his left hand, and spoke a single word, and held it aloft as light flared out from the rune-covered length of the blade. He shook his head as Rhea opened her mouth to speak. She closed her mouth with a snap. In silence, the three left the darkness of the rift for the soft light of the full moon. They freed their horses and mounted in silence, cantering back down the narrow track that marked the old Jodan road.

When they cleared the brush, Rhea kicked her mount level with Oslo's. "Did you recognize it?"

Oslo nodded grimly. "I went over all the gifts closely. It was distinctive."

Cyril drew even with the two of them. "Who sent it?"

"Vehelian." Oslo spat the name.

"We have no way of knowing if Vehelian himself knew what the gift meant. He could have acquired it from someone else. There is a chance he is innocent," Rhea said slowly.

"We can check that," Oslo said. "And we will. After all, we have help."

"Help?"

Oslo spread his hands in an expansive sweep that took in both sides of the road. Movement flickered through the low bushes, as if a horde of small animals paralleled their course. "The Shaped One's Halfcats. The Plague Bearers. They will know the thief. They'll smell the taint of his guilt."

"And then?"

Oslo shrugged. "They'll take it from there."

⇜ ⇝

The city of Conover, seat of the Grand Comte Vehelian, bustled with commerce. Loaded wagons, men on horseback, and men afoot choked the roads. Curses filled the air. Soldiers seemed to be everywhere. Outside the immediate bounds of the city, tents stood in orderly rows.

Rhea smiled grimly. "Looks like Vehelian's planning on annexing some territory."

Cyril, Rhea and Oslo threaded their horses through the confusion in a gray mist of rain. Traffic had churned the roadway to a sloppy sea of mud that reached up to a horse's fetlocks.

"Now would be the time for it." Oslo shifted a silk-wrapped bundle that he carried before him on the saddle as he made his careful way around a bogged wagon and team.

As they passed, a watcher might have noticed flickering movement at the edges of vision, a hint of substance that faded as the eye turned to follow.

Vehelian held court at an estate that had long since grown to a complex of buildings. Ornate gates woven of twisting iron rods stood open. A squad of helmeted guards in black surcoats and scarlet sashes stood at attention in the gateway, long spears held upright in their hands, short stabbing swords hanging at their sides. A bareheaded officer wearing a long sword at his hip held up one hand and stood in the path of the horses. "What do you want here?" he asked as Oslo and the others reined in their mounts.

"We are emissaries from Frederick, Dux of Rejin, Gachet, and the Low Counties. We bear a message to the Grand Comte Vehelian," Rhea answered.

The officer's lips curled into a nasty expression that loosely resembled a smile. "I'm sure that the Grand Comte will be fascinated by what the Young Dux' messengers have to say." He wheeled to face his men. "Bertrand! You have the gates. Thierry! Watch the horses. I don't believe that the emissaries will be staying long enough to require the use of the stables."

Rhea inclined her head. "You may be correct."

As they dismounted and handed their horses over to the quietly efficient Thierry, Oslo noticed several of the guards blinking, their eyes sliding from side to side. He felt sure that they were attempting to track the myriad small movements teasing their peripheral vision. He understood—even after the hard ride to and from the Seat of the Dux, he had not yet become truly accustomed to the presence of his escort.

The guard officer led the three through a maze of covered walkways lined by brilliant walls of lush flowers, every petal a variation of shades of red. To Oslo, the flowers seemed fat with blood. The officer led them up a wide set of shallow marble stairs, and past another brace of guards, and through a short hall. Then the hall opened out into a great banquet room. Rosewood dressed every surface of the huge room, polished to a flawless sheen. Red silk and velvet curtains and streamers had been braided across the walls in intricate patterns, and scarlet crushed velvet carpets covered the surface of the gleaming hardwood floor.

Men and women filled the space of the floor, all clothed in rich shades of crimson. A high rosewood seat occupied the center of the floor, at the confluence of several long carpets. A stocky man, wearing red and black, sat forward at the edge of the seat, a look of expectation heavy on his face.

As Cyril, Oslo, and Rhea entered, a hush swept over the hall, and every eye turned toward them. Oslo saw greed and anticipation in every eye, and knew that these favored courtiers anticipated the rich bounty to come. He saw them in his mind's eye, fighting over the corpse of the Low Counties like carrion birds, and his heart hardened within him.

The guard officer approached and bowed to the man on the seat. "My lord. The Young Dux has sent you messengers."

Rhea and Cyril both bristled at the insult embedded in the informality toward their lord. Vehelian smiled. His dark eyes were cold and devoid of expression. "Has Frederick sent you to ask for assistance against this plague that is ravaging his lands? He should have come himself. Or is he too sick? No matter. I had intended to...assist him in any event."

Rhea smiled as murmurs and titters ran through the courtiers. "The Dux knows of your desire to help, lord. He did, in fact, feel that you might be looking for his fealty, and have the ambition to become more than Grand Comte. Perhaps even a king."

Vehelian's smile widened. "King... I hadn't thought of that, but King Vehelian sounds remarkably good, don't you think?"

The courtiers murmured assent.

Rhea continued to speak pleasantly. "In anticipation of this happy event, the Dux has sent you a gift fit for a king."

Vehelian's smile faded as Oslo stepped forward, blinking against the swarming flurries at the edges of his vision, unwinding the silk cloth that covered the object in his hands. Vehelian scrabbled back into the throne as the covering fell away to reveal the sharp, twisting spires of a crown wrought of a bright, silvery metal. The crowd of courtiers murmured and shifted uneasily as Oslo stepped up to the throne and thrust the crown into Vehelian's nerveless hands. "Long live the king," he said.

Swarms of movement converged on Vehelian, and the would-be king convulsed on the throne. Mottled black spots swelled with terrifying speed under the skin of his throat and hands as he twisted under the unseen lash of the Shaped One's servants. The courtiers stood frozen with horror at the unexpected turn of events as Vehelian groaned on his seat. The crown rolled from his shaking hands and crashed loudly to rest at the foot of the seat.

Oslo bent and scooped the crown up from the floor. When he straightened and turned, his gaze swept the room, and he saw for a brief instant a crouching, ghostly form on the shoulder of each court-ier. They had the vague shape of cats, those ghosts, but their bodies were black with a burden of pestilence, and their yellow eyes held the patient inevitability of death.

Oslo immediately dropped his gaze to the floor, and walked swiftly toward the door of the chamber. The officer of the guard moved to bar his path, his long blade rasping out of the scabbard. Oslo raised his eyes to look the other man full in the face. "Do you want the source of this plague gone from your lands, or do you, like your master, seek to be king for a day?"

The guard officer looked past him to the thing still moving feebly on the throne, swallowed heavily, and slowly withdrew. Oslo led Rhea and Cyril out into the light and toward the horses.

Cyril sighed. "And now we ride like all the furies of hell pursue us, so we can return this wretched crown."

"We ride," Oslo agreed. "And all the furies of hell will ride with us. Or do you doubt it, knowing what is happening in the hall behind us?"

Cyril winced as he heard a distant wailing, and shook his head.

No one stopped them, hindered them, or questioned them as they retrieved the horses and rode out of that place, bearing their burden of death. Behind them, the plague bearers reaped a full harvest of the dead in the name of the Masters, taking their due in blood and pain from the one who had defied them, and all who stood with him.

And in those lands, there rose a great weeping for the dead.

THE BONDA PROPHECY

by Nick Aires

"Those audacious little brats!"

The sorceress Vera had been gazing into her crystal ball, when she received a mildly upsetting vision. She saw her apprentices, Hiro and Cassie, feasting on her prized *bonda* fruits. All week, she'd been snacking on the rare fruits in front of them while they practiced their spells, but she'd never shared her treats with them, much like she didn't share *any*thing with any*one*.

Later that day, whilst munching on the sweet bondas, Vera received a summons from the Queen. She didn't want to dally, but she was concerned about leaving the children alone with her delicacies.

Since her apprentices did not even recognize the fruit she'd been snacking on, Vera fallaciously told them that a man who hated children grew bondas in a magical orchard. She warned them that there was a spell on the fruit that caused rocks to fall on the heads of any children who ate them. Certain that she had sufficiently frightened her apprentices, and having ordered them not to leave the house, Vera went off to the palace.

The magicians-in-training looked at each other, thinking: *Should we?*

After many excruciatingly indecisive minutes, the curious children approached the bowl of bondas. "We'll just look at them," they giggled. "Surely it wouldn't hurt to *smell* them," they agreed.

The bondas smelled delicious, with hints of strawberry, coconut, and kiwi. The children couldn't resist temptation — they greedily gobbled up several bondas.

With full stomachs, the apprentices were aghast by what they'd done, belatedly remembering Vera's dire warning. They dove to the floor, and placed their hands over their heads.

"Hey!" said Hiro after a while. "I don't think the rock shower's coming! She tricked us!"

"Yeah!" Cassie exclaimed. "But she's still going to have our hides when she gets back!"

"Hmm, maybe not..." Hiro picked up Vera's crystal ball and smashed it on the ground.

"*Are you crazy*?!" Cassie shrieked. "For the fruit, she maybe would have made us conjure stinkweeds or something, but for *this*...I don't even want to think about it!"

"Relax! I have an idea—just get back on the floor, and pretend that you're expecting rocks to fall on your head."

Soon, the sorceress returned. Entering her study, she stopped short, staring at the shattered remains of her crystal ball. Enraged, Vera shouted: "What do you have to say for yourselves? And why are you cowering on the floor?"

Hiro stood up nervously, still covering his head, and said: "Great Sorceress, while playing tag, we accidentally bumped the crystal ball."

"We are *sooo* sorry!" Cassie chimed in.

"Because we were awfully upset by the accident," Hiro continued, "we sought punishment for our inexcusable recklessness. So, we ate some of the cursed bondas and were lying in wait of the rocks that we were sure would befall us...." Hiro looked up at Vera coyly, "But perhaps the rocks were unable to penetrate your roof...?"

If Vera had only shared, she would still have some of her bonda fruits left, as well as her crystal ball. The sorceress learned an important lesson that day: Don't take on any apprentices.

CATCH OF THE SEASON

by Vicki M. Taylor

Vicki M. Taylor writes dramatic stories with strong women as her main characters. A prolific writer of both novel length and short stories, she brings her characters to life in the real world. Her memberships include the National Association of Women Writers, Short Fiction Mystery Society, and many more. She has had hundreds of articles published in electronic and print publications. She is one of the founders and past President of the Florida Writers Association, Inc. She conducts regular writing workshops, speaks to local writing groups, and facilitates a Reading Women's Fiction Group at her local Barnes and Noble bookstore.

They started watching him last Earth year. It was only natural they would pick Cap'n Matt Green. He stood the best chance at becoming their squad's biggest and most prestigious catch.

Over the years, they'd intercepted transmissions that identified a species similar to their own in dire straits. Patient, unyielding to every cry for help, they waited. Waited for the perfect target. The ultimate prey. They'd finally found him.

≈≈

Matt Green, or Cap'n Matt, as most everyone called him, grew up in the Florida Keys. His dad grew up in the Keys and his granddad grew up in the Keys. There'd been a Cap'n Green at the helm of the twenty-foot *Coral Beauty* for three generations and in the future, if he had a son, he would make it four. Matt grinned at his paternal thoughts. He'd have to get married first. And that meant settling down. Neither of which he was real keen on at the moment.

Last season, Cap'n Matt and his crew performed extraordinarily well. He amazed friends and family alike with his abilities to master the deep blue waters and return again and again with his limit. He'd become a legend in the Florida Keys. Everywhere Cap'n Matt went he'd regale all who would listen with his enthralling tales of hunting and capturing *Panulirus argus*—the Spiny Lobster.

Of course, the boat really wasn't over thirty years old. Not much in this humid salty air could last thirty years, except the old-timers. Each time the elder Green retired a boat and purchased a new one for their dive business, Coral Divers, it would get christened the *Coral Beauty* out of habit, pure and simple.

Matt recalled that his grand-pappy always said never mess with a good thing. The *Coral Beauty's* unique paint scheme of red, gold, and purple stripes had become a trademark symbol for their successful scuba diving business. Consistency was good for business. It helped bring in the crowds, generation after generation.

The Greens weren't about to mess with a good thing. Not when most of their referrals were word of mouth. Cap'n Matt had a knack for finding the best dive spots on every reef between Conch Reef and Caloosa Rocks. It was kind of eerie the way he'd come back to the shop trip after trip, his boat's guests laden with bug-filled bully nets, even when other dive shops would come up empty handed. When he went on his own, he'd limit out every trip. No one doubted Matt's abilities to hunt bugs. Some said Matt had a nose for the bugs, as if he could smell them underwater.

Men would sit for hours in the local pubs plying Matt with drinks hoping he'd spill some of his family secrets. He never did. Matt never could explain clearly to anyone how he just knew when and where the next bug hunt would be. No matter how much he protested the existence of any special magic the other fishermen wouldn't believe him.

Coral Divers started catering to the desires of lobster divers, or "bug-hunters" as they were known, in the early 50's, long before the population explosion among the Keys. Even longer before dive shops crammed into every available space along Highway 1 so tight that you couldn't drive a mile along any stretch without counting more shops than you had fingers on two hands.

The first Cap'n Green was Matt's granddad. Back in the fifties, he decided to host a contest for the biggest lobster. Every season since the contest continued, it brought more and more contestants all vying for prizes like the yearly first prize that started as $20 and now was $200. Coral Divers recently added the ultimate grand prize of $1,000 if anyone could bring in Ol' One-Eye.

The second Cap'n Green, Matt's dad, and Ol' One-Eye went way back. They first met when both were barely wet behind the ears or antennae. Ol' One-Eye wasn't Ol' One Eye then, he was just one of many lobsters that had made the dangerous trek as a juvenile from the sea grasses close to shore to the sparkling reefs further out in the deeper, cooler waters.

Right before sunset, Matt's dad had dropped anchor off a secret bug-hunting site he'd found the previous season. He'd only taken snorkel gear, anticipating a quick scouting expedition for future trips. Setting out his red and white diver-down flag he slid his mask over his face, adjusted his snorkel, took a firm grasp of his stick, and slipped over the side. He took a deep breath and sunk silently into another world.

In this world, he had a private view into the inner abyss where fish and other critters of the deep, sparkling clear waters hunt, eat, sleep, and hide.

His destination, a shallow reef, teeming with activity twenty feet below his boat. Among the reef's rocky maze of nooks, crannies, and crevices lurked moray eels, snails, corals, and fish of assorted shapes and sizes. Without even a second glance to these amazing creatures, he homed in on his target—the multitude of invertebrates such as shrimp, crabs, and lobster—especially lobster—that called this reef home.

It took only a few seconds to spot the spiny lobster ducking into the shadowy gap at the end of the reef. Matt's dad knew that the only way to catch a bug was to be patient. He waited.

Matt's dad had long, nimble hands that bore the scars of times when he wasn't so patient. He'd had his hands pierced more times than he could remember by their spiny thorns before learning that patience and ingenuity went a long way in catching lobster. Now, he faced this new section of the reef determined to win the test of wit and skill with the sharp-horned bug snuggled into a small crevice with only its waving antennae sticking out.

His patience was rewarded. Very gently, he eased the end of the tickle stick behind the lobster's tail. Skillfully, he watched the antennae, determined to predict which direction the wary bug might bolt. He softly tapped the lobster's tail, urging it to move forward from its hole. One hand ready to capture the bug as it bolted, he tapped again. With lightning speed, he swooped forward and caught the bug just as it moved forward enough to expose more than its swaying antennae. Quick as a flash, the lobster fought for its life. When it was over, Matt's dad headed for the surface, tired and alone, for a much-needed breath of air. In the palm of his hand, a new puncture wound that would definitely need stitches and a tiny eye.

Season after season, Ol' One-Eye, growing to massive proportions, managed to evade capture by staying on the move, traveling further away from shore to the deeper waters. Matt's dad caught sight of him occasionally, as he drifted through the current while on a dive or bug-hunting expedition. Each time, the bug and Matt's dad would face off. Both determined to win. Each time they'd limp away, shaking off the latest battle wounds, fiercely protecting their pride. Matt's dad got slower as he grew older. It was time for the younger Green to try and tame the beast.

～～

They never knew about the first Cap'n Green. By the time they discovered the second Cap'n Green, the third Green, Cap'n Matt, was well on his way to becoming quite a bug hunter. He was their prey. It was imperative that they capture him now. Before he had a chance to breed and possibly produce a fourth Cap'n Green.

They didn't think the Earth species that sent the messages would last much longer. The transmissions appeared more frequently, occurring at almost the same time every Earth year. It was time to take action.

❧❧

Cap'n Matt set out in the *Coral Beauty* across the open water toward Matecumbe Drop-off. He knew of a specific spot on the ledge. Matecumbe Drop-off, with a depth that ranged from 35 to 135 feet was isolated, far from the popular dive spots. Located smack between the 136-foot tower on Alligator Reef and the 49-foot tower on the Tennessee Reef. He mentally checked off the equipment he needed for the afternoon's hunt. Tickle stick, gloves, bully net, full tanks, regulator, mask, BC, and flippers. Everything necessary to catch lobsters.

A lingering thought kept nagging at the back of his mind. Matt knew he shouldn't go out alone, but he'd been making this run since he was big enough to launch the boat by himself. He'd be damned if he'd chicken out now. Besides, he'd make a one-tank dive and be back by suppertime. Saliva spurted from Matt's glands over his tongue as he thought of digging a fork into the cracked body of the biggest lobster he'd ever seen and dipping the succulent white meat into hot, melted butter and chewing slowly, savoring every morsel.

A grin spread across his brown, leather-tanned face. His eyes twinkled behind a pair of dark sunglasses. The lines on his face betrayed his lost youth. He wasn't old, just weathered. Nary a gray strand dared sift through his long sun-bleached hair. He felt like a teenager again. Tonight he'd show them all who the great bug hunter of the Keys really was. He beat his chest as if he were king of his aquatic jungle and let out a raucous roar.

Matt checked his watch after mooring to the buoy to ensure he had plenty of time. He put his gear on quickly and efficiently with the practiced hand of a long-time pro. Mere minutes clicked off the clock by the time he'd slipped into the clear, cool water and sank beneath the surface in a cloud of bubbles.

Instantly, he was immersed in silence. The only noise coming from the air as it flowed through his regulator. He gently bit the soft rubber mouthpiece, fitting it more firmly into his mouth as he kicked to propel himself toward the reef below. With practiced ease Matt checked his watch and dive computer to ensure all was on schedule. Plenty of time. Nearly an hour of bottom time by his calculations for a fifty-foot dive. Plenty of air. And, from the looks of the sand swirling below the rocks, plenty of bugs.

The first two lobsters Matt caught didn't put up a fight at all. No sport in the hunt. He needed more of a challenge. He could have sworn they scuttled right into his net it was that easy. Then he saw him. Ol' One-Eye. Matt's eyes widened at the lobster's gigantic size. He had to be at least twenty pounds if not more. Already, he could hear the cheers and feel the slaps on his back from his buddies on the dock when he got back with Ol' One-Eye.

He congratulated himself on figuring that he'd run into Ol' One-Eye out here. The reefs were older, bigger, crevices large enough to hide such a monster. Even without one of his eyes, he seemed to have eluded capture for what must be sixty or seventy years. He could picture himself holding Ol' One-Eye in both hands as journalists scrambled for pictures. Maybe he'd mount the ol' guy and display him at the dive shop. Wouldn't that be a boon for business?

⁓ ⁓

They watched from inside the craft as Cap'n Matt and The Elder jockeyed for position on the sea floor. The Elder's whip-like antennae stretched to nearly twice the length of his body making the loss of one eye insignificant. They signaled to The Elder to make his move. The Elder's antennae twitched in understanding.

⁓ ⁓

Cap'n Matt watched Ol' One-Eye dance to the left and then to the right on his five pairs of legs, all moving in perfect synchronization. Matt almost felt sorry for the old bug. He'd lived quite a life down here, but his time was over. A shadow cast over him, blotting out the sun. He turned to see what could be so large. Then he saw something big and dark flash to his left.

Matt's eyes widened in disbelief. There it was again. He cleared his mask and looked again. It had stopped. The visibility was so good he knew he could see for a hundred feet. He nearly lost his regulator when his jaw went slack in astonishment. Slow and silent, a lobster bigger than any he'd ever seen before hovered in front of him.

To his amazement, Matt figured the lobster was bigger than his boat. He almost swallowed a mouthful of saltwater as he choked back a nervous laugh. Relief sluiced through Matt as tension drained from his body. It was nothing but a commercial mascot.

Red Lobster₍ₐ₎ must have lost one of their "Clawde" lobsters that they transported around the country to advertise their seafood. It wasn't nearly as big as he thought. The refraction from the water and his mask only made it look big. He thought he remembered someone telling him the thing was really only about twenty-five feet long.

Foolishness washed over him. He felt like such an idiot, but excited at the same time. No way would he ever tell anyone about the fear that raced through him when he encountered the fake lobster hunting Ol' One-Eye. If the restaurant would let them, Coral Divers could mark it with a buoy and it'd quickly become popular with the tourist divers. His old man would be proud of him for thinking of the future of the shop and how to bring in more revenue. First things first. He turned back to Ol' One-Eye.

～～

They watched Cap'n Matt as he first showed terror then relief at their craft's appearance. Their spaceship propelled silently toward him until they could reach one mechanical leg out and touch his back. They relished in watching his face drain to a milky white. His stick and net sank to the bottom in a swirl of sand, clouding the ocean floor for a moment until the current cleared it away.

They watched as he whipped his head left and right looking for an escape. He kicked out his legs trying to force any advantage he could find. They tossed him from one leg to the other, making sure to keep him within reach.

～～

Cap'n Matt fought desperately to disengage himself from the creature that looked to be toying with him beneath the calm surface of the water. All thoughts of catching Ol' One-Eye erased from his mind. His only thoughts were on surviving. His chest heaved as he drew more air into his lungs. With a final lunge he thrust himself forward and kicked violently. Just one more inch. Free! He made it. Without looking over his shoulder he swam as hard as he could toward the overhanging reef. If he made it to the ledge he could find a small cave and hide. He knew of one on the north end of the reef that he could just squeeze his body into. He kicked harder, forcing his flippers to move more water.

～～

They watched him swim away. They were in no hurry. They were patient. The Elder skittered along the sand, leading them to their quarry. They'd catch their prey soon enough. Determined, they knew how to win the test of wit and skill.

They followed his trail of air bubbles. He had backed himself into a small crevice just large enough for his body. Cap'n Matt had removed his tank and clung to it while wedging himself further into the reef, away from their prying legs. He was putting up a good fight. They knew The Elder was proud of their choice. Cap'n Matt would make a prestigious prize.

Silently, they watched the diver wriggle further into the hole in the rock. Patiently, they watched his eyes, gauging which way he might dart. Tentatively, they inserted one long antennae into the hole, past the diver's body until they reached the back. Gently, but firmly, they tapped him, again and again, forcing him to move forward.

⁓⁓

Panic set in. Cap'n Matt lost his slippery hold on the air tank he held in his arms. It sank quickly to the bottom taking his regulator with it. No more air. He looked up disappointed that he was at least seventy feet from the surface. Even swimming as fast as he could, dropping his weights, he probably wouldn't make it. Even if he did, Matt knew he would face a dangerous risk of the bends. He had no choice; he had to try.

Matt pushed at the reef, knocking fragile corals from their tenacious grasp on the rock. A man, who had spent nearly his entire life under the water, never took even an empty shell from the bottom, and could be found verbally berating tourists for touching coral, ripped gaping gashes into the living creatures. Nothing registered in his mind; surviving his only objective. He ripped off his weight belt and tossed it away as he swam. A tiny line of bubbles trailed behind him as he exhaled gently, instinctively knowing not to hold his breath.

⁓⁓

They anticipated his movements. In an instant he was captured firmly in their second set of legs. He would not escape again. The hunt was over. With a flip of their spaceship's fan-like tail they maneuvered toward the bottom. Deftly, they picked up the abandoned tank to return it to its rightful owner. They watched as the diver looked confusingly at their ship then scrambled into his gear. His chest rapidly contracted as he pulled the precious oxygen into his lungs.

⁓⁓

Cap'n Matt faced his captor. He stared in silent horror as he was lifted effortlessly to the head and into the mouth of the large creature. His last look at the sand below, before being pushed into the creature's mouth, was of Ol' One-Eye waving his massive antennae. If he hadn't known better, he would have thought the old bug was grinning at him.

Inside, instead of being digested by some mutant sea creature, Matt was extracted by mechanical pincers that held him tight while another mechanical arm attached a weighted chain to his ankle. It then dumped him into a large see-through tank that looked suspiciously like one he'd seen at the aquarium. Unable to swim to the top of the tank because of the heavy weight, he could only float a few feet from the bottom.

Checking his gauges he realized he only had a few more minutes of air. As if on cue, a hose snaked into the water. Air escaped from the nozzle on the end while it hissed beside him.

A panel opposite the tank opened and an alien creature crept out. It had a large head with huge black eyes atop a thorax-like body with three pairs of arms. Protruding from the abdomen section were four sets of legs. It dragged a large fan-like tail behind that folded and unfolded itself like an accordion.

The alien creature tapped on the side of the tank with one of its claws and mimed the motions to attach the hose to his regulator. Numb with shock and suspicious of their intent, Cap'n Matt did as he was told. Tentatively, he took a small breath. Oxygen. He breathed deep. Without thinking, he made a circle with his thumb and finger and signaled to the creature. Startled, he watched the creature awkwardly return the symbol with its claw-like appendage.

The tank began to shake as he felt pressure building around him. Shock vibrations rippled through the tank. More creatures scuttled about positioning levers and tapping panels of lights with their many claws and feet. Matt felt movement, as if in an out-of-control elevator.

A monitor dropped from the ceiling. One of the alien creatures positioned it in front of the tank. First, only blue fuzziness materialized on the screen. Then the fuzziness cleared. He could see his boat. Then the Keys, then the entire state of Florida. Dizzily, he watched as more and more of the earth dropped below his view.

Matt waved his arms wildly, making strangling noises as he tried to get the creatures' attention. He beat his fists on the glass. Not one of them paid any notice to him. He was left to watch his entire world disappear before his eyes into the vast blackness of space. Activity continued around the tank.

Time passed slowly while he breathed through the tube inside the aquarium. Hours or days passed, he knew not which. He may have slept, he wasn't sure. His mind closed in, forgetting to measure time. Many of the alien creatures stopped for a moment to look at him silently then move on. Some aliens posed in front of the tank while others pointed small flashing objects at him.

Dejected, he hung his head. Depression set in. Lethargic, he barely moved his arms or legs. He floated like a forgotten buoy tied to a reef. For a brief second he agonized over never seeing his family again. Then he blinked several times before realizing he was crying inside his mask.

He had no idea how long the lobster-like aliens left him like that as they went about their life on the spaceship. He prayed hard that whatever they did to him it was quick and painless. His prayer turned into a mantra that continued to repeat in his mind. Nothing else registered.

He stopped watching the activities outside the tank until it appeared that certain actions centered on him. Was this the moment he was waiting for? Anticipation and hope, long forgotten emotions, wriggled tentatively deep inside his soul.

Uncomfortable sensations pushed at him. Gravity squeezed his body as the tank's water drained from below. Before he could gain any bearing on the situation, water from another source refilled the tank, immediately submersing him, once again. Risking his life, he removed the regulator to taste the water. Fresh. The saltwater was gone.

Confused at the sudden activity surrounding him, Matt watched one of the aliens direct a small machine. It connected to the side of the tank with large suction cups, and then effortlessly lifted the tank. The movements so precise not a drop of water spilled.

For the first time, Matt saw another part of the ship. A larger room, with long, high tables. Hope crept into his thoughts. Could they finally be ready to release him? Had they conducted enough tests? He turned his head from side to side, watching every action, trying to understand the alien creatures' intentions.

The machine settled the tank into its new position. With a higher view, Matt could see more creatures gathering into the room. These new events gave him hope. For the first time he allowed himself to think of home again, to think of his boat, of his dad, of the warm Florida sun. Warm beaches. Warm water.

So real were his thoughts he could almost feel the water warming around him. Reality crashed like heavy waves over his daydream. The water was getting warmer. His skin warmed inside his suit. Hot. Hotter. He scratched and pawed at himself to ease the burning sensation. He cast off everything he could only to discover that the water was hotter with his suit off.

He watched tiny bubbles on the bottom of the tank grow larger until they lifted and rose rapidly to the surface. Some of the bubbles broke against his skin hitting him with pockets of burning air.

As he felt the blood in his veins begin to boil, he peered through hazy, pain-filled eyes at the activity outside the tank. The aliens surrounding a large table preparing for a feast.

The last thing his mind registered before shutting down completely was the image on the bib of the alien lobster nearest his tank— a human silhouette, spread eagle.

THUNDERSTRUCK

by C. J. Winters

If I hadn't been born a mouse, I could've been Lana Turner. Now *there* was a woman who understood glamour. Fortunately the Folks in my house like old movies.

It isn't that the Folks are all that dear to my little feminist heart (he calls her "Laurie-putt," isn't that sickening?), but like me she appreciates pretty things.

I suppose you can guess how *my* home is furnished. Once I moved out of Mom's place and into the attic, the only limits are what I can carry. My greatest treasure is a ceezee tennis bracelet. I use it to hold my fiberfill mattress in place. Round beds were very stylish in the 40s.

Yesterday I snipped a couple of purple sequins from Laurie-putt's dress (they look smashing on the mirror chip I keep beside my bed for a quick tidy), and found a gold shirt stud on the floor. I'll keep it for my old age; a man on TV said the price of gold could only go up.

Before Mom disappeared into Hawk Heaven, she told me she'd brought nineteen litters into this world of cats, owls and mousetraps. Seeing my look of horror, she admitted she never could resist a male with a roguish twinkle in his eye.

Well, you can bet your beaded booties that won't happen to ME!

❧❧

"Mornin', Doris." Jessie, the sleepy-eyed twit who lives over behind the boxful of wedding presents the Folks don't know what to do with, yawned and pawed her ear. So gauche. "Whatcha up to today?"

"I plan," I said crisply, so she'd know I wasn't in a mood for tittle-tattle, "to check Laurie-putt's closet. She brought Wal-Mart bags home yesterday, and you never know."

Jessie's black eyes brightened. "Ohhh, that means new cookies! I'm off!"

"Better watch those hips," I shot after her, suspecting the young silly was already in the family way, "or you won't make it back through the hole in the cabinet." For that excellent advice I got a flip of her tail as she ducked under a rafter.

And, yes, she *definitely* had acquired a waddle.

Following a preen (I never leave home with crumbed whiskers), I made my way down the wiring to the Folks' bedroom and slipped through the crack between the floor and baseboard. I paused, sniffing to make sure I was alone. (I'm a Capricorn and therefore cautious. I plan to live a long time, for a mouse.)

Laurie-putt's cologne still lingered in the air. The silence, though, told me they'd gone to work.

I sighed, envious of the fluffy, tumbled bedcovers and the bright Oriental rug angled under the big brass footboard. Lana always slept in a big bed too, though usually with a satin coverlet. For a moment I stared at my reflection in the shining brass. I'm not half bad looking, if you like gray.

Getting down to business, I nosed along the wall to the closet. Its door has a catch that doesn't quite catch, so I can wriggle in and out with no one the wiser.

"And who are *you*, little Miss Priss?" demanded a husky, rough-cut voice in the darkness.

I gave a startled squeak (I hate it when I react in that wimpy, poor-little-female way) before I collected myself. "That's no concern of yours, sir," I replied tartly.

"*Huh!*" This time I felt his warm breath, and I'd swear there was chocolate on it. "I'm new here, but I thought I'd met most of the residents. The *pretty* ones, anyway."

Smarmy creep, thinking I'd fall for such blarney.

"It's too dark in here for you to know whether I'm pretty or not."

"All the better reason to get acquainted," he said, leering. I know he leered.

Well, if that's how he wants to play it, my teeth are just as sharp as his. And so is my tongue.

"Drop the seduction act, Hotshot. I have better things to do than raise your litter of buzzard bait."

"Huh?"

Got a bright one here, Doris girl.

Still it wouldn't be smart to hang around, so I nosed under the door and squeezed out like toothpaste.

"Hey!" His bigger body slowed him down. "Ya didn't tell me your name."

I said, "Call me Lana," and whipped out of sight under the bed-clothes.

Luckily no one knew of my admiration for the real Lana, and the other mice weren't bright enough to put me and my pretties together, so nobody told Moose Mouse where I lived.

A couple of days later, though, I stumbled into the Moose sprawled across the pipe opening under the kitchen sink.

"You!" I sniffed. "Hogging the best opening, just like a male."

I didn't doubt his slow grin won over most unwary females. But not this one.

"Honey-lips," he drawled, "I was just savin' space for you. What say we tackle the breakfast dishes? There's egg left on a plate, and if we're *real* careful, the Folks won't suspect."

I gave an un-Lana-like snort. "I've never seen the male who could resist leaving a trail."

"For you, Honey-lips, I'll control myself."

I might've bought it if he hadn't winked, one of those slow, long-lashed winks that tell a female what a guy has in mind.

"Just don't spoil things for the rest of us. You leave a trail, the Folks bring in a cat, and even the Craft-Barn down the street won't be safe. Come to think of it," I added slyly, "you'd fit in fine down there. I hear the kids drop Cheetos crumbs while their mothers shop."

He looked hurt and I felt a tad guilty, but it's in my best interest to keep my chilly image intact. If *I* don't look after Numero Uno, who will?

So with phony enthusiasm, I burbled, "Hey, you'd like the Craft-Barn. The attic here is cold and drafty in winter."

A crafty look came into his eyes, and I knew I'd made a mistake.

"So *that's* where you live. In the attic."

Needle-sharp, I snapped, "I'm a recluse. My welcome mat is *never* out."

"I thought a recluse was a spider."

Hmmm. Maybe he's not quite so vacant upstairs as I thought.

He twitched a whisker, just one, which is hard to do. "Don't you even *care* what my name is?"

I gave a sophisticated, Lana-style shrug. "Not especially."

"It's Hugo. As in, you know, *Huge.*"

"Tough patooties," I said. I'm not usually crude, but this guy was *so* full of himself.

And *that*, I thought, was *that*.

How wrong I was. Not twenty-four hours later I had to save the Moose's hide.

You just can't teach some mice. Tell them about the ancestors who fried because they chewed a cord strung between a lamp or tv and the wall, it just goes in one ear and out the other. So the next evening I wasn't surprised to find Hugo lying on his back under Billiam's desk with his feet stuck straight in the air, a mouse version of *The Titanic*.

I leaned over to check if he was breathing. Our whiskers touched, and to my astonishment, he gasped, "I've been *thunderstruck!*"

Feeling a little queasy myself, I said, "Roll over and get on your feet before the Folks come in."

"Don't think...I can..."

My hard poke in his upturned belly changed his think. I said, "Lean on me. We have to get over there, behind the stereo."

I don't know how I managed it– he weighed as much as a package of soda crackers– but we staggered over to a sliver of dark space behind the speakers, where I let him collapse.

All night he lay there, still as death except for his unsteady breathing. I felt next to useless, but I couldn't leave him, helpless and alone. So I fussed about, shoring up his broad backside with bits of carpet fuzz, and bringing him mouthfuls of water from the sweaty pipe under the kitchen sink.

It was a very long night.

Then just as it was getting light, Hugo showed signs of life. Strong signs. In fact, once when I was delivering a sip of water I had to give him a tail-swat to keep his paws in line.

As soon as I heard the Folks moving, I left him with a warning. "Hotshot, don't give me another fright like that or I'll do some thunderstriking myself!"

I slept in that morning, figuring I deserved it for playing Florence Nightingale all night.

While I slept, though, The Moose was busy. When I woke, I found *three* salted peanuts lying next to my ceezee bracelet. Why, I hadn't had breakfast in bed since I was weaned. Even Lana didn't get better service.

Naturally I'd have to thank my benefactor. Imagine, making *three* trips from the first floor to the attic just to give little old *moi* a fancy feast.

Still, you can't be too careful when it comes to males and their single-tracks. If hunky Hugo thought his gift would soften me up to accept more than his thank-you present, he had another think coming.

After I finished my breakfast and morning preen I set out to track him, which wasn't difficult. I found him in the kitchen, relating his near-death experience to a bunch of simpering, ogling females.

From the shadows I listened until I couldn't take any more. It wasn't so much what he said, but what he *didn't* say. Oh sure, he mentioned that I'd "looked after him," but who was the real Star of the Disaster? His *Royal Himself*, of course. My supporting role ranked somewhere below Our Hero's near-termination, brave death-vigil and stoic recovery.

I was so furious, I cried. Yes, old stone-hearted Doris-Lana, who hadn't cried since Mom left, raced home in tears, threw herself on her bed and bawled her heart out.

And then I discovered Our Hero had spotted me in his audience and followed me home.

"Golly gosh gee, Lana," said Rat-breath. "Did I do something wrong?"

Golly-gosh-gee? Obviously the rube never stuck his nose into a *GQ* or even *The National Geographic*.

And what made him think I even *cared* what he'd done?

"Go away," I said, snuffling into my fiberfill mattress. "You're from Mars, and I'm from Venus."

"What's that mean?"

"You wouldn't understand."

"Try me, Honey-lips."

He sat slumped on the clasp of my ceezee bracelet, his shiny eyes bracketing a puzzled line between them.

"It means males don't understand females."

"Oh. Then females don't understand males."

"That's *not* what I said!"

"Then what did you say?"

I sighed with genuine regret for the way the Universe worked. "Some things just aren't meant to be, Hugo. Now you go back downstairs and enchant the other females. I'm the house spinster, you see, and spinsters– well, we have better things to do than be enchanted."

He didn't move, though, and I could tell he was doing his best to think hard. Thinking doesn't come easily to males, but the exercise is good for them, so I waited while those teensy-tiny gears whirred and shifted. At last his brow cleared. "You're *deep*, Lana. For a pretty little thing, you're *deep*."

"You're right, Bubba," I said to his departing backside. "And don't forget it."

After that life was pretty quiet for a week or so. Then all hell broke loose.

The CAT arrived.

It wasn't anybody's fault. There were just so many of us now, including Jessie's litter whose incessant squeaks kept me awake all hours. Fortunately I always keep a supply of food on hand for emergencies, and with moisture on the bathroom pipes, Jessie and I didn't have to range far. As long as the Folks didn't boost the monster into the attic, we'd be okay.

The downstairs mice weren't so lucky, and I found myself worrying about Hugo. Big and slow, time wasn't on his side. I knew I shouldn't care (what's one male, more or less?), but snug in my fiberfill bed in the dark, I couldn't help thinking about him.

So after a while I got up, quiet so as not to start Jessie's brats squeaking again, and made my way down to the kitchen.

I edged from under the cabinet door and paused, listening in the dark, ominous silence, before risking a loud whisper. "Hugo?"

At first nothing happened. Then everything happened at once. The hall light came on, a weight slammed down on my tail, and Hugo yelled, "*RUN, Lana!*"

Run, sure— with a monster paw on my tail? Shrieking and yanking, I couldn't get any traction on the slippery floor. Then a searing pain ran up my tail and along my back all the way to my ears. My tail on fire, I lunged...and skidded headfirst into the cabinet. Instantly scrambling under the door, I dashed through the pipe hole and up the wires to the attic.

There, ignoring Jessie's anxious questions, I fell into bed and succumbed to pain. If you've never had an inch of your tail ripped off, you can't imagine how it feels.

Eventually the pain eased some and I fell asleep.

I woke to daylight seeping through the window. My tail felt blistered and raw, but it was bearable, and I was *alive.*

"How ya feelin', Honey-lips?" asked Hugo.

I twisted around, saw him crouched outside my ceezee boundary, and cried, "You're alive too!"

He grinned sheepishly. "I was afraid you'd be mad at me for bitin' off your tail."

"*You* did that? I thought it was the cat!"

"It was all I could think of."

"But—" tears wet my eyelashes "—you could've been *killed.*"

He shrugged a John Wayne 'aw shucks' shrug. "I couldn't just do nothin', Honey-lips."

"Thank you." I gulped. "I—I think you'd better go now."

"Wait, I brought ya a present." He snouted a little red-and-gold ribbon bow onto my bed. "Found it in the Christmas decorations. Thought it would look pretty on your tail, once it heals."

Well, what could I say?

After he left, I yawned and set about making some plans. In a couple of days we'll check out the Craft-Barn. No cats. No drafts. Cheetos. And loads of pretties to go with my ceezee bracelet.

I'll miss Lana, but Hugo isn't the only one who's thunderstruck. I may even let him talk me into a family...just one or two, mind you...certainly not nineteen...

STONES OF DESTINY

by Linda Bleser

The albino never smiled, not once in all the time I'd known him. He woke, walked and made camp an empty man, as if searching for something he couldn't remember losing. I guess we all felt a certain emptiness, but what the albino lacked was something crucial, vital— something that had stolen his smile.

MoJo made it his business to try to coax a smile to the albino's face. He considered it a challenge. I guess that's what kept MoJo going long past the time most of us were ready to give up. And Vesta...well, Vesta said the albino's white-lashed, staring pink eyes gave her the creeps. She couldn't stand to be near him and wouldn't even look into his face when dishing meals.

There are five of us now—MoJo, the albino, Vesta, myself, and Dake. Dake is our leader. He had gathered us, one by one, to follow on a path whose destination only he knew. Dake never told us where he was leading, or what we would find when we got there. But we followed him. What else was there to do? We trusted him and he held us together with secrets and a weathered map.

At first it had just been me and Dake. We'd been traveling for two months before picking up the albino and MoJo, a harlequin pair of shadow and light, who had been travelling in roughly the same direction, more or less together. Shortly after, we'd found Vesta trailing us. Dake invited her to come, and even convinced her to stop chewing the leaves so she could think clearly. I think Vesta loves Dake.

I think I do, too.

Day by day our ragged group traveled this hollow land. At the last settlement there were two others who wanted to join. They were young and strong and looked as though they could be of help on our journey, but Dake saw something dark in their eyes and said we hadn't provisions for more. Vesta suggested trading the albino for the two young men and swished her ample form provocatively at them. Dake said she could stay with them or come with us.

She came.

Although youngest among us, I am the only one who can read and write. My mother had taught me to read before I was thirteen. Mother showed me how to write words with a stick in the sand, but my lessons were washed away each morning. We had three books she cherished—*I Sing the Body Electric*, *The World According to Garp*, and *Marathon Man*.

Every night we would read together from these books after scavenging. I asked her once how the people in these books could be so much like us, yet their worlds were so different? Was one of those worlds out there lost somewhere? Her only answer was that the books were made up, and if our world had ever been like theirs, she didn't know what had happened to change it. But I saw her eyes cloud over and knew there were memories hidden deeply, too painful to recall.

Mother and I had lived alone for as long as I could remember. Over the years we'd seen others pass by, but we avoided them. Mother said it was impossible to tell who was diseased, so it was better to let them pass.

When Mother lost her footing at the crater's edge one day while gathering firewood, I tried to survive on my own, but with time found the loneliness too much of a burden. One night a man camped nearby. I watched him for signs of disease, but he seemed healthy. He ate only what berries he needed, not stripping or harming the plants, and he chewed no leaves. In the morning I let him find me and he treated me kindly.

Desperate to share words, I allowed him into my cave and gave him drink. He invited me to join him on his journey, but remembering Mother's warning, I hesitated. When he saw my books, he said he had seen others like them but could not understand their meaning.

Others? There were more than these three? I made up my mind then and decided to go with this man Dake, if only to find more books. That decision brought a secret joy to my heart, for despite my reasoning, I knew I would walk in his shadow to the ends of the earth and back, if only for one of his smiles.

We haven't yet found books, but in one settlement MoJo brought me a present.

Paper.

Paper and pencils!

With this gift I keep track of the days and record our journey. I carry my papers in a bag called Brunswick. I hope somewhere to find more paper because I have only a few sheets left and I fear there is much more to write.

We've traveled at a comfortable pace for several seasons, covering many miles. Yesterday, though, Dake pushed us harder, as if sensing an ending in the air and anxious to reach it. When we thought we could travel no further and complained of exhaustion, he allowed us to make camp for the night, rationing our waning supply of water and fruit. As he slept, Dake's legs twitched as if anxious to move forward on their own.

In the morning I was the first to waken and took my privacy beyond the camp. Noticing a clearing ahead, I walked further than my needs warranted and came upon a sight I will never forget. Below me was a valley, and nestled like a jewel within, a city teeming with life. I called to Dake, excitement making my voice shrill. Soon they were all gathered around, gazing in awe at the city below.

Dake was the first to speak. His voice held a touch of reverence and something else I couldn't identify. "Our journey is over."

An owl screeched overhead, and as one we all looked fearfully to the sky. That's one thing we seem to have in common, our instinctive fear of things coming from the sky. We all sky-watch automatically, lifting our eyes, then reassured of its calm, going on our way.

When we looked back to the city, it seemed a group had formed and spotted us, perhaps alerted by my screams. We started down the valley, meeting them halfway, never taking our eyes off the city, which grew more incredible with each step taken.

The first to greet us was a man in woven cloth the color of the sea. I tried not to stare at his face, hairless like a woman's, but his smile made me feel safe. "My name is Kacee," he said. "I'm leader of this city. Welcome."

Dake stepped forward. "I am Dake." He turned and introduced each of us by name. "I've led these people many miles to find you."

"And now you have."

For the first time Dake seemed unsure of himself, but Kacee smiled to put him at ease. "You've heard stories of our society?"

"Yes."

"And you've brought these people with you hoping to join us."

Dake nodded.

Kacee motioned for us to sit. With legs folded I listened to him explain about the new society they'd rebuilt from the ruins. I found it hard to believe most of the wonders he told about, but he spoke so convincingly that my doubts soon dissolved. Could it be true? And how had Dake known to lead us here? I forced my attention back to what Kacee was saying.

"...but most of all we were determined to avoid the corruption that destroyed our world before. If you are sure you want to join us, you must each pass a test. Are you willing to be tested?"

Test? What kind of test, I wondered. But Dake, the albino, Mojo, and even Vesta all bobbed their heads in agreement. I found myself nodding too, wanting more than anything to be a part of Kacee's city.

He stood and pronounced words that seemed like a riddle, but had the feel of being spoken in just this way many times before. "You are not the first, and not all who come are accepted. To become one with this society you will make two choices, one of your own and one beyond your control. The choices are three—to be, to not be, or to remain the same. But always remember that the final choice is yours."

Dake nodded. I felt as if he'd already known that this would be our greeting. I read fear and hesitation on his face, but *need* too. I knew that whatever decision Dake made we would follow, as we had followed him all these months to get here.

Kacee spoke again, directly to Dake. "We will prepare for the ceremony. Until then you are not allowed to enter the city. There are ample quarters outside where all your needs will be met. Come." He beckoned with a wave of his hand.

He led us to a small shed more grand than any I had ever seen. There we were given clean clothes—similar to those worn by the city dwellers—which smelled like the flowers in the field. I happily discarded my rags to bathe. After washing the thorns from my hair, I wound it away from my face with a strip of leather. The robes I'd been given were smooth against my skin, emphasizing the recent changes in my body.

That afternoon Dake came to me. He smoothed my hair, in silence. I waited for him to decide whether to speak, too frightened to voice the questions in my heart.

"You tremble," he said finally. "Do you not trust me, little one?"

"Yes, Dake, I do. Of course. It's not you that I fear." How could I tell him that now that our journey had ended, what I really feared was change? What if I failed the test and was sent alone back into the wilderness?

Dake pulled the map from his pocket, unfolded it carefully and smoothed its wrinkles. "I wasn't sure I would ever find this place. Sometimes I even doubted its existence." He spoke quietly, as if to himself, but he held my hand and that was enough.

Perhaps I dozed, leaning against his chest, wrapped in his security. When he spoke again I jumped, though his voice was barely a whisper.

"We could die here, little Emmah," he said.

"They would kill us?"

Dake stared into the distance. "Perhaps."

"Then we must leave," I said, perhaps more bravely than I felt.

"Leave? To go where? Should we continue to wander without even the hope of something better to comfort us? No," he stated. "Better to take our chances here."

I stared, numb, remembering Kacee's warning of choices to be made. What to choose? How to choose? I didn't understand. All I knew was that wherever Dake was, I wanted to be. I asked Dake where he had gotten the map that led us here.

"From a dying man with a strange story to tell," he replied. "I knew that if his tale were true I had to find this place, because it is the place of the rebirth of our world. Since the map led us here, I can only assume the rest of his story is also true and tonight we will be given an opportunity to be a part of that rebirth."

"But what choices did Kacee speak of?"

"Choices that we each have to make on our own. As of now you must no longer look to me to make your decisions. I am no longer your leader. The choice is yours, Emmah, and only you can make it."

"You speak in riddles like Kacee now."

Dake smiled, but his eyes burned with intensity. "Just remember that the choice is yours alone and you may decline it if you wish. Even at the last moment. By that time I may not be able to help you." He brushed a fingertip over my cheek with a gentleness that made me yearn for the comfort of my mother's touch. "Good luck," he whispered. "Good luck to us all."

The messenger came too soon. I wasn't ready. I didn't know if I ever would be, but Dake went and so I followed. Within moments, I was too amazed by the sights within the city to wonder. We were led into a gathering room lit as bright as day, even though it was now evening. The tables were laden with platters of food, the variety and proportions of which I had seen only in my dreams. I watched people working together, busy yet content.

I held my breath in wonder at the abundance all around; food, clothing, and tools. But most of all paper—glorious reams of paper; white pages full of blank expectancy. And books! A wealth of books. I reached for one, but a woman stayed my hand with kindness etched in the lines of her face.

"Not yet," she said. "There will be time for that later."

I stared at her, unable to hide the hope in my heart.

"Or there won't," she continued. "In which case it doesn't matter."

"When?" I asked.

She patted my hand and whispered. "After the choosing." With a final glance in my direction, she turned and walked away.

Although our group was separate, the city dwellers occasionally looked over and smiled encouragement. I felt that they were hoping we too could belong—as much as I found myself yearning to be included.

They had much to offer us, but what could we give them in return to gain admittance? Our skills were nothing compared to theirs, and although Dake was the smartest among us, even he had little to add to their collective knowledge and skills. We were simply nomads, and our greatest accomplishment so far was our ability to survive.

Soon I noticed something else that held them apart from us. Each of the city dwellers wore a crimson mark on their brow, the lack of which branded us as outsiders.

Kacee came up beside me and glanced at the ground where my mother's treasured books had spilled from my bag. He looked deeply into my eyes, a look that made me feel naked inside. "You read." It was not a question.

I nodded, having no voice to answer.

Quietly he said, "Perhaps you will find much to read within." His statement filled me with wonder and desire. I tried not to *want* too much, for experience had proven that the greater the desire, the more painful the loss.

We ate. Flavor upon flavor, textures and colors and smells never before experienced. With dinner finished, we were led into a court-yard where our cups were filled with liquid heat. Vesta danced sugges-tively, her body making swirling patterns in the fire's flickering shadow. She tilted her body before the men of the city, dipping her hand greed-ily into their bowls and brushing their food over her lips. The men wore the embarrassed smiles of young boys watching dogs mate. The women looked away.

I didn't realize how accustomed I had become to the chatter of people until suddenly all talking ceased. An air of anticipation sur-rounded us. Suddenly Kacee called out and twin crones entered the circle, their bodies hunched over a basket held between them. They looked to be a hundred years old, and the weight of the basket was surely more than their own weights combined.

They lowered the basket to the ground. A woven cloth the color of moonlight hid the contents inside. I stared at the cloth, mesmerized. Glittering threads seemed to dance by the light of the fire, almost form-ing words. The more I tried to decipher them, however, the less sense they made. If I turned away, I could almost grasp their meaning, just out of reach like a name at the tip of my tongue. Closer inspection, however, showed them to be only designs, nothing more. Intricate and beautiful, yes, but telling no tales.

Kacee lifted the cloth, revealing the treasure inside. Stones of ev-ery color filled the basket. They captured the light of the fire and sent it back in bursts of living color. He reached in and swirled his hand through the stones, which seemed to speak in clattering murmurs.

"We've all been in your place at one time," Kacee said to our group. "If you wish to become one of us, you must choose a stone." A moment of reverent silence followed, but my gaze remained riveted on the mound of stones. Choose one? How could I possibly choose only one when each rivaled the last in beauty?

"There is no guarantee you will choose the right stone, or that the memories found will suit our needs," Kacee continued. "When the stones are gone, our memories will be complete and the doors to our city will close."

I looked again into the basket filled with stones and couldn't imag-ine an end to them. There seemed to be more than enough stones to people a hundred more cities. Could this be the test, simply picking the right stone? It seemed more luck than skill was involved.

A table was set up on the other side of the basket, facing us. Chairs were brought and five city dwellers in black robes took their places before us. They watched us with blank eyes that gave away no secrets. On the table sat an earthen bowl and each judge carried five white sticks, which looked like bones.

Kacee's voice changed, becoming deeper, ceremonial. "Who leads this group?"

Dake stood. "I, Dake, lead these people."

"Do you choose to be one of us?"

Without hesitation, Dake replied. "I do."

Kacee nodded to the basket. "Then choose your destiny."

Dake reached in, all eyes upon him. He searched, either unwilling or unable to make a choice. I held my breath as if the fate of the world awaited his choice. I knew that the fate of *my* world did. Finally, Dake closed his eyes and let instinct guide him. His hand closed around a single stone.

Dake straightened, opened his eyes, and stared at the stone nestled in his hand. It was brilliant green, the color of grass caught in a ray of morning sun. He turned it and the stone glowed, bathing our upturned faces in emerald hues.

"Is that your choice?" Kacee asked.

In answer, Dake placed the stone in his mouth. Moments passed as I watched his face take on meaning, his eyes fill with understanding.

"Tell the council what you would give to this society, and what wisdom the stone has imparted," Kacee said.

Dake turned to the table. "I remember the terrain of the land, the hidden places where lost souls cower waiting to be coaxed to the safety of a new society. My skill will lead them back to the family. I am a journeyer, a missionary."

The judges put their heads together, then each threw a bone into the bowl, which flared briefly.

Kacee nodded and smiled at Dake, then reached into the bowl, swirled his hand within. With a flourish, he placed his thumb on Dake's forehead, leaving behind a stain of crimson.

"Welcome to our city, Dake," he said, embracing him, and the chorus was taken up by the multitude, welcoming Dake into their fold. He took his place on the other side of the fire, an eternity away from me.

Then Kacee turned to face our group. "Who would be next?"

The albino stood so quickly that I didn't have time to wonder if I would have the courage to go. He strode to the basket, a solemn look of yearning on his face. Reaching in without the slightest hesitation, he pulled out a stone of crystalline translucency unrivaled by the purest mountain ice. I couldn't remember seeing a stone of such clarity when I'd looked in the basket, and despite the hundreds of stones in view, could not see another like it.

The albino made a reverent gesture with his hands and placed the cool, clear stone on his tongue. Immediately a look of peace smoothed his features and I knew with certainty that he had found what his soul had been craving.

After a moment of silence, he turned to the judges. "The stones have given me back the faith I had forgotten. If it is thy will, I shall serve you as a healer of souls. I will comfort your sick and guide those who would go astray. My mission will be to spread the teachings of love."

Again the judges conferred briefly before filling the bowl with the second of their five judgement bones. This time, however, Kacee reached for a purple sash. He draped it around the albino's robe before marking his forehead. Instead of an embrace, Kacee knelt on one knee before the albino, who made the same symbolic gesture he'd made earlier with the stone. Then he turned and sat among them.

Vesta slithered up to the basket next, making a show of picking stones and discarding them with mocking laughter. No one spoke. No one rushed her. She turned her back on the basket and asked Kacee what would happen if she chose not to take a stone. He said she would have to leave the city, since only those who have earned their place were welcome.

Vesta searched the watching faces around the fire. Then, as if doing them a favor, reached inside and pulled out a stone the color of blood on fire.

A shiver ran through me and I wanted to call to her, beg her not to put it in her mouth. The stone shivered in scarlet shades of hate and pain. Vesta devoured it before I could utter a warning. Her eyes seemed to glow, but perhaps it was just the fire reflected in them. She whipped her head around, baring her teeth with sounds of both pleasure and pain, and sparks caught in the tips of her hair, which became a blaze of swirling flame around her head.

With more quickness and strength than I would have imagined, the twin crones covered her with the stone's shroud, smothering her depravity. Beneath it I could hear Vesta's guttural moans and see her struggling, though no one held the tapestry's edges around her.

The judges each broke their third bone in half and tossed the pieces over the shroud. Vesta's struggles stilled and the bones made connections on the tapestry, forming words of damnation I dare not repeat and hope to soon forget.

The albino stepped forward and murmured a prayer over the cloth. When it was lifted, nothing of Vesta remained but an oily, star-shaped ash, while all around was silence and heads bowed in sorrow.

It was time to go on. MoJo looked to me and I shook my head. *No.* Not yet. So little time left to steel my courage. He patted my head and walked to the basket. Like Dake, he closed his eyes and waited for the stone to choose him. When he opened his palm I was sure he held a piece of the sky, so brilliantly blue was his stone. He touched it to his cheek and sighed, cradled it near his face and exhaled an "aah" of delight. Finally he placed it on his tongue and swayed from side to side like a branch on the breeze.

When MoJo next opened his mouth, the stone was gone. He raised his voice in what first seemed to be a question, but then became a circle of sound rising to the sky, rivaling the call of the sweetest bird. His voice rose and lifted me to the top of the mountain, winter gales whistling through my hair, then fell in a rush, a waterfall's splash, trilling and rippling over the rocks to bubble and splash below. I closed my eyes as his voice swept me away with a sweetness I'd never felt outside of my mother's arms.

I knew instantly that my life had been missing song.

MoJo sang, with heart-rending beauty, a melody so powerful I felt myself filled with emotions—ecstasy, sorrow and joy. Others felt it too. When I opened my eyes I saw theirs, like mine, glistened with tears.

And the albino was smiling.

Before MoJo's song ended, the bowl was filled with the fourth bone of the judges. He never needed to state his case, for his music spoke for him. The judges realized, too, that a world without song was a dead world indeed.

And now, finally, it was my turn.

I walked with slow, hesitant steps, careful to avoid the ashy stain of Vesta. Did I, like her, carry corruption hidden inside me waiting to be brought forth by a stone's intent? I looked at the faces around me. Serene and sure, they seemed aware of something I was not. All eyes held encouragement, urging me forward. Still I hesitated. What could the stones hold for me?

MoJo, Dake and the albino beckoned me wordlessly. I could see now that the stones enhanced each of their inner qualities, but I felt I had no strengths to draw a stone to my calling. I wondered again about the source of the stones. Were they the building blocks for all of humanity, or the essence of those who passed before us, seeking like souls to continue the traits necessary in this new world?

It was a riddle with no answer. Do the stones carry the imprint or does the person imprint the stone? We would probably never know.

Kacee smiled at me. "Come, little one. Choose your destiny."

I reached into the basket of stones, hoping one would reach back for me. But they all felt the same—smooth, cold, round like berry nuts. With hundreds of possibilities to choose from, I closed my eyes and remembered Kacee's warning, "The first choice is yours, but the second is beyond your control."

I took a deep breath and lifted a stone to my mouth, afraid to look at the color for fear it would reflect only a dull void, a black smudge with no soul glowing within.

The cool stone lay on my tongue. As it warmed in my mouth, images swirled through my mind like colored veils, each one revealing a new one beneath—hundreds of stories, tales that had to be told, information crying to be shared, a history to be written.

I saw children gathered around me, eyes rapt with wonder, and elders who laid their lives at my feet to be chronicled. I smiled with gratitude, since that which I loved most could be of use to this society. Somehow, the stone had chosen, enhancing what I hadn't even known I possessed.

I'd passed the test.

As the stone slowly melted into my soul, Dake's hand closed over mine, and this, more than the bones rattling into the bowl and the mark touching my forehead, told me that I'd found my destiny.

UNMARKED PLANET

by Nick Aires

Chailld was the only planet in the Farso System that hadn't been overrun by the ruthless Muckras. We traveled many light years to find out why.

The Muckras had decimated hundreds of human outposts, and their fleets would soon reach the larger planetary colonies—where our planet peacefully laid. Since no one had yet survived any of their vile, unprovoked attacks, we held precious little intelligence upon which to build our defenses. We had to figure out why there wasn't a Muckra beacon planted in the soil of this fertile planet.

A small but elite team of five Reconnaissance Rangers accompanied me on the mission. We set down somewhere along Chailld's equator, in a grassy meadow lined with gnarled, quarter-kilometer-high trees. It was my turn to stay behind, as protocol required that someone always remain with the ship.

The ship's external monitors were my eyes and ears as the rest of the team disembarked and headed towards the tree line. They were halfway there when a loud, garbled cry coincided with the appearance of a ten-foot alien that jumped out from behind a tree.

Renault, the unit leader, signaled for the others to halt and draw their weapons.

The bipedal alien looked almost humanoid, but with plated skin, and it was primitively clothed at its groin region with some sort of leaves. It held a club-like weapon in the large four-knuckled fingers of its left hand. "Geeuhuh raizai," the alien screamed, as it rattled the club menacingly.

"Translation?" Renault asked me over the com.

The ship's computer had a universal translator that I'd switched on ahead of time. The translator's speaker was silent. "I've got nothing," I replied.

"Damn." Renault took a step towards the alien. "Hello!" he called out. He proceeded to give the official *Earth Alliance greeting*.

The alien gurgled some more gibberish in response, but the ship's computer still offered no translation.

"Anything?" Renault asked me.

"Give it time. The universal translator needs more distinct words to form a basis for comparison."

Renault instructed each member of the unit in turn to attempt to converse with the alien. For its part, the alien seemed intent on trying to talk to them as well. Within a matter of minutes I was sure that I'd heard enough different sounds from the alien's mouth to make the translator happy, yet it remained silent. To the best of my knowledge, this had never happened before.

"I'm sorry, Captain, but I've still got nothing...and I'm starting to think that we're not going to get anything anytime soon."

"Damn. Okay, I guess we'll have to do this the old-fashioned way." Renault turned to the woman on his right. "Trier," he said, "Go back to the ship and get the *E.A. goodwill package*."

Trier turned and took a couple of steps, then froze. The alien blocked her way with its club.

"Neh ggehw," it wailed.

"Back away," Renault said.

Trier took a hesitant step backwards.

The alien suddenly grabbed Trier's left arm with its free hand. "Mmayen!"

Trier, acting on instinct, swung her blast-rifle around and dealt a sharp blow to the alien's right arm. The blow had the intended effect—the alien cried out in surprise (or pain) and let go of Trier, who stumbled back a couple steps before regaining her composure.

The alien seemed to almost laugh, then it took its club and whacked Trier on her right arm, causing her to drop her rifle.

Crewman Langley, who'd been having a not-so-secret torrid affair with Trier, reacted brashly. He blasted the alien's weapon-hand, before Renault belatedly told him to stand down.

Such a close range hit would have vaporized a human hand, but the alien's hand appeared to have only sustained minor burns. Nonetheless, the alien screamed in agony for several seconds, then put its seared fingers into its mouth and sucked on them.

All of a sudden, a loud commotion came from somewhere in the direction that the alien first appeared from. The crashing sounds grew louder and louder as something rapidly approached the clearing.

The rangers all took an involuntary step backwards as the cause of the commotion strode into view. It was another alien. It looked very much like the first one, except that it appeared to have six mammary glands concealed under more leaf-clothing. And it was about a hundred feet tall.

"Mmaie bhambheen*kill!*" the new alien bellowed. Then it attacked.

It picked up Renault and Trier and bashed them together.

Before I could even consider breaking protocol to go to my team's aid, the enraged hundred-foot alien had already stomped on Damascas and Reagan, and had ripped off all of Langley's appendages.

I launched immediately, but the giant alien dove at the ship and nearly got a hold of the aft burner.

As I left Chailld's orbit, the ship's computer finally proffered a translation of the aliens' vocalizations. Everything still sounded like gibberish to me—albeit, English-sounding gibberish—until the second alien's words boomed through the speakers:

"My baby!"

ORACLE OF CILENS

by Kathryn Sullivan

Kathryn Sullivan began reading science fiction and fantasy not long after getting her first library card. Very soon after that, she tried writing. Stories about girl agents defeating alien bad guys and tales of wizards' apprentices looking for forgotten treasure filled school notebooks alongside her regular homework. She is owned by two very bewildered birds and lives in Winona, MN, where the bluffs surrounding the Mississippi River also double as alien landscapes and fantasy forests.

The haruspex was awaiting the word of the gods when a mule-drawn cart stopped with a clatter beside the merchant ship. The pretty, black-haired matron within signaled her driver to wait, her dark eyes watching the ritual. The Umbrian slave spared the seer only a brief glance. "Etruscan fakery," he muttered disgustedly in his own tongue.

Ramtha Partunu ignored his comment, her attention on the high conical hat and brightly colored cloak of the skyreader.

The haruspex had stationed himself in the middle of the afterdeck, facing southward as he watched the clear blue sky.

South was where the gods of nature and earth dwelled, west and north were the abodes of the gods of death and the underworld, and east the home of the celestial gods, the most powerful of the three forces. Ramtha scanned the sky, but saw no omen for the haruspex to interpret. Skyreading was time-consuming, but Arnth preferred that form of divination to reading the livers of animals. Ramtha finally located her husband beside the lean figure of the captain and stifled a sigh. Where had he found that old tebenna?

Cloaks aplenty he had with his status to maintain as master trader, but he had to wear that stained one in the presence of the seer. People would next be saying that Arnth Visnai was disdainful of the gods.

She had heard rumors already of the growing belief among the traders that Arnth's recent wealth was due not to his skill as the master of four ships but the fact that he had married a witch. His witch wife adjusted the wool mantle draped over her shoulder and stepped down out of the two-wheeled cart.

She walked slowly up and down the dock, occasionally touching the rough timbers of the ship as she attempted her own form of divination. So intent was she on summoning the Partunu gift that she did not notice her husband leave the ship and steal softly up behind her.

Arnth tugged gently on a curl that had escaped from her long elaborate braid. "What brings you here, child? You of all people need no instruction from the high hats."

She glanced up at the patient haruspex, but did not smile at their private joke. "I had a foreboding feeling today."

Arnth tensed. "About what? Ramtha, did the goddess send you a warning?"

She shook her head, uneasy at his concern. "You know that I cannot see my own future."

"Your father and his father could."

"Only on the day of their deaths." She wished her own gift was so limited. Why had Cilens taken her blessing to the Partunu—that of knowing the hour of their deaths—away from Ramtha, of all her family, and given her instead the ability to see the fate of others?

Ramtha looked away from the sympathy in her husband's eyes. Why was he always pretending that he cared about her? She knew he did not. He loved That Woman, not Ramtha his wife. And to think that she had once believed he could love a girl twelve years his junior. Three years of marriage had proven her wrong.

She looked up and found him still watching her. "No vision brought me today. I merely thought your captains might begin to wonder why you always bring them to me before a voyage."

"Ah, but Vel has solved that little mystery. He has decided that you cast spells against shipwreck."

"And you did not correct him? Arnth, why?"

Arnth smiled at his young wife. "What matter what others believe? Your seercraft has brought us much good fortune, and I prefer to keep that secret, rather than have you become haruspex for all of Caere."

He glanced up at the seer still scanning the sky. "Not that that skyreader couldn't use some competition. Come, sit out of the sun and tell me what you would like if this voyage proves as successful as the last. A new pair of red shoes? A gold necklace? A bronze coffer for your cosmetics?" He took her arm to lead her back to the cart.

Ramtha started at the wave of dizziness that followed swiftly upon his touch. She felt the aura of *otherness* abruptly close about her as if Cilens, spinner of fates, now stood beside her.

Arnth looked closely at her, then released her arm.

"What do you see, Ramtha?" he asked patiently.

Her voice came from far away. "The ship will not sail today."

"Why?"

The piercing eyes of a goddess were turned upon him, and he recoiled a step before their gaze. "What is fated, will be. You will lead part of the crew up to the city. The captain and others of the crew will search the docks, keeping Cumaei ships under close watch. The Dorians will steal from you."

"What? What will they take?"

But the goddess had gone. Ramtha spread her hands apart. "I am sorry, Arnth. I did not see."

Arnth frowned. "Dorians stealing from a ship while it is in harbor? That is not like them. They are pirates upon the sea, but honeyed-tongued on land. Now, the Carthaginians—"

"I saw one of the thieves, one whom you will find. He is a hooknosed Dorian, and he wears the tunic of a freeman, although his feet are bare."

"The tunic of a freeman, but the bare feet of a slave," her husband repeated. "I will remember that."

He studied the distant masts of Dorian ships in the harbor. The Dorians, like his own people, owed allegiance to no single king. Each city-state was independent of the other, and Cumae was said to be the oldest of the Dorian city-states. Arnth disbelieved that tale, having in his younger years sailed to the distant islands of the Dorians' origin and seen older and far more beautiful cities there. The Dorians were a clever people, talented with stone as well as with words. They were also contenders for the mastery of the sea, a title claimed by the Carthaginians as well as Arnth's own people, the Rasena.

Arnth frowned and steered his wife toward her cart. "Much as I would rather have you stay, Ramtha, if the Dorians plan to attack the ship, you had best return to Caere."

"Go quickly, Septem," he told the slave as Ramtha settled herself within the cart. The Umbrian obeyed, the cart rolling away so swiftly that Ramtha had time only for a wave back at her husband before Septem had skillfully maneuvered the cart through the traffic of the dockfront and out onto the plain.

She looked back to where Arnth stood on the dock and in her memory saw once again the vision Cilens had sent her during her wedding rites. A young woman—beautiful, Ramtha knew, although the woman's face was turned away from her—was held tightly in Arnth's arms. Her blue mantle had been flung back to her elbows revealing a short-sleeved cheton of rich green. Her long black hair was falling out of its ribbon binding, forming a second mantle down her back.

Despite the woman's unkempt appearance, Arnth was looking at her with so much love in his eyes that the then 14-year-old Ramtha had known that her new husband would be forever lost to her once those two met. As they were fated to.

Arnth was still watching her from the dock. She waved, ignoring the tears stinging her eyes. No one could change what was to be, not even the gods. But Ramtha, oracle of Cilens, dared to desire the unthinkable. If only there was some way to thwart the goddess of fate!

She turned around and sat stiffly upright, biting her lip to keep from sobbing.

She did not see the flock of sparrows dip down out of the sky and wheel as one over her. Arnth did, however, and took it as a good omen. Everyone knew that sparrows were the favorite birds of Uni, goddess of marriage. Perhaps Ramtha's odd moments of sadness over the death of her father would lessen, he mused. Perhaps Uni meant that they would have a child.

He smiled at the thought. He had been richly blessed by the gods. He had a clever and beautiful wife whom he dearly loved and a thriving business with her help. And the goddess', he quickly added.

Smiling fondly, Arnth watched until the cart was out of sight.

The captain cleared his throat respectfully beside him. "Sir, the haruspex has made his prediction."

"At last! What does he say about your voyage, Vel?"

Vel hesitated. "I think you had best hear for yourself. I don't think you're going to like it."

The haruspex waited majestically for them to approach. Arnth eyed the little skyreader, a faint amusement at this pompous fellow tingeing his normal respect for seers. "What say the gods, holy one?"

The haruspex looked up at the sky and spread his arms wide in supplication to the gods. He lowered his gaze and looked sorrowfully at Arnth. "A treasure of your home will be taken from you."

Arnth frowned. "What do you mean?"

"Did you not see that flight of sparrows? They came from the east, from Uni's, goddess of the hearth, sector, then turned and flew into the northwest, into the realm of the underworld. I say again, a treasure of your house shall be taken from you."

The pieces of the mosaic abruptly fell into place. Arnth turned and looked across the plain toward the red tufa cliffs below Caere. The birds had turned above Ramtha's cart, he recalled with a sudden stab of fear, before flying into the northwest. Into Cilens' sector!

Somehow he knew that he was right. Ramtha had never been able to see her own future. And Uni was the goddess of marriage as well as the home. "No, holy one, not just a mere treasure," he groaned aloud, "but my wife!"

❧ ❧

Ramtha shivered suddenly and wrapped her wool mantle over her linen tunic. The sunlight seemed oddly cold. She clutched at the side of the cart, feeling a familiar whirling sickness as the vision struck.

Charun, Bringer of Death, laughed as he strode toward the oncoming cart. Sharp teeth shining whitely within his black beard, the giant nodded to her and raised his hammer.

"No!" Ramtha protested. The Umbrian, unhearing, continued to drive the cart straight at the god.

Laughing, the giant pointed his hammer towards Septem, and the slave cried out, doubling over. Blood flowed from his death wound, and Ramtha saw a sword gleaming faintly.

"Are you all right, Lady?"

Ramtha stared wildly at Septem. He was alive, turning towards her from the front of the cart, the reins held tightly in his hands. "Yes," she gasped. "No! We must be inside the city before the storm breaks!"

The slave glanced at the faint line of clouds on the eastern horizon and back again at her white face. He shrugged and started the mules moving again. These Etruscans and their gods! He would never become accustomed to the Lady's strange fits.

Ramtha stared at the solid back before her and shuddered with fear. He was going to die! Before they would reach the safety of the city, he would die!

She tried to still her trembling. She had seen Charun and his hammer many times, but never before had he struck so near to her. She took a deep breath. What was fated, would be. But who would wish to kill Septem? Why?

Her visions of the morning returned, and she fumbled under her mantle for her belt knife. Her eyes studied the orchards set back from the road, and she held her knife ready, hidden under folds of cloth.

Dark clouds rolled swiftly across the sky. The fading sunlight turned greenish. Shivering anew at these ominous signs, Ramtha tried frantically to picture the road to Caere, a road she had traveled all her life. They would be attacked while on the road. Where?

Caere, like all the old Rasena cities, was set on a hilltop overlooking the harbor and thus easily defended from the pirate raids common in its early years. The small stretch of plain between the harbor and the hill was clearly visible to the guards posted on Caere's outside walls, as were the two neighboring hills, Caere's cemeteries. The best place for an attack, then, would be on the hill road, where the roadway often wound out of sight of the city guards.

Ramtha glanced at the distant city walls and slipped her knife back within her belt. They still had some distance to go before she need fear attack; the mules had only now trotted past the turnoff for the road to the hill Abaton and its tombs.

The thought of warning Septem was dismissed as quickly as it appeared. He had not been expecting any danger in her vision, therefore she could not warn him. Any interference in Charun's comings caused the god to change a swift passage to the underworld into a slow and painful dying. She was helpless to alter what was to be. She could do nothing but place herself in the hands of her goddess. Her fingertips brushed the hilt of her knife.

The cart rolled briskly along under the darkening sky. Thunder muttered irritably in the east.

The road widened, branching off yet again towards green-topped Banditac and its tombs. Ramtha tensed as they neared the gentle slope of the hill road to Caere.

A rider on a mule came down the road, waving his sword slowly over his head as he neared them. "Danger! Rockslide ahead!" he warned.

Muttering under his breath, Septem pulled the mules to a halt. The rider stopped beside the cart. "Is the road completely blocked?" Ramtha asked, glancing up the slope.

The man pointed his sword back at the cliff. "My companions will soon have a pathway clear. By Hermes! Are you not the wife of the master trader Visnai?"

Ramtha froze at the Dorian word. She glanced quickly towards the rider, looking past the sandaled feet to a face from her vision.

The hook-nosed Dorian lost his false smile. He cast his left hand up as if to shield himself from her gaze. "The witch knows!" he shouted and ran Septem through with his sword.

The slave cried out, doubling over, and Ramtha lunged forward to snatch the reins from the Umbrian's dying grasp. She found herself instead fighting to disentangle herself from the folds of a cloak cast over her head from behind. She struggled to fling aside the cloak and rise, but was pushed to the floor of the cart again, the cloak held firmly over her head.

"Don't look at her eyes!" she heard Hook Nose shout. "The witch will enchant you if you look into her eyes!"

"You've made a mistake!" Ramtha protested, ceasing her ineffectual struggles. "I am not a witch!"

She felt the restraining bite of rope as it was wrapped about the cloak, fastening it securely over her head and binding her arms to her sides. Yet her hands remained free.

"Our master says you are a witch," a cold voice commented next to her ear. "But, as he is paying us to either deliver you to him or kill you, what you are makes no difference to me. Now, you will either stay quietly where you are or I will kill you. Understand?"

The cart rocked, and Ramtha heard him land on the road. "Help me with the body, Grypos," he ordered. The cart rocked again and Ramtha felt her throat tighten at the memory of the disrespectful, grumbling slave and his patience with her strangeness. "Swift passage, Septem," she whispered softly. "May Charun soon lead you to the halls of music and feasts."

She waited, listening intently in order to locate each of her captors. She quickly discovered that although she had only heard two voices, there was one other, silent so far. She could hear the sound of something being dragged off to her left, the quick step of sandaled feet on the road behind the cart, and harsh breathing towards the front of the cart.

She tested her bonds, growing accustomed to the strong smell of mule that clung to the cloak. Its rough fibers scraped her skin as she cautiously tried easing one hand to her belt.

The cart rolled forward. "No, Leanderes," came a cold reminder far behind the cart. "Hold the mules' heads."

The Dorians spoke their own language among themselves; but Ramtha, wife and daughter of traders, knew that tongue well. She wondered where they would take her. Who was their master?

"Hurry, Grypos, before anyone comes."

Ramtha's fingers brushed the hilt of her knife. She heard footsteps nearing her and froze.

"The body is hidden, Theronos," Hook Nose's voice came.

"Good, Grypos." Ramtha blinked, and a slow grin spread over her face as she realized that that Dorian name translated as "Hook Nose". The cart rocked as someone climbed into the driver's seat. The cart began to move backward.

"Grypos," came the cold voice of Theronos before her, "ride your mule and take mine up to Caere. Find Physkonos—he should still be watching the Visnai home—and have him ride to the ship. He's to tell the captain that we have the witch and that he should be ready to sail tonight."

Ramtha's mind reeled. A ship! Merciful Uni, how was she to escape from a ship?

"...don't see why I can't ride to the ship myself," Grypos was saying when Ramtha could hear again.

"Because I want you to wait and watch for Visnai. The moment he arrives at his home, you come and tell us. We can't travel with her until dark and I don't wish to run into him on the road. You remember where our camp is, don't you?"

"Yes," Grypos said sullenly.

"Wait, Grypos." The voice was dangerously mild. "Take off your sandals."

"What?"

"I said, take off your sandals. If the Tyrrhenoi see you with that one blood-soaked sandal, they might forbid you to even enter their city. They see bad omens in everything; no sense for you to provide them with one. Take off your sandals."

There was a pause. "Grypos," said a hoarse, raspy voice, "Theronos told you to do something."

"Now, now, Leanderes," Theronos chided. "Grypos is no fool."

Ramtha reached carefully for her knife as the silence seemed to lengthen. Her movements hidden under the cloak, she slowly drew her knife from her belt and tried to work it under both the cloak and her bonds.

"Good, Grypos," Theronos said finally. "Try not to forget your instructions. Come along, Leanderes. We have wasted enough time." The cart turned on the wide stretch of road and headed back the way Ramtha had come. She could hear a single mule following the cart.

The Dorians rode along in silence for a time. Then Ramtha felt the cart turn to the right and realized that they were on the road to the neighboring hill of Banditac. They traveled swiftly through the small valley separating the two hills.

Ramtha's muscles were growing cramped in her crouched position and she longed to straighten. Cutting through both the cloak and the rope was taking longer than she had expected.

"Dorian," she tried, raising her voice over the rattle and squeak of the cart. "Your master is wasting your time. I am not a witch."

"Not a witch, Lady Visnai?" Theronos mocked. "How, then, do you explain the fact that your husband has managed to avert or lessen disasters that would have broken another man? No, Lady, you are a witch."

Ramtha scowled, the familiar frustration at being misunderstood rising within her. How could she explain that her 'witchcraft' was possible to any Rasen who consulted the gods? If a haruspex said that a particular ship would be wrecked in a storm, then one chose a less valuable cargo to load. When the gods warned of a pirate attack, one sent more men to defend the ship and take the pirates' own. How to explain that to a Dorian? Their own oracle at Delphi was only consulted on matters of grave importance, not on everyday occurrences as were the haruspices.

"I am not a witch," she insisted. "Dorian, my husband is rich, as you say. He will pay more for my safe return that your master will for my capture."

"Visnai is more liable to kill me once you are safe with him. I know you Tyrrenhoi."

"You know little of us, then," Ramtha said angrily. Thunder rumbled, echoing her mood. "Uni will punish you for this deed."

Theronos laughed. "Hera has attempted to punish me before. Always I have thwarted her. She may be a goddess, but she is only a woman."

Thunder growled again above them, and Ramtha heard Charun's laughter. She fell silent, too shocked at the Dorian's disrespect to attempt to reason with him any further. The thunder seemed to be drawing closer, and with it the feeling of *otherness* that she had always associated with the gods. "In which direction is the lightning?" she asked.

"You Tyrrenhoi and lightning." Theronos chuckled. "But I will humor you, witch. Whose sector of the sky is due east?"

"Uni," she said, and dazzling white light suddenly exploded before her eyes.

The cart seemed to be tossed aside by a giant hand. Her ears ringing, Ramtha found herself on the grass, the rope and cloak falling away as she struggled to rise. Somehow her knife was still clenched tightly in her hand.

The cart was tumbled wreckage not far from her. The still harnessed mules galloped off across the plain, dragging the broken cart pole between them. She climbed unsteadily to her feet, looking for the Dorians. Near the wreckage of the cart was a blackened, smoking hole in the ground.

"Thank the gods the bolt struck no closer," came the hoarse, raspy voice of Leanderes. Ramtha turned and saw the Dorians not far beyond the ruined cart. A big man, heavily muscled, supported the slight frame of the other, who held a hand to his head.

"Never mind the gods," the slighter one said, shrugging off the big man's support. "Find the witch, or all our efforts will have been for naught."

Ramtha squared her shoulders. There was no place for her to hide. They believed her to be a witch; very well, she would play the part. "All your efforts were for naught, Theronos," she announced.

The Dorians turned in surprise.

"She knows your name, Theronos," the big man said slowly. "And how did she get free?"

"You toy with powers you do not understand, Dorians." Ramtha flung her hands skyward in the manner of a haruspex. Thunder answered.

"Take her, Leanderes!"

Leanderes hesitated. "Grypos said she would enchant me."

"Leanderes! Take her!"

"Do you so fear me, Theronos, that you must send others to do your work?" Ramtha asked mockingly.

"I fear no woman, be she witch or goddess," Theronos answered.

She raised her knife as the slight man approached. "Touch me at your peril, fool." Thunder rumbled menacingly and she heard the cold tones of the goddess in her voice. "You are dead men. You," the point of her knife flicked toward Leanderes, "will die at the feet of your master. You the goddess will spare for now to carry the news of her anger to him."

"You, however," her knife returned to Theronos, forcing him to back away, "have only moments to live. Uni is very displeased with you."

"Only Zeus controls the thunderbolts, witch," Theronos snarled. "Not Hera."

"Behold the cart," Ramtha countered. "Or was that merely accident?"

"Give me the knife, witch," Theronos commanded. His sword rasped from its sheath. "Do not force me to kill you."

Ramtha eyed him mockingly. What would a witch do? She laughed and tossed her knife up into the sky.

He raised his sword to shield himself from the knife as it fell back to earth, ignoring her for the moment. The knife clattered against his blade.

Lightning streaked down out of the sky, bathing him in its cold fire. His dying shriek was drowned out by Charun's laughter, rumbling in Ramtha's ears like thunder.

Lifeless, he slumped to the ground. Ramtha faced Leanderes over the body. The big man looked down at his companion. His eyes were full of fear when he raised his head.

"Behold Uni's wrath," Ramtha intoned. "Do not tempt her anger further. Go now, and inform your master of her curse."

Leanderes backed a step.

"Go!" Ramtha gestured, and the thunder answered.

Leanderes turned and dashed toward his mule. He scrambled onto its back and, without a backward glance, rose away as if the Furies pursued him.

Ramtha leaned against the wreckage of the cart, feeling limp and giddy with relief. A faint laugh escaped her. After all her protests to Arnth not to make her out to be a witch, she had just proved all the rumors true!

She felt the warmth of sunlight upon her and looked up to see the dark clouds rolling away, following the Dorian towards the harbor. "My thanks, Uni," she said gratefully.

Her eyes still on the clouds, she had a sudden vision of Leanderes arriving at the dock to find that his ship had departed without him. She had no fear that he would not find another ship out of Caere. The harbor seemed abuzz with activity, all centered about the Dorian ships. As she watched, three ships lifted anchor, scurrying out of the harbor as if their captains feared attack from the approaching storm clouds.

A breeze tugged at her hair as she looked across the plain.

Adjusting her mantle about her, she started walking, following the road towards Caere.

She had not gone far when she saw a lone horseman in the distance, riding swiftly towards her. "Ramtha!" came his shout.

"Arnth!"

The horse thundered up to her, and her husband swiftly dismounted. "Beloved!"

He caught her in his arms, holding her tightly. Ramtha relaxed into his grasp, feeling too safe and secure to wish to recall That Woman. Suddenly the goddess put a vision into her mind, the same one that Ramtha had seen on her wedding day. But now the face of That Woman was turned toward her. It was the same face that looked out of her mirror each morning. She had been jealous of herself!

Stunned at the revelation, Ramtha glanced downward and saw that she was indeed wearing the green cheton and blue mantle of her "rival". And her hair was a wild mess. A giggle escaped her.

After a few moments, Arnth looked down to see his wife laughing and crying into his cloak. "Now what is wrong?"

"Oh, Arnth, you *do* love me!" came the muffled reply.

Arnth raised his eyes skyward, then lowered his gaze and began stroking her hair. "That, wife," he said gruffly, "is a comment worthy of a high hat, not my talented witch."

He tensed at the sound of approaching hoofbeats and swung her behind him as the horse and rider came into view. "Vel," he said, relaxing as he recognized the rider.

"What have you to report, Vel?" Arnth called as the captain neared.

Vel dismounted. "Thank the gods you are safe, Lady." The captain looked a trifle sheepish as he turned to his master. "I fear the thieves' ship has escaped us, sir. That fool haruspex babbled his prediction up and down the docks, and one Dorian ship left the harbor not long after you left in search of the Lady. Later my men came across a Dorian with a message for that ship's captain."

"Was his name Physkonos?" Ramtha asked, translating 'Grypos' into their tongue.

Vel looked warily at her. "Yes, Lady. Once I heard what he had to say, I came at once to warn you, sir. I am sorry the ship eluded us."

Ramtha felt Arnth take a deep angry breath and hurried to forestall his outburst. "When you come upon that ship tomorrow, Captain, the scrolls you will find in the captain's chest will be apology enough."

"My ship will capture that one? With that ship's lead?" Vel interrupted.

Ramtha heard the distant thunder and knew that neither the ship nor the one who sent it would escape Uni's vengeance. "As any witch knows," she said, smiling mischievously up at her husband, "a spell against shipwreck and piracy can easily be turned into a spell *for* shipwreck and piracy."

THE TAKERS

by Loren W. Cooper

The soldiers and servants of the lady's retinue bustled silently around the courtyard, preparing for departure while the innkeeper stood before the carriage, pleading. "Please. Listen to me. I know that you are here on the word of the Young Dux, but you do not have enough men to brave those hills. You have only enough to tempt them."

In the light of the rising sun, the stone and timbers of the inn cast long shadows over the carriage and team, as well as the horses and mules of the train. The steward leaned past the lady to look down out of the open window and smile at the innkeeper. "Them?" Subtle mockery twisted his words. "Them who? Bandits? The hills couldn't support a large force. The Dux Frederick sent us to dispel exactly these rumors you seem so fond of spreading. We'll undoubtedly find nothing more than a small, ragged band of poorly armed peasants. Or perhaps a pack of mangy wolves."

The innkeeper shivered. "Your guesses are closer than you know. And farther than you think. What finds you in the Ash Hills will be less interested in your money than your meat."

"Cannibals?" The lady's face appeared at the open window, her eyes a sparkling green, her mouth a curve of distaste.

The innkeeper sighed. "They would first have to be human to qualify as cannibals, Lady. Oh, they're close enough to pass, or so the stories say. In the darkness. In the distance. Why do you think these hills have such an evil reputation? Why do you think that the arm of the fine Jodan highway that leads into those hills is so rarely traveled?"

"I'm sure that you'll tell us," the steward murmured in a voice delicate with irony.

The innkeeper ignored him. "They were there before the Jodan, who called them the Takers. The Jodan cleaned them out, of course. Twice. The second time they drove a highway through the middle of Taker country, just to prove that they could. They even built an old way station back in there, but travel fell off the highway, and the Takers outlasted the old Empire. They're survivors. It's the essence of them."

"Children's tales," the steward scoffed.

"Believe what you want," the innkeeper replied quietly. "I can't stop you. But you should at least go into this with open eyes. An old man passed through here a fortnight ago, and vanished into the hills."

The steward snorted. "Probably crossed through to the other side. Trust me, our eyes are quite open. We see more than you realize."

The innkeeper placed one hand on the sill of the open window of the coach. "Lady, please go back to the Young Dux Frederick. Tell him to send a division or more of hardened troops. You are not enough. I know that the plagues have hit the interior hard, and the Young Dux needs more victories to keep the people's minds off of their troubles, but this journey will bring you, and him, only sorrow."

The lady settled back into the shadows of the coach, and the innkeeper threw his hands in the air. "I tried to warn you, truly I did. I wash my hands of this. I pray only that those who follow will find more than your bones, lying next to the old wanderer's gnawed remains."

The steward nodded coldly. "Thanks for the warning."

The driver snapped the reins, and the coach rolled forward as the steward leaned back to be swallowed by shadows. The train of soldiers, servants and supplies followed after, the sound of clopping hooves and creaking leather filling the air. None of the servants or soldiers said a word. None of the animals made a sound other than the sharp noises of their hooves on stone.

The innkeeper stood in the dust of the courtyard a long while, watching the silent procession.

The broken fingers of ancient Jodan markers stood upright at the sides of the road as the carriage began the long climb into the hills. Cyril, not as careful with his role of steward once they had passed out into the empty hills, leaned across Rhea to peer out over the folds and protuberances of the rough terrain, his eyes searching for signs of habitation, current or ancient. He saw nothing so clearly definable as signs of life, noting the lines of snow still held in the shadowy places on the flanks of the hills. He shivered as a gust of icy wind swirled into the carriage and pulled the window back up.

"See anything?" Rhea asked mildly.

"Not what we're looking for."

"Perhaps Oslo will have more luck." She closed her eyes and settled back into the seat.

"It should be there for him to find." Cyril absently tapped his front teeth with the neatly manicured nail of the forefinger of his left hand. "After all, it's a standard device for any Jodan fortification. But they did tend to conceal their escape hatches. And who's to say it survived the last thousand years of abandonment?"

Rhea shrugged. "No sense worrying about it. If it's there, it's there. If not, not. Even if it is there, it still doesn't insure that we make it out of this intact." The lovely green eyes opened to regard Cyril, sparkling ferally. "That's what makes it interesting."

Cyril grinned at her. "Sometimes I think you live more on the edge than Oslo."

She laughed. "Close. I live for the edge. Oslo lives for the hunt."

The coach and escort wound deeper into the bare hills as the sun waxed and began to wane. The soldiers, servants and animals of the train made no noise but the sound of their passage, never speaking, never stopping. In the middle of the afternoon, the procession found the first obvious sign of life. A stocky man, bundled in a large gray cloak, watched them pass from the side of the road. No hands were raised, no greetings exchanged, and the coach and its escort passed on, following the smooth Jodan road ever deeper into the barren hills.

The pedestrian moved back into the middle of the road as the procession passed, and he began following the procession with long, distance-eating strides.

Cyril, Rhea and the rest of the procession reached the old Jodan Way Station while the sun still hung well above the horizon. The tall walls of the small fortress loomed above the road, but the stone gates had been shattered to ruin. The vanguard rode through the shattered gates without hesitation, and as servants silently dismounted to begin busily unloading pack animals and setting up camp, half of the soldiers left their horses behind to take up station around the walls. Those still mounted drew themselves into a defensive semicircle behind the gates and barricades, and waited silently. The animals stood in equal silence, uncomplaining, unmoving.

Cyril and Rhea, abandoning all pretense at steward and lady, scrambled out of the coach, unlocked and threw open the strongbox on the back of the coach, and began working their way into full sets of mail, every cold iron scale marked with a small rune. Weapons followed—a long sword for each, and two braces of long knives. Rhea buckled a small shield on her left arm while Cyril settled for a heavy set of vambraces. Last they removed bulging waterskins, bags of provisions, and a small hooded lantern apiece, set swinging from straps at their belts.

Cyril looked over at Rhea. "Feel better?"

"Less naked, anyway." One of the servants caught her eye, and Cyril followed as she stepped in front of a young girl. The girl's pretty face was expressionless, her blues eyes wide and unseeing in her flushed face. Something had caught her blouse and ripped it, pulling the top awry to expose the upper mound of her left breast and the chain of runes running like a black snake across her chest. Under and around the runes her skin was a mottling of red and gray, and pustules spread across her skin in a swath that stretched up to her collarbone.

While Rhea carefully pinned the blouse back into place, Cyril turned away, his face pale and sweating. He saw the edges of black traceries marking the hides of several horses, just visible under the shifted coverings from the day's travel, and swallowed heartfelt curses. When Rhea finished and the servant had fallen back with the others to continue her duties, Cyril muttered audibly, "I hate necromancy. I hate it."

"It's a good plan." Rhea led the way to the central building of the way station, pausing to light her lantern.

Cyril fumbled with his tinderbox. "I never said it wasn't a good plan. I just hate necromancy. Even in the best of causes. Even when practiced by two of the people I trust the most. Necromancy is a filthy business."

The air inside the building tasted dusty, old, and gray. No doors still stood between rooms, no furniture remained, no sign could be seen that anyone had lived in that place for years. The two of them searched systematically, beginning with the lower floors and working their way up the inset stone stairways to the rooms in the two floors above. On the third floor, in a small storeroom in the back of the station, Cyril found the object of their search. Two cunningly concealed stone panels swung away to reveal a spider web of tiny runes taller than a man and twice as wide as a normal doorway.

Cyril eyed the doors speculatively. "Pity we couldn't manage to coax a horse up all of those stairs."

Rhea raised an eyebrow as she made her way to an empty room across the way to settle by the nearest window with her back against the wall. "Those horses? I thought you didn't like necromancy."

Cyril shuddered. "On reflection, you're right. It's undoubtedly better this way." He settled down beside her to wait.

As the sun set and long fingers of darkness began to stretch out of the deep places between the hills, the traveler in the gray cloak came striding up the road. Cyril watched from the high window as the traveler walked without pausing through the ruins of the gates. The captain of the waiting horsemen rode forward, lifting his blade in challenge or salute, but the man in gray raised one hand and passed in silence through the company.

He walked through the servants without pausing. The servants had built several small fires around the courtyard and were going through the motions of cooking and eating—a shadow play that seemed relatively transparent at close proximity. But then, they were relying on the hunger of the Takers, not their discretion.

Cyril watched the traveler walk on through the camp, past the empty carriage, and disappear into the station. Cyril stepped away from the window and touched Rhea lightly on the shoulder. She lifted her head from her knees and rose to meet the traveler with a smile as he stepped into the doorway of the room where Cyril and Rhea waited.

After the first startled glance at his face, Cyril laughed. "Good disguise, Oslo. Anything moving on the road after us?"

The lined face of an old man, his face seamed with years and the weather, creased into a smile. The traveler bowed his head, scrubbing vigorously at his face, and a fine dust of sparkling runes sifted like ashes to the floor. When he raised his head, the face of a much younger man, somewhere in his mid-thirties, regarded them. "Nothing and no one, that I saw. They're probably gathering. We may not even be hit the first night. How went the journey?"

"Not bad," Rhea said. "People see what they expect to see. As long as we didn't spend too much time anywhere, we were fine." She stepped close and hugged him. "Did you find it?"

He returned her embrace. "No. I don't know where the Jodan have hidden it. Perhaps it's been destroyed. My nights in the hills were uneventful." He pulled his cloak around himself and settled into a corner, pulling Rhea down beside him. "Maybe the Takers thought that an old man such as myself would taste too stringy. Maybe they didn't notice me."

"And maybe the Takers are gone."

"I don't think so." He reached into his cloak, pulled out a small flat bone, and handed it to Cyril. "I found most of a skeleton in the hills. Small woman or a child, I'd say. Fairly fresh. It had been gnawed clean, the long bones splintered for the marrow."

Cyril turned the bone in his hand. "It could have been an animal." His voice trailed off. "Surely those aren't teeth marks!" he exclaimed in sudden alarm. He held the bone up into the light. Myriad small grooves striated the surface of the bone neatly.

Oslo nodded. "That's not a pattern made by any human or animal I'm familiar with. The rows are close together, almost like a shark's teeth, but no shark feeds thus."

"And we're miles from any ocean," Rhea added dryly. "What did you think of the innkeeper?" she asked suddenly.

"Down at the crossroads?" Oslo leaned forward. "I spent little time there. But the man never smiled."

"Always careful not to show his teeth," Rhea said thoughtfully.

Cyril's eyes widened. "But he warned us away."

Oslo shook his head. "Doesn't matter. He could still have Taker blood. If they can breed with humans. He might be following local custom, if Taker blood is in the local community. But if the Takers are most obvious because of their teeth, anyone in the area should be always smiling if they have nothing to hide."

"My thought exactly," Rhea said. "It would show that they're human."

Cyril retched. "Interbreeding? With those things?"

"We haven't seen a Taker, yet. We don't know how close they are to human. All we have to go on are disappearances, old tales, and Jodan records. To the Jodan they were monstrous both for what they did and what they were. Even the Jodan spoke of Taker half-breeds in the Ash Hills, and of certain Taker...habits."

"Do you think they'll take the bait?" Rhea asked mildly.

"I hope so," Oslo replied. "We're along to provide a good, clean, healthy human scent. The rest are pretty neutral. The sickness in our bait is held static by the runes. When the runes are broken, the Takers will release the most virulent plague in recent history back into their dens."

"Plus the extra nastiness you added," Cyril noted. "Unclean methods for an unclean war."

"This isn't a war," Oslo corrected him. "This is extermination. Monster hunting. You poison rats, you don't declare war on them. But for intelligent vermin, both trap and poison need to be more elaborate."

"What about portal stones," Rhea asked impatiently. "Did you find any?"

"None intact," Oslo said. "Doesn't mean that more aren't out there. I should be able to tell from the master here if any are left intact."

Harsh, wet sounds rose through the open windows of the Station, and the three hunters rose as one and ran across the building to look down into the courtyard below. In the flickering light of the servant's fires, the line of horsemen could be seen bowing back before the pressure of a mass of shadowy forms. The observers could make out little detail in the poor light, but some armor and weapons could be seen in the chaos. The attackers pushed with savage determination against the line of horsemen, who in turn chopped methodically down with swords and axes from the height of their saddles. None of them—the watchers, the animals, the servants, the soldiers, or the raiders— made any outcry as the battle sharpened, casting an eerie pall of silence over the scene, broken only by the scraping of blades on armor and the softness underneath that, the impact of heavy bodies, the ripping of torn flesh and the splintering of broken bone.

The dismounted troops came rushing into the fray as the first horse fell, borne over backwards by the unceasing pressure of the raiders. Then the next horse fell, and the next, and then the footmen filled the gap, and it seemed for a moment as if they would hold against the tide of bodies, even though the circle kept stretching further and further back into the courtyard. Then dark shapes could be seen flowing silently over and down the walls, and always more reinforcements filled the gate, pushing forward hungrily against their fellows.

"They mustered a considerable force, and more quickly than we thought. And they're picking up weapons where they've fallen," Cyril said thoughtfully.

"They also eat their own dead," Oslo noted, clinical distance in his voice. "That's good for us. Indicates a none too discriminating appetite, and assures the spread of the plague."

Rhea watched the first of the Takers break through the line and rush into the huddled servants. "Don't you think you should be working on that portal?" she asked Oslo pointedly.

He nodded, turned, and strode back into the room across the way where the runes waited. Rhea followed Oslo, while Cyril stayed at the window, watching the battle unfold.

At the portal, Oslo bent forward, placing his mouth almost on the runes, and spoke a quiet, breathy phrase. Light spread outward from his mouth, sparkling along the pattern in threads of color. Oslo stepped back, and struck the pattern with the nail of his middle finger. A single musical tone rang through the chamber.

Cyril cursed from the window, ran out of the opposite room with a long knife in his right hand and his sword in his left. He met the first Taker in the hallway. He took it through the body with his sword, and finished it with his knife as it scrabbled at his armor with clawed fingers and a mouth filled with jagged teeth.

"We need to move," Rhea called to Oslo impatiently.

Another tone sounded from the runes. "I'm searching for a good transfer point, love. We don't want to try a broken marker stone, trust me."

Rhea joined Cyril in the hallway as two more Takers appeared. Wide mouths gleamed with too many teeth in the light of their lanterns. The heavy maces they carried were dark against their pale skin.

Rhea lunged under the first stroke of the Taker on the left, driving the point of her blade under the raised arm and through lungs and heart. It vomited bright blood and fell, but its mace came down on her hip, the shock of impact deadening her right leg.

Cyril deftly took his opponent's hand off at the wrist, closed, and drove his dagger through its right eye. The Taker folded like an empty suit of clothes.

Behind them, a cascade of pure sweet music rose from the storeroom. "Let's do it now," Oslo bellowed.

Cyril saw Rhea leaning against the wall, put his arm around her, the bloody knife still jutting from his fist, and half-dragged her through the door. Oslo waited before a doorway opening into shadows, dim moonlight, and bare stone. When he saw them, he crossed the room as Rhea sheathed her blade. He caught her free arm. Together the three of them stepped through the portal and found themselves standing in the throat of a cave.

A word from Oslo, and the portal closed behind them.

Cyril looked around, saw the spiral webs of runes that faced each other from opposite sides of the cave, and then looked down to see the stacks of bone neatly arranged before each transfer marker. "This is not a good place to be," he said softly.

Oslo nodded, taking one look behind them into the impenetrable darkness of the deeper cave before turning his face toward the dim glow filtering through the cave mouth. Together, he and Cyril helped walk Rhea to the open air. The moon stood high above the looming rock walls that enclosed a narrow crevice, casting light down on the three. Cyril and Rhea paused to dim the light of their lanterns. Seeing no activity, they began following the long, winding crevice of rock that sheltered the cave mouth, moving as quickly as they could with Rhea's leg and the need they all felt for stealth.

After a few minutes of progress, Cyril and Oslo could feel Rhea easing her weight back on her leg. Once a little more time had passed, she gestured for them to stop, and began roughly massaging her leg and hip. After a brief rest, they continued, Rhea limping alongside the men in silence. About a thousand paces further down the way, the crevice opened out onto a hillside.

Oslo studied the terrain critically. "The portal didn't take us as far as I would have hoped."

"And it dumped us right in the mouth of a den, it looks like," Cyril said. "If they track by scent, we're screwed."

"We'll have to make good time." Rhea gave Oslo a sidelong glance. "They're denning in old Jodan shelters?"

He nodded as they started walking again. "And it looks like the Takers have expanded them. These hills are probably one big warren. We need to move fast." He put one hand on Rhea's shoulder and spoke in a worried tone. "Can you make it?"

She shook his hand off. "Nothing broken. I'm just bruised. You two try to keep up."

Cyril chuckled as Oslo nodded and set a hard pace across the hills.

Two days later, Cyril took a long drink from his water skin, lowering it with reluctance to look down at the distant farms nestled among the trees. "Three days, and I long for civilization."

Oslo shook his head, grinning. "There are hunters, and there are hunters." He sobered. "We take the long way out, and stay apart until we reach some fortifications. We don't know who, if any, of the locals were in with the Takers, and we don't want to bring the Takers down on anyone unprepared for that kind of confrontation."

Rhea looked back up the scrub and brush covered slope of the foothills. "I haven't seen movement for a while."

"It's closer here, away from the bare rock of the Ash Hills." Oslo cocked his head, listening. "Don't underestimate them. They're excellent hunters. In this terrain, we won't see them until they're on us."

His words might have been prophecy. As they stepped into the next clearing, an easy score of thick forms rose around them from cover. Seen clearly in the daylight, the Takers were pale, lean, and strongly muscular, their arms and legs jointed oddly, giving them a crouching posture not natural for a man. Large eyes opened above a gash of a mouth bristling with small, pointed teeth. They were just close enough to human to make a human observer uneasy.

All bore weapons, all seemed to be male, and all were covered with open, running sores—the most obvious early sign of the plague. One, larger than the rest, stepped closer to Oslo. A glaive dangled casually from one massive, filthy hand. Runes covered the four foot haft and the three foot blade of the weapon. Piecemeal chain armor had been split to provide at least partial cover for the Taker's massive limbs and torso. His free hand rose to point at the three monster hunters, and he rumbled a string of words.

Oslo answered immediately in the same language.

Cyril leaned closer to Rhea. "Jodan?"

She nodded grimly. "They've been tracking us since the first signs of sickness hit. They know that we're responsible."

Oslo spoke again, his eyes locked on the glaive in the leader's hand. The Taker rasped something akin to laughter and began walking toward Oslo.

Oslo turned quickly to the two of them. "Stay here. Watch yourselves. He's not quite taking my challenge seriously, but they do seem to have a pack mentality, and he's the leader."

Oslo walked out to meet the Taker, shrugging a pair of twenty-inch blades into his hands from under his cloak. The big Taker paused, wheeled the glaive through a vicious circle, and charged Oslo. The other Takers shifted where they stood, but waited and watched.

Oslo met the leader's charge, deflecting a thrust with crossed blades. He stepped back and circled to avoid a slash, then closed as his opponent turned, driving down with one knife in an overhand blow that fell inside the chain where it draped over the Taker's shoulder. The Taker slashed as he turned, then paused, the hilt of Oslo's knife projecting grotesquely up from his collarbone. Oslo's cloak flapped loosely, split lengthwise by the Taker's blade. The hunter unfastened and stepped out of the cloak in a single movement, rune-etched scale armor shining dully as the gray cloth fell away.

A low murmur passed through the Takers, and they took a collective step forward, tightening the circle. Rhea reached for her blade, but Cyril stopped her with a gesture. "Don't mess with the balance. Let it happen. We move only if the Takers do."

Abruptly the leader charged Oslo again. Oslo slipped inside the arc of the blade gracefully, caught the haft of the glaive with his free hand, and struck past the shaft as the Taker instinctively pulled the weapon closer.

Again Oslo struck down through the collarbone, inside the chain mail, this time on the side opposite to his other blow. Bloody foam burst out of the Taker's mouth. Oslo stepped back, twisting the haft of the glaive, and broke the weapon free of the Taker's grip.

The Taker groaned deeply. His hands rose fumbling for the hilts of the knives jutting from his shoulders. Oslo stroked the blade of the glaive lightly with one hand, spoke a word, and the blade burst into white flame.

The Takers swayed back as Oslo spun the glaive into a fiery wheel, half-turned, and drove the burning blade through his adversary's body. The big Taker bent double, the head of the glaive visible through his skin like a candle shining through wax paper. Then his entire body exploded into flame, and Oslo stepped back, drawing the blade out of his enemy's body. The big Taker folded forward, collapsing on himself like a burning house.

Oslo swung his gaze around the ring of Takers. "I am your death," he told them in Jodan. "Go. Or not."

The Takers faded back into the underbrush, but not before one paused to answer Oslo in broken Jodan. Oslo watched them go, quelled the flame of the glaive with a word, and walked slowly back to Cyril and Rhea, his face thoughtful.

"Are they done with us, then?" Cyril asked.

Oslo nodded. "They'll try to make it back to their homes, to die with their families, if any remain."

Cyril frowned. "You sound almost sympathetic."

"You heard what the last one said to me?" Oslo asked Rhea.

"'We pass away, and you come to replace us. I have faith that this is nature. But what will replace you, I wonder?'" she translated softly.

Oslo considered the glaive in his hands. "The works of the Jodan remain. We know nothing greater than the art of their hands. Yet nothing of them lingers but a few records, some broken buildings, a few scattered artifacts, and a dead language. What will time do with us?"

Cyril snorted. "Philosophy from ghouls, now! To blazes with that. Let's go tell the Young Dux that the road through these hills should be clear, at least for a time."

"Sounds like a good idea," Rhea said. "I need a bath and some hot food."

Cyril laughed. "And something to drink besides water."

Rhea looked curiously at the silent Oslo. "What do you need, love?"

He gave her a half-smile. "More faith, perhaps."

Cyril shook his head.

Oslo regarded him curiously. "What?"

Cyril chuckled. "Oh, I was just thinking about that innkeeper. You know, the one we suspect might have had Taker blood?"

Rhea raised a single eyebrow. "What about him?"

Cyril grinned. "How much joy do you think he'll have of his heritage, if our speculations are true? As the ghouls die, which will take him first, the plague or his neighbors?"

Rhea and Oslo looked at one another without speaking for a long moment.

Nothing more was said as Oslo led them down to the lowlands. For some little while, at least, the hills would again be clean.

SURVIVAL INSTINCT

by Elaine Corvidae

*Elaine Corvidae has worked as an office assistant, archae-
ologist, and raptor rehabilitator. She is currently earning
her Masters degree in Biology at the University of North
Carolina-Charlotte. She lives near Charlotte, NC, with her
husband and three cats. Her first published novel, WINTER'S
ORPHANS, was the recipient of the 2001 Dream Realm
Award and the 2002 Eppie Award.*

Later on, Coyote thought he should have known something strange
would happen the day the girl fell out of the sky.

He opened his eyes in the dark, going from dream to waking so
fast that he lay still, listening hard for anything that might have disturbed him: the shuffle of a step, the sound of breathing, the sense
that the shadows had taken on weight and substance. But there was
nothing.

Huh. Just jumpy, I guess.

When he felt certain that it was safe, he sat up and pulled the
cover off the chemflash beside his bed. Its pale, greenish light illuminated the confines of his den, an enormous, round cylinder made
from a single piece of concrete, either end blocked by rubble. CrashFox
had claimed it was part of a storm drain leading away from the old
spaceport, but Coyote had been living here for years and it always
stayed dry even in the heaviest rains, so he figured maybe it had been
something else after all.

A shaky ladder built out of old steel pipe bonded together with
epoxy leaned against one rubble-fall, leading up to a ragged hole in the
ceiling. Coyote climbed up and stood with his head just level with the
opening, listening and smelling. A lizard slithered away from the edge,
darting deeper into the cover of the sage bushes that hid the entrance
to his den. The sun was starting to set, but the heat of the day still
clung to the dry land.

The wind was out of the west, and that was safe, so he climbed
the rest of the way out. You didn't go out when the wind came from the
south—that was death, just to breathe it, or at least it used to be

according to the old timers. Still wasn't good for a body—stung your skin like acid and made your eyes redden and burn. Maybe it just killed you slower these days.

The western sky was turning a deep purple, streaked with red and gold, and the ruined towers of the old spaceport looked black against it, like fingers reaching for the stars. Coyote stopped for a moment to look at it, and as he did so he caught a flash of brown and gray out of the corner of his eye. There was a real coyote there, just a little down the rise, its amber eyes fixed on him like it was waiting to see what he would do next.

He grinned. "Hey, brother. Don't got nothing for you tonight. Got to find your own dinner."

The coyote was used to him and so it didn't run off when he spoke. It had figured out a long time ago that he'd throw it any scraps he could spare. CrashFox said people had tried to kill off its kind years ago: poisoned 'em, trapped 'em, shot 'em. But nothing worked, cause coyotes knew that there were only two rules in the whole world that mattered.

Adapt.

Survive.

Just then the coyote jumped and looked towards the west. Instantly on guard, Coyote looked too, and saw something new against the sunset.

There were lights in the sky, like the stars you saw sometimes on nights after a calm day, when most of the dust had gotten a chance to settle. But these stars moved, swarming like insects, flaring up bright and going dim. As he stared at them, wondering what they might be, he realized they were getting closer—or maybe he could just see them better as the sun went down.

There came a faint, far-off boom, an explosion he could feel vibrate in his bones more than hear with his ears. The stars turned into comets, streaking across the sky, tails of smoke reflecting back the very last light of a sun that was already invisible to him. Horizon to horizon they raced; then, far in the east, he saw a flare a few moments before he felt the deep shake of another explosion.

What the hell?

"The stars are coming down to dance," that's what CrashFox would've said if he were still alive. And then M8r would have thrown a pot at his head and told him he was stupid, that the stars weren't nothing more than far-away suns and couldn't come down to dance, and that if his ancestors thought different it was because they were just as drunk as he was.

The shooting stars lessened in number and became smaller, fiery wisps that burned out before they touched the ground. But just as Coyote was about to turn away and head back to his den, the biggest one of all came into view. Only this one wasn't racing across the sky—

it was coming down slow. And in the hot, angry red of its glow, he caught sight of what looked like a parachute spread out behind it, slowing its plunge even further.

He took a nervous step back. Damn thing looked for a while like it was going to come down right on top of him, but instead it landed a few rises over, out of sight of his den but near enough that he felt the thump in his feet when it hit earth.

"Shit. Now what?" he asked, but he was alone. Real coyotes were smart enough to get the hell out of the way when pieces of the sky started falling.

Uncertainty gnawed at him. He didn't know what it was—that alone was a good argument for leaving it untouched. But others had to have seen the falling stars, and they had probably tracked the last one down, too. Regular folks and maybe even bounty boiz would be out here as soon as the sun was up, poking around for whatever they could find that might be useful. But they wouldn't come out here at night—he was the only one loco enough for that, they said—so if there was anything good to salvage, it was his clear and free.

And if it's something that's gonna kill you, that's yours clear and free, too.

꒰꒱

It was some kind of pod, the heatshield on the bottom ticking softly as it cooled in the desert night. The huge parachute draped out behind it, half hung-up on a stand of cactus. Coyote approached slowly, the whole idea seeming worse and worse with every second that passed. The pod had landed hatch-side up, and he stood there for a long while waiting for something to move. When nothing did, he cautiously came close and touched his fingers lightly to a recessed handle with an emergency symbol over it. The metal was still uncomfortably warm, but not hot enough to burn, so he popped the hatch and peered inside.

The figure within was all bundled up in a jumpsuit of some kind, a helmet and facemask covering its head and gloves over its hands. The inside of the little pod reeked of burned insulation and wiring, and there were charred patches on the jumpsuit.

"You alive in there?" Coyote asked, but the figure didn't stir. Hoping that the damaged pod wasn't going to blow up or something, he climbed inside and carefully pulled off the facemask and helmet.

It was a girl. Fresh bruises ringed both eyes, and a trickle of drying blood traced a track from nose to chin. His first thought was that she had to be dead, because he'd never seen anybody as pale as her, but when he touched the side of her neck he felt a pulse flutter like a baby bird under his fingers.

Damn. He sat back on his heels, wondering what to do. No telling how bad she was hurt, and the nearest doctor was a few days away by motor, which he didn't have. If she was banged up inside, there wasn't anything he could do, and he didn't like the idea of sitting around watching her die slow. Not that dying fast was such a great thing, either—sure hadn't been when CrashFox had gone down in a spray of blood and brains.

Well, he couldn't just let her lie there all night, either. Maybe if somebody like M8r found her in the morning, she'd be okay, but if Strik9 found her first, then Coyote might as well just cut her throat now. Strik9 and his boiz sure wouldn't hesitate to.

He didn't want to hurt her worse by moving her, though, so he started checking for broken bones, hoping like hell she didn't wake up in the middle of it and take his feeling her up the wrong way. He kept his touch light as he could, starting with her legs and working to her head.

And for a minute he figured she'd been hurt bad. The skull under her short-cut hair felt lumpy to his touch, and he thought for sure she'd been smashed up in the fall. But the small bumps and ridges were hard and smooth and regular, not like injuries at all. More like she had something extra under there.

She moaned, and he moved back quick, not wanting to scare her. Her eyes opened, and just that fast she was conscious, her gaze wary and alert and locked on him. It didn't seem normal to him, that sudden waking...but what the hell did he know about girls who fell out of the sky?

"You okay, *muchacha*?"

She didn't say anything, just stared at him. Taking in her surroundings and trying to decide what to do next, he figured.

"I seen you fall out of the sky," he added, pointing up. "You hurt? No doctors around here, but I got some bandages and stuff. Or I can take you over to Watertown if you want."

For a moment he wasn't even sure she understood him. Then she said, "Who are you?" Her voice was soft and a little raspy, and she had a funny accent, but her words were clear enough.

"Coyote," he said. "Who're you?"

But she didn't answer, only looked around, her expression getting more and more frantic. She was scared, he decided. Maybe the desert seemed like a strange place to girls who fell out of the sky.

Anyway, they couldn't sit there all night, so he got up and held out his hand. She drew back and shook her head.

Didn't trust him, but he couldn't blame her for that. "You know your way around here?" he asked, although he knew by the look on her face she didn't. "Know where to find good water? How to get to town? Where the safe places are if the wind turns around and comes out of the south?"

Confusion and fear in her pale eyes. Then she shook her head.

"Then you got no choice but to trust me."

She looked sick, but after a long moment she put her gloved hand out and let him help her up.

Adapt.

Survive.

୬ ୧

He'd meant to take her straight to M8r in Watertown, but she was shaky on her feet and looked like she might pass out again, so instead he led her back to the den. He hadn't had anybody else there with him since CrashFox had died. It felt weird to have another presence nearby; the air was suddenly filled with all the little sounds a person makes just by living.

There was a ledge about four feet high on both sides of the gigantic culvert, and the sky girl perched on it while he made them dinner. Hopper stew with some chunks of fresh cactus thrown in; a couple of heat tabs warmed it up so that it steamed in the rapidly-cooling air. She kept her gloves on when he handed her a bowl made from a turtle shell he'd found bleached white by the sun. The look on her face was one of faint horror.

"God," she whispered. "It's like I've gone back to the Stone Age."

Maybe she was still rattled or something. "No way," he said. "I got all kinds of good stuff here. Best you're gonna see this side of Watertown."

Although he wasn't boasting—or not much—the statement didn't seem to cheer her up at all. She ate her stew listlessly, then wrapped her arms around her knees, a sad, huddled thing made of despair.

"What's your name?" he asked, hoping to cheer her up a little.

She blinked slowly…then spat out a long string of numbers and letters that he couldn't even begin to follow.

"Okay," he said, wondering if that was supposed to be her name, or if she was just cussing him out. "Um…you got anything shorter than that I can call you?"

The swelling around her eyes seemed to have gone down a little. She stared at him like he was something she'd never seen before…and slowly shook her head.

The movement was stiff, and he realized that she was in pain, so he suggested they get some sleep. His bed was a mattress stuffed with sage and herbs that kept the bugs down, and he offered it to her since she was hurt. Distrust flared in her eyes, and although she lay down, she kept all her clothes on, down to her boots and gloves. He made a nest of blankets in a far corner and covered up the chemflash before stripping down to his pants. The concrete floor was hard, and he missed his mattress. In the silence, he could hear the sound of her breathing, and knew that she wasn't asleep. Despite her injuries, which she wouldn't let him look at, she wasn't about to let down her guard.

Maybe he shouldn't, either. Maybe he was as loco as everybody said. After all, what did he know about girls who fell out of the sky? Hell, she might kill him in his sleep.

As he lay in the dark, he tried to remember everything CrashFox had told him about the stars and the sky. But the only stories he could think of were ones that involved people being thrown up in the heavens to become stars, or climbing up tall trees to reach the sky. Going up, not coming down, which didn't help him a damn bit so far as he could see.

Course there were always the stories that said falling stars were an omen of death, that somebody died for every one you saw. Falling stars and falling girls didn't necessarily mean the same thing, of course.

Did they?

⁓ ⁓

The girl fell asleep anyway, whatever her intentions might have been, because she was snoring softly when he woke up around dawn. Dawn and dusk, those were the best times, the safest times, to go out, so he did. On his way to a small, well-hidden spring of good water, he spotted his neighbor the real coyote again. It lay near the base of a tall cactus, eating some small thing it had caught, and looked at him with an expression that seemed to say he was damned stupid for taking in some girl who barely spoke, who didn't seem to know anything about surviving. Wherever she came from, up there in the sky, things were obviously a hell of a lot different than they were down here, and he'd bet that she didn't know about finding food, or that you could get water out of cacti if you were desperate, or anything that he took for granted.

On the way back to the den, he stopped in the cover of the sagebrush and watched the western horizon. As the sun got higher, he could see a plume of dust heading in the direction of the girl's pod.

"What is that?"

He jumped, because he hadn't heard her climbing up the ladder, even though it should have creaked and groaned and made a hell of a lot of noise. In the morning light, she looked paler than ever. The bruises around her eyes had turned an ugly brown, and the whites had gone almost red. Something to do with her fall, he guessed, remembering the blood that had come out of her nose and mouth when he first found her.

Coyote turned his attention back to the dust plume. "Motor. Probably Strik9 and his crew—they're the only ones with a rambler big enough to kick up that much sand. Going after your pod, I guess."

"No!" Her face went white, and she lunged half-out of the sage, as if she was going to take off running across the desert in the heat and the sun and everything.

Startled, he grabbed her gloved wrist, yanking her back. "Stay down! You crazy or something? That Strik9 wants to be a bounty boi—

he's gonna see that pod and be wondering where the person in it went."

"But it's mine, it's mine, they have no right!" she shouted at him, and he could see tears starting up in her swollen eyes. But she sat down again, and after a minute he let go of her wrist.

"I'm sorry," he said. "I am. But there's nothing we can do. You can't fall out of the sky in a big streak of light and think nobody's gonna notice, *muchacha*. That's why I busted my ass getting out there—cause I knew Strik9 would be coming as soon as the sun was up. He's bad news. Why you think I live all the way out here, if not to get the hell away from the likes of him?"

He didn't know whether she understood what he was saying or not, because she didn't react, just huddled into a ball and shivered, obviously fighting back tears. But at least she was smart enough to listen to his first warning and not just take off half-cocked, without knowing the dangers. Maybe she was starting to learn.

Adapt.

Survive.

⁊≈

They were in the middle of dinner that night when the girl went crazy.

As the sun sank over the horizon, the wind had started coming up with a vengeance, and Coyote could hear the eerie singsong that presaged a sandstorm. As it built in intensity, the girl had started glancing up worriedly, unnerved by the howl of the sand around the rocks and through the sage.

"It's okay—we're safe down here," he started to say. "It's just—"

Her eyes went blank suddenly, as if he wasn't there, or she couldn't see him at all. An expression of joy lit up her face, and she sprang to her feet, dumping her bowl to the floor. *Wopati* went everywhere, and the shell cracked in half.

"Yes! I'm receiving you, Base One!" she yelled at nobody he could see. "Come in! Come in!" She rattled off the long string of numbers and letters that might have been her name, her entire body taut with anticipation, her gaze locked on nothing.

But then, suddenly, she shook her head, like a fly was buzzing around it or something. "I'm not getting you—the transmission is garbled—"

Her eyes refocused on the room—and lit on the ladder. A second later she was scrambling up it, yelling and chattering and demanding that somebody talk to her, answer her, tell her something that made *sense*.

The whole time, Coyote'd been sitting there with his mouth hanging open. The girl was past loco—sun-touched or god-touched or something, talking to people who weren't there. But seeing her head up the ladder into the sandstorm broke him from his paralysis.

"Stop!" he yelled, and went after her, scared that she was going to just disappear off into the storm, following ghosts or mirages, and he'd find her bleached bones lying in a wash someday.

The screen of sage kept down the sand, and this wasn't one of the killer storms that sometimes blew up and savaged every living thing in its path. But it was bad enough—the night was utterly black, and even the chemflash that he'd grabbed on his way up the ladder didn't show anything past a few feet. Grit stung his skin and eyes, and he swore furiously, thinking maybe he ought to just leave her to her madness and save his own damn hide.

But he held up the chemflash and took a couple of steps, and there she was, standing at the edge of the sage, one hand up to block the sand from her face.

"I don't understand you!" she shouted at whatever ghosts plagued her. "It's just gibberish. Is it a code? I wasn't briefed—"

Then suddenly she fell silent, head cocked to one side. A look of utter confusion passed over her face. "I don't...I don't understand," she mumbled in her raspy voice, so quiet he could barely hear her over the wind and the sand. "I'm getting a targeting image—but I'm not hooked up, there isn't anything to feed it in."

He had no idea what she was talking about—figured it was just the kind of nonsense that crazy people said sometimes, when they couldn't help themselves any. "It isn't safe out here, *muchacha*," he said in what he thought was a reasonable tone of voice. "We got to go back—"

Then she was yelling and cursing, her whole body bent over double, her hands clawing frantically at her head. He couldn't understand half of what she was screaming about—electromagnetic interference, and shadow images, and echoes and implants and he didn't even know what. Grabbing at her wrists, he forced them down, trying to keep her from hurting herself the way she was tearing at her head. She looked up...and for an instant he thought she was going to attack him in her wildness, for reasons that maybe made sense in her crazy brain and maybe didn't.

But all the fight suddenly went out of her, and she collapsed, crying in great, wracking sobs that shook her whole body. With a sigh he picked her up—she was a small thing—and carried her back down the ladder and out of the wind.

Her sobs were louder away from the noise of the storm, and she beat ineffectually at his shoulder with one fist. "I hate this," she moaned in her broken voice. "I hate this, I hate you, oh gods I just want to go home."

And wasn't it just his luck—a girl fell down out of the sky, just about on top of *his* head, and turned out to be damn crazy, and hated him for something he had no part of at all. Wasn't his fault she was down here. Maybe he should have left her for Strik9.

But though she was hitting him with one hand, she was clinging with the other, her fingers gripping a lock of his long hair so tight that it made his eyes water. *She's hurting, that's all. Misses the sky and everything up there. And who can blame her?*

The girl leaned her head against his shoulder and cried and cried. Not knowing what else to do, he just sat down on the ledge and rocked her, stroking her head and making little shushing noises. After a while she relaxed her grip on his hair and fell asleep, worn out from sheer exhaustion and hurt. He rocked her for a little while longer, though, liking the weight and feel of her body in his arms.

And wondered what he'd do if she did manage to climb back up to the sky and leave him alone again.

༄༅

"We ought to go into town today," Coyote said the next morning, in that gray time between night and dawn.

She seemed to have recovered from her craziness…and of course had gone right back to being quiet. Like she could only talk much when she was nuts, and the rest of the time had to stay shut up tight like a turtle in its shell. Now she just looked at him curiously, maybe like she was wondering about *his* sanity.

"Strik9 will still be out messing around with your pod, if we're lucky," he went on, despite her look. "I didn't know I was gonna have a guest, so I don't have much supplies on hand. Sure don't have anything a girl might need for her monthlies or nothing like that."

The puzzled-as-hell look stayed on her face. "Why are you doing this?" She looked around, seeming lost. "Helping me?"

"Well," he said, not sure how to put it in a way that would make sense to a girl who fell out of the sky. "CrashFox used to tell a lot of stories about people in trouble. Guests showing up at the door with no warning, strangers in need on the road, stuff like that. And they'd always turn out to be disguised gods, or fairies, or angels, or animal spirits, or something like that. Rewarded or punished depending on how they'd been treated. I figure you aren't nothing like them, even if you did fall out of the sky, but I still got CrashFox's message. You see somebody in need, especially somebody who seems helpless, you do right by them. And maybe someday somebody will do the same for me."

He could tell she didn't understand. Thought he was loco, just like everybody else, probably. So he just sighed and picked up a backpack stuffed full of things he would try to barter in Watertown. "Come on. The sun will be up soon."

༄༅

Normally it was only a couple of hours walk into town, but the girl was either still hurting or just wasn't used to a lot of walking.

Maybe people who lived up among the stars went everywhere by motor, or just flew around in ships like the ones that CrashFox said had used the spaceport before the plague.

At any rate, it took them until almost noon to get to Watertown, and by that time Coyote was sweating and the girl looked about ready to faint. He'd given her an old blanket to shield her from the sun, seeing how pale she was, but even so she was stumbling a little by the time M8r's place came into view.

Watertown wasn't much to look at. Its biggest attraction was the heavily-guarded well of safe water, which was sold at outrageous prices to travelers who didn't know how to find water on their own out here, or who had to stick to the roads where most of the old wells had gone bad. Just a cluster of dusty buildings, some of them made of concrete and prefab, others of adobe. Antennae and dishes sprouted from most of the roofs, black against the harsh glare of the noonday sun.

The inside of M8r's place was cool and soothing. Letting the thick blanket that served as a door drop back into place, Coyote waited a moment for his eyes to adjust. The little building served as a way station for travelers and a trading post for locals, and the front room was lined with shelves. Machine parts, electronics, vac-packed sweets, jars of pickled cactus, first-aid kits, and clothing all jostled for space, spilling over onto the floor in some places.

A low hum announced the arrival of the little cart M8r used to get around in. She'd been born without any legs, something CrashFox swore could have been corrected a hundred years ago, either with gene therapy when she was an embryo or with vat-grown grafts later on in life. But Coyote figured that was just another of the 'things used to be better way back when' stories that old folks liked to tell to make it seem like the current generation was sending the world straight to hell. Probably wasn't nothing to it, and anyway M8r made due with her little cart and seemed to do pretty damn well for herself, so far as Coyote could tell.

The girl shrank back against Coyote's side, and he felt a weird flush of pleasure. Not that she was needy, but that she trusted him, at least a little. "It's okay," he said, and patted her on the shoulder, which drew a confused look.

M8r's dark eyes didn't miss much. But Coyote trusted her—she wasn't one to go mouthing off to bounty boiz and grrlz, not after what had happened to her kids. "Haven't seen you for a while, Coyote," she said neutrally.

"I need some stuff," he said, shrugging his backpack off. "Got some good trade today." Useful plants he'd gathered and dried, a pretty pair of earrings he'd found just lying in the sand one day, all kinds of things he scavenged and scrounged up from the desert.

She just nodded, like he walked in with strange, nameless girls everyday, and they started haggling. Gave him a real good deal on some extra clothes and blankets and such for the girl, too, so he figured that she probably knew there was something weird going on and wanted to help out a little, maybe just cause she liked him and maybe just to spit in the bounty boiz faces.

The sky girl didn't say anything the whole time, just watched with her pale, bloodshot eyes. Coyote wondered if her brains had gotten rattled loose in her fall, or if it was just another part of her craziness, or if it was just all so different from what she was used to that she didn't know what to do.

M8r gave them some free water to drink on the way back, "in memory of old CrashFox," she said. And added: "You watch out, Coyote. Strik9 went out yesterday, so he might be on his way back."

He just nodded. He hadn't planned on taking so long to get here, not realizing the girl couldn't go any faster. And it would probably take even longer to get back, seeing as how she was all worn out now.

A long, exposed walk back into the desert...and Strik9 and his boiz out there somewhere.

≈≈

Coyote knew his luck had run out when he saw the plume of dust coming over the rise.

They weren't even halfway back to the den, in an open place with no cover, and he cursed furiously even as fear iced his veins. The girl froze and frowned at him, obviously unsure as to what was wrong.

Well, it wouldn't take long for her to find out. "Drop your things and get ready to run," he advised.

"Why?"

He swallowed, watching helplessly as the plume got closer. The feeling of an animal in a trap closed over him, and his heart beat harder and harder, until he thought it might rattle straight out of his chest. The sound of bolt fire seemed to echo in his ears, along with CrashFox's dying scream.

"That's Strik9's rambler," he said through a throat that felt so tight he could barely breathe. "He wants to be a bounty boi."

Come back, come back little rat, yelled the voices in his memory. Bolt fire kicked the sand up as he ran, heart pounding, knowing that if Strik9 caught him he'd end up sold off or worse. And then CrashFox shouting at them to stop, coming in between and catching the bolt meant for Coyote.

The rambler growled up the slope and creaked to a halt. Heavily-armed figures were already jumping off the sides, their goggles reflecting the sunset like insect eyes. Within seconds, they had surrounded Coyote and the girl.

Damn it, no!

"I'm sorry," he whispered to her. What had he been thinking, dragging her out here with him? Why hadn't he left her safe in the den?

Strik9 climbed down out of the rambler's cab, strutting slowly across the sand until he stood in front of Coyote. His goggles were shoved back, and his eyes were hard and cruel and filled with hateful laughter.

"We meet again, little rat," he said. His eyes flicked to the girl, and he smiled viciously. "And what do we have here?"

"Leave her alone," Coyote said desperately, even knowing it wouldn't do any good.

Strik9 gave him a look that said he was a fool. "We've just gotten back from a crash site, rat. And now you turn up with a bit dressed all funny, like she isn't from around here. I guess you're going to tell me she doesn't have anything to do with that pod in the back of the rambler?"

"Give it back to me!" the girl said, blowing any chance Coyote might have to talk their way out the situation. Her eyes were cold and wild, and her hands balled into fists. She had taken off her gloves and tucked them into her belt. Coyote thought he saw a flash of metal, like maybe she was wearing rings.

Strik9 and his boiz laughed. "Sure thing," Strik9 said. "We'll chain you to it, if you want. Or even if you don't. There's people who'll pay good to have you along with that piece of metal." His eyes flicked disinterestedly over her charred and dirty jumpsuit. "Even if you aren't much to look at. Some folks like novelty, you know."

Fear and rage surged through Coyote, and he flung himself at Srik9 with an incoherent yell. A second later, Strik9's fist connected hard with his gut, and Coyote fell to his knees in his sand, all his breath knocked out of him. Out of the corner of his eye, he saw Strik9 draw his gun, and he had a fleeting instant to wonder if it would hurt, if he would have the chance to scream like CrashFox had before he died.

The low whump of bolt fire sounded, and something wet and sticky hit Coyote in the face. Startled, he raised his head just in time to see Strik9 hit the ground, half his head missing and his hands empty of any weapons.

The girl stood protectively beside him, one hand holding the gun, the other held out like a shield. The metal Coyote had glimpsed earlier wasn't rings at all, his confused mind told him. Some sort of implants, instead, decorating her palm and running out to the tips of her fingers.

For a moment, everybody just stared at her in shock—and then the boiz let out a collective yell and charged her.

She moved fast, like a dancer, like a song in motion. Her empty hand struck the nearest boi, landing flat on his chest, and there came a little flash of light from her palm. He screamed, his whole body jerking once, wildly, before collapsing into a spasming heap.

But only a fraction of her attention was on him, because she was too busy putting bolts through everyone coming up on her right. She never missed, every shot right through the head or the heart, perfect and deadly. And when the survivors started to fall back, she followed them, dealing death with both hands.

It was over within seconds. The dying sunlight turned her into a golden statue, taut and still, a weapon resting a moment until she found more enemies to destroy. Strik9 and his boiz lay at her feet, most of them in bits and pieces, and the smell of blood mingled with that of electrocuted flesh.

Coyote staggered to his feet, stumbled a few steps—then fell and vomited helplessly.

Oh gods oh gods oh gods...

She...what is she?

Then he felt fingers stroking his hair tentatively, the same gesture he'd used with her last night. "They hurt you," she said, and there was real anger in the words.

She thought he had thrown up because of the punch to the gut, not because of the carnage around them. Couldn't even conceive that taking apart a bunch of human beings right in front of him could make him ill, no matter what kind of lowlifes they had been.

"I'm all right," he muttered. Still queasy, he sat back. She withdrew her hand from his hair quickly, and he caught a flash of the implants as she pulled her gloves back on.

Turning towards the rambler, she gestured at it. "We got my pod back," she said brightly, as if oblivious to the bodies all around. "And look—we don't have to walk now!"

And flashed him a smile that was happy and—gods—oddly innocent. Like a child.

Whatever she was, wherever she came from, she didn't seem to comprehend that there was anything unsettling about what she had done. And maybe that ought to scare him to death. Maybe he ought to act like a sensible person for once and run screaming in the opposite direction.

But she'd saved his life. And maybe taken revenge for CrashFox, even though she didn't know it.

He remembered the way she'd touched him moments ago, awkward expression of caring, trying to comfort him. The way she'd cried last night, so lost and scared.

And besides, crazy girls didn't just fall out of the sky every day.

"That's great," he said, dredging up a smile from somewhere. "Let's see if one of us can figure out how to drive this thing, huh?"

Adapt.

Survive.

MR. FATE

by Kenneth E. Baker

Kenneth E. Baker worked for the Telephone Company for thirty years. He retired in 1999 and took up writing full time. Kenneth lives in a very isolated area along the West Virginia, Kentucky border with his wife, two dogs and three cats. He tries to write as he see the world, so a lot of what goes into his novels are his perceptions of how the world should be. After thirty years of working with the public, Kenneth finds living in an isolated area very relaxing. He believe that your imagination can take you to many places, and to be able to write about those places only makes them better.

I don't know how to begin this story, because it is at once plausible, possibly true, and totally insane. I have no facts to corroborate any of what I am about to tell you. The only thing I can say is that the man who told me this story was quite believable. When he first contacted me by phone I put him down as a crank caller, and forgot about him. A few days later I received another call from him and this time I was rather rude before hanging up.

As the day went on I could not get the call out of my mind. I began to regret being so brash with the caller. Although the small bit of information given to me by the caller was bizarre, I kept dwelling on his words. I gave up trying to write the piece my editor assigned me for the next week and left my office.

Over a drink at a local tavern, I kept mulling over the man's words. No matter how fantastic and bizarre they sounded, there was a ring of truth to them.

I was on my second drink when a well dressed middle aged man sat down on the stool beside me. I paid him little attention until he leaned close and said, "The Fate of the world is in my hands."

I was about to sip my whiskey when he spoke and his words caused me to spill some of it down my front. Taking a napkin from the bar I wiped away the spilled drops, and turned to the man. He was a little taller than my six foot and about thirty pounds more than my one eighty. The striking thing I noticed about him was his eyes. They were deep sea blue and old, incredibly old. His uplifted smile set me at ease for the moment.

There was no mistaking that voice. A low gravely voice, grating yet soothing at the same time. This was the man I talked to on the phone.

Politely, I asked if he was following me.

He answered yes and no, which confused me. I asked him to explain.

"You see, I have inquired as to where you went after work and was told that you frequently visited this establishment. On the off chance that you would drop in here today I decided to come over and wait for you. I came early and was surprised to see you here already," he told me.

An eerie feeling settled in my spine at these words. The man didn't look dangerous; yet you could never tell in this age.

My concern must have been written on my face, because he placed his hand on my arm and told me to relax. He stated that he meant me no harm.

I did relax a little, but the words he spoke on the phone kept beating the inside of my head.

"I am here to give you one more chance to hear and tell my story. If you refuse I will go out the door and you will never see me again," he told me.

I leaned back and studied him for a long moment. There was nothing striking about him. Middle aged, graying around the temples, with a slight bulge around his middle. Yet there was an indescribable air about him. Something I couldn't put my finger on. If he was a lunatic, then he was a well dressed and mannered one. After several minutes thought, I told him I was willing to hear what he had to say.

Over the next few months we met every evening at my apartment and he told me his story. In the end, before he left to go his way, I almost believed his every word. Still living in this world makes every-one a cynic to one degree or another.

I missed his voice and the way he gestured while telling me his story as I put into my own words what he had told me.

At last I am finished and can publish his story.

I never learned his real name, he just said to call him Mr. Fate. Here is his story.

～☙☙～

I was killed in the year of our Lord 1918 outside a small town in France. I was resurrected an hour after my death and given a task which would drive a sane person mad. As it did those who preceeded me.

I was a German soldier at the time of my death, and many times since then I have wished I had died a true death. Time is meaningless to me. Days become months and months become years, passing in the blink of an eye. Emotions such as love, hate and anger do not affect me anymore. The things I have done leave no room for emotions. I have become an automaton. Existing for the single purpose of choice.

However, in the back of this cranial cavity, I sense these emotions lurking, waiting to come forward and leave me a hopeless wreck. Will I ever know peace? I don't know the answer to that. Can I die? I hope so, but time will only tell. Time is my ally and enemy both. No longer do I hate the things I do that affect so many people. I look at it as a game and ignore the cause and effect that happen from my choices.

The one thing that burdens me the most is the loneliness. To neither be loved or love is a curse and a blessing at the same time. Oh I am still human in every sense. I bleed when cut and I die when shot. I feel the agony a normal human feels when hurt or dying. It doesn't last however. A few hours after I die, I am again resurrected in a different location on this planet called Earth. I have died dozens of times. Sometimes by choice, most often not.

What is my task you ask?

My task is simple, yet complex. You see when God said man must make his own choices, he meant that quite literally. One man on this teaming planet makes the choices for all of mankind. In this instance I happen to be that man.

You may think that things that happen in the world are left to chance, but you would be mistaken. I and I alone guide mankind's destiny, for either salvation or destruction.

How is this done? That is the simple part, all I have to do is make a choice. The complexity comes from making the choice I feel mankind will benefit from. You see, there are as many destinies as there are choices. A word spoken here, an accident there, alter the lives of everyone. The spoken word or accident must occur in the right place in order for one future to happen.

At times this is not an easy task. In some instances, many and varied are the obstacles placed in my path. At other times, it is as little as a few words spoken into the ear of the right person. Forgive me; I am starting to ramble.

Mistakes, I have made a few. The most notable was Adolph Hitler. He would never have came to power had I made another choice. The upside as they say, if it can be called that, is that now we have space travel and all the things associated with it. The downside is that all those people had to die.

You see, had I made another choice, man wouldn't have walked on the moon yet. Many of the modern conveniences we have today would not exist.

The cold war would never have occurred. However in that future death and disease would have decimated the planet. Mankind would have literally regressed back to the Stone Age.

Do you think it an accident that the U.S. developed Atomic Weapons first? No, my hand was there guiding events so that this country would have them first. I deemed the U.S. would never use these horrible weapons. Alas, there I was mistaken also.

Had Hitler developed Atomic weapons first, do you doubt he would have used them? I don't. As a matter of fact in one of the futures Hitler won the war, but killed all life on the planet. In that future Hitler also took his life.

I hope you understand by now that the choices I make aren't easy ones. I am not complaining, just stating a fact.

Why was I chosen for this task? I don't know, but when you get to Heaven, tell God that I am tired, so tired. Perhaps he will see fit to release me and let me rest.

At this point Mr. Fate sat slumped in his chair for an hour without uttering a word. His face looked sunken and his hands trembled on the chair arms. I got up and made some coffee. After handing him a cup, I asked if he was all right.

You know if God was just and benevolent why couldn't he remove my memories after I make a choice. Your memories are of happy times and loved ones. My memories consist of the millions and millions I have killed.

"When I leave you at night, so that you can sleep and rest, do you know what I do?" He asked.

I shook my head no.

I walk the city streets, trying to forget. Sleep, which is common for you, no longer exists for me. If I slept, an opportunity to change something might occur and I would miss it. I haven't slept in years. I used to day dream of laying my head on a pillow and drifting away into blissful unconsciousness.

Even as we talk, I see many possible futures to chose from. Before you ask, yes even now I am working. Sifting through this or that future to find which will benefit mankind. In this one only a few will die, he said pointing to a place in the air. This one will bring much benefit to mankind, but many will die, he pointed to another place in the air.

Would you believe that before I became what I am today, I couldn't make decisions. Getting me to make a decision was like having a tooth pulled, he said skipping to a different subject.

I had noticed that his attention span on one subject seemed limited. He would talk about one thing and in the middle of a sentence start another subject. I could tell that he didn't realize he had switched subjects. If what he was telling me was true, perhaps this was a flaw in his character that kept him sane. Unable to dwell on some terrible thing he had done enabled him to continue functioning.

I asked what his life was like before all this started?

He pulled a picture from his breast pocket and handed it to me.

That was my wife and child, he said.

A slightly plump blond woman holding a child of three or four, stood on a doorstep in the picture. What happened to them, I asked as I handed the picture back.

After I was resurrected the first time I made my way back to the town we lived in. This took several months because I kept getting captured by the Americans and Germans, depending on whose line I was behind at the time. Twice I was shot and killed for being a deserter. Once by the Americans, and once by the Germans.

When I finally got home much of the town had been ravaged by the war. The house my wife lived in had burnt to the ground. Asking around I found that she was living in a refugee camp outside of town set up by the British.

Picking my way through the rows of tents, I spotted my wife's head a few rows over. As I was about to step from behind the tent she was on the other side of something held me back.

I heard her talking to another man. She was telling the man a letter arrived last week from the army saying I was dead. At that point she broke down in tears. Oh I wanted so badly to step out and say I wasn't dead, but still something held me back.

That was the first time visions of different futures appeared to me. In one future I saw my wife and child die two years from then. I stood grieving by their grave. In another future I saw her remarry and lead a long life. I stood there for a few moments longer, listening to her sob, then turned away. With breaking heart I left the camp. By doing so I changed the future and my wife lived until 1984.

My son is still alive and doing quite well in Hamburg, Germany. Over the years, when I could I went back to Germany and watched him grow into a fine man. The last few years I grieve for him. He has turned into an old man, while I remain the forty five I was when killed the first time.

I poured him another cup of coffee as he sat there with a far away look in his eyes.

Sipping my coffee I tried to imagine what it felt like to watch your wife and child grow old, while you remained the same age. Undoubtedly he loved them or he wouldn't have walked away. The pain and suffering this caused was etched on his face as I watched him think about them.

To watch loved one's grow and not share in those experiences except as an observer had to hurt deeply. That ended my first evening with him. I found it hard to sleep that night.

༄ ༄

Mr. Fate called the next morning, saying he had to be out of town for the next few days, but would return at the end of the week. All day at work I wondered what future he was guiding us to. Then I thought about my son and wife. Although divorced, my ex-wife and I got along fine. I didn't get to see my son as much as I liked, but still we had a good father-son relationship. At least I could participate in my son's life to a small extent. Which was much more than Mr. Fate was able to do with his son.

Weekends and a few weeks in the summer weren't much. They were better than standing on the sidewalk and watching your child at play, without him realizing who you were.

Over the next few days I began to wish that I had turned Mr. Fate away. I felt myself settling into a depression. The more I thought about his situation the heavier the funk became.

When he called Friday afternoon I almost told him I didn't want to listen anymore. On hearing the deep loneliness in his voice I relented and agreed to another meeting at my apartment that evening.

On opening the door to admit him, I was shocked by his appearance. He looked washed out and drawn. His eyes were listless and his arms shook like he had palsy.

"My God, what has happened to you?" I asked.

Another future made in which many will die, he answered in a hoarse whisper. Making his way across the room he plopped down on the chair, and held his head in his hands.

I handed him a steaming cup of coffee, but his hands shook so bad I set it down on the table in front of him. I busied myself putting fresh batteries in the recorder while he recovered.

A half hour later he was able to lift the coffee and take a drink of the cold liquid. I emptied his cup and filled it with hot coffee.

"Thank you," he said.

"Is it like this every time you choose a fate for humanity?" I asked him.

"No, but it gets worse every time. You can't even comprehend the tortured suffering I go through with each decision I have to make. It is horrible."

"What if you make no decision?"

"Ah, you still don't understand. Not deciding isn't an option. I and all the ones before me have tried this once and I must say once was enough. By not choosing we allow the most terrible of choices come to the front and that path is followed. Believe me that choice is beyond all human comprehension. In order to get things back on an even kilter I had to make many more choices. None of which were easy. No, it is better to make one choice than to make many."

Color was returning to his pale face and most of his shaking had subsided. I could still hardly look into his tortured eyes. Eyes that carried pain and suffering the way no human should.

"Has this event already occurred, or will it occur in the near future," I asked?

He laughed in a horrible cackle. "No my friend, I wish that it were already done. If so then I would be a part of the event and not know about it. Whom ever picked me and the others deemed it necessary that we must watch the consequences of our choices. As to your question, the actions of my decisions will become apparent to you over the next month. Remember, no actions of this world are random. I imagine such is true of other worlds or lives as it may be," he said with a rueful shake of his head.

"So you believe in reincarnation"?

"I must, for it is all that lets me hold on to what little sanity I have left."

"What do I get from listening to these stories. Whether true or false I with hold judgment for the moment. Most of all, why me? I mean of all the people on this planet you could have told this to, why me?" I asked.

"It is quite simple. I have read several of your articles over the years. I enjoy the way you state the facts without embellishing them. Clear and concise reporting, now that is something that is rare in today's world, you have to admit. Oh, I realize that if you write what I tell you ninety five percent of those who read it will chuckle and say, 'what a nut case.' The other five percent are fringe people who are thought to be a bubble or two shy, so their believing will be shrugged off." He took a long sip of coffee and had that far away look in his eyes again.

"My goal if you decide to put this to paper is to have written word of what I do. Oh I know it won't be relevant today or in the near future. My hope is that in the future, when mankind has evolved a little more, historians will find what you have written and it will have some meaning for them. A long shot, I know, but nothing lost all the same.

He became quite for a while with a far away look in his eyes. Every now and then I saw a flicker of pain cross his face. I busied myself making another pot of coffee, giving him time to compose himself.

As I refreshed his cup, he shook his head and muttered something in a foreign language.

I was getting used to these lapses in our conversations. While Mr. Fate made his choice of actions that guided humanity, I watched him. His eyes flickered rapidly as the eyes of a person in REM sleep would. He covered his right hand with his left as it began to shake. A low mournful moan escaped his lips. His left hand clamped down on his right hand so hard it turned white.

He shook so hard, I wondered should I call 911 and get an ambulance. As I picked up the phone, he let out a long low sigh and the trembling stopped. I watched as color came back to his face and he loosened his grip on his right hand.

"Is there anything I can do," I asked?

"No, no, I will be ok in a moment. Perhaps a strong drink if you have any," he softly said.

"All I have is a year old bottle of Vodka. Would that do?"

"That will be fine. Make it a heavy belt, would you please?"

I went to the kitchen cabinet and got the bottle of Vodka off the top shelf. I poured a couple of ounces into a six ounce water glass and added ice. As I handed him the drink I noticed that he had composed himself. He downed the drink in a single gulp, then sucked on an ice cube.

"Thank you, my friend," he said his voice a lot firmer.

"You have done something terrible. I can tell by your reaction."

"No, not really. I had a choice to make and an anomaly forced me to make my second best choice."

"What type of an anomaly?" I asked.

"Before I explain, could I have that cup of coffee."

I poured two cups of steaming coffee and gave him one. He sipped the hot brew and leaned back. He finished the coffee and set the cup on the coffee table.

"The Anomaly, yes. How do I explain it?" He mumbled to himself.

"Let me put it this way. There are people who, no matter what I do, will not change. Not only that; I can't eliminate them. To alter the future with them as the focal point would cause instant chaos. Now these people are normal in every way, and don't realize the role they play in the fight against chaos. My speculation is that they are thrown in to create a randomness that somehow places a check on Chaos.

These people—or anomalies as I refer to them—very seldom get sick and live a long life. The number of these anomalies ebbs and flows according to the amount of chaos in the world. At present I would say there are less than a hundred in the world. For a reason I can't define more and more of the choices I make have some connection with these anomalies."

"What makes these people so special?" I asked.

He shook his head. "That I can't answer."

"Would I know one of these people if I saw them?"

Another shake of his head. "Let me put it this way. Have you read or heard of someone that has been in an accident or had a heart attack and against all odds survived?"

"Every so often I hear of something like that," I answered.

"Those who are chosen will not die no matter how dire the circumstance. I believe this is why they don't know what they are. Some wouldn't be able to handle it, while others would go hog wild and create more chaos than could be handled."

I sat back in my chair and thought about what he had just told me.

"You mentioned they would not change. What do you mean?"

"Suppose there were a squad of soldiers that had to die in order to bring about a future I choose. Now suppose in this squad was one of these anomalies. All the soldiers would die except for the anomaly.

The future I chose would be altered because he still lived. Even a small alteration can have cataclysmic results and give Chaos the upper hand. Now you see why my choices must be decisive and final."

"You speak of Chaos as if it was an entity you were acquainted with."

"Yes and No. I can't physically see Chaos, but I know it's there. Chaos is all around me all of the time. The acquaintance comes from all the different futures I have to make a choice of. One choice for a set of futures presented to me. Think of Chaos as the dark side. Chaos is everything we despise and can't tolerate as civilized humans."

"That brings up an interesting point. If Chaos is the dark side, what is the light side"?

He shrugged his shoulders.

"Perhaps you are the light side. Just as God is supposed to have angels to counteract the devil, perhaps you are the one to balance Chaos?"

He chuckled. "An amusing thought, but not true."

"Why not?"

"Think about it for a moment," he said.

I went over what he had told me and could think of no reason why he couldn't be the light side. He seemed to be the logical choice, and I told him so.

"I have to make a choice of one future from a multiple choice of futures. Where do these futures come from?"

He had me there. "I don't know," was all I could say.

"Think of balances. For eons Chaos ruled this planet. You might say Chaos made this planet what it is today. Then along came a life form that needed conformity to exist."

"Humans!" I burst out.

He nodded. "With Chaos running rampant humans were doomed to extinction. Now comes the tricky part. Whomever or whatever be it God or something else that created all this had a problem. Let the new life forms die thereby giving Chaos full reign, or placing a check on Chaos. I think the choice is obvious."

I was puzzled now. "How does your choosing a future place a check on Chaos," I asked?

"Chaos is random and illogical. There is no rhyme or reason for it's actions. For some reason when I make a choice of which future I prefer that future happens. That doesn't mean that Chaos is eliminated from that future, just that Chaos can't run rampant."

"When you chose a future how far can you follow where that future leads and the effects it will have."

"If it is a person, I usually see the future till they die. If it is a natural event it gets tricky. There are many more futures when a natural event occurs for some reason. Usually I can see a hundred years into a particular future. There have been a few times when I saw hundreds of years into the future." He gave a body trembling shudder. "None of these futures did I choose. They were all so gruesome."

"One thing puzzles me. If as you say you are making choices all the time, why don't some of your choices cancel out previous choices?"

He chuckled deep in his throat. "For many years I sought to answer that question. I came to the conclusion there is no answer. Whoever or what ever supplies me with these futures makes sure they don't cancel each other out." He got that blank look on his face again and didn't speak for several minutes.

I opened a couple of cans of soup and put them in the microwave to heat. Taking lettuce from the fridge I made salad. Occasionally I glanced to where Fate sat with that blank look on his face. Placing the hot bowls of soup on the table next to the salad, I got what bottles of dressing I had and placed them on the table.

Taking a seat I watched as he came out of his trance like state. He sighed and flexed his arms. His face became animated again.

He looked at the food on the table such as it was and said. "You didn't have to prepare food for me."

"I was hungry and as you see opening another can and throwing together a salad wasn't a hardship." I said with a smile.

He came over and sat down at the table across from me. He ate the soup and salad with relish. Pushing back his chair he reached into his jacket pocket and pulled out an old briar pipe. "Would it bother you if I smoked?" He asked.

"Not at all. My Dad smoked a pipe for years. I loved the smell of pipe tobacco." I answered.

He pulled out a leather pouch and stuffed tobacco into the large bowl of the pipe. Pulling out a kitchen match he flicked it with his thumb and held the flame to the pipe. Several puffs later a billow of smoke crossed the table and hit my nose. It brought back memories of a younger me sitting with my father and inhaling the same fragrance.

We talked trivialities for another half hour and then Me. Fate took his leave for the evening.

The next morning I sat down at my computer desk and stared at the screen. There were so many questions I needed to ask. How to put them into the proper order was the problem. I thought back to the major events that happened over my lifetime. How many of them did Mr. Fate have a hand in. What if they had never happened.

I got on the net and started researching the Challenger disaster back in early 2003. Everything was ok on the space shuttle until twenty three minutes before touchdown in Florida. As the shuttle entered the earth's atmosphere something drastic happened and it broke up killing all seven of the astronauts. No definitive cause was ever found.

Other conflicts that happened over the last twenty years got a good look from me. I wrote down questions as I went.

Before I knew it, it was evening. I made a pot of coffee and ate a light meal. The doorbell rang at 7PM on the dot.

I opened the door and ushered in Mr. Fate. He looked much better this evening. He even had a bounce in his step.

"I see by the gleam in your eye that you have plenty of questions for me." He said with a smile as he took his seat.

I sat down on the couch across from him and turned on the recorder.

"First; can you tell me how you are chosen to do what you do?"

He sipped on his coffee for a moment then said. "Back before World War I, a stranger sought me out in a beer garden in the town I lived in. This fellow sat down and told me a story, much the way I am telling you my story. I thought nothing of it at the time, but later, after I become what I am, his story made sense. You see, I believe he recruited me without my knowledge. Back then I sluffed off what he told me as the workings of a demented mind. Harmless, but still demented."

A chill went down my back, cold as an Arctic iceberg.

He must have noticed because he said, "Do not worry, my friend. I have no intention of placing this burden on your shoulders. Everything is as it seems." He gave me a big smile.

I felt the back chill recede a little. Not all the way, but enough to not be uncomfortable. There was still a nagging part of my mind that kept telling me there was more to this than just the telling of a story.

"Where was I. Oh yeah, how I was recruited. This fellow never mentioned his name, he just sat down and bought me a mug of stout. According to him, he was chosen in 1815 by a woman from Italy."

"That answers one of my questions." I broke in.

He arched his eyebrows in puzzlement.

"I was going to ask if any women were ever chosen to do what you do." I said.

"Ah, I take your point. Let me think a moment." He said. He sipped his coffee and got a far away look in his eyes.

I stopped the recorder and waited.

Several minutes later, he sat the coffee cup down and said. "There were six women that I know of. Most of them were between 500AD and 1500AD. The reason for this is that women are longer lived than males. You have to realize that in that time frame women only lived until their mid thirties and the males were lucky to reach their mid twenties. All of these chosen women lived to be well over a hundred years old. Which for the time was an overwhelming feat. Every one of them was killed at least once for their longevity. You see, like me, they didn't age after being chosen. While those around them aged, they stayed the same. This caused the normal people to assume they were possessed in some way by the Devil. Believe me when I say death back then was neither quick nor easy."

"How do you know these things. Records from that era are spotty and non existent at best?" I asked.

"Ah, I understand your confusion. For some reason, when we are chosen we gain some of the knowledge of those who have preceded us. Not much, but enough to keep us from making the same mistakes they made."

"Do you mean that you can access their memories?"

He smiled and shook his head. "It doesn't work that way. Say I am going to make a choice on a future that will have cataclysmic results. At that time the conscious thoughts of one of my predecessors will pop into my mind and advise against that choice."

"So you can't go back and see how they lived and worked their choices?" I asked.

"Not at all. If that happened they would be brought back to life in a way. No, they much deserve their blessed death; and it would be unconscionable to do that to them."

I shook my head. More confused than ever.

He saw my confusion. "Let me explain it this way. What are you, or better what is your essence?"

"My soul is the essence of me." I answered.

"Leave out the soul for the moment. What is your essence?"

I thought for a long time and the only thing I came up with was my ability to think on a rational level and told him this.

"You are partially right. Your mind is the essence of you. The mind can take you back in time, or it can take you into the future. If I went back and used their conscious thoughts it would be the same as bringing them back to life. In this way they would live again."

I shook my head again. "But that doesn't make any sense." I said.

"Have you ever wondered what happened to yesterday?" he asked.

"Whoa, you threw me a loop there. Yesterday is just yesterday. A part of the past."

He gave me a big smile. "You will agree that yesterday existed?"

I nodded my head yes.

"Today is tomorrow's yesterday. Now if today exists then all the yesterdays exist also. They occupied time and space and for all purposes they all still there. Say I could access your thoughts of yesterday or for that matter last year. I would live your experiences so ergo you would still live. That is, if you were dead in the present."

I got up to fill our coffee cups and brought them back to the coffee table. "If you went back and accessed my thoughts or essence as you put it I would still live. I find that hard to believe," I told him.

"Of course it would not be you as you are now. There would not be a body. Only your thoughts or as I say the essence of you, but it would still be you. Like most people you think of the past as a blank. The past exists as it happened. It is still there at this moment. In that time frame you are doing the same thing over and over, except you don't realize it.

"It would be like saying that because you moved from one house to another the former house no longer existed. No, my friend, we are still alive in the past as we are at this moment."

"Let me think on this overnight, perhaps I can make some sense of what you have told me," I said.

"Of course. You have other questions?" he asked.

"Do all your choices come out the way you first perceive them?'

He laughed out loud at the question.

"Hardly, my friend. Remember Chaos. Chaos has a way of altering things, no matter how much I would wish them to go a certain way. I choose a future and that future works its way forward. Very rarely does the future I choose come out the way I perceive it."

"Then why choose a future?"

"Because without a somewhat planned future, Chaos has free reign. There are many things I don't understand about my purpose and why I do what I do. That is part of what keeps me going. Searching for the answers to these questions keeps me somewhat sane."

"I am puzzled. If what you say about the past is true, why can't the you of that time frame pick a different future?"

"The answer to that is simple. What we do in the here and now is fixed, so that when it becomes the past it can't be changed. The future however, is fluid. You have choices to make, such as, will I go to work today. Will I see that movie I've wanted to see. Will I get a haircut, etc, etc. Once you do these things they become fixed. Until then it is a matter of choice."

"So that makes you the ultimate choice chooser. Instead of choosing for just yourself, you choose for all of mankind."

He hung his head and I barely heard him say. "Guilty as charged."

"I still don't understand when you say there are multiple choices and you have to pick one. Can you give me an example?"

"Ok. Here we have a male baby being born." He pointed to a space off to the left of him. "This boy will grow up to be a very prominent scientist. He will enter government service and work on a major gene splicing project. Inadvertently he will create a mutant strain of virus that will wipe out half the world's population.

"In this future, I see his mother killed by a mugger on her way home from work. In this future he is never born." He points to another space."

"Here I see him have an accident when he is 12 that causes him to go in a different direction in his future. In this future he goes on to become President. As President he accomplishes world peace. However, because of his love of space exploration he causes an asteroid to leave its orbit and crash into the earth causing extinction of all life."

"In this future the same child grows up to be an explorer. He goes to the Congo and catches a very virulent form of Ebola and brings it back to the United States. This disease wipes out all but a few hundred people in the US. Half the world's population will die before this disease mutates into a harmless germ."

"I must chose from one of these three. Do I choose number 3 and let the United States cease to exist as a country? Or do I choose number two and see all life on earth wiped out? How would you choose?" he asked.

I sat back shocked. Until now this had all been a very strange conversation. I felt a crushing weight come crashing down on my shoulders. My God, is this what Mr. Fate felt every second that he lived? I began to shake uncontrollably. I found it hard to breathe. Try as I might, I couldn't seem to get enough air. I felt a sharp blow to my cheek. I looked up and saw Mr. Fate staring into my eyes.

"It is not easy, is it?" he said as he sat down.

I cupped my face in my hands and sobbed like a baby.

"That is the same way I reacted the first time I had to make a choice."

"For Gods sake; how do you stand it!" I cried in anguish.

"The knowledge that these futures aren't set in stone helps. Remember our friend Chaos. Sometimes Chaos inadvertently rights a wrong by trying to make it worse. Do you wish to know the choice I made?" He asked.

"Gods, no." I said with a deep shudder.

"It is just as well. My time with you is over. It is your choice to publish what I have told you or not. My time talking to you was a pleasure. I doubt that you feel the same way."

He stood and shook my hand. I stood there still in shock as he closed the apartment door behind him.

꧁꧂

For two weeks after Mr. Fate left I couldn't sleep and went into a deep depression. It took me another month to get back on my feet. I spend a lot more time with my son now. Every moment I can as a matter of fact. My former wife and I have been out on a few dates and things are looking up between us. My outlook on life has changed so drastically that for the first time I feel like a truly free person.

I now see how foolish all of the problems are that I thought I had. Nothing can even approach the chains that surround Mr. Fate. When something comes up that used to make me mad I shrug it off and chuckle.

People are beginning to notice the change in me. When they ask the reason, I tell them I've had a vision. They give me strange looks, but that is ok. I've made my peace with the world. Most of all I've made peace with myself. You see, if you like yourself and are honest, others will like you also. Those that don't, well, they don't matter.

THE OLD GREEN DOOR

by Julie D'Arcy

Julie D'Arcy was born in Australia in 1957. She studied Art and Design at Monash University, majoring in Ceramic Art and Design in 1980. Julie, who began writing seriously in 1994, has had two short stories, and two books published with LEGACY OF THE BLACK DRAGON being her third. Her novels have been shortlisted for several prestigious awards, and her first novel won the 1999 Dorothy Parker Award for Fantasy.

Sherry awoke with a start, her body drenched with perspiration. She swung her legs over the edge of the bed and stumbled to the bathroom. She could remember nothing of the dream except...a golden idol.

The statue had been beautiful and ugly all in one, depicting a man and woman in an embrace of what could have been love, or the throes of death. She shook her head trying to clear her mind, and looked into the mirror. The face that peered back seemed like that of a stranger's: the eyes huge pools of desolation, the skin ghostly against a back drop of brilliant auburn hair. She ran a washcloth over her face, dragged a brush roughly through her hair and turned for the door. She needed air.

She had to get out of the motel room or she would surely go insane. She had been held up here for five days...waiting. Now, there would be no more waiting.

Tears came to her eyes and she hastily wiped them away. This was supposed to be her honeymoon—yesterday her wedding day. But that had been a dream, and this was another day.

She stepped from the motel lobby into the main street of Rio de Janeiro and was struck by the heat. Slowly, she pushed her way through the crowd, and moved down the congested sidewalk. She had forgotten about the parade. It was evening and the Mardi Gras was in full swing.

The humidity made her feel uncomfortable and dirty. She flicked her damp hair back from her eyes. If there were anything she hated more than this relentless heat, it would be the laughing, noisy, crowd which jostled and pulled her in every direction.

A man in a garishly painted mask of a blue wolf lowered his face to hers and laughed harshly. She shoved him away and squeezed through a narrow gap in the crowd.

An elbow struck her ribs and she staggered into the doorway of an old shop.

Plucking her shirt away from her overheated body she sighed and leaned against the wall. The sign above the entrance read, 'The Old Green Door.'

Curiosity motivated her to reach for the door handle. To her surprise it opened, and she stepped inside.

Her head was pounding in time to the beating drums in the street. She knew there would be no escape from the noise outside until the parade was over. And as she had seen no schedule, she was not even certain when that would be.

The door closed of its own accord with a soft click behind her. Silence. How curious, not a sound from the Mardi Gras intruded.

She shivered as a chill feathered down her spine. The temperature had dropped considerably since she entered the shop, yet she could see nothing to indicate any type of cooling device.

The store, although tiny, was cluttered with all types of bric-a-brac. From antique furniture, medieval armor, idols of all kinds—from dark teak wood to precious metals. Mirrors and paintings hung on the walls, depicting great battles, beautiful women and handsome men. But not as handsome as her man. Jarred's image flashed through her mind, raven black hair, brilliant blue eyes, the body of a god. Yet he'd done nothing extraordinary to keep his body in shape, except live a healthy lifestyle. Although a politician, he'd found time to take her horse riding, bush walking, and water-skiing. She remembered those times now with tears in her eyes.

She spied an overstuffed green sofa in the corner of the room. There still seemed no one about, so needing a moment to catch her breath and settle her nerves, she sank into the sofa and leaned back, lapping up the comfort.

Her mind began to wander once more.

She had been so excited when Jarred had rung her at her apartment in New York after his meeting in Mexico five days before, and proposed.

From the moment she and Jarred met eight months ago, both had known that there would be no others. It was as if they were destined to be together. A feeling hard to explain, yet it had been there.

Now he was gone. His plane had been lost that same day in the desert and the Search and Rescue Service was unable to locate him. Believed dead, they told her. Her Jarred, dead! How could that be? They had planned so much—their whole life together. They were to be married here during the Mardi Gras. They even arranged the wedding with a small chapel on the outskirts of Rio.

Now all her dreams, her hopes, were no more than whispers in the wind.

Forcing herself to her feet, she wandered down one of the confined rows of merchandise, examining but not touching. A scent came to her on the air. She raised her head, her nose twitching as it picked up notes of sweet spice and roses. She smiled sadly, remembering the bouquet of red and white blooms Jarred had arranged to be waiting in the motel room on her arrival. The card had read: Love you, now, and forever.

Sherry wiped the tears from her eyes that threatened to overflow and glanced down. Through a haze of blur, an unusual golden idol caught her eye. Its familiarity caused the hair on her nape to stand on end. It was the idol from her dream. With a mixture of dread and curiosity she reached for the statue to examine it closer, but was halted by a voice.

"Are you sure that is the one you want?"

Sherry glanced up, her hand hovering above the statue, her gaze going to a man at the end of the row. He was tall and wizened, a long white beard hung to his waist and his long royal blue robes were embroidered with tiny silver stars. If it hadn't been for the serious look on the man's face, the hint of warning in his tone, Sherry would have laughed. He appeared, as if something out of an Arthurian tale.

"Sorry," he said, "for startling you. I suppose I must come as a bit as a surprise, but my clientele has come to expect a certain amount of eccentricity from me." He smiled. "Hence the gown."

Sherry smiled back, warming to the old man. "It's a lovely piece," she said, indicating the idol and lowering her hand back to her side. "Is it gold?"

"Yes, but coated only." His gaze met hers as he moved closer. "That piece is not for you. Already you have suffered much tragedy, you have no need for more."

Sherry frowned. "You must be a seer."

"I read people," he said, now standing at her side. "You have lost your parents and...someone else you loved dearly."

"Then tell me. What is my future without Jarred?" Sherry glanced away from his deep violet eyes, so bright and lively in a face so weathered.

The man took Sherry's hand and held it between his two. "Do you really wish to hear that? The truth can be painful."

She nodded.

He squeezed his eyes closed and began to speak in a deep harmonious tone. "The future has many paths," he said. "But on one path only do I see your man. You both live happily to a ripe age and have several children.

"On another path, your man dies and you must carve out a life on your own. You never marry and your life is lonely, but you go on to become a brilliant historian."

He opened his eyes and dropped her hand.

"Is that all?"

"I could go on, but as I have told you, only in one of your futures did I see your man. And that is the question you wished to ask, was it not?"

Sherry pulled away in disappointment. For a moment the stranger had her believing in the unattainable; however, as much as she would have liked to give credence to his reading, she was certain there was no truth in the telling.

Leaning forward, again she reached for the idol. But her hand was caught in his.

"If you could ask for anything. Anything at all, what would it be?"

She eyed him suspiciously. "Why is it, that twice you have stopped me from touching this idol?"

He gave a short laugh. "A question for a question. Ah, I was not expecting that. I think I am beginning to like you. What can I say except to leave you with this one thought. True happiness is like a warm breeze that touches your life when you least expect it."

Sherry sighed in resignation, knowing there would be no happiness for her without Jarred. "You must know what I would choose," she said "To see Jarred alive. But that would be impossible."

"And if you could select any piece in my store, what would that be?" He spread out his free hand indicating the goods in his shop.

She frowned, making no sense of his words. "I have already chosen…this idol."

"Then let it be upon your own head. It was not that you were not given a choice." He smiled sadly and released her hand.

Her fingers grasped the idol. "I don't understand—"

But her sentence was never finished. Sherry felt herself falling, down…down into a pit of darkness. She burst through, into a tunnel of bright whirling lights and still she was drawn along. This time she was spinning faster and faster until all thought, all reality diminished and there was only a feeling of terrible dread. She closed her eyes and ceased her struggles, allowing her mind and body to float freely. Of a sudden, she stopped. She felt her arms gripped and opened her eyes to a nightmare.

Before her was a yawning pit. The two creatures that flanked her and held her arms in a deadly grip wore masks like those from the Mardi Gras. She peered into the face on the right. "What am I doing here?"

The creature grinned and Sherry felt her blood turn icy despite the heat that rose from the pit. With dawning horror she realized the face was not a mask, but in reality truly belonged to the creature beside her. The beast's features were that of a pig; half human, blue stripes running from its forehead to chin, its hair standing out like a lion's mane, its smile pure evil.

She tried to pull away but the beast's grip tightened. She turned to the creature on her left, hoping for help. But found none. Scarlet plumage covered its face. Bright birdlike eyes darted its gaze across her body, lodging on her breasts.

Sherry flushed and looked down. Her body was barely covered. Somehow in her travels her clothes had changed. She now wore a dress of shimmering white cloth with skimpy straps tied at the shoulders, tight fitting at the waist and cut roughly at the knee.

The material left nothing to the imagination, nothing at all

Jeers came from across the pit. On a high ledge stood a crowd of around fifty. Garish faces chanting for her death.

Fear touched her then, deep and jarring. She realized they meant to sacrifice her. She didn't know where she was, how she had got here, but she knew if she didn't get away within minutes, she would be dead.

Twisting, she glanced behind her for a way of escape.

A huge golden throne stood fifteen feet away. On the throne was seated another of the creatures. She imagined him to be their king.

The back of the throne was carved in the image of the idol. On both sides at the top of the throne stood two smaller idols. With effort, Sherry reached down to pinch herself, certain this was all a hideous dream. But her pain brought her no relief and reality hit home. She was in a huge cavern, to the side was a large cage with a pulley attached, and before her she could feel the heat of flames rising from the pit. They intended to burn her—to place her in the cage, and lower her into the pit in some bizarre ritual.

What had the old man done to her? What was this place?

She swung to glare at the king, all the while searching her mind for a plan. "Who are you? I demand you let me go." Swiftly, she brought her leg around in front of the pig-creature and pulled him forward. He lost his balance and fell screaming into the pit. She shoved against the other guard and found she was free, but the bird creature leapt after her and caught at her legs. She fell heavily, unable to protect herself with her bound hands.

The guard dragged her unceremoniously back to her feet and pulled her toward the pit.

Then he was there. Standing before her. Jarred. Her Jarred...yet not. He wore an armor plate, bronze and molded to the shape of his chest. His hair was longer than Jarreds and held back by a leather strap. He wore leather breeches and in his hand he carried a short sword.

"Stand way from my woman, or feel the weight of my blade across your throat."

The creature on the throne laughed out loud. "You can try. But first, who are you?"

"I am Chardon, of the Celti Tribe. Free my woman and I shall let you live."

"I cannot do that," returned the creature, smoothly. "She has been chosen as the bride of Kaligi."

"Then you and your men will die."

The king nodded to the bird-like creature holding Sherry. "Terros, get rid of this scum."

The bird-man released her, drew his short sword, and stepped out to face the warrior.

Chardon took a deep breath, then advanced. "I will send your love to your wife, Terros," he said, his voice warm and friendly.

For a moment only, Terros froze. Then Chardon was upon him. Terros parried desperately, but Chardon's sword tore into his belly, ripping up through a lung and out through his back. Terros sagged against Chardon, letting go his sword and resting his massive head on his killer's shoulder.

Chardon tossed him aside.

Another creature gave a hideous cry and raced toward the warrior. Chardon was ready for him. He hefted the creature into the air and tossed him screaming into the pit.

The crowd bayed for blood.

The king leapt up from his throne. "Seize them," he roared and charged Chardon, a knife in his hand.

Chardon stepped to the side allowing the king's momentum to carry him past. The king came to a halt at the edge of the pit and swung to face the warrior.

Sherry, on seeing the beast's move, was spurred to action.

She skirted the warrior, knowing now that he was not Jarred, yet still worried for his safety. She scanned the cavern for a weapon; not even a loose rock lay upon the floor. Her gaze alighted on the small idols atop the back of the throne. She raced toward them.

The king charged Chardon again. This time their blades crossed. Chardon landed a powerful left to the king's jaw, and the creature staggered back, trying to right himself. He stumbled and fell. Chardon leapt forward and plunged his sword into the king's throat, then looked around for Sherry. "Hurry," he bellowed.

She grasped up one of the idols and raced toward him.

"Quickly! This way!"

Sherry followed him out of the cavern and into a tunnel that branched to the right, lit at random by flaming torches in iron wall brackets. In the distance the disembodied sound of shouting and booted feet echoed in her ears.

"We must reach the street," he said, waiting to take her hand.

She placed her hand into his, noticing he was not even breathing heavily. His hand was strong and firm. Even in the dimness of the underground tunnel she couldn't believe the uncanny resemblance to Jarred. "Who are you"" she asked, softly. But there was no time for answers. His hand closed tightly over hers and she was dragged along.

A set of carved steps loomed toward them and hastily they began to climb as the cries of their pursuers grew louder.

"You know who I am," he said, still climbing. "I am Chardon and you are Cara, and we are to be wed."

Sherry breathed deeply trying to gain her breath. "Then what was I doing about to be sacrificed?"

Chardon stopped for a moment only, his hands going to her shoulders, his brilliant blue eyes staring into hers. "What have they done to you, Cara? Do you remember nothing?"

Sherry shook her head. Who was this Cara he spoke of? And who was this man who looked so much like Jarred. And more importantly, where was she?

Chardon seemed about to say something, but instead shook his head and took her hand again. He urged her up the steps, the sound of pursuit even closer.

"The Eildons are a rogue race of Elves, banished for their deformities," he said at last, still moving. "Usually they are peaceful. They worship Kaligi, the Fire God, and this is their festival day. We will find a great celebration in the street above. Which, thank the gods, will be to our advantage."

"A deformity you say? Why?" Sherry asked, breathing heavily.

"I have no time to go into Elfish History, but I believe it has something to do with a witch and a curse." He stopped suddenly and reached forward to kiss her soundly, then released her. "I have wanted to do that since I found you again."

Sherry touched a hand to her lips and was about to speak, but he silenced her with another quick kiss. "Enough talk now, we must hurry."

They came to a portal, which appeared to be made of solid rock. Chardon felt for the trigger hidden in the ledge above the door, and the stone rolled silently aside. They stepped into the light, from the side of a cliff, and the door rolled quietly shut behind them.

It was just on evening; tall oil lamps lighted the streets. Sherry was surprised to see hundreds of the creatures mingling with humans. Vendors had set up tents and trestles to sell their wares and the village had the same carnival atmosphere of the Mardi Gras in Rio.

"Wait here," Chardon said, disappearing into the crowd. A few moments later he returned. In his hand he held two light-weight cloaks. He placed one on the ground momentarily and threw the other around Sherry's shoulders, then drew the cowl up over her hair and kissed the tip of her nose.

She smiled. "Thank you, but why the gift?"

His eyes darkened. "A disguise. With that bright hair of yours you

stand out like a beacon. Besides, cannot a man buy a gift for his be-
trothed."

Chardon unbuckled his breastplate and dropped it to the ground,
then retrieved his cloak and tossed it casually about his shoulders,
fastening it at the throat with a golden pin. Sherry thought he appeared a cross between an untamed wild Indian and a god from a
Greek painting. His skin glistened in the heat, his long dark hair fell
to his waist and she'd swear she could feel an aura of masculinity
radiating from his body. He caught her staring at his chest and grinned.
She flushed and looked away.

He took her hand again and began to pull her along.

"Wait!" demanded Sherry, hauling back. "If these people are peaceful, why did they abduct me?"

Chardon's features hardened. "The creatures who pursue us, who
held you captive are a breakaway religious cult, who unfortunately
worship Kaligi in their own bizarre way. The death of their High Priest
will slow them down, but they will soon elect another. Now, we must
keep moving."

Sherry wiped her hand across her brow as they wound their way
in and out of the crowd. The noise and the heat were as bad here as
they had been in her world. But there was an extra element added.
The stench. She peered through the gathering at the deep drains running each side of the street, and grimaced. It seemed sewers had not
yet been invented in this world.

"I thought the man in the chair was their king," she said, covering
her nose with her hand.

Chardon laughed. "The stench can be a little overpowering, until
you get used to it. No. The king here is a good man. He has outlawed
the rebels, but they are forever changing their venue."

Suddenly a creature, its face covered in brown hair like a dog,
ran at Sherry's back with a dagger. Chardon knocked her to the side
and swung a fist into the creature's face. Dog-face fell into the stall of
a vender hawking earthen pots. The pottery crashed down about the
cultist's head, knocking him cold.

"Are you hurt?" Chardon asked, helping Sherry to her feet and
brushing her down. "Can you go on?"

She nodded as she rubbed her elbow and gave him a brave smile,
and they took off through the crowd, cutting into a side street and
across a park. They forded a small stream to enter a fairground and
Sherry pulled from his grasp and stopped. She gasped for breath.
"Enough! I've followed you this far, but no farther, until I know where
you are taking me. I cannot keep running."

Chardon circled her waist with a well-muscled arm and brought
her against his chest, running a knuckle gently down her heated cheek.
"Forgive me Cara. I know you have been through much. But we are
almost there. Then we can rest."

Sherry swallowed the lump in her throat. He was so much like her man it made her heart hurt. She allowed herself the luxury of resting her cheek against his warm skin. She could hear the rapid beat of his heart beneath her ear, and feel her own beat in time. Perhaps this was why the old man had sent her here. Perhaps this was her last chance at happiness.

"Do you not remember Aquato?" she heard Chardon ask.

She shook her head.

"Then come and I shall introduce you again."

He led her through the fairground and around the back of a large tent. "Stay here. I will be back."

He lifted the flap of the tent and stepped inside. A moment later, true to his word, he returned, but with him was the ugliest creature she had ever seen.

Sherry took a pace backwards. The creature had the tall body of a man like all the other beasts, but his face was covered with orange scales. His eyes bulged like a great goldfish, and his mouth gaped; drool hanging from both sides. Small fins sprouted from each cheek.

He wiped his shirtsleeve across his mouth before he spoke. "Sorry if my appearance offends you, my lady. Chardon has explained your lapse in memory and it saddens me. We were once good friends." He held out his hand and she placed hers gingerly within his larger one. He squeezed her hand gently and released it. "Come, you must be in need of refreshments and rest."

Sherry looked nervously behind her. "What about those hunting us?"

"They will not come here. This fair belongs to me." Aquato glanced pointedly to the side. Several more of the mask-like creatures stood at a distance posted at intervals of around ten feet. Each wore a sword at his side. "They will not pass my men," Aquato turned into the tent, and took Sherry's arm and followed.

The tent was divided into three sections, two sleeping chambers and a dining area. The dining area was scattered with large soft cushions, and several low side tables placed at intervals. Two guards stood just inside the entrance. Aquato gave a quiet order, and one of the men slipped from the tent.

"I have sent my man for refreshments and food. "Please," Aquato invited, "make yourself comfortable, and tell me of your adventure."

Chardon and Sherry settled themselves on the cushions and Chardon began to speak. He related the day's events, along with the details of Cara's abduction, and his own plan to save her. From his words Sherry learned that Chardon was the Lord of the Celtis' son, and Cara, her likeness was his third cousin, Lady Cara of the village, Nosta. Cara had been traveling to the Celti Village to be wed when her caravan had been attacked.

"So you took them on single-handedly. You should have called upon me for help," chastened Aquato.

"My father argued that point, but I convinced him it would be easier for one man to sneak through the tunnels undetected rather than..." The talk was interrupted by the entrance of three women carrying trays laden high with food.

Sherry was surprised to see they were human. The girls placed the food on the tables, then turned to go.

"Wait!" she called unthinking.

The girls stopped and peered back at her in surprise.

"You did not introduce your friends, Aquato," Sherry berated.

"They are not friends, Cara. These women are handmaidens." Aquato clapped his hands and the girls hastened from the tent.

Sherry frowned. "Handmaidens?"

"Slaves, Cara. And Slaves are not introduced," said Chardon in a hard tone. 'Tis not the custom of our people, but—"

"My people still practice slavery," finished Aquato. "I know you look on slavery as barbaric, you have expressed your opinion many times, however, to my people it is a way of life."

"I did not mean offense, Aquato. You have shown us a great kindness today and for that I will be eternally grateful."

Aquato smiled as he rose, the fins at the sides of his face flaping back and forth. "No offense taken, my friend, but I shall bid you good sleep." He ambled toward one of the partitions on the other side of the tent and pulled back the flap covering the entrance. A large bed stood in the center of the chamber. Aquato gave a slight bow. "I hope you will find the bed to your satisfaction." He waited for them to enter, then turned to leave.

Sherry lifted the flap and watched him exit the other side of the tent with a sense of awe, distaste and something else. She examined her feelings. Although the creature had been kind and had helped them, as Chardon had expressed, she couldn't quite bring herself to trust him.

She stepped back into the bedchamber allowing the canvas flap to drop into place, then watched as Chardon removed his cloak, sword and boots and dropped back spread-eagled onto the bed. "Come, woman," he said softly, rolling onto his elbow and patting the place beside him.

Sherry remained standing. She allowed her gaze to wander over his wide chest and shoulders, down his flat stomach, to his muscular thighs still encased in brown leather breeches. He fair took her breath away. Never had she seen a man that stirred her blood more. He was her Jarred, yet not. He was more rugged. Jarred with the smooth edges removed. A lock of raven hair lay low on his forehead, almost in his eyes—brilliant blue eyes, which she could lose herself in and never wish to return. His masculinity was raw, sensual, calling to her. She took a step forward, then another.

"Take my hand," he whispered, "I would never hurt you. If it was not for your abduction, already we would be wed, and tomorrow we will be. What difference is one night? And with what you have been through, I think you need my arms about you."

One night, Sherry thought. Just one night. One night to say goodbye to Jarred. One night with this warm beautiful man. Then she would start her search for a way home.

Just one night of love.

Another step took her to the edge of the bed, but as she stepped a great weight seemed to drag her down. Her hand went to the pocket of her cloak and closed around the idol she had taken from the High Priest's throne. She drew the statue out and set it on a table beside the bed, then unclipped her cloak and dropped it at her feet.

"You may be great warrior," she said, with a soft smile, "but no man to my knowledge can make love with his pants on."

Chardon eyed her solemnly and rolled from the bed, his hands going to his belt. "Anything that makes my lady happy."

She slid her gown from her shoulders and went into his arms.

Next morning, Sherry woke to the sound of a low growl, and opened her eyes to stare up into the face of a nightmare. A creature with the visage of a spotted frog stared down at her. "Lie still," ordered a voice from across the bed. She turned to see the fish-faced Aquato, a short sword leveled at Chardon's chest. A creature resembling a cat stood behind the bed holding the warrior's arms.

"I knew we couldn't trust you."

"Clever girl. You should have told your lover."

"I'll see you dead for this," snarled Chardon.

"Too late." Aquato nodded to the creature staring down at Sherry. "Take her, while I finish this one."

"Wait!" demanded Chardon.

Aquato's fish mouth tightened. "Yes, what is it?"

"Why are you doing this? I thought we were friends."

"I pretended friendship for my own gain." Aquato's face twisted in a cruel smile. "I knew one day it would pay off. Never could I really care for one of your insignificant race." He turned and spat on the floor. "And I had noted the look of disgust in your woman's eyes many times, even when she professed friendship. He glanced at Sherry. "But she shall pay. Pay dearly. First I shall have some sport with her, then once more she shall be wedded to Kaligi through the pit of fire." He seemed to rise in height. "I have been elected new High Priest."

"No!" Sherry's finger's closed around the idol, she brought it around and smashed it across Aquato's sword. It spun from his hand and Chardon twisted his body to the side, and dived for the sword. Sherry brought the idol back, striking the frog creature in the jaw. She heard the bone crack. He grunted and fell to the floor. She glanced around for the cat-man, but too late, she was struck to the side of her head, and fell into a deep abiding darkness...

Again she seemed to be falling, then she picked up as if on an air current and sped through a bright tunnel of multicolored lights. Her body felt light as if it had no substance. Her mind a fuzz. Where had she been? Where she was going? She knew it was important to remember something...yet no memory came.

With a sense of déjà vu she awoke on a bed, staring at a ceiling. A white ceiling. She frowned, wondering why that should seem so strange, then realized the ceiling in Rio had been blue.

She squeezed her eyes closed, knowing there was something she must remember, but she felt nauseated and her brain refused to work. She slipped her legs over the side of her single bed, at the same time her knuckle coming into contact with an object, cold and hard. Her hand closed over the object and she lifted it to her lap.

It all came flooding back. This time it had not been a dream. The cold metal of the idol brought home the cold truth of reality. Jarred's proposal, Jarred's death, 'The Old Green Door', the sacrifice, Chardon's rescue and the attack. Her heart sank. What had become of the courageous man she had met in that other world? Had he lived or had he perished at the hand of Aquato and his henchmen? If only there were a way to help him. But she knew she couldn't help him, he was in a world lost to her.

She glanced around the room. She was back in her apartment in New York, and the calendar on the wall read April 5th. The day Jarred's plane had gone down. Jumping off her bed, she reached for her bedside clock. 9:30 in the morning. She was gripped with a sense of excitement. At 9:35 on the 5th of April, Jarred had called to propose and suggest they elope to Rio.

It might be too late to help Chardon, but perhaps not to save Jarred.

Sherry paced the room, each second seeming like a countdown of her own heartbeats. The phone rang and she dived for it, knocking the receiver from its cradle. Hastily she gathered it up and held it to her heart, then her ear.

"Yes. Yes, is that you, Jarred?"

She heard him laugh, the sound sweet to her ears, and say, "Are you all right darling? You sound flustered."

Flustered? If only he knew... She took a deep breath to calm her nerves. "I'm fine, how about you? You're calling early. Something wrong?"

"No, nothing wrong, but I've been thinking..."

"Yes," she prompted, smiling inwardly and remembering this was just how that first conversation had gone. When it came to public speaking Jarred could command thousands. When it came to proposing, he was just like any other man—hesitant and shy, afraid of rejection.

"I was wondering if you might like to hop a plane and get married in Rio." His voice was low and hopeful. "I know how much you love carnivals. And what could be better than the biggest carnival of all. The Mardi Gras in Rio."

Sherry squirmed, knowing if she ever attended another Mardi Gras this side of eternity, it would be too soon. "Yes to the wedding, no to Rio," she answered, softly. "Why don't I fly to Mexico and we'll discuss it. I have a hankering for something a little more exotic for a honeymoon, perhaps a cruise. Give me two days to tidy up loose ends here and see my boss about extending my holiday."

"Anything to make my lady happy."

Sherry stilled, heart skipping a beat. Jarred's voice had sounded so much like Chardon's it brought a lump to her throat. They were the same words he'd spoken to her before they had made love for the first, and last time.

She couldn't feel guilty, just sad, for she knew somehow the men's two souls were intertwined.

"Sherry? Are you still with me?"

Sherry smiled. Always, she mused. "Have you ever thought of growing your hair longer?" she asked out loud.

She heard him laugh. "I'll see what I can do while we are away. I've got to go now. Remember I'm counting the days."

"Not as much as I," she replied, replacing the receiver with a warm feeling.

Her man was alive. Alive! And she had the old man in the shop to thank. She promised herself she would fly to Rio and thank him personally. Perhaps he would know what had become of Chardon. And why had he brought them together only to have torn them apart? Yet, she knew she would never really lose Chardon, because for her he would always exist in Jarred. Perhaps Chardon had really been Jarred in a parallel universe, and for a short time she had been lucky enough to share that world.

≈ ≈

Several weeks later after a quiet wedding on the high seas and a dream cruise of the Greek Islnads, Sherry alighted from the taxi and paid the driver. She had taken the cab directly from the airport, leaving her luggage in storage. She stared across the narrow street where 'The Old Green Door' had stood. Instead of the small antique shop, a brick wall stared back at her.

It was almost evening and the street was deserted. This evening resembled not at all the crowded night that she had first stepped inside the establishment.

She felt slightly unnerved and turned hastily to leave.

Behind her stood an old man.

For a moment her heart lightened. She had thought the man was the old timer from the store, for his bright violet eyes were nearly identical. But where her old man had been tall and sported a long beard, this man was short and his beard close cropped.

"Are you lost?" he asked, his voice so low she almost missed his words.

"No, not lost. Just confused." Sherry pointed across the road. "A short time ago I visited this place. An old antique store stood where that wall now stands. *The Old Green Door.* Do you know of it?"

"Sorry my dear, but you must be mistaken. No store has resided on that corner for near on two hundred years. Except ..."

Sherry frowned. "Except?"

"Which night did you say this was?"

Sherry hesitated. "It may seem strange, but it was Mardi Gras night."

The old man nodded. "I see."

Sherry turned away, disappointment lacing her words. "I'm sorry to have wasted your time."

"It is said," the old man began.

Sherry swung back, hope in her eyes. "Yes?"

"That every fifty years an old store appears on the corner. And that the store keeper has the power to grant one traveler their dearest wish." He smiled, the mauve of his eyes deepening. "Perhaps you were that traveler, lass."

She matched his smile. "Perhaps, I was."

"And was this wish everything you could have dreamed of?"

"And more."

The old man nodded, bid her good day, and moved on quietly down the street.

For a moment more Sherry stood staring across the road, the old man's words running through her mind. Wish—dream. She brought her hand to her head. Of course! If he had the power to send her into another world and grant her wish, it would be nothing for him to change his appearance. She swung about to scan the street. He was gone.

"Thank you," she said, whispering the words onto her hand and releasing them to the wind. A small warm breeze blew up from the south, caressing her cheeks and carrying away her words, and she smiled and walked on, remembering something an old man had once told her. In what seemed a time long ago.

True happiness is like a warm breeze that touches your life when you least expect it.

ALL THE FIRES OF HOME

by Loren W. Cooper

Lights burned down steadily into the arena as Antaeus spun and hit, his legs flexing to take the impact. For an instant, hanging parallel to the floor and staring up into the night sky, he could forget the familiar patterns of the constellations and fancy the stars as countless small fires, waiting for men and women and children to come close and huddle around them, turning their backs on the terrifying darkness to bask in the life-giving warmth.

Contempt touched his face with bitterness, and he pushed himself away from the wall before Luna's sluggish grip could end his routine. The bitterness faded from his face as he flew across the open expanse of the room, his shadow sketched starkly below him by the light of the stars and the rising Earth. He flexed his limbs, turning as he flew, to hit again with his bare feet, but absorbed the force of his rush with bended knees to rebound from the curving side of the clear dome gently, allowing Luna's grasp to settle around him and pull him down to the warm, slightly resilient floor of what had once been an observation dome, and would be again, once he left that place. He turned his gaze toward the Earth, nearly full and glowing with light. The sun still lay below his horizon, but he could see the terminator, that stark line between planetary day and night, drawn across the fat curve of the Earth's bulging waistline. Against the darkness, away from the face of the horizon, he could just see the East Pole turning into view, lights clustering around Earth's Second Folly. The gargantuan construction project had become more of a tourist attraction than anything else, though it also served as an excuse to keep Outworld ships from entering Terra's atmosphere. The Beanstalks (East and West Poles) had proved to be a failed expensive gamble: little more than up before breakthroughs in clean propulsion and power had rendered them all but obsolete.

"What do you think? Beautiful, isn't she? It's been a long time, yes?"

Antaeus spun, the startled motion still graceful in the light gravity, but he could feel the degree of lost control by the time he spent drifting back down to the reassuring contact of a surface. He hadn't heard Devlin enter.

He hadn't been so helpless in years.

He turned to face his watchdog, his features an expressionless mask. "Mars is prettier. Blue skies, red sand, and the green traceries spreading from the poles and Mariner Cliff City. We haven't had time to screw up what we've started there, yet."

"Cheerful this morning, aren't we?"

"What do you want, Devlin?"

The smaller man tilted his head, his eyes glittering and reptilian. "Why such a dislike of me, Antaeus? I am, after all, your appointed Earth Liaison. I'm here to provide whatever you want. You're a hero down there."

Antaeus' mouth twisted. "You mean I will be a hero, if I give them what they want."

"You need to understand how important this is to everyone. To Earth." Devlin sighed. "A victory could help close the distance."

"Or increase it." Antaeus turned and began walking briskly toward the arena exit, falling naturally into the smooth skating stride required by the light lunar gravity. He derived some satisfaction from watching Devlin fumble clumsily into an undignified bounce as he hastened to keep the pace.

Antaeus caught Devlin's eye as they crossed through and into the tube corridor. "You know as well as I do that Earth's SenseNet propaganda machine will make what they want of the outcome. None of the rest of it matters. The Gradient is a game, Devlin. A game played at every colony, and broadcast to every world. This is just another match."

"You couldn't be more wrong," Devlin said firmly. "This is the ultimate match, a battle between the Outworld champion and the one Earth Scion who went to the colonies and beat them at their own game. They want this match here so they can humble you, and through you, all of the rest of us."

"You're paranoid, Devlin." Antaeus laughed. "There is no us and them. They are us. We're all the same. The only resentment the colonies have is against the Federalist Movement on the home world. You can't blame them for that. Earth clings to the colonies like a jealous woman. More gates are constructed now with colony funds and materials each year than Earth financed in the first hundred. Earth can't expect to maintain political control and impose taxes on a transport system already in the hands of the colonies. It doesn't matter where the technology for that transport system originated, or that it paved the road for successful colonization of the outworlds. Earth's drive for the impossibility of continued political and economic control will widen the breach growing between her and her colonies. Perhaps to the point where war itself could follow. And I can't believe I'm even discussing this with you, Devlin. Just back the hell off, and let me play, and make your use of it."

Devlin stopped. "Why haven't you gone to Earth?"

Antaeus slowed, and turned. "That's the heart of it, isn't it?"

"You requested only the use of this old complex, and the privacy of isolation. You haven't even made the attempt to contact anyone on the place of your birth." Devlin cocked his head. "Why?"

Antaeus' lip curled. "Afraid I'm going over to the other side? Afraid I'm throwing the match?"

Devlin shook his head. "I know you too well for that. You're too much of a competitor to do anything but win. Why haven't you gone home?"

Antaeus blew out a harsh breath. "Earth doesn't hold anything for me, anymore. I have no home but the stars and the spaces between them. This place is just another stop, just another game." His brow creased. "What are you bothering me for, anyway? I still have a little while."

"The bureaucrats are jumpy. Eyes have been watching from the ridges, recording your workouts in the dome from a distance. Did you know that? At any rate, there's concern about security. Threats from dissidents or crazies."

Antaeus snorted. "Earth has plenty of those."

"Be that as it may." Devlin pushed away from the floor with too much force, his Earthborn reflexes leaving him exposed in a long floating hop. "They've come for you early. If you need anything from your quarters..."

"All I need I carry with me. I probably won't see you again." Antaeus bounced down the corridor in a sudden lunge of motion, using walls and floor and ceiling for control and speed.

"Antaeus!"

He stopped at the tube junction, settling as always into a slight crouch, and turned to look back down the distance to where Devlin still stood, making no effort to catch him. "Yes?"

Devlin cocked his head. "Do you know what your name means?"

Antaeus chuckled. "As I recall, Antaeus was a figure out of Greek myth. A wrestler who lost to Heracles."

Devlin nodded. "Heracles won by holding Antaeus above his head and strangling him. You see, Antaeus grew stronger when he touched the ground, for he was a son of Earth."

"A little heavy handed, Devlin, even for you."

He straightened his legs and flexed his back, brushed the sloping roof of the tube with one hand, turned to plant his feet against the corner of the junction, then shot off down the tube and out of Devlin's sight. His face hardened as he flashed down corridors at rates of speed rarely associated with unpowered movement in the moon's lazy gravity.

They wondered at his request for isolation, but he felt hemmed in enough on Luna, with Terra hanging overhead like a reproachful memory. And, of course, he could never have moved with such speed and efficiency had crowds enclosed him, but the empty tubes let him fly across the passageways in a crisscrossing course that never took him out of reach of any surface. To the inexperienced eye, his brief touches against the walls of the tubes would have seemed no more than light brushes of hands or feet, and such an observer would have thought that he moved in the absence of gravity, not in a pull some one-sixth of Earth's solid grip.

By the time he had covered the five or so kilometers of secured and cordoned corridors to the shuttle complex, a light sheen of sweat covered his body, his breathing had deepened noticeably into a long, steady rhythm, and less than ten minutes had passed. He slowed at the curtain of light that marked the boundary between his private areas and the public terminal entrance. Through the field he could see the crowd, individual shapes blurred into one mass by the ripple of the security field.

The security field faded as he approached, and they closed around him, the natives easily discernable from the visiting Eyes by the slow, sliding grace of their movements, making them look like dancers on a floor invaded by the clumsy rush of misshapen beasts. The Eyes, a combination of freelance and contracted representatives of the larger media houses, fought to get closer to him. The closer they were, the more clearly their wired systems would pick up the sounds and smells and feel of his presence in the moment. They threw questions that blurred together, about the Gradient, about his training, about the worlds he had seen, about his diet or his sex life, or else they stared and shambled closer, absorbing the sight and the scent of his presence and the close warmth and dusky smell of the crowd all overlaid by the gentle net of Luna's light gravity, so that they could bottle the experience and sell it later to the crowds of Earth and Mars, and the ones rich enough to afford the cost in the colonies, charging so much for a sip of sensation, some set value for a taste of stolen memory.

In the silence of his mind he cursed them all, but he made his escape as gracefully as he could, never speaking, streaking through the crowd to the safe cordon of Lunar Security that marked the entrance to his waiting shuttle. The crowd pursued, their voices blending into an incomprehensible roar, like the sound of surf beating against a rocky shore. The LunSec officers closed in behind him, the blank masks of their armored visors providing enough deterrence to make the crowd hesitate, and that was all the opportunity he needed. Antaeus slipped through the opening door and into the shuttle link, and as the doorway irised shut behind him, cutting off the sound of the crowd with knife-edge abruptness, he paused to breathe a heavy sigh. Back on Earth, only the wealthiest could afford the space for privacy.

Shaking his head, he skated down to the door opening at the other end, and laughed aloud as he saw who waited for him there. "Rosalee! Ah, Rose, I never thought that you'd make it down here."

He scooped her up as the door shut behind him and jumped, hurling them both further into the ship. Startled heads tilted, the light of their controls and screens flashing on the pale ovals of their faces as he kicked off from the doorway and hurtled down toward the cabin section, Rose's bright hair whipping across his eyes.

He stopped them in the cabin and let her go, grinning into her scowl. "It's good to see you."

She caught her hair and wound it back into a tight knot at the nape of her neck. "I would never have known."

Antaeus winced in spite of himself at her dry tone. "It's been a few weeks. I'm allowed."

Her mouth twitched, the beginnings of a smile visible in her eyes. "So you say. You've been picking up bad habits."

He felt the low rumble of the drives kicking in. "I've been training."

Her knees flexed as the hand of acceleration, even damped by the compensators, fell down across everyone in the ship. "So has Drake. He's been on Mars and Earth, I understand."

"Drake hasn't been training," Antaeus snorted. "He's been touring. He's lucky no one's shot him yet."

She cocked her head. "Is that the reason you gave for the isolation? Security?"

"Of course. Though if anyone had wanted me on Luna, all they would have had to do is blow the dome or one of the tubes while I was using it. I never bothered with a suit."

She settled into the slung seat. "Careless."

"I don't like to be confined."

"Do you think Drake's time in the heavier gravities will give him an edge?"

Antaeus snorted. "At least he's been smart enough to keep moving, and vary the gravities, but no, I don't believe he'll have any advantage to speak of from the heavier gravity. I haven't been on Luna long enough to lose any muscle mass, and pushing a lighter gravity can beat you into shape faster than anything short of a constant two gravities if you know what you're doing as long as you don't spend too much time. Besides, in the Gradient control is more important than raw power, and a lighter gravity is better for working on control." He paused at the far wall. Light folded out from the wall, his hands skated through checkerboard patterns, and the wall ghosted to a field of stars. Satisfied, he dropped into the seat next to hers. "One of the corporate shuttles, I see."

"Father likes me to travel in comfort. And I'm not as much the rebel as you."

His face hardened slightly. He deliberately smoothed any traces of tension from his face before answering. "And how is he?"

"Settling into place to watch the game in comfort from the Gate station. He'll be one of the first to see the results, outside Earth, Mars and Luna, of course. He's offered you a ride back with him. He's leaving directly after the game, but he'll wait for us to rendezvous. Unless you're planning on sticking around in Earth space for a while."

Antaeus smiled. "I might just take him up on that." He reached over, caught her hand, and pressed her fingers to his lips. "It's my last game."

She dropped her gaze. "Are you going to offer to settle down? I won't believe it."

"Settle down into a ship of our own, maybe," he said, grinning. "Your father offered me a job, you know. Troubleshooting for him. Political representative of the corporation, more like. He knows I don't know any more about Gate technology and quasimatter than any man on the street. But he thinks the image could be useful. And I'd have all the travel I could justify. Which would be considerable."

"I heard you talking. The two of you." She raised her eyes to his. "On your last visit. You mean to lose."

His eyes narrowed. "I won't let them use me, Rose. And yes, I still believe that my winning will move us away from reconciliation, not toward it."

"Do you? Think that, I mean? I know my father does."

"Do you think I'm lying? That I want this to grow toward war?"

She shook her head, her face serious. "You believe your justifications. And even your justifications are good. They always are. It's one of the many reasons I love you. All I'm asking you to do is know why you're doing this. Is it because you want to close the growing distance between Earth and her colonies, or is it because of the resentment you still have against your home and family? Because of the past you've spent all your time running from? Because when you were looking up, they were looking down, and when you were looking out, they were looking in, or because when you were dreaming, they were scheming? You're on the largest stage anyone's seen in history, and at a pivotal moment. People on every world will be watching this game of yours. And when you decide what you decide, I want you to be thinking about where you are and where you're going, not about where you've been. Not about whatever it is that's been going on between you and your parents for the last couple of decades. Ultimately, the war will happen or not, apart from the game. Any propaganda victory will be a thing of the moment."

He pulled back, studying her for a moment in silence. "Sometimes you scare me a little."

She grinned impishly. "That's how every man reacts to a woman who makes him think."

His chuckled wryly. "Truth." His face lost any sign of mirth. "A lit fuse is a thing of the moment. Propaganda can light that fuse. I don't want to be the one who provides the spark. We're on a slippery slope, Rose. Stuck in the point of balance, we can't climb for fear of falling.

Whatever we do, we're afraid it will be wrong. We're riding our own gradient, and all of us know it's a steep and unforgiving son of a bitch. And I am not the kind who can refuse to act. I have to try something, no matter that it may be wrong. I have to follow my instincts, and let my judgment guide me. And through all that I rely on you to keep me from wandering astray of the path, and sliding over the edge. I don't know if anything I do up there today will make one damned bit of difference. In all probability, it won't. But I have to try. I can't let them use me. Do you see?"

He reached out, touching her face gently, and pulled her close against the steady weight of constant acceleration.

"Sir?"

Antaeus frowned, and turned to see the long face of one of the ship's crew forming in the middle of his star field. "Sir, I hate to interrupt your reunion, but you have a call. From Earth."

Antaeus' mouth hardened. "I should have expected this. I'll take it in the back."

Rose caught his hand as he pushed himself upright. "Take it easy." He chuckled. "I'm careful."

His steps were light, even with the pull of what he reckoned at roughly one and a half Earth standard gravities. He palmed the door to the private cabin open, and shut it carefully behind him. He walked past the bed, and the door to the privy, and through to the circular den. He closed that door as well, and sat carefully in one of three molded chairs extruded from the floor of the room without increasing the illumination past a gentle background glow.

He hadn't been sitting long before light folded up from a central well dominating the middle of the room to sculpt a woman's face. His eyes met hers. "So. Has the owner and director of FieldTech come to persuade me of the vital importance of the upcoming match to the welfare of Terra and its place in the Universe?"

The merest glint of mockery burned in her eyes. "Why should I bother convincing you of anything, when it seems that you have already convinced yourself? Do you intend to lose?"

"I don't lose. But that says nothing of my convictions."

She showed her teeth in an expression resembling a smile. "Does it matter, so long as you have convictions?"

"Have you noticed that we don't so much hold conversations as slip seamlessly back into that continuing argument we've had for the last few decades?" he asked mildly.

Her face smoothed to a blank mask. "And how is Rose?"

His eyes became hooded. "Well enough. Worried, like everyone else. Everyone with eyes to see, at any rate."

She cocked her head slightly. "Have you heard from your father?"

He shifted topics easily, long accustomed to her mercurial conversational style. "Last I heard, he'd passed through the first leg of the far Rimward Loop. He's still focusing on the Corporate Colonies, his gaze yet captive to his vision of Oligarchy."

Her smile faded. "However it goes, the family will prosper."

His eyes narrowed. "You always took the long view. Both of you did. What do you see?"

A hand rose into view, absently brushing a lock of hair back from her face. "We can talk more about it when you come home."

He stiffened, but said nothing as she continued. "I've aired out the old place. It's autumn in the mountains, you know. Geese are beginning to stir overhead. The leaves are just turning, and the air has that crisp taste you always loved. We still have the grounds, of course. I've had the gardeners exclude them from their rounds for the last year or so. They're getting wild again, the way you wanted them. I thought that you might want to go walking. I've cleared a couple of days on my schedule, though you can stay as long as you wish."

His jaw tightened. "I don't know that I'll have the time. My own schedule doesn't have much room, particularly now and after. Commitments, you understand. Another time, perhaps."

She smiled sadly, the first time he had seen her facade slip in years. "No hurry, of course. We have all the time in the world." Her eyes flickered from his face, as if she were reading a message coming in on her screen. "Well, I must be going. Some little problem with the holdings on Crete. At least it's close to home."

He nodded. "Obligation."

Her smile faded. "Sometimes I think we understand obligation better than we understand one another."

He sighed. "Sometimes I think you're right."

Her eyes sought his. "Luck."

He watched the patterns fade to chaos, and then to a gentle glow, and then to darkness. And he sat in the shadows, listening to the silence, until a gentle rapping came at the closed door, and he rose to open the door and let in the light.

He had a solid day with Rosalee before they came for him. He used the time as well as he knew, drawing strength from her presence, not allowing himself to examine his own motives too closely.

Not allowing himself to doubt.

He dropped from the corporate shuttle into the bay of a liner that usually made the Earth-Mars-Belt run. The lights chased visible shadows from the hallways of the liner, and a select group of Eyes met him as he came aboard. He ignored their questions, and they quickly settled into a watchful silence, shadowing him as he walked through the long hallways gleaming with inlaid patterns of opalescent pearl and set with a rainbow glitter of precious stones. Screens opened intermittently, all showing different angles of a disk swarmed over with the pinpoint glow of ships and shining in the harsh sunlight streaming across one face of the disk. A smile came unbidden to his face as he felt the lightness of adrenalin brush his stomach, a sensation more familiar than even the touch of a lover. Two pods waited in the bay, black eggs not much larger than the men who would ride in them. Beside one of the ships, surrounded by his own crowd of Eyes, stood a tall figure clothed in the same regulation skinsuit that Antaeus himself wore, lean ridges of muscle visible through the transparent patches of the suit. Grudgingly, as if impelled by some invisible force outside his body, Antaeus made his way between the ships, and the tall man, moving in much the same fashion, met him halfway.

Antaeus looked up into the pale, molded features of his opponent. "Drake."

"Antaeus." Drake's nostrils flared.

Antaeus smiled, and proffered a hand.

Drake took it gingerly, maintaining contact only briefly before pulling his hand away. "And what was that for?"

"Luck."

Drake's eyes flickered with disdain. "Luck has no place in the Gradient."

Antaeus' mouth twisted as Drake turned on his heel and stalked back to his ship, his movements lithe and pantherish in the Earth standard gravity of the bay. Antaeus turned back to his own ship, and caught sight of a small, gray man standing beside the molded curves of the pod. Antaeus stepped over to him, noting that his face did not hold the avid hunger of the Eyes'.

The gray man held out one hand, palm up. The thin patch of a bonephone lay in his hand. "I will be your referee, Antaeus. You will need your link before we can begin the game. Drake already has his."

Antaeus nodded, took the bonephone from the referee's hand, and placed it against the curve of his mastoid process. The patch spread out against the skin, there was a moment of tightness and then no sensation of anything at all behind his ear. He heard a slight crackle, then the referee's voice. "Is everything working?"

The referee's lips moved only slightly, and Antaeus knew that the other man must be subvocalizing. He responded in kind. "Seems to be working fine."

The referee nodded. "You may have some interference with all of the signals passing through the Gate's booster lens. You can tap the 'phone off, but it will automatically revert to active status when I broadcast. Understand?"

Antaeus nodded.

"Good." The smaller man stepped away from the ship. "We should begin."

Soundlessly, the egg split, opening to reveal a molded seat. Antaeus sat, pulled the webbing over himself, and turned to glance at Drake as the egg closed around him as silently as it had opened. He sat for a moment in darkness before fields of light flickered to life around him.

Stars drifted at either side of him, and of course the disk of the Gradient spun before him. Two long fields framing the center rolled with information.

His eyes flicked across the displays and his jaw tightened at the fact that even here, FieldTech's display interfaces surrounded him. No matter how far he went, he always felt the touch of the family's hand, like the weight of distant memory. Anger clenched in him like a fist, amplified by the adrenaline. How dare she! How dare she turn from his childhood, and reach for him now that he had managed to leave the family behind.

Absorbed in his thoughts, trying to bury the rage, the jolt of acceleration caught him by surprise as the liner threw the eggs into the velvet darkness. A mighty unseen hand pushed him evenly back into the cushioned seat of the egg until his vision blurred, and then the pressure faded. The display in front of him flickered, shifting to a field of stars centered around a dot that rapidly grew larger, giving him a view from the egg's perspective rather than the view from the remotes the displays had shown him before. The disk turned, the image clarifying until Antaeus could see the bulges of the field generators in the center of the faces of the disk. Even as he found himself hoping that the programmer who had set the flight plan had a steady enough understanding of the controls of the quasimatter powered field generators to prevent the kind of lurch the liner's launch had provided, he felt pressure force him forward and to the side, against the webbing.

The disk shifted in the display in front of him as induced fields of force gripped his egg and swept it on a long decelerating curve toward the cradle of his docking station at the rim of the disk. He had a momentary glimpse of the other egg crossing the bright reflection of the disk as Drake's pod broke away toward the opposite side of the disk. Then the bulk of the arena loomed over him, and he felt the gentle bump of the docking cradle, and for the first time in the last few days his gut lifted to the sensation of weightlessness. He could just feel the smooth motion of the docking cradle retracting as he pulled himself out of the webbing, and then the egg split, and he floated out into a small tube, every surface polished to a high, reflective sheen..

He kicked himself down the tube, skimming one wall until the tube opened out into a room small enough to be little more than a large box. A hatch sealed itself behind him, and light flared from strips laid along the edges of the box, lighting the room with a warm yellow radiance. Floating in suspension, his hands skated lightly along the cold smooth metal of the entry cell. Reflections stared back at him from every wall as his bonephone crackled to life. "Cells sealed. Gradient secured. Commencing spin. Brace for acceleration."

Slowly, he floated down and to the right, settling into the lower corner of the cubicle as the arena spun up to competition speed. A light crackle heralded crossover from one of the announcers broadcasting from one of the cluster of ships surrounding the disk. "...imagine a disk two hundred meters in diameter, placed temporarily in a vacant Lagrange point. Spin the disk to an angular velocity of just over thirty-one meters per second. At the outside edge of the disk, centrifugal force will provide a pull toward the edge approximately equal to Earth gravity. This pull decreases toward the center, where zero-g conditions prevail. This is the Gradient, the constantly varying simulated gravity that is the players' primary opponent. The engineers tell me that the course laid out for this competition is one of the toughest nonlethals ever seen. Of course, a competitor could choose to move along the side of the ring, but this is the longest path to the other player's goal."

Another voice broke in. "The Gradient has a great many variations, of course, but I've heard that this is to be a relatively straightforward game."

"That's right." Antaeus winced at the forced joviality in the woman's voice. "The terms of the game were set nearly a year ago, before the course had even been constructed. Three rounds will be played, with victory conditions determined by the first player to palm his opponent's trigger plate. The trigger plates are located by each competitor's entry door."

"I understand that in the colonies, the Gradient has become little more than ritual combat, with the competitors entering the arena armed..."

Antaeus' lips tightened at the thinly veiled bloodlust mixed with condescension in the man's voice, and touched the pad behind his ear, deactivating the 'phone.

He'd seen such variations of the game. They were perversions, gladiatorial combat, a spectacle of butchery compounded by the treacherous gravitational slope of the arena. This race between himself and Drake would be so much more civilized.

His lip curled at the irony, and he shook off despair, knowing that nothing he did could keep the powers on either side from using the game for their own ends. He had once thought to deny Earth a propaganda victory by throwing the game. He had come to understand in the last few days how he had been fooling himself. Anything he chose to do would ultimately be used by both sides.

Antaeus settled down to his haunches, wedging his back in the corner of the room, gauging the acceleration. As the pull crested, he felt the acceleration slowing, easing the pressure on his back as the pressure against his feet steadied. When he could no longer sense any acceleration, the inner door irised open, and he straightened into a leap, using the lip of the doorway to leverage himself neatly out of the compartment and roll smoothly into the arena chamber.

He looked up, across the expanse of the arena. He seemed to stand at the base of an arching hoop, bounded by walls three meters apart and alive with rich, buttery light. A maze of seemingly randomly placed polished metal cylinders of varying sizes stretched between the walls, casting distorted images of himself across every visible surface.

He kicked off the slippers they had given him, took two quick steps, jumped, bounced off a beam as broad as his chest, caught another the diameter of his index finger, and swung himself up and toward the center. The pull diminished as he moved, gauging the shifting balance of forces instinctively, nearly unconsciously. Noting the almost frictionless surfaces of the beams he had touched, Antaeus grinned. It would be a tough course. Not the toughest he had played, but tough.

He saw a hint of movement, a flash of reflection to his left, and he threw himself up and through the weightless zone, dodging from beam to beam, flying headlong down through the forest of unforgiving reflection, dropping down in the steadily increasing pull to flip and land on the outside wall of the arena. He spotted the closed iris of Drake's entrance less than two meters away. The light of the switch burned steadily beside it. He hesitated, then lunged for the light, only to see it wink out in the instant before his hand slapped down on the unforgiving surface of the arena.

He couldn't have told anyone, right then, where that hesitation had come from. He didn't know himself.

He rolled slowly to his feet as the patch behind his ear crackled to life. "First round to Drake."

Behind the referee's impersonal announcement, he could hear a heated discussion between the two 'casters. "...disagree. A basic first round, testing the arena and the relative speed of the competitors."

The referee broke in again. "Proceed along the outer wall to your goal, players."

Antaeus jogged along the outer wall, slowing as he saw Drake's lean shape come into view.

Antaeus held out his hand. "Well played."

Drake stopped, eyed the hand, and shook his head, the skin around his mouth and eyes tight with animosity. "You still don't understand, do you?"

Antaeus dropped his hand, his blood heating. "Understand what?"

Drake looked down his aquiline nose at the shorter man. "No matter how much dust you shake from your feet, you still stink of Earth. Try as you will, you will never be one of us."

Antaeus stepped closer to his opponent, eyes narrowed and his jaw clenched. "We are all the same, as much as I occasionally hate to admit it. There is no us and them, you stupid bastard."

Drake's fists bunched, and Antaeus laughed in his face. "Save it for the arena. Anything else is a foul."

He stepped past Drake and stalked back to his gate. He felt tired under the rage, knowing that their conversation would be heard by everyone wired into the game, and on the lips of everyone interested in driving Earth and the colonies further apart. In the end, it seemed, nothing he could do would make any difference. Drake and his faction had all of the fanaticism of the Federalists, and just like the Federalists, the colonies would use a victory to fan the flames of resentment and hatred into the fire of open conflict.

Antaeus settled to wait in the circle of his door. Rage and frustration boiled within him. He had thought that he could have some impact on the course of events. What a blind, arrogant fool he had been. The game itself that should have been his focus was trivial in the course of events. The game had become a beautiful propaganda opportunity for both sides, because of the audience, because of the competitors, because of the metaphor the media on both sides could twist out of it.

What a fool I am to play, he thought savagely, looking out blindly toward the unseen audience, and what fools you are to watch.

When the light of his trigger plate blinked to life, he hurled himself again into the heart of the arena. He picked up speed as he moved, using what he had learned the first pass, skimming through the tangle of crossbars at nearly twice his previous speed, using the sliding lift of his stomach to measure the constantly shifting forces gripping him, compensating automatically to each change in the Gradient's invisible slope.He began decelerating as he dropped out of the weightless zone and began to fall. Bounding from beam to beam, he spotted Drake's sudden rush in a flicker of dancing reflection, and rolled away from it, catching the other man's arm and flinging him out toward the edge of the arena as he rolled.

Drake caught a nearby beam and spun back, but by that time Antaeus had dropped further down through the beams, bouncing in to land feet first on the trigger plate. He somersaulted aside as the light blinked out and Drake landed where he had stood an instant before. Antaeus smiled into Drake's red face as the referee's voice crackled to life in his ears. "Second round to Antaeus."

Antaeus slipped past Drake, jogging toward his gate. He had seen the heat in Drake's eyes, and he recognized the move Drake had used. Drake intended to disable him, shifting the nature of the game from race to conflict, a strategy perfectly legal under the rules. Antaeus rolled his shoulders as he ran, welcoming the sparkling coil of a rising predatory rush, perfectly willing to escalate the conflict. At least he would have a tangible outlet for his frustrations, and gladiatorial perversions be damned.

He stepped back into the circle of his entrance into the arena, and watched his trigger plate. As soon as it lit, he jumped up and into the arena proper once more. Antaeus adopted a more cautious approach than his last headlong rush, easing his way into the fractured reflections marking his progress into the heart of the Gradient, toward the place known as the sweet spot, where the pull of the spin-

ning disk faded to weightlessness. A quarter of the way across the
arena, he paused, balancing on a beam, listening. The scattered placing of the crossbeams effectively created cleared spaces as well as
sections so densely crosshatched with obstacles as to be nearly im-
passible. Wanting to maximize both control and visibility, he moved
cautiously further toward the center, gliding along the inside edges of
the dense sections, studying the reflections in the beams carefully as
he passed. The Gradient's pull had eased to a tendency to drift when
he saw Drake. Drake waited at the opposite edge of a large area clear
of beams that centered on the area of the disk where the force created
by the disk's spin approached null—the sweet spot.

Drake waited inside the ring of the clearing, making no attempt to
conceal himself from Antaeus' eyes. Antaeus smiled tightly, recognizing
the challenge, and met it in kind, easing through the beams until he
drifted out into the open, on the side of the clearing directly across from
Drake. He saw the beginnings of a smile on Drake's face, swallowed
quickly back into the mask of his face, and Antaeus resisted the urge to
shake his head. All the years of progress, and even this still came down
to a couple of overgrown children playing deadly games.

The antagonists moved gracefully, with deceptive unconcern, circling around the edge of the clearing, the space between them changing in fits and spurts, until Drake closed the distance in a sudden
rush, and they came together, moved swiftly, and passed apart, as if
dancing. They hung quietly between the walls of the disk for a moment, studying one another. Drake held himself stiffly, and Antaeus
could see beads of blood spiraling lazily toward a nearby beam. He
could feel his right eye swelling, and knew that he had to finish the
matter before he lost his vision on that side.

As if by common agreement, they came together again, bounding
back and forth between the walls to build speed, using the torque of
spins to lend momentum to blows made in lightning passes. Once
again they separated, both breathing heavily, the walls and crossbeams
of the arena splotched with blood, and dark droplets spun in the air
between them. Antaeus could feel a fire in his ribs when he moved,
and he could see the dark blotches of bruises already beginning to
mottle Drake's flesh through the transparent patches of his skinsuit.
Antaeus was trying to assess the damage in a tired way, wondering if
Drake's longer reach made this a losing battle, when Drake kicked off,
hit one wall of the disk, then the other, lunging toward Antaeus in a
sudden furious rush.

Antaeus set his feet, caught Drake's leading arm, thrust with his
legs, ignoring the scream of protest from his ribs, and used the leverage of the beam behind him to spin Drake in a circular throw. Drake's
body rotated through a quarter turn before slamming into a beam no
wider than a man's wrist. His legs kicked once, convulsively, and he
cartwheeled slowly back toward the center of the arena.

Antaeus saw how limply Drake floated, and an icy dash of fear hit him. He eased out to Drake and slowed him gently, watching how the arms and legs and head moved only in response to his light touch. He hesitated, knowing he could simply drop down and trigger the patch, ending the game, then bent closer to Drake's face, to see if the other man still breathed.

Drake's eyes popped open, and he took a sudden convulsive breath. Antaeus kicked away, then saw that Drake still floated, arms and legs splayed in the nearly nonexistent gravity. Antaeus drifted back. He could see the white around the edges of Drake's eyes. The bigger man squeezed his eyes shut, diamond tears clinging to his lashes, then opened them again, and caught sight of Antaeus. "I can't feel my legs."

Antaeus heard the pain in the whisper. His first thought was to stabilize Drake in the center of the sweet spot, then slide down and slap the patch, ending the game. Injuries were part and parcel of the game. Floating in the sweet spot, Drake should be safe, with only the slightest chance of drifting far enough to begin an uncontrolled fall down the gradient's slippery slope before Antaeus returned.

Antaeus studied the pain and fear in Drake's eyes. To hell with the game. "Relax, Drake. You'll be all right. We'll get you out of this."

He tapped the link behind his ear. "Spin us down."

The referee's voice came back immediately. "The game isn't over. Both patches are still active."

"Drake is hurt," Antaeus said sharply. "Broke his neck, I suspect. I know that you have monitors in here, for the benefit of the audience. You take a look at those, and spin us down."

"We've been watching." The referee's voice didn't change. "We know that Drake is hurt."

"Then you spin us down."

"Do you forfeit?"

He could have laughed at the outrage that rose within him at the suggestion. Instincts die hard.

Drake sighed. "Go hit the plate. Take the game. I'll make it or I won't. I wouldn't have stayed for you."

"I don't care," Antaeus snarled. "I forfeit."

After a moment's hesitation, the referee's voice came back. "Antaeus forfeits. Drake wins by default. Spinning down. Medical teams disembarking."

Antaeus reached up, peeled off the bonephone, and let it drift out and down, toward the edge of the arena. He settled at Drake's side, and kept him steady against the delicate pull of the cariolus force, touching him only when necessary, and then only gently. He waited until the medical teams made their way in, and stood aside as they cocooned his former opponent, securing his spinal column from shifting before they moved him. Two of them peeled off to look at Antaeus, who availed himself of their painkillers, and allowed himself to follow along behind them to the waiting ship. The painkillers comfortably blurred the next few hours, the Eyes and the touch of strangers, the bustle and the noise.

When Rosalee came for him, the medical team thought to make him stay for observation, but she was convincing, and he was adamant. When he made it back to the comfort of the shuttle, he smiled, and pulled her close.

She laughed. "I think it worked out well, in the end. You made it up your slippery slope without falling. It'll be hard to make good propaganda out of that. Father thinks so, too. He's waiting for your call. He wants to know if you still want that ride out of the system."

"If they want the conflict badly enough, they'll make it out of whatever comes to hand," Antaeus said wearily. "I'm sure that they'll have plenty of opportunity. And in the end, do you know I forgot all about my plans and calculations? I forgot about the war."

She kissed him. "I know. So does everyone else." She paused. "Did you want to make that call?"

He gave her a lopsided smile. "In a minute. I need to call someone else first. How would you like to accompany me for a little while? I have a place in mind, a place I haven't seen in a long time, where a tired wanderer can find a little of the beauty once natural to Earth, with plenty of privacy, wonderful food, and crisp, smoky air that tastes like life."

"Of course," she said softly. "I'll let the crew know where we're going."

Antaeus rose to his feet, and made his way gingerly back through the private cabin. He paused at a wall, touched a section, and let his fingers dance through fans of light. The wall smoothed and opened like a window to a brilliant web of stars, the golden glow of the sun just rising in the background as the ship rolled, changing course. He stepped over to the terminal, and sent the authorization and request, then leaned back comfortably against the molded side of the chair, his eyes on the dancing stars.

He shifted against a distant twinge of pain rearing through the muffling drugs, tilting his head to keep the sunlight on his face as the view turned slowly to include the soft colors of Earth, embraced by the sun's fierce yellow rays, burning defiantly against the backdrop of night. He smiled when he saw the reflected radiance of the terminal fields rise past him, and he spoke without turning. "Mother? Have some logs split for the fireplace and set two extra places for dinner. I'm bringing Rose with me. We should arrive at the East Pole within the hour. Have a lift meet us at the terminal when we finish our descent." He turned to face her, sunlight warming his back like the heat of an open flame. "I'm coming home."

DRINK MY SOUL...PLEASE

by Rie Sheridan

Reviewers compare Rie Sheridan to J.R.R. Tolkien and Terry Brooks. Works include fantasy, sci fi, and horror, ranging from children's stories to adult novels. An award-winning poet and short story author, Rie is sure to give you a smile or a shiver, depending on your mood.

—what dreams may come must give us pause....
Hamlet, William Shakespeare

The machine sat on the scarred oak counter...a tiny monitor with battered keyboard. It looked so innocent, its cursor blinking steadily, a little green pulse tallying electronic heartbeats. A single word of text glowed on the screen invitingly. "Engage...?"

Daniscar Zenov jerked upright with a gasp, staring around him in the darkness.

Just another dream.... He buried his face in his hands. *Dear God...no more dreams. Please...no more dreams.*

꙰ ꙰

Elianora Vaire could only just remember a time before the War. She had been ten when it started. When it began, they predicted it would be over in days—ending with the long feared destruction of the world. Instead, it took eighteen years.

The problem of radiation poisoning had been licked with the invention of the Doomsday Bombs. Cities might fall, but the air would be safe for the Powers-That-Be when they crawled out from under their rocks, so they didn't hesitate to use the weapons. Civilizations that had stood for millennia were rubble in weeks.

Of course, there were things that those in power had failed to take into account. Such as the fact that military bases weren't the only things housed in cities. So were factories and refineries, universities and banks....

By the end of the second year, the armies were fighting on horseback and on foot. By the end of the third year, the major fighting was down to desultory strikes by bands of roving commandos. The ordinary citizenry who managed by luck or curse to survive the initial destruction of their world began to pick up the broken threads of tattered lives.

Elianora and her father, Tikardo were near nobility in the tenuous power structure of the New World economy. Tikardo had two horses to draw the sawed-off truck bed that served as his traveling showroom. He was a metal dealer who sold most of his wares to farmers struggling to revitalize the countryside. A used car salesman in the Before War world, the gleanings from his devastated lot had seen them through the worst times with relative ease when his neighbors started trying to rebuild. Scrap metal was a precious commodity in a world thrown back to its roots.

Stepping out of the three-room cinder block home that seemed palatial compared to others in the neighborhood, Elianora swept dark hair from her forehead with the back of a well-tanned arm. Her hands were covered with flour. It was a day of celebration. Word of the Cease-Fire had come through with the morning's news-crier, and she had decided to bake a cake. Not a true light and frothy confection like she vaguely remembered from childhood, but a treat for her father nonetheless.

He was late. She expected him long before this. The day had been scorching hot. There might be no radiation, but dust clouds rising into the atmosphere from myriad bombings had never fully settled, making semi-tropics of formerly temperate areas. The cinder block dwellings stayed fairly cool, but having a cook fire inside would turn one into a kiln.

She set the pan containing her cake batter in the center of the outdoor convection oven and blew on red-hot coals. With a satisfied smile, she dusted her hands on her white linen shift and stood up, scanning the horizon once more.

On the edge of sight, she glimpsed a horse-drawn cart...but it was single harness, not her father's double rig. A salesman's signature toga fluttered in the light breeze beginning to stir as he waved to the girl by the cook fire. Her tall figure was well known to the whole village.

Elianora waved back and turned to step into the house. A piercing whistle stopped her in her tracks, and she spun to see Tikardo's cart approaching from the south. She ran to meet him. Her mother had died when she was five—long before the War started—and Tikardo was the only constant she remembered.

"Papa, is it true?"

He didn't need to ask for elaboration. "Yes, Angel, it's true. The War is over." He leapt lightly from the cart and enfolded her in a bear hug. "The War is finally over."

Tikardo was a big man, darkly handsome. When the War had begun, he was the same age that Elianora was now, and it had taken numerous favors and all of his pre-War savings to be mustered out as a single parent. Many friends and relatives were not so lucky—a pain that gnawed at him daily—but one look at Elianora's shining face proved the cost worthwhile.

Thankfully, she remembered nothing of those first terror-filled War years...and he had paid dearly again to make it so.

"I have a surprise for you, Lia."

"What is it, Papa?" She glanced eagerly toward the rear of the cart.

"You'll get it tomorrow," he said laughing.

"What is it?" she repeated, an edge of impatience rising in her voice—she was unused to delayed gratification.

"Dani's coming home."

⋙ ⋘

In a temporary camp halfway across the village, War-weary soldiers enjoyed the first safe sleep many of them could remember. There was nothing left worth fighting for by the end of the fifth year...but duty dies hard, and no one ever said "stop." So the raids had gone on...and on...and on. Until the Powers-That-Be finally remembered the word "cease-fire."

There was a wistful quality to the air as the sun managed to break through the dust clouds just in time to set. The low arcing beams gave the utilitarian buildings fleeting warmth they aesthetically lacked.

Daniscar Zenov closed his eyes and breathed in the spring sunset.

Maybe tonight I'll sleep.

Lately he'd been too tired to sleep...and too afraid. With sleep came dreams, and dreams were definitely something to be feared.

Dani could remember the time before the War much more clearly than former neighbor Elianora. He had been seventeen when the War began, and keen to fight. It had seemed like the ultimate adventure to a headstrong teenager.

For more than half his life he had been a soldier. The adventure had worn off with his first scavenging mission into a newly bombed city. The death and destruction had left him violently ill—to the raucous amusement of his older comrades—and he had vowed then and there to survive the War at any cost.

It hasn't always been easy either, he reflected, absently massaging the right arm he had nearly lost three years ago.

But the scars he bore on his body could never touch those on his soul.... Dani sighed, with a wry half-smile. Such thoughts did no one good. His left hand strayed to the chain around his neck and the battered locket that hung from it.

The talisman had kept him going through more than one rough spot. Without opening it, he could see the images inside it. In one half of the locket rested a family portrait of a happy couple and a grinning blond teenager—how very long ago that photo session seemed—images from another life.

In the other was a picture hastily cut and wedged into the opening. It showed a dark-haired solemn-eyed little girl, trying so hard to look older than her ten years.... He ran his good hand through lank blond hair that lay like bleached straw across his leathery forehead. A jagged scar ran from left cheek to temple. His gray-green eyes no longer laughed.

Will she even know me...?

He stepped to the doorway of the cinder block hut he was assigned to with the rest of his squad. With a sigh, Dani pushed aside the tinkling curtain of scrap metal serving as door, stooping to go inside.

Tomorrow I will find out....

❧ ❧

Elianora pulled back in her father's arms. "W—what?"

"Dani's coming home. I saw him this afternoon. We're the closest things to family he has left, so I invited him to lunch. He'll be here tomorrow about noon."

She walked to the cook pit in a daze, automatically checking the progress of her cake.

"Lia...?"

"Dani's coming home..." she whispered, one hand straying to neatly braided hair. "Excuse me, Papa." She pulled the cake out of the oven, setting it on the edge of the pit to cool and continuing into the house.

She drifted into the small alcove Tiko had partitioned off for her. Going to the far corner, she knelt before a rickety shelf upon which sat a small carved wooden box—one of the few mementos of her mother she still possessed.

She carefully unlocked the casket with a tiny key she wore around her neck. Inside the box was what she possessed of Daniscar. She made herself comfortable on the floor and spread out her treasures one by one. There was a larger copy of the family photo in his locket, heavily creased from years when she had slept with it clutched tightly in hand. A second photo showed a younger Dani tossing six-year-old Lia into the air as she squealed with laughter. A crumpled piece of paper wadded up in anger many years ago, then lovingly smoothed out, declared LIA LOVES DANI FOREVER in careful block print. And there was the letter.

Tikardo had read it to her gently the first time because she wasn't able to decipher the scrawled cursive yet...and he held her close as she cried herself to sleep, only able to grasp that her beloved Dani was leaving her, and not the reason why. Not that she fully understood even now why the seventeen-year-old had lied his way into the army.

Later that night, she had stolen out of the house and run barefoot in her nightgown to tap urgently on his window.

Tearfully, she had forced her photograph on him, promising to wait forever...and now he was coming home. At last. She had never forgotten—or betrayed—her promise, but long ago despaired of keeping it when no word came.

Her vague memories were now older than Dani was when he left.

Does he even remember me after the horrors he must have suffered?

Tomorrow she would find out....

✍ ✍

Sleepless eyes of gray and brown greeted the hazy red dawn.

On opposite ends of the cinder block city, grateful sighs were heaved that daylight had finally come. For her part, Elianora pulled on a tunic that fell to mid-thigh, carefully dyed deep sky-blue with precious reserves scavenged from the old city. She fussed restlessly with her waist-length hair until Tikardo threatened to cut it off, then quickly plaited it into its customary braid.

Having no option but his uniform, Dani was already dressed, but even more apprehensive about his appearance. He took stock of it dubiously in a piece of polished tin. His uniform hung on him after six months of shortened rations. His face was hollow and gaunt—the grinning teenager all but wiped away from the grim soldier. His right arm dangled awkwardly, good for little more than steadying his rifle. He needed a haircut, but couldn't bear to waste time.

I have to know. And I have to know now.

Taking up his rifle from habit too ingrained to lose easily, he started across town, following the directions Tikardo Vaire had given him. The merchant had offered to fetch him, but Dani had declined, wanting to get a feel for his new surroundings.

So much had changed since he was a boy that he wasn't ready yet to call it "home." And there was no denying he felt uncomfortable in the older man's presence—as if he had left something undone it might be too late to repair. It was a dreadful shock to glance up from the campfire at noon yesterday and see Vaire staring at him as if he were a ghost. He recognized Vaire at once. There was much less change in a man between age twenty-eight and forty-six than there was between seventeen and thirty-five.

Seeing Vaire had brought so many memories flooding back—memories not tinged with the blood of the horrific War....

He had gone next door to Vaire's the night before he left to join the army and nervously approached Tiko. Lia was only ten—a baby—but he'd loved her all her life.

More afraid of being turned down than he was to fight, Dani had asked for Elianora's hand if he returned. Since no one expected the War to last more than a week or two, it was rather silly of him to ask.

Vaire kindly told the blushing teen as much—but gravely promised not to stand between them when she was old enough to decide for herself.

Dani wrote the letter then, sitting at Tiko's kitchen table, unable to face telling her in person he was leaving...

...And then the child had come to him on her own, tearful, but older than her years. She pressed the solemn-eyed portrait on him as a good luck token and vowed to wait forever if she must....

But eighteen years *was* almost forever. He'd tried to contact her at first...but the messages never seemed to get through.

In time, he gave up; sure she was dead...or married. It was too much to hope that her feelings remained unchanged.

Vaire did not mention a lover, but she is twenty-eight years old—surely she's had many suitors if she fulfilled the potential for beauty she showed as a child.

Dani shook his head to bring his thoughts back to the present.

In minutes he would know. He found the correct street among dozens that were the same by absently counting those he passed.

The cinder block structures were more elaborate here than those near camp, denoting wealth and status in the new economy. He slowed as he continued up the street, reluctant to finish the journey now he was so close.

There's the house.

Heart rose into throat at the sight of a lithe figure bending over the cook pit.

She is so beautiful...more beautiful than I ever could have imagined.

He almost turned and walked away—but she caught sight of him and raised a hand in tentative greeting. The gesture froze him in his tracks.

≈≈

Lia glanced up from the cook pit to see a blond man in ragged uniform standing a few yards away, rifle held loosely in one hand as he stared hungrily in her direction. Her first thought was he merely wanted food, and then she looked more closely. There was an echo of the boy in the man—faint, but distinctive.

Her heart skipped a beat and she raised a hand in greeting.

He is home. After what seems an eternity, Dani is really home!

The paralysis holding her broke, and she ran to him, flinging herself into arms that automatically encircled her, and then tightened painfully. She didn't mind.

"Dani, you came back!"

"Didn't I promise?" His voice was hoarse as he dropped his chin into her hair. "How could I have stayed away?"

"I was so afraid...but I waited. I always waited."

"I would have understood if you hadn't," murmured Dani softly.

She drew back enough to look up at him, bewildered by the remark. "How could I not? I promised too."

"I'll release you from your promise if you want me to."

She stared into his eyes, her confusion deepening. "But—"

"I don't have anything to offer you, Lia. A crippled soldier who doesn't even dare to sleep at night for fear he'll die in his dreams...."

"Please." She put fingertips to his lips. "Don't talk about it. Not now. Come, let's eat." She took his right hand, chin tilting defiantly as she did so, and drew him to sit beside the cook pit. She casually adjusted her table arrangement to put things in easy reach of his left hand. Flicking a smile his way, she went to the fire. After a cursory check of the stew bubbling in its kettle, she slipped onto the bench beside him, ducking her head shyly.

"Lunch is almost ready."

"Thank you."

"You haven't tasted it yet," she replied ruefully, with a wry little grimace.

"No, I mean...thank you for being here to come home to." He raised his hand to her cheek, drinking in her face eagerly. "The hope you would be waiting eased me through more nights than you'll ever know."

She covered his hand with hers. "It's like a dream—"

"Please." He closed his eyes with a shudder. "Don't say that."

"Dani, what's wrong?"

He smiled wanly, in a vain attempt to reassure her. "Nothing, I'm fine."

"I think the stew should be ready." She rose in one smooth motion and moved back to the cook pit.

Lia stirred the stew, then ladled some into a large bowl and set it in front of him. "I don't claim to be a good cook," she warned, serving herself a smaller portion.

He blew on a spoonful of the stew and tasted it. "It could use a little salt," he admitted.

"Oh!" She raised hand to mouth, eyes wide. "I forgot."

He laughed—a lilting chuckle gone rusty with disuse. The sound grew into a full-throated roar, tears rolling down his cheeks as he tried vainly to control himself.

Lia looked on in puzzled bemusement, one finely shaped eyebrow cocked. "Dani—?"

"Oh, Lia," he finally managed to choke out, "how I've missed you." He held out his hand, and she moved eagerly into the circle of his arm.

"I've missed you too, Dani," she sighed, resting her head on his shoulder.

His laughter suddenly died in his throat. He gulped, tilting her face towards him and gazing down at the trust in her eyes. Suddenly, as if reaching a decision, he bent and kissed her parted lips.

Lia gave a muffled little cry. Dani jerked back.

"No—" she protested, "don't stop!" Throwing her arms around his neck, she pulled his mouth back down to hers. "I've wanted to do this for so long," she murmured against his lips, returning his kiss hungrily.

Dani lost himself in the kisses. His hands strayed to her hair, face, and breasts, as if to convince himself she was real.

With extreme difficulty, he reined himself in before he allowed it to go too far.

I have to remember she is only a—but then, she isn't a little girl anymore, is she? She is a grown woman, with needs and desires of her own.

What are those needs? And will I be able to fill them?

He pulled away from her, looking down at her closed eyes and parted lips. A delicate flush of rose glowed beneath tanned cheeks.

She was eminently desirable.

God, how I want her...in more ways than one.

But in his mind's eye, he kept seeing that solemn-eyed little girl, and not this beautiful woman.

"Dani, what is it?" Her voice held tentative hurt. "Don't...don't you want me?"

"Oh, my precious girl—more than you could ever know!"

"Am I doing something wrong? I—I haven't had any practice." She swallowed hard, the flush in her cheeks blooming scarlet, "but I can learn—"

"Oh, Lia!" He hugged her to him fiercely, wanting to protect her, never to let her go. "Sweetheart, we have plenty of time for me to teach you what you want to know. Now, I'm just glad to be home." He sighed deeply, searching for the words to help her understand. "It isn't you. It's me. I—I'm just not ready yet."

"Make it soon."

The words were whispered so softly that he almost missed them.

"I will. I promise. But there's something I want you to have first." He reached to the bottom of the thigh pocket of his worn fatigues and pulled out a small paper-wrapped object.

"What is it?" she asked, taking the packet with trembling hand.

"Open it."

She carefully unfolded the paper to reveal a simple gold band with a tiny diamond inset. "Oh, Dani—I can't take this. It's too precious!"

"There is nothing more precious to me than you, Lia. It was my mother's. I know she'd want you to have it."

"Dani...."

He slipped the ring onto her left hand. "I know things are less formal these days, Lia—but I've been waiting to ask you this for such a long time now...." He got down on one knee with a self-deprecating laugh. "Lia, will you marry me?"

"I told you before, silly. Don't you remember?"

"I wasn't sure *you* would," he replied seriously. A fleeting glimmer of something half-recalled flickered behind her eyes then was gone.

"Of course I remember. You proposed to me the night you left— and that's when I promised to wait. Of course I'll marry you. Why else would I have waited all these years? Now, get up off the ground and eat your stew before it gets cold."

She picked up the saltshaker and shook it vigorously over his bowl.

"I think that ought to do it," he commented ruefully, swinging a leg over the bench. "You don't do anything by halves, do you, girl?"

"No," she replied, her intensity charging the words far beyond the question, "I won't."

He noticed the change of tense, but forced himself to focus on the stew. Otherwise things might rapidly slip beyond his control.

※※

The afternoon passed in a blur. They had so much to say to each other—little things that had been stored away like jewels to be taken out and exclaimed over. Lia told him everything she could remember about how things had been at home. He told her the few things about the forefront that weren't horrible.

She sensed volumes lying unspoken behind the light anecdotes, but dared not press him. *If he wants to tell me in time, he will. Though he doesn't have to suffer the memories himself either.*

"Dani," she began hesitantly when the sun was sinking once more towards sunset. "What do you know about General Cardikof's Stand-Down Edict?"

He tensed, left hand gripping hers with bruising force. "More than I want to know," he replied brusquely, the words charged with emotion. She couldn't quite decide if it was anger—or fear.

"I don't want to talk about that tonight, Lia." He tried hard to smile, but managed only a twisted grimace.

"But, Dani—the Desensitizer—"

"No, Lia! Please...." He jerked his hand free and leapt to his feet. "I-it's getting late. I should go."

"But Papa will be home any minute—"

"Give him my regards, and my regrets." Dani snatched up his rifle and fled towards the road.

What did I say? The Desensitizer is a Godsend. It has done so much for so many people...and it seems to me like the soldiers will benefit most of all.

She rubbed absently at the base of her neck. *It didn't do me any harm. What is Dani so afraid of...?*

༄ ༄

Dani jogged through the darkening streets as if demons were at his heels. And, in a matter of speaking, they were. Even the thought of the Desensitizer terrified him.

Created in the early stages of the War, the machine's weapon potential was soon declared inefficient. It didn't generate a wide enough field for mass application, and subjecting individual enemy soldiers to the process was too time-consuming and impractical.

In the most basic terms, the Desensitizer erased memories, much like a computer program could be used to wipe a chip. The memories thus eradicated were irretrievably gone...and they would never even be missed.

That was the claim, at least. The doctors running the machine boasted the ability to remove as small a segment as a day, or a whole lifetime, as the situation demanded. It had become quite common for parents to exorcise the specters of War for their children through the miracle of the Desensitizer.

This was what Tiko had scrimped together credits for in those first tragic years of the War—he had paid to excise Lia's memories from her eleventh birthday until she was fourteen. Those were the days of worst destruction; without them, she remembered only the plodding day-to-day tedium of the raids. He had not tampered with the years before the War, but the gap helped dull the edges of her childhood....

Tiko confided this to Dani yesterday over a watery beer in a dimly lit tavern. It had sent a chill reverberating through him to hear the man speak so matter-of-factly about destroying a part of her soul. No matter how evil the memories, they belonged to *her*. To hear Lia casually suggest Dani do the same—it froze his blood.

God knows I can't sleep at night because the memories haunt my dreams...but they are a part of me. Can I live without them? Do I even want to try...?

Now General Cardikof, established as World Commander of the Unified Armies under the cease-fire, wanted all former soldiers to undergo treatment. His rationale was that removing the trauma of the War would make it easier for the men to rejoin society and lead productive lives.

Most of the War-weary combatants were jumping to sign up for the expensive treatment at government expense; his comrades in the barracks this morning could talk of nothing else.

But the thought that Dani kept coming back to—no matter how he tried to avoid it—was that with the memory of the War deleted from the world—and submission to the Desensitizer was ordered for *all* the Unified Armies—there would be no deterrent to starting it up again.

Now, the horror is so raw the very thought of another battle makes grown men shudder. Such immediacy might wear off in time, and the seeds of dissent blossom again in future, but the present— the here and now—is safe for the moment.

The General's Edict might jeopardize that...intentionally or no. And deeper below that fear lay another. An insistent whisper in his very core asked, *What will he fill the void with if he takes away the War? What will happen to armies of men with eighteen years of their lives ripped away?*

Dani kept hearing a chorus running through his head—an old, old rock song that told of the headless specter of a mercenary stalking the night and firing his machine gun with the single-minded purpose of a zombie. Dani feared desperately that the General's plan would lead to the creation of an army of such soulless fighters.

The doctors won't be able to spend time picking and choosing among good days and bad for thousands of soldiers. They'll simply take away the entire block of time...and what will prevent them from wiping the rest of the slate clean while they are at it, giving the General those armies of zombie puppets for his amusement....

Dani found himself back at the barracks, and ducked to enter.

Holding back the tinkling curtain, he stopped short in the doorway when he caught his name in the conversation going on just beyond the opening.

"Zenov could be trouble," growled a voice he couldn't place.

"Nah, Dani's a good guy," protested his friend Alexi.

"He's publicly questioned the General's order. It might make others question."

"He'll change his mind. Once he sees how much better it is for everyone, he'll come 'round."

"What if he doesn't see?"

"Don't worry, I'll talk to him."

Dani eased the curtain carefully into position and backed away from the hut. Things were slipping away from him. Soon he might be forced to "come 'round"—whether he liked it or not. He had to think.

Tightening his grip on the lifeline of his rifle, he began wandering the dark streets of the ravaged city, searching for anything that might remain of his childhood. He passed the ruins of the school where his mother used to teach, abandoned playground marked by the jagged teeth of sawed-off metal poles, which once supported swings and monkey bars. Everything that could be scavenged for rebuilding had long ago been spirited away. He could almost hear the echoes of children playing, and it caused him to hurry past with a shudder.

He passed a burnt out husk that had once been the neighborhood library, and he gritted his teeth at the senselessness of it all.

There hadn't even been the excuse of political necessity for the War. The War need never have occurred at all.

The Consolidation had almost been complete before the first missile was launched. It had been a token protest from a handful of dissidents to begin with—and then bloodlust had taken root.

Finding a secluded corner with twisted trees that had survived the War by virtue of decay, Dani huddled on the ground beneath their branches, resting head on bent knees. Thoughts whirled through his tired brain as he tried to make sense of things.

He hadn't slept at all the night before, worrying about Lia's reaction to his rebirth, and it had been days since he'd slept well...if not years. He hated sleep—fought it as long as he was able before slipping beneath its waters. Finally, however, despite all resolves, exhaustion won out, and Dani slept....

The War had just entered its first winter. While the largest cities had been leveled months before, there were still smaller population centers like this one seeing their first bomb strikes. The squad was sent into the remains of a newly bombed apartment building to scavenge anything of potential value. Already food and ammunition were getting harder to count on as supply lines were constantly broken and reformed. Anything they found to supplement official rations was considered fair game.

Dani was gestured into a gaping doorway as the rest of the men fanned out. He had just passed his eighteenth birthday, and already the glamour of war was beginning to pale. This was his first scavenging mission.

Ducking into the bombed-out apartment, gun clutched tightly in trembling hands, Dani moved slowly through ruined rooms. He picked up a small glass ornament and stowed it in the pocket of his fatigue jacket. It might fetch a few credits on the black market.

He started to relax a little. The dwelling appeared to be empty, and he breathed a sigh of relief. He was not really paying attention as he stepped through the kitchen doorway.

The crack of a pistol split the silence. Pain exploded in the side of his face, and his finger tightened convulsively on the trigger of his rifle as he fell backwards. He came to his senses to find his squad leader looming over him. "You alive, Zenov?"

"Y-yes, sir," he mumbled thickly, sitting up and reaching with fumbling fingers to explore the pain in the side of his head.

"It's just a crease, boy. Lots of blood, but no real damage. It'll scar though—you'll have a nice memento there. Continue with your salvage, son. By the way—good shooting."

The sergeant clapped him on the shoulder and was gone. Dazed, Dani stumbled into the kitchen and dropped to his knees, swallowing hard against rising nausea. Losing the battle, he was violently ill. Across the room, a small figure clutched a pistol in one lax hand.

Half the child's face was gone as she slumped over a woman's stiff-ened corpse. The girl was no older than Lia...and he had killed her. She had been alone and afraid—no telling how long her companion had been dead—just trying to survive....

Dani moaned in his sleep. *How many nights must I see that blasted face in my dreams?*

It had gotten easier to accept the dead as the War dragged inter-minably on, but he never got over that little girl. To him, she symbol-ized the whole useless War. It was memories like this that haunted his dreams—that made the Desensitizer so alluring—but he couldn't give up the large part of his personality those memories shaped.

Without them he'd no longer be Daniscar Zenov, but someone, or some*thing*, else.

෯෧

Lia's sleep was peaceful, her dreams of the future rather than the past. Lips curled in a smile, she dreamed of Dani and a little cottage of their own somewhere far away from the cinder block city....

In her dream, Dani was trying to plant a garden, "hepped" by a sturdy little boy about two with dark hair and gray-green eyes.

She sighed happily and turned over in her sleep—the dream shifted.

She saw herself cradling a baby in her arms as she corrected the pronunciation of the same little boy, now about five, while he read from a book clutched in chubby hands.

Dani came to stand behind her chair, laying his good hand on her shoulder and bending down to kiss her cheek....

There were no shadows in her dreams—Tiko had seen to that.

Her War memories were only of frustrated attempts to put to-gether daily grocery needs and organize life around the deprivations. She didn't miss the images she no longer remembered. As far as she was concerned, she was the same Elianora Vaire she had always been, and grateful to be so.

෯෧

Dani woke when birds began to chirp in the predawn light.

He was stiff and cramped from sleeping sitting up all night, and he rolled his head on his neck to ease the tension, wincing at the resulting pops. "I'm too old for this," he muttered, levering to his feet with his back against the tree. He straightened his uniform and shook his hair into place, running a hand through it as a final touch, and his toilet was complete.

Slinging rifle across his back, he started back toward the main section of town. It was easier to think when he was moving, though he wasn't at all sure where to go. If he returned to the barracks, he would face Alexi's attempts to win him over—and if he continued to resist, the persuasion would not remain so friendly.

Every fiber of his being longed to head straight for Lia, but he hesitated. She did not understand why he was resisting the device any more than the army did.

His thoughts were whirling endlessly. He couldn't stop their roulette spin long enough to focus them on a solution. He had to center himself, before it was too late.

He spied an early morning cantina with smoke curling lazily from its cook fire. The heady scent of brewing coffee permeating the air made him decide to stop and rally his resources.

Digging in his pocket for a worn 5-credit disk, he flipped it on the table as he swung onto the bench. "Black, please."

The coffee was a fragrant cup of instant revival as he gratefully took a healthy swallow, then held the cup to his forehead. Somehow, despite the devastation, the world had managed to keep the coffee brewing—a testament to where priorities lay—and this was good coffee.

The thin, watery army brew was nothing like the deep, fresh taste of his youth, and this was. The scent brought on another wave of memories. His mother in her sunny kitchen, turning to him with coffee pot in hand as they made ready to head for school in the morning. His father and Tiko arguing politics, steam from their mugs rising between them while he and Lia played a complicated game of the child's invention. That first bitter sip of stolen caffeine, snatched from his father's cup when he was seven....

Memories.

He kept banging up against that wall. His memories were so much a part of him that he couldn't conceive of life without them.

Even the bad ones. He absently fingered the scar on his cheek. *What am I going to do...?*

He gulped the rest of his coffee and set down the cup with a deep sigh. The first thing he had to do was tell Lia goodbye.

It was the kindest thing to do. Knowing she was alive and well would have to be enough for him. *I need to disappear, and I can't ask her to go with me. It wouldn't be fair....*

≈≈

"What do you mean it wouldn't be fair to you?" Lia's eyes snapped fire. She tried to contain her anger, but it spilled over the top. "Daniscar Zenov, I've waited almost twenty years for you—wasted two-thirds of my life dreaming of the day you'd come home, and now—a few kisses, a little groping and you say 'okay, it's been fun, but I'm leaving now.' Well, you can rot in Hell for all I care, if that's the way you feel about it!" Her anger dissolved into bitter tears, and she shook with the violence of her emotion.

Dani stood before her, shoulders bowed, reaching out, but not touching her, as if afraid of her reaction. He had surprised her when he knocked on the door—she hadn't been expecting him until later in the day, and was flustered enough to see him. His news struck her to the core.

"I know I'm not very experienced, Dani—but I can learn. I don't know a lot about life, but I can keep a house neat and comfortable for you. I can cook...sort of. I—"

He held up a hand and shook his head. "Lia, it's not you. It's me. I can't stay. Don't you see?"

"No. Frankly, I *don't* see! Tell me. Explain it to me. I want to understand...."

He sank down onto the bench beside the fire. "I can't stay because I can't give in to them. I can't submit to the machine. I-I have to keep my memories—they are all that I have."

"You have me," she murmured softly, looking down at her hands so she wouldn't cry any more. "Aren't I enough?"

"Oh, baby, I wish I could say yes...but it would be lying to you and to myself."

"Did you or did you not give this to me yesterday afternoon and ask me to marry you?" She thrust out her hand and the tiny diamond flared like a beacon in a shaft of sunlight. The light danced as her hand trembled. "Didn't you mean it?"

"Oh, yes...more than anything...." He caught her hand in his, "but I hadn't thought it through."

"Either you want to marry me or not. Whatever your decision, I will try and accept it, Dani...but let me say just one thing. I didn't wait eighteen years for you because I wanted a few kisses and a pat on the head. I waited for you because you meant more than anything else in the world to me...except maybe Papa. I waited for you because you told me you'd be back for me, and you never, ever lied to me, even when the truth hurt—like the time my kitten was run over and Papa said it ran away. You told me the truth, and held me while I cried.

"You see! I haven't forgotten everything, just because of some silly machine. But if you think you need to run rather than accept the treatment, fine. Let's run. But, *please*, Dani—I beg you—let's do it together!"

"Oh, Lia, I do love you so." He held out his arms and she fell into them. "If you want to come with me, you can come. The thought of leaving you again was killing me."

"I can be ready in five minutes."

"No. I need to go by the barracks first and pick up my things...talk to some people. You need to speak to your father. He isn't going to like this...."

"I think you'll find him more sympathetic than you think, Dani." She grinned impishly. "Besides, this way he won't have to pay for the wedding."

"Meet me at the old school at sunset." He rose to go, lifting her to her feet as he stood. "We'll have to travel light and go quickly...and we probably won't ever be coming back."

"As long as we go together, Dani. That's all I ask."

He kissed her hard. "The old school—at twilight. I love you, Elianora Vaire."

"And I love you, Daniscar Zenov—now go, before I decide not to let you."

He laughed and snatched up his rifle. "Twilight!" he called out as he backpedaled down the street.

"Turn around before you kill yourself!" she yelled back, one hand lifted in farewell.

When he was out-of-sight, she lowered her hand and clasped both of them in front of her. "Please let this work out," she prayed softly. "He's been through so much."

"Miss Vaire?"

She turned at the sound of an unfamiliar voice behind her. "Yes?"

"I need you to come with me. I'm afraid there's been an accident."

"Dani—?" Her eyes flew to the direction in which he'd disappeared. Surely he hadn't been gone long enough to—

"No, Miss. It's your father."

"Papa! What happened?"

"There was an accident with his cart. I think you'd better come."

"Yes, of course." Without a second thought, Lia let herself be led away.

⁂

Dani made it to the barracks without seeing a single man in uniform. That in itself might not be so unusual...they had but newly returned to the city, maybe everyone felt the same need to re-familiarize themselves with their surroundings that had struck him the night before....

But the barracks themselves loomed empty as well. Not a single soldier stood sentry duty. No one lounged in front of the hut enjoying the sunlight. No one called out a greeting as he ducked inside the building.

Where is everyone? Did they all succumb to the lure of the Desensitizer? Even Alexi?

The thought shot a spur of pain through him. He and Alexi had been the youngest in the squadron—the other but a year ahead of him. They had banded together from the first against the tyranny of the older men. He had shared everything with Alexi, from his dreams to his rations. Without him, Dani lost his closest companion....

But will it really matter any more? After all, Lia and I are running away at dusk. I'll probably never see Alexi again anyway.

Dani sighed, hurrying to collect his meager belongings. He needed to get out of here and find some way to provision this flight. His credit case was woefully thin. The coffee for breakfast had almost cleaned him out.

He hadn't worried at the time, because he didn't need credits to go alone, but with Lia....

Where can I get more credits—fast?

He glanced at the small pile of possessions lying on the bunk. Nothing of much value: a comb, a letter of commendation, a couple of medals he couldn't yet bring himself to part with, the glass ornament picked up on that first disastrous raid and kept as a kind of penance.... The only other things he owned were the clothes on his back and the blanket on his bunk. The army owed him three months' back pay, but he guessed he'd better not hold his breath for that.

With a shrug, he bundled his possessions in his blanket.

"You there!"

Dani whirled—tensed to spring—and relaxed when he recognized Alexi. "Am I glad to see you, Alexi! I need to ask you some questions, and...I wanted a chance to say goodbye—"

"What are you doing there?" The grim voice bore no resemblance to Alexi's usual breezy cheerfulness. "These quarters are for military personnel only."

Dani glanced down at his worn uniform, and then back at Alexi. "Technically, I guess I still qualify. Alexi, listen—"

"I don't know where you stole that uniform, or how you know my name, but I intend to find out." Alexi lifted his rifle. "Come with me."

"Alexi, it's me...Dani—"

"I've never seen you before in my life," Alexi replied harshly. "Now move."

Dani's heart sank. His worst fears proved true—the Desensitizer had changed Alexi from a happy-go-lucky draftee counting the days till release to a grim mercenary with the flip of a switch. So much for "I'll talk to him."

Alexi had been the only hope Dani had left in camp. The only possible source of information, and maybe a few credits. Now, who could say?

Dani gathered up his blanket. At least he'd be prepared when he had the chance to slip loose from Alexi. And the chance *would* come. It had to.

≈≈

Lia followed the stranger through the hot sunlit streets without a single thought except that her father was in trouble. All plans to run away with Dani were shoved to the corners of her consciousness by the overwhelming prayer—Let Papa be all right. The slim figure in front of her moved quickly and efficiently through the maze of the central market square, easy to spot in his crisp, green uniform.

Lia wanted to ask what had happened, where was her father, any of a hundred questions, but he hurried onward, confident that she still followed him. Finally, she could take no more. "What kind of accident was it?" she asked breathlessly. "Where is Papa?"

He glanced back over his shoulder briefly. "We're almost there, Miss. They will answer all your questions when we arrive."

Where was "there?" She gazed around her curiously. This part of the city was unfamiliar to her. Buildings gleamed with the raw look of fresh concrete before the inevitable patina of grime had clogged up its pores. This was new growth, and miles from her side of town. She would have a difficult time getting home without her escort....

The soldier had stopped before a squat building with a windowless facade. He opened the door politely and gestured inside. "In here, Miss."

Lia hung back. "This isn't a hospital—or even a clinic. If Papa's hurt, why would they bring him here?"

"Just step inside, Miss." There was a trace of irritation in the smooth voice, the first emotion she'd heard from him.

"I think I'd better go home," she murmured, beginning to back away slowly.

The soldier drew a pistol. "I really think it would be better if you didn't try that," he snarled, the polite mask discarded. "Get inside."

Lia's eyes widened, and her mind swiftly weighed the pros and cons of flight. Deciding that she could never hope to outrun a bullet, she stepped past him into the dimly lit interior.

He followed, the pistol held level with the middle of her back. She could feel it behind her as surely as if it actually touched her. "Answer just one question," she murmured softly. "Is my father all right?"

"I wouldn't know," he replied. "I've never met him."

"It was all a lie?"

"Think of that as the bright side."

Lia seethed at her own gullibility—she should have asked questions, demanded proof...something!

Instead, I blindly followed a stranger merely because he told me to. What will Papa say? And Dani will think I am still a child!

Dani.... Does this soldier have something to do with Dani...?

"Why have you brought me here?"

"The General will explain."

"Why would the General want to see me?"

"Save the questions." He shoved her through an open doorway, and she barely kept her feet. When she'd recovered her balance, Lia studied the room she found herself in. It was large and rectangular, empty except for an oversized desk and chair with the flag of the Consolidation hanging behind it.

The top of the desk was clear except for a pen and pencil set placed precisely in the center of the leading edge. Before the desk stood the most important man in the Consolidation, General Merisford

Cardikof.

Despite the nominal leadership of the Consolidation Governors, everyone knew that the true power in the world lay with Cardikof. After all—his efforts had almost single-handedly ended the War. His suggestions were sure to find their way into laws without opposition. In fact, a gratified Board of Governors had offered to make him King of the Global Consolidation—twice.

The great man had modestly declined, of course—he knew the real power to lie on the fringes of the government. Instead he had accepted the post as head of the Unified Armies, and issued his edict. All soldiers would submit to the De-Sensitize Process for "their own good," or face court-martial and internment. There had been no provisions for individual circumstances.

But if Dani doesn't want the treatment, I'll stick by him. And if that means we run, we run.

Caught up in her own thoughts, Lia was startled to realize the general was speaking to her, and she hadn't heard a word he said. "Forgive me, sir...I was concerned about my father. They said he had been in an accident?"

"No problem at all, my dear." He snapped his fingers. Her guide rolled in a fine leather chair and placed it before the desk. "Thank you, Frezon."

The man nodded curtly and started from the room.

"Oh, and Frezon..." the general purred.

"Yes, sir?" There was a trace of anxiety in the man's voice.

Lia frowned. *What is he afraid of?*

"It was unfortunate how Miss Vaire almost fell entering the office. Please check and make sure there is no trip hazard in the doorway. We wouldn't want the incident repeated."

"No, sir," mumbled the soldier, his face white as paper. "It won't happen again, sir."

A threat was just made and received, Lia mused, *without a word of it being spoken.... This is a powerful man indeed.*

"Please, sit." The general gestured toward the chair

Lia perched on the edge of it, her hands laced on the top of the desk. "I was told my father was hurt, sir. Is this true?"

"I'm sorry, my dear. There seems to have been some kind of an error. I told Frezon I had something of importance to discuss with you, but no mention was made of your father at all. He must have misunderstood my request. I will have to speak to him about that."

Something in the man's tone sent a chill through her, and Lia shivered. "No, I'm sure it was an honest mistake. Please don't bother on my account. What did you wish to speak to me about?"

The general moved to sit behind the desk, steepling his fingers under his chin as he leaned toward her. "I believe you are acquainted with one of my men, a Captain Zenov."

Dani is a captain? Lia felt a thrill of pride run through her. It was an honorable rank for a foot soldier to attain. "Yes, I know him." She twisted the engagement ring on her finger nervously. "He's my fiancé." It was the first time she had said it out loud. *It feels good.*

"Really? Congratulations, my dear. He is a lucky man indeed."

Lia felt her cheeks reddening. "Thank you," she murmured. "What is it that you want from me?"

"Have you heard of the Desensitizer Edict?"

"Of course."

"Have you discussed it with Captain Zenov?"

"Briefly."

"Did he tell you that he has refused the treatment?"

"Yes. He is afraid it will change his personality."

"And what did you tell him about this fear?"

"I told him that I thought he was wrong, but it was ultimately his decision and I would stand by him, whatever his final choice might be."

The general shook his head with a sad little smile. "Ah, my dear. You are only fueling his delusion. His compliance is for the good of the entire Alliance. Zenov is one of a handful of holdouts. As long as he continues to refuse the treatment, the public will question why. And I would rather that not happen."

"I don't understand. Why should anyone care what Dani does or doesn't do? Surely a captain is not so important in the grand scheme of things."

"It's his importance as a symbol that I am concerned about, my dear." The general studied a sheaf of papers he retrieved from the desk drawer. "My sources say that there are those among the populace that consider the Desensitizer to be an instrument of the devil. They have the mistaken idea that its use will somehow diminish them as individuals. This belief was waning as they saw the soldiers eagerly embracing the treatment...until Zenov refused to submit. Now they are beginning to question again. I can't have that."

"We'll go away. No one needs to know that Dani hasn't undergone the procedure."

"I'm afraid that won't be good enough. I'm sure you can understand my position." He rose to his feet and came to lean against the desk before her. "You are my bargaining chip. He will do it for you."

Lia stared up at him. "What are you saying?"

Cardikof reached down and cupped her chin in his hand, lifting her head. Lia felt her soul contract at the touch. The general's eyes were flat yet hungry as his glance raked down her body. "I think any man with a pulse would do anything you asked."

She tried to pull free of his grasp, but his fingers tightened with bruising force. She gulped. "I won't force him."

"I didn't intend to give you a choice, my dear." The general's voice was smooth and cold. She felt as if ice water were being poured into her veins.

What can I do? How can I warn Dani? He won't know where I am. He won't understand...he'll believe them....

"I won't help you," she reiterated.

"That is too bad. You are such a pretty girl." He shrugged. "But it is unimportant. All that is important is that he believe you desire him to cooperate. When he finds out the truth, it will be too late. And he will no longer care." He jerked her to her feet by the jaw.

Lia was thrown off balance by the movement, falling forward into him. His other arm tightened around her waist, and he pulled her against him. She could feel the hard, muscular lines of his body beneath his uniform.

The arm around her waist slipped lower, and he ground his hips against hers. Lia struggled against him. Her heart pounded in terror.

He bared his teeth in a mirthless smile. "You are a little innocent, aren't you? Did you save yourself all these years for your knight in shining armor? Isn't it a letdown to find that armor tarnished? To see him hold his own well-being above that of the entire population? Do you think he cares one jot for you, you silly little fool?"

Lia forced the words past her dry throat with difficulty. "Dani loves me. Dani has always loved me."

She felt his hand groping beneath her skirt, and raked her nails across his face.

With an outraged oath, he swung her around and pinned her against the desk, bending her backwards until she must collapse or her spine would snap. Lia continued to struggle, but he was much stronger than she.

Wrenching sobs of disgust and terror wracked her as he fumbled free of his uniform and tore aside her skirt. She felt a hard, hot bar against her thigh, and then an agonizing pain as he shoved himself to the hilt within her, ripping through all barriers. Lia screamed, and the general laughed like a madman.

He continued to rut inside her, his thrusts growing harder and faster. Lia sobbed like a child. *Dani will hate me. He will never forgive me. I didn't fight hard enough. I have betrayed his trust. Oh, God! What will become of me now?*

Suddenly, the general stiffened then ground his hips one last fraction tighter against her. She felt a rush of hot liquid inside her, and something within her died.

Cardikof pumped his hips once or twice more then slid out of her. His eyes glittered, and a cruel smile twisted his lips. "No one's little virgin now. Tsk, tsk...what will your precious Dani say to that? But you won't care. No, no, my dear. You fit me well. I think I'll keep you for myself. At least until I tire of you."

The tears that pooled in her eyes and spilt upon the desktop blurred Lia's vision, making his face a grotesque mask. "What will you do to me?" she whispered, her heart broken beyond repair.

"I'll soon make you forget that you've ever even dreamed of anyone but me." He stepped back and adjusted his clothes.

Lia lay across the desk, too wounded in body and soul to move.

He grabbed her wrist and dragged her from the office. She stumbled after him, her thoughts whirling like leaves in a millrace. *What will Dani think of me? I'm dirty and used...broken. How will he be able to love me after this? I tried so hard. I waited so long. He will hate me! Dani will hate me....*

Her mind kept repeating the same thought over and over again, as the tears streamed down her face.

❧ ❧

Alexi kept his rifle pointed squarely in the center of Dani's back. Dani could feel it there as surely as if it touched his spine. His gaze darted from side to side, searching for an opening—for some opportunity to break away from his former friend.

That's what hurts the most. Alexi was the only real friend I had in the entire United Forces. Why did they have to send him? Is it part of the plan to break me? Why can't they leave me in peace? Why is a single man such a threat to the United Forces? All I want is a little hut somewhere with Lia at my side...maybe a garden. I am so tired of war. Why won't they leave me in peace?

Preoccupied by his thoughts, Dani was shaken out of his reverie when Alexi slammed the barrel of his rifle home between Dani's shoulder blades. "In there, Zenov." He jerked his head toward a concrete Quonset hut set on a square of bare earth.

Dani stepped through the doorway, blinking to adjust his eyes to the dim interior after the late afternoon sunlight. A corridor stretched to either side of him, and a doorway stood immediately opposite. Hesitating over which way to go, Dani received another shove from Alexi's rifle barrel. "In there."

Dani stumbled through the doorway into a nearly empty office. His eyes were still adjusting to the change of light, but he could see the figure seated behind the desk, and his heart grew cold. Forcing himself to remain calm, he snapped to attention, hand going to his forehead in formal salute. "General Cardikof, sir."

The general leaned forward on his desk. "I don't think there is any reason to pretend you still consider yourself a soldier, Zenov." The words were cold. "I know that you were planning to desert rather than follow orders. Did you really think that I would not find out?"

Dani lowered his hand to his side, clenching his fists to hide his trembling. "What do you mean, sir?"

"Your little plan has been discovered. You might as well submit to the inevitable now. You have no reason left to hold out. Comply with the edict, and you will retain your position in my army—in fact, I will see you made Major. A nice promotion, a handsome raise in pay...."

"All I want is to be left alone, sir." Dani could hear himself pleading, but could not stop it—despite the fact he knew it was to no avail. *I have to try. For Lia....*

And then the blow that drove him to his knees...the general held out his hand, and a woman stepped out of the shadows to take it. A beautiful, doll-like face exquisitely made up, with hair coiffed to perfection. Her gown was silk, and fell in graceful swirls about her sensual body. She was stunning. She looked at him in polite disinterest, her lovely eyes devoid of all emotion. Lia didn't even recognize him.

The general reached up to fondle the underside of one of her breasts. Dani leapt forward, and received a rifle butt in the temple. He staggered, dazed by the blow.

"I believe you've met my new companion," the general commented, his expression feral. "Elianora, my dear, this is Daniscar Zenov. You've heard me speak of him."

"Of course, Merisford." She held out a dainty hand, her nails perfectly manicured. "How do you do, Captain Zenov?"

Dani choked back a sob.

"She is a quick study, this one is." The general pulled Lia into his lap, then gave her a long, deep kiss. His hands roamed freely up and down her body, and Lia arched against him.

Dani buried his face in his hands. *No...no...he has taken the last precious thing I had in this world...there is nothing left. Nothing.*

The general broke the kiss with a satisfied sigh. "Yes, she is a marvel this one is. Too bad you never had a chance to find that out for yourself. But then, it's never too late, is it? Lia, my dear, would you be so good as to give Captain Zenov some idea of what he is missing?"

Obediently, Lia came around the desk and stopped in front of Dani. She let the silk dress fall from her shoulders, and stood, naked to the waist. Her gaze was focused on the wall behind Dani, and there was no trace of expression in her eyes.

"You may touch her if you like," the general offered. "I certainly have."

Dani groaned low in his throat, shoulders sagging in utter defeat. *Oh, Lia...my precious girl. What have I done to you?*

He rose to his feet. Every movement was like wading through quicksand. He reached out and drew Lia's dress back onto her shoulders. For a heartbeat, he let his hand linger on her cheek, and she smiled. His breath caught in his throat then he realized the vapid smile did not reach her eyes. *She doesn't know me. She doesn't know me at all.*

"See what a marvelous job the Desensitizer can do, Zenov? Look at your friend, Alexi—the perfect soldier. Look at Elianora—the perfect mistress. You, my friend...you could be the perfect commander.

You have intelligence; you learn quickly; you adapt well. Without your crushing emotional hang-ups, you would be invincible. Join me, and I will even give you back your lovely lady. The two of you can live happily ever *new* after."

Dani looked from General Cardikof to Lia. *We will be strangers. She may never love me again...but I cannot bear this pain. He's won at last.*

Squaring his shoulders, Dani took a deep breath. "Drink my soul...please."

JUST DON'T

by Eolake Stobblehouse

One fine day on Planet Earth, I was sitting in my own comfortable home in my own comfortable chair in my own comfortable body. And just as I had leisurely turned a page in my book, and was about to leisurely take a sip of my coffee, the doorbell rang.

I raised my body, squinting at the sunshine outside, and went to the door.

Having opened it, I found myself looking at a spaceman. I knew immediately that he was a spaceman from his different looks and his suit.

Now, I was quite dumbfounded. I had a funny feeling in my stomach, and didn't know what to make of the situation. But this spaceman seemed quite as cheerful as any sergeant handling civilians.

He looked up from his clipboard, said, "Follow me, please," and turned around.

I hesitated, looking back into my comfortable home, and then stumbled after him.

"Hey," I asked. "What gives? What's happening?"

"Oh," he said, "they are going to give you guys another treatment. Some of you are regaining your memories."

"What memories?"

"Don't think about it," he said.

Mundania Press LLC

www . mundania . com

books @ mundania . com

KEY TO HAVOC, the first book in the ChroMagic series, is a brand-new epic fantasy from the Master of Fantasy and Best-Selling Author Piers Anthony. Mr. Anthony is best known for his wonderful Xanth series with its creative magic, colorful characters, fantastic monsters, and of course—the Puns! But beware! ChroMagic is not Xanth! It is an adult-oriented epic fantasy thriller from the imagination of Piers Anthony.

1,000 years ago Earth colonized the planet Charm. But the population of Charm is now far removed from their ancient ancestors. Technology has been lost over the years but the people have something better--Magic!

Charm is a world covered by volcanoes, each erupting a different color of magic. Everything within a particular Chroma becomes that color. Plants, animals, insects, and even humans all become one color and can perform that color of magic. Traveling is dangerous because a person leaving their native Chroma home can no longer perform their color magic.

Havoc is a barbarian living in a non-Chroma village, where no one has magic. As a boy, he rescued a dragon that rewarded him with special magic; to sense pending danger. His gift becomes more valuable than he can imagine as he is suddenly drafted and forced to become the new king of the planet. He must perform his duties or be executed for treason. To make matters worse, the assassin who killed the former king is now after Havoc!

Hardcover . ISBN: 0-9723670-7-1

Trade Paperback . ISBN: 0-9723670-6-3

eBook . ISBN: 1-59426-000-1